SNOW Angel

CHANTLLY WHITE

Also by Chantilly White

"Chantilly White writes amazing sexual chemistry wrapped in modern romance."
–Lucy Monroe, *USA Today* bestselling author

~ Novels ~
Pearls of Pleasure
Cupid's Mistake
Unwrapped

~ Collections ~
Christmas Wishes, Valentine Kisses:
Unwrapped & Cupid's Mistake In One Volume

~ Short Stories & Novellas ~
Pearls of Passion
Pearls of Wisdom
Tempest

~ Coming Soon ~
Remember Me
Desert Damsel

SNOW Angel

CHANTLLY WHITE

For Yolanda –
I hope you love reading Snow Angel as much as I loved writing it! ♡
Chantilley White

Snow Angel Copyright © 2014 by Chantilly White. Published October 2014 by SnapDragon Press. All rights reserved. This book, or parts thereof, may not be reproduced in any form without the prior written permission of the author.

Edited by Laurie Temple

To obtain permission to excerpt portions of the text, other than for review purposes, please contact Chantilly@ChantillyWhite.com

Cover Design Copyright © 2014 Chantilly White
Cover Images Copyright © T.Tulik, via Fotolia. Copyright © Alexandr Vasilyev, via Fotolia. Images used with licensed permission.
Interior Book Art Images Copyright © mtzsv, via Fotolia. Copyright © agrino, via Fotolia. Images used with Licensed permission.

This book is a work of fiction. Names, characters, places, and incidents are the product of the author's imagination or are used fictitiously. Any resemblance to actual persons, living or dead, business establishments, events or locales, is purely coincidental.

Discover more at ChantillyWhite.com. Please join Chantilly's mailing list at www.chantillywhite.com/contact.html#newsletter

ISBN-13: 978-1502860033
ISBN-10: 1502860031

Dedication

To friends—
Young and old, new and established,
Male and female, human and furry.
Cherish them all.

To my friends—you are loved.

It was not in the Winter
Our loving lot was cast;
It was the Time of Roses…

~ Thomas Hood, *Ballad*

1

"Melinda Anne Honeywell, are you packed?" Her mother's voice rang along the upstairs hallway, moving closer.

Grimacing, Melinda switched her teary gaze from the handsome photo filling her cell phone's screen to the empty suitcase on her bedroom floor.

"Um..." Crap.

"Melinda?" Her mom's voice, closer now, rose in volume, drawing her name out in an I'm-coming-to-check-on-you-and-you'd-better-be-busy warning tone.

Melinda hunched her shoulders against the imminent intrusion, feeling four-years-old again instead of twenty-one. She clicked her phone off and swung her legs over the side of her unmade bed to stand up.

Too late.

Her mom, Karen, thrust open Melinda's bedroom door and stood in the opening, her arms cocked and exasperation covering her pixie-esque face. Her big blue eyes narrowed as her gaze swept from Melinda's guilty expression to the open suitcase.

"Just as I suspected," she said, shaking her head and making her glossy sweep of dark brown hair swing. "Come on, Mel, chop chop. The Tanners are here, dinner's almost ready, and I want everyone packed before bed. Five o'clock comes early."

"I know, Mom, I—"

"No, now listen. You earned your couple days of hibernation after busting your butt helping me get ready for Christmas, which I really appreciated—"

Melinda sighed, but Karen simply held up a hand and kept talking, "—so I haven't wanted to push too much the past few days."

It was a challenge not to roll her eyes. Her mom, in fact her entire family, had a great talent for pushing and poking and nosing.

Out of love, of course, but still.

While it was true no one had prodded her overtly since The Christmas Day Disaster, Melinda would hardly call it hibernation when her mom, dad, three cousins, aunt, uncle, two dogs, and various family friends had been in and out of her room in a steady stream on one pretext or another.

Checking on her.

Keeping her company.

Cheering her up.

Love, in her family, was not exactly subtle.

Her cousin Rick had even performed a complete scene from Shakespeare's *Hamlet*, playing every part himself, and had made her laugh 'til she cried with his over-the-top versions of each role. So hibernating she had not been, even if she might have preferred a little more privacy to lick her wounds.

Still, she didn't argue the point.

"I know you're upset right now, and you have every reason to be." Genuine sympathy shone in her mom's eyes, and a healthy dose of anger on Melinda's behalf, though it couldn't quite overcome the hurry-hurry vibe humming beneath the surface of her words. "But we're on a deadline here."

Echoing down the hallway outside Melinda's room came the sounds of a small horde of people rushing frantically around the house. Melinda's dad, Stanton Honeywell, called orders from downstairs in his best war-general imitation, rallying the troops—

now including her best friend, Jacob Tanner, and his parents—who seemed hell-bent on making enough noise to raise the dead in Australia, let alone in Pasodoro, their small Mojave Desert town in southern California.

"Don't forget your thermals," Karen added, pointing at the suitcase and raising her voice over the din, "and—"

She broke off as the sound of a loud cheer, followed by maniacal laughter and the ecstatic barking of their two-year-old black labs, Buddy and Baxter, rolled into the room.

Stepping into the hall, Karen put her hands on either side of her mouth like a megaphone and hollered, "Get to work, you hooligans!"

A chorus of male voices answered her with the equivalent of a "yeah, yeah, yeah," and more laughter. Somewhere, a door slammed shut, and the dogs' barking faded slightly as they raced outside.

Her dad's voice boomed its way to her room next. "Hon, where're the bungee cords?" he yelled.

Melinda imagined her handsome father—just short of six-feet tall and starting to go a bit pudgy around the middle—standing at the base of the stairs, arms akimbo and his head thrown back as he called up to her mom. His hair, a lighter shade of brown than hers and her mother's, and sun-streaked from decades of working outdoors, would be raked into spikes after running his fingers absently through it all day long.

Staying on top of the packing and organizing for their winter trip was a huge job. One her dad took seriously—at least to a point. While he might sound like a military master, his moss-green eyes would still be twinkling with good humor, and if the opportunity presented itself for a bit of mischief, he'd be first in line.

"Honestly," her mom muttered beneath her breath. She stepped farther into the hallway to yell back to her husband over the noise of way too many people and the reentrance of the barking dogs. "Third drawer down in your tool chest!"

"Thanks, hon!"

Raising her hands heavenward as if begging for patience, Karen turned back into the room. "My word, they get louder every year."

Melinda assumed her mother meant the people, not the dogs, but she only nodded.

Five women, counting herself and her mom, and—holy hell—eleven men, aged eighteen to forty-seven, filled the house to the rafters, all preparing to depart on their annual post-Christmas, multi-family, week-long skiing trip. The racket seemed to underscore her mother's agitation. The slightly manic gleam in her usually calm gaze warned she was near the end of her travel-planning tether.

No matter how many years they'd been making this trip, the night before departure always devolved into a three-ring circus.

"I don't know why I believed any of this would get easier once you kids were all grown up," Karen added. "When you were little, we could park you in front of cartoons, out of the way. Now there are people everywhere."

Yeah.

Everywhere.

Melinda wished they'd all go home. Aside from their forays into her room, she'd managed to mostly avoid her extended family members and their friends over the past two days, but once on the trip, avoidance would be impossible. The last thing she wanted was to be surrounded by a bunch of people having a good time.

And didn't that sound whiny and self-pitying.

Flopping back on the bed, Melinda drew her knees to her chest and hugged her arms around them with a groan, her face buried against her legs.

"I don't even want to go," she mumbled, knowing she sounded childish. This was not the way her Christmas break was supposed to go.

"Oh, honey," Karen said, huffing out a breath. "I know."

Her mom sat beside her on the bed and draped a comforting arm around her shoulders. Though Melinda topped her mother's compact five-foot-two by a good four inches, they had the same delicate features and curvy build, the same coloring—the dark hair, pale skin, and deeply blue eyes inherited from their Black Irish ancestors.

Karen smelled faintly of her signature floral perfume, leftover Christmas cookies, and the zesty spaghetti sauce she was making for dinner. Melinda inhaled deeply, but even the promise of a favorite meal didn't sound all that appetizing.

Her mother stroked gentle fingers over Melinda's hair, scooping the dark-chocolate strands into a long ponytail down her back. Melinda sniffled.

"He's not worth it, you know," Karen said.

Melinda swiped a hand beneath her nose. "It still hurts."

Blowing out another breath, Karen pressed her head to Melinda's and squeezed her shoulder in a one-armed hug. "I know it does, sweetie. The first real heartbreak is always the worst."

"What about Kenny?"

"You didn't love Kenny, honey. You just thought he was hot."

Melinda acknowledged that silently, knowing her mother was right. Hating that it made her seem so shallow. Kenny had been the first guy to ask her out, back when she'd been sure no one ever would, and he was hot. Very. He'd appealed to her vanity. When he'd broken up with her, it had hurt, but he'd wounded her pride more than her heart.

Karen kissed Melinda's cheek. "This one'll hurt for a while, there's just nothing you can do about that. And I know it's only been two days, but you're not going to sit here moping over that asshole all alone—"

"Mom!"

"—so get started packing. Then come do the garlic bread for me, the salads are up in ten."

Melinda set her teeth. She couldn't care less about the garlic bread. The asshole in question might not be worth her tears, but Mitch Gaveston had broken her heart, and there was no stopping the constant flood of pain in her chest. It made it hard to breathe.

"But—" Melinda broke off at the sound of approaching footsteps.

"Hey, chicken legs," Jacob Tanner called out as he bounced into the room. "Oh, sorry." He stopped short on seeing the two women perched on Melinda's bed. "Everything okay?"

"Of course," Karen answered. "Did you need something, Jake?"

"Ah, no. Just wanted to say hey to Mel."

Both juniors at Cal State Fullerton, she and Jacob had been friends their whole lives, as welcome and comfortable in each other's homes as their own—not to mention all the shared family trips, weekend barbecues and pool parties, movie or game nights, and most holidays, including every single Halloween and Fourth of July. Jacob and his parents were part of nearly every milestone and major memory in her life, as she, her brother, and her parents were in Jacob's.

"Hey," Mel said, dragging up a weak smile.

Though they'd driven home for break together, Jacob had been busy since then with a volunteer project for their local fire department, and she'd spent most of her time either helping her mother or out with Mitch. She'd only seen Jacob once in the past ten days. Prior to Christmas. Back when she and Mitch had still been she and Mitch.

Jacob jerked his chin in acknowledgement of her greeting, though his whiskey-colored eyes scanned her face with concern. They'd talked on the phone and texted a few times over break, but normally they saw each other every day. He didn't know about her breakup.

He quirked an eyebrow. She gave a small shake of her head. Later.

Accepting the silent message, Jacob turned a megawatt, deeply dimpled grin on Karen. "Is that your awesome spaghetti I smell downstairs?"

"It is."

"Meatballs?"

"It's not spaghetti without meatballs, son."

"Hot damn!" he said, punching both fists in the air. "When are you going to drop Stan and run away with me?"

"As soon as you make your first million," Karen answered, as she always did. Her blue eyes twinkled. "In the meantime, why don't you grab Eddie or Wendell and set the tables for me."

"On it!" he said, flipping them both a casual salute. "Later."

"He's such a dork," Melinda said after Jacob bounded back down the hall.

"Yeah, but he's a nice dork. And a cute one, too."

That was true enough. Jake was a cutie, and he'd always been one of the good guys. A good friend.

Her *best* friend.

"Cute or not, he has an awful lot of energy for such a big guy." Melinda sniffed.

His energy she was used to, though at the moment it made her extra tired by comparison. The handsome thing was a relatively recent, post-high-school development.

It still took her by surprise sometimes, though she'd always thought him way cuter than most girls their age had given him credit for in their school days. Then he'd grown out of his gangly-colt stage and into his long limbs, great big puppy feet, and six-foot-four height. His skin had cleared of its adolescent havoc. The strong features that had sat awkwardly on his teenaged face looked good on the man, as did his well-muscled physique, and his smooth, deep voice had made more than one girl's eyes go soft and dreamy in Melinda's viewing.

Jacob's exterior finally matched the guy he'd always been inside.

But he was still a spaz.

Karen chuckled, brushing Melinda's hair out of her face. "You're only saying that because you've been holed up here for days like a slug. You need fresh air and exercise and company. This trip will do you good."

Melinda shrugged. That remained to be seen.

"Jacob isn't bringing anyone, is he?" she asked.

The face of his current squeeze, Nicole something-or-other, popped into her head. Melinda twitched her shoulders, hoping he still planned to travel solo. Nicole was not her favorite person. He'd brought a girl on the ski trip for the first time last year, much to his mother's displeasure and his dad's barely concealed amusement. Kimberly or Kylie or somebody. Kayla? She couldn't remember, although they'd roomed together at the condo. Some bleached-blond with a high, squeaky voice, who snored like a lumberjack. She'd seemed nice enough, if extremely possessive of Jacob. And about as bright as a plastic jewel.

Thankfully, Jacob had broken it off with her not long afterward.

He hadn't been planning on a guest this year, male or female, the last Melinda had talked to him, but with Jacob that could change from one hour to the next.

"No," her mom said absently, her gaze now wandering the room, a slight frown pulling between her brows. No doubt cataloguing all the things Melinda still needed to pack. Which was everything. "He and the rest of the boys have been busy making up their strategy for tackling the slopes during the day and chasing all the hot-tub bunnies by night. Rick made a pie chart and everything. Why?"

Melinda shrugged again, noncommittal. "Just wondering."

If he had anyone with him, especially a girl, it would seriously cut down on any time they might have together. She didn't want to have to compete for his time. She needed her friend.

Jacob's dating pool now was huge, a far cry from his nearly nonexistent love life in high school. He unabashedly enjoyed every moment of it, too, though he was still so wide-eyed with surprise over his change in status that he managed to remain adorable about it.

Not that most of his dating choices were worthy of him, in Melinda's estimation, but at least he hadn't become one of those love-'em-and-leave-'em jerks. He kept things casual and fun, never promising more than he intended, and when he or the girls moved on, they usually remained friends.

Unlike herself and Mitch. She never wanted to see his lying face again.

"There's plenty of room," Karen reminded her for the umpteenth time in the past two days. "Are you sure you don't want to ask one of your girlfriends instead? It's a little last minute now, but if they aren't busy—"

"No," Melinda interrupted. "Really. Thanks, but I'd rather keep things the way they are. They've all got plans, anyway."

Besides, as much as she loved her girlfriends, she wanted to talk things out with Jacob first.

"Okay," Karen said. "If you're sure."

"I am."

The girls would want the full breakup experience, and she wasn't ready for it. Cartons of ice cream, tear-jerker movies, the ritual shredding of Mitch's character, his looks, intelligence, and future prospects, plus plenty of tears, tissues, and endless talking. Jacob would listen, make a couple of pithy remarks, then give her a hard hug, tell her she was better off without the jerk, and get down to cheering her up in his usual Jacob way.

Both traditions were important, but Jacob's version had the power to actually make her feel better.

She and Jacob had seen each other through their middle- and-high-school years with plenty of late-night phone sessions, coffee dates, and trips to their special spot looking over the Mojave River. Once upon a time, those trips had often included their third musketeer, Seth Mazer, a tradition she and Jacob now missed terribly with Seth's absence.

They'd emerged from high school's social hell mostly unscathed, though Jacob's awkward phase was nothing compared to Melinda's. He'd been well-liked by the other guys, and popular enough—even with a lot of the girls—if only from deep in the Friend Zone.

Melinda might have bloomed sooner than Jacob had, but the blossoming had been a different sort of torture. She'd not only dealt with a developmental loop that rotated between gangly and chubby, with no happy medium, she'd also been that worst of all combinations—really smart and painfully shy. It was the kiss of death to her elementary school and junior-high social life. With her snaggly teeth, thick glasses, and bad skin, she'd borne the brunt of a lot of teasing through the end of eighth grade.

Then the real trouble began.

As a freshman, she'd gone from a life in the shadows, vacillating between bully victim and periods of safe invisibility, to being thrust into the spotlight of extreme popularity almost overnight. Learning to navigate treacherous high-school waters filled with girls who only wanted reflected attention—but secretly hated her and her new looks—and guys who only wanted her body had taken its toll.

Jacob alone had stayed faithfully by her side from infancy to adulthood, never wavering. Their assorted emotional traumas from that roughest of time periods had cemented their already-strong bond.

Though Melinda had a wide, trusted circle of girlfriends now, when she needed someone to confide her deepest secrets to, more often than not, Jacob fit the bill.

Which made her extra glad he wasn't bringing anyone this year, even though she wasn't ready to talk about the thing with Mitch yet. Jacob would spend most of his time with the other guys, as usual, and that was okay. He'd be around when she needed him. When she was ready.

Plus, it would feel less awkward. Her cousins had their usual friends coming along—who were practically family, anyway—but with no one coupled up this year, it would make it a little easier to bear the group as a whole now that she was single again, too.

2

Once out of Melinda's room, Jacob frowned. Something was up with her. Her big blue eyes were redder than the garland on the Christmas tree downstairs, and it was totally weird for her to be holed up in her room instead of in the middle of everything.

It made him want to do something about it, something to make her laugh and wipe the hurt off her face, but he knew his friend. She'd seek him out when she was ready to talk about it. If she didn't, he'd drag it out of her.

If all else failed, he'd ask one of her cousins—Rick would know.

Satisfied with that bit of strategy, Jacob paused at the top of the stairs and put his hands out. He was half an inch from grasping the wide, glossy banister and throwing his left leg over to slide down its smooth, curved length to the ground floor, when he caught the glare. Melinda's aunt, Pat Carlisle, stood at the foot of the stairs, hands on her hips and looking as fierce as her Viking ancestors, a don't-even-think-about-it gleam in her light blue eyes.

"Ah," he said, straightening. All innocence, he sent her a

winning smile, and with hands now tucked safely in his pockets, strode down the steps two at a time. "How's it going, Aunt Pittypat?"

Wagging an admonishing finger under his nose, she continued to glare at him, though a smile tugged at her stern lips. "You're the only one who can get away with that."

He bent forward to kiss her on the cheek. "That's 'cuz I'm your favorite," he said, winking.

With a dramatic sigh, Aunt Pat fluffed her hair. "Just don't tell my sons."

Coming up behind her, his arms full of gear for the trip, Wendell Page—best friend of Aunt Pat's youngest son, Christian—said, "Whoa, whoa, whoa. I thought *I* was your favorite."

"Now see what you've done?" Aunt Pat said to Jacob, tossing her hands up in the air. To Wendell, she said, "You're my favorite redhead. Now, both of you, beat it. I have work to do."

And she sailed off.

Wendell frowned after her. "I'm the only redhead."

"Come on, young Padawan," Jacob said, draping an arm around Wendell's shoulders and ruffling his very red hair. "We're on table duty. I'll regale you with the many reasons why I am, indeed, Aunt Pat's favorite."

Obliging, Wendell dropped the gear in the middle of the walkway, where someone was sure to pick it up, and headed into the dining room with Jacob.

"Goodie," Wendell said, rubbing his big, freckled hands together, "story time. Will there be milk and cookies?"

"Of course," said Jacob, grabbing one of two long, silver serving spoons from the dining room table and tossing the other to Wendell. "But first, we battle. *En garde!*"

"You haven't been helping Rick rehearse his play again, have you?"

"Mayhap," Jacob said, trying to put a British spin on his accent. "Why dost thou, um, query?"

"Don't quote Shakespeare at me. I hate it when he does that."

"Appreciation of the Bard separates us from the animals,

dude."

Wendell scoffed. "And here I thought it was reason and opposable thumbs."

"Cocky," Jacob said. "Very cocky. I like it. Defend!"

They crossed spoons and prepared to duel, but from the hallway came the sounds of a crash, a curse, and an adult male yelling, "Who the hell left all this crap in the middle of the hall?"

Wendell hunched his shoulders, his abundantly freckled face flushing. His mouth drew down in a guilty grimace.

"On second thought," Jacob said, grabbing Wendell's spoon out of his lax hand and tossing both back on the table, "methinks retreat's the better part of valor. To the yard!"

Melinda and Karen both jumped when they heard the pained yell from downstairs and held still as startled deer, waiting.

"That sounded like my klutzy brother," her mother said, meaning Melinda's Uncle Allan. His wife, Aunt Pat, and their three boys had been at the house since the week prior to Christmas.

When nothing more was forthcoming, Karen breathed a sigh of relief. "I guess no one's hurt, at least."

"Don't jinx us," Melinda warned. "It's early yet."

"Ha," Karen said. "Yeah. Well."

In tandem, they leaned over and knocked twice on top of Melinda's wooden bedside table. When they sat up, they grinned at each other over their superstition.

"Better safe than sorry," Melinda said.

"Very true." Briskly now, Karen gave an encouraging pat on Melinda's knee. "Okay. Time to get back to it."

In whirlwind-mode once more, her mom hustled out of the room. Her shouted, "Stanton Honeywell, don't even think of propping those skis against my freshly-painted walls!" brought a small smile to Melinda's lips, though it faded quickly. Her gaze snagged on her phone's darkened screen.

Picking it up, she twisted it in her hands, then simply held it in her lap. She didn't turn it back on. She didn't want to see Mitch's face smiling up at her again, all handsome and lying.

For three of the happiest months of her life, her now ex-boyfriend had been the center of her universe. He'd made her feel special. The way it was supposed to be, the way it always was in the movies. He'd made everything beautiful and fun and important.

Worst of all, he'd made her believe in him and in their future.

Mitch had said all the right things, had claimed to want everything she wanted. Marriage, family, settling in Pasodoro. Now it all rang hollow. Scripted. She hadn't been the only one convinced they were headed for a happily-ever-after, either. He'd fooled everyone into thinking he was The One, including her parents and all of her friends.

Except Jacob, actually. He'd been friendly enough to Mitch whenever they were together, but he'd never jumped on the We-Love-Mitch bandwagon.

Melinda frowned. She'd never really thought about that before. Well, whatever Jacob had recognized in Mitch's character, he'd never said, and she'd been blind to it.

Then two days ago, on Christmas-freaking-Day, with no word or warning, Mitch had dumped her. Not like a man, either. Oh, no. He didn't have the tweedle-dees for that. No, he'd stood her up.

On *Christmas*.

At first, when he didn't show on time, she'd been afraid something had happened to him on the way to her house. An accident or an emergency. It was a long drive from Pasadena to Pasodoro, after all, and holiday traffic could be dangerous.

The day had worn on, everyone wondering where he was. Her mother had even held dinner an extra hour. Mitch never called or answered his cell. The inability to contact him had finally tripped Melinda's worry into panic. She'd checked online and even called the highway patrol to ask about road conditions, already crying a little, convinced they'd tell her about a massive pileup in the Cajon Pass.

She hadn't understood the tone in the woman's voice on the other end of the line when the dispatcher said the roads were clear. Not until later. But she knew what it was now.

Pity.

Pity for the poor stupid girl, too dumb to realize she'd been dumped on Christmas.

Melinda had only found out the truth by tracking down Mitch's sister, since the jerk wouldn't return her frantic calls and texts. She hadn't been quite brave enough to call his parents.

Those last hours between blissful ignorance and painful reality had played through her mind on an endless loop ever since.

The supposed love of her life had called her on Christmas Eve, as he did every night, and had confirmed their plans for the next day. He'd said, "I love you," to her as he hung up. He'd sent her to sleep with a smile on her lips. She'd dreamed about their perfect first Christmas together. And within that same hour, eighty miles away, Mitch wiped her from his mind and went back to Christina, his psycho ex-girlfriend.

The bastard.

As if it wasn't bad enough that he'd broken her heart and ruined Christmas, he'd also been invited on the ski trip. God, she'd been looking forward to that—the romance of it, the fun, spending New Year's Eve slow dancing under the mistletoe.

Now, instead of spending the week on the slopes with her boyfriend, playing in the snow or cozied up in the lodge in front of the fire, she'd spend most of the time on her own, like usual, while everyone tiptoed around the breakup.

They'd pity her, or worse, want to talk about what a jerk he was and how it was for the best that she'd found out now, before it was too late. But it was already too late.

Mitch had broken her heart to pieces.

Maybe the other guys wouldn't want to talk about it, but the women would. And Jacob would. He'd let her be for a few days, but if she didn't cough it up soon enough to suit him, he'd harass it out of her, then try to tease her into a better mood, like he always did when she was upset.

Usually it worked, and she was counting on him doing exactly that. Just not yet. She wasn't ready to be teased out of her grief. It was too raw. Too painful. She hadn't told any of her girlfriends yet, either. Picking up the phone, saying the words. It was too awful. She wanted to be left alone to cry in peace.

"Melinda!" Her mom's voice cut through all the commotion from downstairs, impatience now starting to boil.

Resigned, Melinda got up, swiping her cheeks and hitching her ancient red cheerleading sweatpants higher on her hips, tugging down her wildly mismatched blue-and-orange Cal State Fullerton sweatshirt. Her slippers were purple and furry and even older than her raggedy sweats.

If she was going for hobo-chic, she'd nailed it.

"Coming!" she shouted back, her throat rough and raspy.

A glance in the white-painted oval mirror hanging above her matching dresser reflected her eyes, big and blue like her mother's, were wet, red-rimmed, and dark-circled. Her skin was pale and blotchy from crying, and her hair... her hair. Wow.

"Ugh," she said out loud, disgust ripe in her voice. She sniffed hard. "You could give Medusa a run for her money."

No wonder Jacob had looked at her the way he had.

Moving into her adjoining bathroom, she blew her nose and splashed cool water on her face, dabbing it dry on a bright blue hand towel. She brushed her teeth, alternating squats and heel raises in front of the sink to get her blood moving for the first time in days. She wasn't used to laying around like that slug her mom had mentioned. Her muscles felt stiff and sore, as if Mitch had not only beaten her up emotionally, but had taken a bat to her body, too.

She was so not going to put up with *that* feeling.

Grabbing a brush, she dragged it through the heavy, tangled length of her hair, pulling the dark mass into a messy top knot to keep it out of her way.

Her eyes still wanted to tear up.

Melinda groaned at herself in frustration. The crying had to stop. Her mom was right. The bastard wasn't worth it. The pain might linger for a while, but she would bury it down deep, not let it show. Vanity had her grabbing her blush brush and fluffing it over her cheeks, then swiping on a thin layer of mascara and a dab of rosy gloss on her lips.

Heartbroken hobo didn't have to mean ugly-fugly, too.

"Ready?" she asked her reflection. She still looked wan—

"Melinda!"

"Oh, my God, I said I was coming," she muttered, rolling her eyes in the mirror. Raising her voice, she called back, "Be right there!"

Once she stepped into the upstairs hallway, the din seemed to increase tenfold. Shouted instructions, more laughter, the occasional curse word, and doors opening and slamming shut both upstairs and down assaulted her ears. It made for an ungodly amount of noise in a home that was generally quiet these days. At least since her older brother, Zach, had moved out. Now, the decibel level seemed almost as loud as a Friday night in her dorm.

And that was before adding the dogs to the mix.

Thinking of Zach missing the ski trip for the third year in a row made her sad again, so Melinda pushed the thought away. Her brother was doing work he loved and mentoring under his idol, having the time of his life, learning everything he'd need to have a long, wonderful career. That had to take precedence over family vacations, even if she did miss him like crazy.

Plus, it was too expensive to fly home from Japan more than once a year. He'd be home for camping over the summer. He'd promised her when he called on Christmas Day.

Melinda edged around the corner and peered over the loft railing to take in the chaos below.

Jacob's parents, Bill and Lois Tanner, came into view, dodging everyone else as they followed her Uncle Allan, her mother's older brother, toward the laundry room where boxes of trip supplies waited to be loaded into the cars. Two family friends—darkly handsome Gabe McConnell and sweetly serious Eddie Thomas—followed the adults, both weighed down with gear. Trailing closely behind were the dogs, tongues lolling and looking for handouts.

Their house wasn't small, yet it seemed tiny and cramped with so many people scrambling in every direction.

Going for stealth, Melinda moved quietly down the wide, curving staircase, hoping to avoid as much attention as possible.

Intent on their own agendas, no one took any notice of her.

She kept her footsteps steady and soft, and for a moment, as everyone scurried about their business, the front room emptied of people. The only motion came from the twinkle lights and a few battery-operated spinning ornaments on the giant Christmas tree gracing the bay window at the front of the house. She had a clear path to the haven of her mother's kitchen, until—

"It lives!"

Damn it.

"Shut up, Rick," Melinda said, narrowing her eyes as her cousin rounded the corner and zeroed in. She stopped on the bottom tread with a frown as he bounded forward.

Richard Carlisle leaped the back of the living-room couch, his outrageously long legs stretched out as though the sofa was a track hurdle, then dropped to one knee before her, sweeping an imaginary hat off his head and giving an elaborate bow.

"Your majesty," he intoned in regal voice, "your humble servant lives only to serve and wishes to thank you for gracing us with your—"

Melinda leaned forward, placed the palm of her hand against his bent head, and shoved, knocking him sideways. "Save it for the stage, fool."

Rick rolled dramatically onto his back, legs and arms waving in the air like a stranded blond turtle.

"Help!" he warbled. "Your worship! I've fallen and I can't—Hey!"

His words choked off on a snicker as the dogs streaked around the opposite corner and spotted one of their favorite playmates on the floor. They jumped in with joyful barks, squashing Rick's stomach and covering his face with enthusiastic doggie kisses.

"Hey, Buddy, how's it—*oof*—down, Baxter!"

"Good boys," Melinda said, clapping her hands to egg them

on. "Get him."

"Well, well, look who's out of her cave." Coming down the stairs behind her, Rick's older brother, Danny, nudged her out of the way, suitcases tucked under both arms. "Done sulking?"

He stopped beside her to survey Rick's flailing limbs.

"Leave her alone," said Christian, the youngest of the three Carlisle boys, trailing Danny and equally burdened with luggage.

Christian blew a lock of blond hair out of his eyes and frowned at his oldest brother. Then he winked at Melinda and trudged past her and Danny on the wide base of the stairs. Stepping around Rick and the tussling dogs with a wordless shake of his head, he continued on his way toward the front door.

Ignoring Christian, Danny whistled to get Rick's attention. "Come grab some of these suitcases, moron."

"In a minute," Rick said, his arms full of fur. "Can't you see these guys are starved for attention? Aren't you," he said to the squirming dogs. "Yes, you are, all this running back and forth and no one playing with you, poor fellas."

Rick descended into a stream of pathetically lame dog-baby-talk while he rubbed bellies and noses and sent Baxter and Buddy into throes of doggie delight.

Melinda and Danny exchanged a glance full of the sort of disgust one can only share with a fellow family member.

"Mom!" Danny called in the tattling singsong voice of a five-year-old. "Rick's not helping!"

"Don't call her, I was attacked," Rick protested, struggling a bit beneath the weight of the dogs, still laughing. "Look at these vicious—*ack.*" He broke off to wipe away the slobbery licks raining all over his face. "Vicious animals. Quit it, Baxter, you got me in the mouth."

"Stop Frenching the dogs and grab a load, man," Danny said, aiming a kick at his middle brother as he finally followed Christian out the front door.

Though their father, Uncle Allan, had the same dark hair and blue eyes as Melinda and her mother, her Carlisle cousins had inherited their Norse-god statures and chiseled good looks from their mother, whose real name was Petronilla but everyone called Aunt Pat if they wanted to live a nice long life with all their limbs attached.

All three boys were well over six feet, muscular, blond, and blue-eyed. American-born Thors. They looked enough alike to be mistaken for triplets at a distance, though Danny and Christian's sandy-blond hair was waterfall-straight, while Rick's was a curly mop.

Melinda adored them all, though she and Rick had an extra deep bond, having spent most of their youth ganging up on—or losing to—the other two.

The front door closed behind Danny and Christian just as Aunt Pat swung into the living room, her arms full of ski jackets bound for the waiting cars, and a frown aimed at her middle son.

"Richard Dean Carlisle, quit fooling around with those dogs. Your Uncle Stan needs help loading the skis."

From beneath the dog pile, Rick snapped his mother a smart salute. "Aye, aye, Captain, my Captain."

Aunt Pat turned her back on him. To Melinda, she said, "I think your mom was looking for you," then she moved on toward the front door. Over her shoulder, she yelled, "Rick!"

"Captain!" he shouted back. Then, more quietly, "Slave driver."

"Put the dogs in their pen first," Aunt Pat added, "and I heard that."

She sailed outside, slamming the front door behind her and sending the jingle bells on the Christmas wreath hanging on it ringing merrily.

With a smirk for her cousin, which he answered with crossed eyes and a stuck out tongue, Melinda finally descended the last step. She made her way into the relative quiet of the kitchen where her mother worked, alone for the moment, mustering the meal together like a professional caterer preparing to serve a large group of unruly savages.

Which was about right.

"Finally," Karen said, wiping her forehead with the back of her wrist. Brandishing the salad tongs in her other hand, she pointed to the bread board, where four loaves of French bread sat already sliced and waiting. "Just mix up the spread, slap it on, and get them in the oven, please, then help Jake and Wendell finish setting the tables. I think they were having a sword fight with the candlesticks."

"Everyone's a slave driver," Melinda said under her breath.

"What's that, honey?"

"Nothing, nothing," she said, starting on the garlic spread.

Though her heart still weighed heavily in her chest, her lips bowed up at the corners. Immersed in the utter chaos of pre-vacation family life, it was impossible to hold on to the black cloud she'd been sailing under the past two days.

Jon Bon Jovi belted a Christmas rock ballad from speakers hooked to her mom's iPod while Karen sang along, badly off key, and finished tossing the salads. Melinda joined in on the chorus, shimmying to her mother's side to share the salad-tongs-turned-microphone for the big finish.

Everything inside her seemed to loosen and settle for the first time since Christmas Day, and a genuine smile bloomed fully across her lips.

Though it was shy of six o'clock, night pressed firmly against the windows over the kitchen sink. The sun had set while she'd been holed up in her room, but everything in the kitchen was bright and warm and full of the comforting scents of home-cooked foods, now a rare luxury Melinda missed wholeheartedly when she was at school.

Karen shifted to the stove to stir the truly staggering amount of spaghetti sauce bubbling in a giant pot.

"Are you sure there's enough?" Melinda teased.

"Haha," her mom said. "You've seen these people eat. Besides, I made extra to take with us for dinner later in the week."

That, too, was a homey tradition. To keep costs down on the annual trip, each family took responsibility for several group meals—breakfasts and dinners—which they served family-style in one of the three condos they shared. Lunches were usually grabbed in the main lodge as people came off the mountain for a break from skiing. Karen's spaghetti and meatballs was a group favorite.

Once she'd dealt with the bread, Melinda grabbed a giant

salad bowl in each arm and headed for the dining room.

The large, formal table was set, somewhat haphazardly, for twelve, though Jacob and Wendell were nowhere to be seen. A festive trio of Christmas centerpieces ranged down the middle of the table, their fat red candles already lit.

From the adjacent family room, a widescreen TV blared the soundtrack of an '80s movie through the dining room's twinkle-lights-and-garland-bedecked archway.

An ancient card table, its scarred surface covered with a festive tablecloth, sat at the foot of the similarly-adorned formal table, in the middle of the arch between the two rooms, set for four to round out their party of sixteen.

Melinda made a mental note to snag a seat with three of the guys at the smaller "kid's table" where she'd be less likely to suffer through an interrogation about Mitch by any of the other women.

With her brother Zach once again absent, and since Melinda and Jacob didn't have additional guests attending the trip this year—thanks to that bastard Mitch backing out—there was an even split between adults and kids—eight each.

The fact that all of the kids were now legal adults meant little when it came to dividing up the party. The kids would always be the kids, even when they were in their forties with kids of their own.

However, there was only room for four at the kid's table, and although none of them really cared where they sat anymore, snagging those seats had become something of a game.

Setting the salad bowls in the middle of the big table, one on each end, Melinda straightened the place settings, then moved through the arch and crossed the family room to stare out the back sliding door.

Buddy and Baxter were in their pen in advance of everyone sitting down to dinner. It spanned the length of one side of the property, giving the dogs plenty of room to frolic. An enormous barn-style doghouse sat on their own covered patio where they could escape the elements, along with a plastic kiddie-pool to laze in during the blisteringly-hot desert summers.

Melinda frosted her breath on the glass door and drew a

heart inside the fog, then wiped it away.

Summer's heat seemed a long way off. The lawn lay dormant and crisp beneath a light layer of frost, crisscrossed with the dogs' paw prints. She tapped on the glass, and Buddy barked in response before chasing after Baxter, who had their favorite tug-rope dangling from his mouth.

No one else was in sight.

The backyard stretched for nearly an acre beneath a clear, star-studded sky, the grounds well-lit thanks to the landscape lighting her mother had installed herself. The many shade trees, her mother's beloved rose bushes, and assorted shrubs reached toward the stars with winter-skeletal arms, waiting for spring to green them up again. They wove in and around artfully designed pathways and river-rocked beds of indigenous cacti, including a few majestic desert sentinels—the spearing Joshua trees.

California's drought conditions would play havoc with the yard again this year, yet somehow her mother always managed to keep it looking gorgeous.

Her parents owned the local nursery, and Karen also hired herself out for landscaping jobs, so their yard served as both a testament to her mother's first love—gardening—and as a living advertisement for the family business.

An above-ground pool, covered for winter, took up a portion of the back half of the property, along with a wide deck and plenty of chairs for sunning. Bright-orange California poppies would blanket the ground around the pool in summer, and evergreen California junipers clumped along both sides of the back fence.

Melinda liked to lightly crush ripe juniper berries in her hands and inhale the scent. Aunt Pat used a different variety of the berry—actually not a berry at all, but a seed cone—in some of her favorite recipes, which had been passed down in her family for generations.

Some people found the desert climate too harsh, too dry, too brown, and it could be, for sure. Especially when the winds blew—burning hot in summer or freezing cold in winter—which was most of the time. It wasn't a lush, tropical paradise by any stretch of the imagination, and they had their share of nasty critters—rattlesnakes, scorpions, and more. But life in their small town of Pasodoro was everything Melinda wanted and loved.

It was home.

"Dinner's ready!" Her mom's voice sounded from the kitchen.

Instead of heading straight for the table, Melinda rested her forehead against the sliding door, her gaze focused on the oasis of the yard.

Beyond their fence line, the Mojave Desert rolled toward the foothills fronting the San Bernardino mountains, visible now only as a deeper black against the night sky. During the day, the desert would spread wide for miles, plentifully dotted with houses, yet somehow still barren-looking.

Melinda exhaled slowly, rubbing her forehead against the chilly glass.

Eventually, she would forget that Mitch ever swam in their pool, or played with Buddy and Baxter on the lawn, or kissed her under the shade trees.

Wind-tossed piles of tumbleweeds mounded against the outside of the fence, waiting to be swept along with the next strong gust. Her memories of Mitch would be like that someday. Dust-dry and easy to blow away with a breath.

She hoped.

3

Behind her, as though a switch had been flipped, the sudden influx of chatter announced the arrival of the hungry horde.

Melinda watched their reflections in the glass as her family and friends filtered in from the kitchen and the hallway, everyone talking over each other, the women carrying serving dishes, bottles of wine, and pitchers full of iced tea.

Her dad carried a basket mounded with garlic bread and, with a furtive glance over his shoulder, set it conveniently next to his place at the table. Melinda grinned. Her mom would make sure he didn't hog it all.

Jacob approached in the slider's reflection, stalking toward her with his arms straight out and rocking side to side like a drunken Frankenstein's monster. He grabbed her by the elbows and lifted her straight up off her feet.

"Parsnip!" he said, bellowing the word and giving her a little jiggle before lowering her back down.

"Rutabaga," she answered with a smile.

He wrapped one arm companionably around her neck and placed his chin on top of her head, his golden-brown eyes glinting like topaz-colored jewels as they met hers in the glass. "Sweet potato."

"Rump roast."

"Hey!" He straightened, hands on hips, feigning indignation. "Don't talk smack about my rump roast. It's grade-A, baby."

Melinda made a face meant to take him down several pegs. "Please. Control yourself."

"Come eat, you two," her mom called, aiming the clicker at the giant TV to shut it off. Pushing another button, she turned soft, instrumental Christmas music on from the stereo instead.

"Your chariot, milady," Jacob said to Melinda, turning and flexing one leg into a lunge for her to use as a foothold. He patted his left hand on his own ass. "Watch the roast."

Ignoring that last comment, she tucked her purple-slippered foot into the crease between his hip and thigh and stepped up, boosting herself onto his back. His black cable-knit sweater bunched warm and nubby beneath her fingers. He grabbed her by the legs and jogged the fifteen paces to the dining room.

"Oh, man," Jacob and Melinda whined in unison, surveying the seating as she slid off his back.

The chairs at the kid's table were already filled by her cousins, Danny and Christian, as well as Danny's best friend, Gabe McConnell, and the carrot-top, Christian's best friend, Wendell Page.

Jacob put on a pout worthy of Rick's stage career and kicked at Christian's chair leg. "I don't wanna sit at the grown-ups' table."

"Suck it up, buttercup," Christian advised, smiling his extra-cherubic smile.

"Yeah," Wendell chimed in. "You snooze you lose, and all that."

"You're twenty-one now, Jakey, you can handle it," Danny said.

"You're twenty-three," Melinda pointed out to her oldest cousin. "And so are you," she added to Gabe, who only grinned, his emerald eyes gleaming.

Next to her blond cousins, black-haired, green-eyed Gabe

looked more like her relative than they did. Well... if her relatives had descended from fallen angels, maybe. Though he was a marshmallow underneath the tough-guy act, and a geek at heart, Gabe's chiseled features, too-long hair, and dark-angel looks suited his self-created reputation.

"Yeah, but we're faster than you two delinquents." Danny stuck an uncooked spaghetti noodle—pilfered from the kitchen canister—in the corner of his mouth like a strand of straw and chomped on it, smirking at them and tipping an imaginary cowboy hat in their direction.

Melinda shared an exaggerated grimace with Jacob for form, then they slumped into the two remaining seats at the bottom of the table across from the rest of the younger generation—her theatrical middle cousin, Rick, and his best friend, Eddie Thomas.

"Stuck with us, are you?" Eddie said with a wink.

Jacob crossed his eyes and stuck out his tongue at Eddie, who was also Jacob's roommate at Cal State Fullerton.

"Hey," Rick said, sitting up straighter and casting an offended glance at Eddie. Affecting a superior mien, he raised a dramatic hand to his chest, nose in the air. "These are places of honor. Someday, people will pay the big bucks to sit next to *moi*."

Eddie rolled his eyes heavenward. From the kids' table, all four guys burst into laughter along with Jacob and Melinda.

"That's a good one, Ricky," Danny hooted, pretending to wipe tears of mirth from his eyes.

"Is that the bedtime story you tell yourself every night?" Gabe wondered.

"That's right, laugh it up, chuckle-heads," Rick said, unoffended. He pointed at them each in turn. "See if I invite any of you to my future red-carpet events."

"We'll risk it," Danny answered, still chuckling.

"Speak for yourselves," Wendell said before turning to Rick. "Can you introduce me to some leading ladies?"

"I might be persuaded," Rick said, studying the fingernails on his left hand. "For those who've proven to be loyal supporters."

Wendell ignored Christian's muttered, "Don't hold your

breath," and gave a fist pump. "Yes!"

Eddie clapped a hand to Rick's shoulder. "Whatever you say, big guy."

Melinda grinned at Eddie. He was such a good guy, but she always felt a bit sorry for him.

Though quite handsome in his own right, Eddie became a shorter, brown-haired, gray-eyed duckling in the circle of swans that included not only her Thor-wannabe cousins, but also Jacob, Gabe, and even the not-quite-as-handsome-but-exuberantly red-headed Wendell.

When her brother was around, Zach added his dark good looks to the swan's numbers.

With his quieter personality, Eddie tended to fade into the background in this particular group of guys, especially with women. Girls went for the swans, or Wendell's goofy charm, never realizing the treasure they were overlooking.

If he hadn't become like a second brother to her from the first day they'd met, she might have gone for Eddie herself.

Melinda took a long drink of water and avoided looking at Jacob. Some people might think she had a sister-brother relationship with him, too, growing up in each other's pockets the way they had, but with Jacob, it was different. As close as they were, she'd never considered him sibling material.

When they were kids, she'd fully intended to marry him one day, because what could be better than being married to your best friend? Even when they bickered, there was no one she had more fun with than Jacob.

It was too bad they wanted such different things.

Jacob's path would take him far from Pasodoro. Her goals planted her smack in the middle of it, where she was happiest, surrounded by friends and family. A romantic relationship with him would never work, much as she might have wished otherwise growing up. Their futures waited down different tines of the coming fork in the road.

Mitch's lying face danced in her mind's eye for a brief moment. Maybe if they'd been better friends, not just a couple... If Mitch had been more like Jacob...

Well. Melinda took another sip of water. There wasn't

anyone else like Jacob, and besides, one of the most important parts of any friendship, any relationship, was mutual trust. Mitch had proved he was untrustworthy.

"Jackass," she said under her breath.

"What?" Jacob asked, an eyebrow raised.

Melinda brushed off the nagging thoughts, her cheeks pinkening. She hadn't meant to say that out loud. "Nothing, sorry."

Uncle Allan's boisterous guffaw drew her attention to the grown-up's end of the table.

Eddie's parents, Nancy and Peter Thomas, sat on the other side of their son, deep in conversation with her still-chuckling Uncle Allan.

For Melinda, the Thomas family's Desert Rogue Horse Ranch formed the backdrop for some of her favorite memories—days spent on horseback with family and friends or fishing in their small lake. Nights camping beneath the stars.

Next summer, the ranch would host the third annual Seth Mazer Memorial Scholarship Rodeo, and they'd all go out to help, as usual.

Melinda's chest constricted a little, thinking of Seth. It seemed incredible he'd been gone nearly three years. His death in the spring of their senior year of high school had nearly brought the entire town to its knees.

Seth Mazer had been one of those guys everyone loved, no matter what social group they belonged to. He had friends everywhere, was whip smart, multi-talented, and super cute, with a smile that could light a city block. He was a shooting star, the great-grandson of the founder of Pasodoro, and one of Melinda and Jacob's closest friends.

Now, though the event was bittersweet, the annual rodeo brought the whole community together for a celebration of his life and to keep his star shining.

Every person in their dining room had known and loved Seth, and he'd often gone along on their family trips. They missed him every year.

Because thinking of Seth's wacky sense of humor and devilish grin made her want to laugh and cry at the same time,

Melinda blinked the moisture from her eyes and focused again on her tablemates.

Their party of sixteen was rounded out by Lois and Bill Tanner, Jacob's parents. They sat across from the Thomases, wine glasses in hand, going over lists with her mom and dad.

"Jake, did you grab the camcorder?" Bill asked, raising his voice over the low roar of conversation flowing across the two tables.

Jacob, in the middle of waging a fierce fork battle with Eddie, answered without looking up. "Already in the trunk."

As the salads began making the rounds of the table, Melinda studied Jacob's parents. Bill Tanner was an almost-identical older version of his son. He had the same strong features, the same rich coloring. They were of a height, as well, and like Jacob, Bill stayed tanned year-round. The sun had woven copper streaks in his thick, sable-brown hair, still as lustrous as Jacob's, and his topaz eyes sparked with the same golden lights, especially when he laughed, which was often.

Jacob's mother, at nearly six-feet herself, was a bit of an Amazon—big boned, broad shouldered, and as strong as many men—and gorgeous, with big hazel eyes, high cheekbones, and the full mouth and charming, deeply dimpled smile her son had inherited.

They made a striking family portrait.

Bill caught Melinda staring and raised an eyebrow, exactly the way Jacob always did. She merely smiled at him and turned her attention back to the boys. Jacob and Eddie had called a truce on their utensil war and were now discussing the pros and cons of adding a psych minor to their respective majors.

"It's midway through junior year," Melinda said, surprised.

"Yeah," Eddie answered with a small shrug as he forked salad into his mouth, "but we've got half the requirements met through our majors and gen-ed stuff already, so it's not like it would be a big deal."

"Do you need it, though?" she wondered.

Jacob's major—kinesiology—suited his goals as a premed student. Eddie already had a double major—business administration and childhood development. Adding a minor to his heavy course load seemed like a crazy idea.

"Are you kidding?" Wendell asked from the other table, grinning at Melinda. "Jakey could use some serious head shrinking—don't they make psych majors go through all those evaluations? Could save us a helluva lot of trouble down the line."

Jacob gave Wendell the stink eye. "Thanks, man," he said. "Great sweater, by the way. Speaking of crazy."

"You like?" Wendell asked, checking out his violently orange-and-red cable knit with a grin.

"Goes great with the hair," Christian put in, a smile wreathing his baby face. "I especially like the flames."

"Say the word, you can borrow it any time," Wendell said. "It's a chick magnet."

"I didn't know chicks dug burning pumpkins," Danny commented as he took a sip of wine.

"See this?" Wendell rubbed a hand over his ginger head. "Like moths to the flame, baby."

"I don't need a sweater for that," Jacob scoffed.

Wendell scoffed right back. "Dude, you need all the help you can get."

Gabe said, "Too right," and her cousins added a simultaneous, "Amen."

Shooting a finger-pistol at Wendell, ignoring the others, Jacob focused on Melinda, getting back to his topic.

"It'll be good to have something extra to offer," he said. "Working with injured athletes, there's bound to be mental components to their care. Eddie's gonna need all the help he can get with his camp. And actually—"

"I think it's a good idea," Eddie's father broke in, patting Eddie on the shoulder.

Melinda raised her eyebrows at Jacob, wondering what he'd been about to say. He looked away from her, though he exchanged a weird look with Eddie. He didn't finish his sentence.

"No doubt," Rick agreed, still on the psych topic. He reached across Melinda to snag garlic bread from a basket. "Kids these days. Worse than Jake." He twirled a finger around his ear, smirking when Eddie and Jacob rolled their eyes.

"Says the banana brain," Danny said, tossing a napkin at his middle brother.

"Takes one to know one, dog breath," Rick shot back without looking his older brother's way.

"Who was it smooching the pooches earlier?" Danny asked.

"Whatever," Melinda interrupted, "as long as you guys don't start trying to head-shrink me."

"Noting wrong with a good shrinking now and again," put in Jacob's mom, Lois, who was herself a psychologist. She winked at Melinda.

"It's a shame you weren't able to do more for your own son, Mama Lois," said Wendell sorrowfully, rubbing an imaginary tear from his eye.

Bill snorted into his wine glass, but Lois nodded in agreement, her lips twitching. "Yes, it's a tragedy, but even the most talented therapists have a checkmark or two in the loss column." She smoothed a graceful hand over her hair and shrugged regretfully.

"Thanks, Ma. Dad. Appreciate it," Jacob said, aiming a look at his parents.

Lois blew him a kiss in return, and Melinda giggled, drawing a frown from Jacob.

"Anyway, you're beyond anyone's scope, Mel, don't worry," he said, crossing his arms in front of his body to block the elbow she tried to land in his belly. "I've already got your checkmark in the loss column. Been there for years."

"Too right." Rick grinned around a mouthful of bread as his cell phone went off.

"Richard," Aunt Pat said reprovingly. Her blond brows drew into a pointed frown. "No phones at the dinner table."

"Sorry, Mom," he said, standing with an air of suppressed excitement, "it's the one I've been waiting for."

Rick excused himself to take the call in the other room, fist-bumping Eddie and smiling when Eddie's mom squeezed his arm and whispered, "Good luck," as he hustled past.

Moments later, a loud *Whoohooo!* from the family room drew everyone's attention, and Rick came dashing back to the table, his handsome face flushed, blond curls bouncing.

"I got it!" he crowed, fairly dancing as he took his seat. "I got it! I got *Hamlet!*"

Congratulations flew, and Aunt Pat stood to toast her son, echoed by everyone at both tables.

The guys, his brothers especially, might tease Rick about his career aspirations unmercifully, but when it came down to it for real, they were behind him a thousand percent, his greatest supporters.

It was one of the things she loved best about her cousins.

Uncle Allan stood to give Rick a hug, and for a second, her middle cousin looked like he might actually tear up. He paused and took a deep breath to control himself.

"Thanks, Mom, Dad, everyone," Rick said, taking a big drink of his wine. "It's off-off-*off* Broadway, but this is a big one for me, and the director's a genius. You all have to come!"

Wendell leaned up from his seat so he could reach across to the big table, his hand raised to high-five Rick. "Dude, red carpet!"

Her mom brought out another bottle of wine, and her dad helped carry in the serving bowls full of spaghetti and meatballs, along with more baskets of garlic bread. People dove in as though they hadn't eaten in months, reminding Melinda of the unruly savages she'd envisioned earlier.

Dinner continued, a festive affair with plenty of laughter. When they weren't discussing Rick's new play, they ribbed each other's skills, or lack thereof, on the ski slopes. Melinda heaved a mental sigh of relief that Mitch's name never came up.

As the meal wound down, they got back to finalizing trip plans. Her mom went over the driving arrangements for the next day, and her dad ran down the schedule and the list of everything that still needed to be done.

"Eddie, be sure your phone's charged, please," Nancy Thomas said to her son, and everyone snorted in unison while the tips of Eddie's ears reddened. He had a well-earned reputation for porting around a useless rectangle of constantly dead phone.

"I don't have your suitcase, Mel," her dad said, leveling a look at her down the length of the table.

"Working on it," she answered around a last mouthful of spaghetti.

Stan gave her his stern-daddy-general look. "Hop to it, Sunshine," he said, then turned to her mother. "Where are we on the cold stuff?"

"All set except for the spaghetti sauce, I have to freeze it overnight," Karen answered.

"More meatballs, anyone?" Aunt Pat asked.

From the kid's table, all four guys raised their hands.

When everyone had finished, Melinda rose with the rest of the women to begin clearing, while the guys prepared to finish loading the cars.

"No, not you," Karen said to Melinda. "Go pack. Jakey, go with her and see that she finishes, please, then take her suitcase straight down to Stan. Rick, you and Eddie take the dogs to the sitter's and pick up the rest of the ice."

Everyone moved to comply with their marching orders, and the noise level rose to roar once again.

Jacob pointed one long finger at her and sent her an evil grin.

"Ready, Brussels sprout? Race you!" he shouted, and took off, laughing like a loon.

Melinda ran, hot on Jacob's heels, though she had no hope of overtaking his extra-long stride. He took the stairs three at a time, his endless legs gifting him with a totally unfair advantage.

She grabbed one of the dogs' toys on the fly and chucked it at his feet, hoping to slow him down, but he only laughed when her missile sailed harmlessly past his left knee.

"Nice try, apple seed!" he yelled over his shoulder as he cleared the final step.

Instead of continuing down the hall to her room, Jacob stopped abruptly at the top of the staircase, whirling to face her and tapping his foot.

"My God, you're slow," he said in a snooty French accent, then grabbed her around the waist before she could respond and whirled her into a fast dance step.

Tangoing the two of them through her bedroom door, he dropped her into a deep dip over the threshold, making her squeal and clutch at his arms.

Jacob raised her partway up one-handed, both of them laughing, and for a moment their faces brushed close together, their breaths mingling, his sparkling topaz eyes staring deeply into hers.

Everything went quiet.

Melinda's smile faded. Her lungs stilled. Her heart rolled over with a heavy thud, then picked up its pace, pounding frantically, and something at the base of her spine snapped like an electric jolt.

Whoa, her brain stuttered. *Sexy much?*

The relaxed camaraderie from dinner vanished as her whole being thrummed with a sudden, outrageous burst of lust.

She licked her lips. Swallowed. Her pulse scrambled.

If the house hadn't been brimful of people, she might have leapt up, might have pounced on him right there in the doorway. Might have ripped her best friend's clothes off in a fever and had her way with his luscious body, never mind their friendship or their impossibly divergent goals.

Or the consequences.

"Good to know you haven't lost your moves," Jacob said into the throbbing silence, the heat pumping from his muscular body enveloping her, their clasped hands still raised above their heads.

The pulse points on her inner wrists, inside her elbows, and at the base of her neck beat a wild rhythm.

"You, too," she managed. She'd meant it to be teasing, but the words came out all breathy and flirtatious, not at all like her normal voice.

Poised in their half-dipped position, with Jacob looming above her, surrounding her, his chest almost—not quite—touching her aching breasts, every muscle in her body melted like warm wax.

She couldn't have raised herself up if she'd wanted to.

And she didn't want to.

Gaze intent, Jacob's eyes swept along her flushed cheeks, up to her forehead, then slowly down to her chin, with a long, potent pause on her mouth that robbed her already starving lungs of oxygen entirely.

He said, "You're so pretty," in a musing sort of way. Almost as if he were talking to himself.

"I am?" She said it stupidly, and could only marvel at her own ridiculousness.

Her brain fogged over, the intensity of the need rocketing through her body turning her mind to sexually charged mush.

She couldn't think clearly.

It wasn't as if he'd never called her pretty before. Only there was something different in the way he'd said it. In the way his eyes traveled over her face.

As if...

"Jake?"

"Hmm?"

"Why are you looking at me like that?" Her voice, light, wavery, softened to a hush.

Jacob's gaze dipped to her mouth, then slowly, ever so slowly back to her eyes.

"Like what?" His words rumbled in her ear, a low timbre that shivered through her body.

Like you're about to kiss me.

"Like that," she whispered, unable to articulate the dreamy wonder stealing over her, breathless desire mixed with a tiny drop of nervousness.

Her eyelids slid half-closed, heavy and slow, like blinking through syrup. Her lips parted. Went soft.

Oh, God, please kiss me...

Jacob blinked, as though waking from a dream. Shaking his head and straightening, he pulled her upright with him and flashed a sudden smile, his dimples winking into view. He seemed to throw off whatever mood had taken them both for a spin in a single heartbeat, while Melinda struggled to stand on her own, to silence the screaming need, to force air back into her empty lungs.

"All part of the dance, *ma cherie*," he said, eminently casual. He drew her hand to his mouth and gave her a friendly kiss on its back.

She had no breath to reply.

Jacob grasped her shoulders, turned her in the general direction of her closet, and with both hands on her ass, pushed her forward, all business now.

"Pack," he directed, mimicking her mother.

Pack. Right. I'll just—

"You don't want your mom to come back up here."

That got through the daze, and gave her the impetus she needed to snap back from the edge of the sexual cliff she'd almost plummeted right over.

Clearing her throat, she said, "Yeah, yeah," forcing herself to go casual when all she wanted was to drag him over that cliff with her, the consequences be damned. She gave thanks for the nearly normal quality of her voice.

Had she seriously just been swept under by a wave of molten lust for her best friend?

Melinda counted the beats of her frenzied pulse, still banging away at the base of her throat, and her body answered, *Oh, yeah.*

Giving herself a shake, she grabbed for inner control. If Jacob could act like nothing had happened, so could she.

Probably.

She had to consciously resist the urge to fan her heated cheeks.

Ordering herself to calm down, to throw off the deep pang of disappointment now that the moment had ended, Melinda focused on her clothing. She pulled jeans off hangers and obediently tossed them next to the suitcase still yawning open and empty on her bedroom floor.

She stared straight ahead and tried to ignore the still-sparking nerves tingling all over her body. She'd never experienced such a powerful response to anyone in her life, not even Mitch.

It had to be a rebound thing. Like those people who had crazy sex after a funeral. Because it was life affirming or something.

A breakup was a type of death, really. The demise of a relationship.

Sexual energy was just a release.

Purely physical.

With relief, she latched onto the explanation her spinning brain had supplied.

Rebounding.

Yes, of course.

Jacob was a handsome guy. Hot, even. She might be heartbroken, but she wasn't dead. He was a man who'd flip any woman's switch. Especially one feeling a little lost and needy, one who'd just been dumped.

It was just physical.

So there was that issue settled.

Whew.

Behind her, Jacob prowled her room. He came into her peripheral vision and toed the pile of Christmas presents she'd yet to put away. They sat on the floor beside her small artificial tree and included the gorgeous floral necklace-and-earring set her brother had sent her from Japan, and her prized new camera, a gift from her dad for their shared passion in photography.

She put the silly little tree up every year and decorated it with ornaments she'd made out of family photos and friends' school pictures. Instead of a star or an angel on top of the tree, she always perched her favorite cuddly animal—a fuzzy black-and-white stuffed kitten Jacob had given her for her tenth birthday. She'd added a tiny Santa hat to its head for a festive touch.

Jacob flipped idly through the ornaments, taking one off and holding it up for her inspection, a lopsided smirk on his face.

"Really?" he said.

"What? I like that picture."

The photo had been taken on a camping weekend at the Thomas' horse ranch when they were seven. Eddie's folks had hosted a pie-eating contest that year. She, Jacob, and Seth sprawled side-by-side on the summer-green grass, hands tied behind their backs, faces covered in blueberry pie, and identical, gap-toothed grins stretching from ear to ear.

"I had such a belly ache after that," Jacob said with a chuckle. "And Seth hurled all over."

"God, me, too. And we didn't even win."

"No one can beat Wendell's big mouth."

They smiled at each other, the happy memory shining between them. Melinda went back to packing, relieved to feel her system finally leveling out. He was just Jacob once again. Her best friend, nothing more.

Jacob continued to wander her room, rifling through her books or picking up and setting down random knickknacks he'd seen a thousand times. He told her the latest jokes he'd heard or ones he'd come up with himself, until she begged him to stop. Her stomach hurt from laughing so hard.

She'd missed him over the last two weeks.

Lifting a framed photo from her dresser, he said, "I like this one," turning it so she could see which one he held. "You looked very pretty that night."

Melinda stared at him. He seemed sincere, not like he was teasing her, but... "Are you drunk?"

It was a photo from the night of their eighth-grade winter formal, with her dad carefully pinning a corsage he'd bought for her to the shoulder strap of her dress. She'd framed it because it was one of her favorites of the two of them together, but she'd looked like a chubby chipmunk covered in melting pink icing. That shiny satin had not been a wise choice.

"No, I mean it," Jacob insisted. "My dad thought so, too. I remember he said something about how you'd become a young lady all of a sudden. I thought he was crazy because you were just Mel to me, but he was right. That was the beginning."

"Of what?"

"Of you turning into a girl," he said with a shrug, as though it were obvious.

"I was always a girl, lamebrain," Melinda answered with a laugh.

"Yeah, but I'd never really noticed it before. Or thought about it. After that you were a *girl*. A girl-girl, not just a kid. It took some getting used to."

Canting her head, she considered her friend. "Was it a problem?"

Still looking at the photo, Jacob shook his head. "No. Just weird for a while. Then you pushed me off the swings and it pretty much went back to normal."

Melinda huffed. "I didn't push you, I nudged you. It's not my fault you weren't holding on."

"Uh-huh," he scoffed, the gold flecks in his eyes dancing.

"Anyway," she continued over his laugh, "you were hogging them. It was my turn."

Jacob looked back at the photo in his hand. "We should've gone together," he said, changing track. "It would've been a lot more fun."

"You seemed to have a good enough time with Sherry Simpson," Melinda said tartly, remembering the pangs of jealousy she'd suffered, especially since she'd gone to the dance alone.

"Sherry Simpson," he said with a heartfelt groan and a devilish grin. "I only took her 'cuz she promised to teach me how to French kiss, and none of the other girls would come near me."

"Yeah, well, you got what you wanted, typical man that you are, so don't complain."

"Eh," he said, lifting his shoulders in a casual shrug. "She wasn't as good at it as she claimed. Not that I had a point of reference at the time."

Melinda, who'd heard that story more times than she cared to remember, sniffed disdainfully. "Ungrateful."

"Never say so," Jacob protested, smiling widely. He placed a hand over his heart. "I'll always hold a special spot for her right here. Everyone's got to have a first kiss, right?"

Not for all the fresh, powdery snow in Utah would she ever confess the way she'd fantasized about him being her first kiss during one of her Jacob-crush periods.

Instead, she'd gotten her first real kiss from Kenny, who'd slobbered all over her like a Saint Bernard.

Studying Jacob's cheesy grin, Melinda said, "You're in an exceptionally good mood."

"It's Christmas. Good food, good friends, good memories. That equals good mood to me."

Tweaking her nose, he set the photo back on her dresser, then flopped his big body down in the middle of her messy bed. He stretched out on his side, his head propped in one hand while he watched her go back to sorting through her closet.

It really was unnerving how handsome he'd gotten, and his

perma-tan made her look pasty-white by comparison. If she didn't know better, she'd suspect him of a membership at a tanning salon, but like his dad, he was an active guy, always outside.

The ski bunnies at the resort would probably be all over him again this year.

Because the idea suddenly irritated her, she twitched her shoulder blades and sidetracked herself with more conversation.

"Speaking of Christmas, how was yours?" she asked.

"Well, no coal this year, so, you know. Can't complain. You?"

Melinda shrugged, already regretting her choice of topic. Her Christmas could have been better.

"I heard the prince turned out to be a prick," Jacob said, watching her keenly now and zeroing in on the source of her misery. "Rick told me. Sorry."

"Oh." The knife in her chest gave another twist. For a little while, she'd been able to put Mitch out of her mind. "Yeah."

"His loss," Jacob added.

She huffed out a laugh and smiled because she knew he wanted her to. "Damn right."

"Mine did, too."

Not really following him, Melinda raised an eyebrow. "You had a prince?"

"—*cess,*" he corrected, pointing a stern finger at her. "Princess. Nicole. Whatever. More of a toad-ess, as it turns out."

"Oh. Really?" Sitting on the edge of the bed, Melinda ran her fingers through the dark, burnished brown hair falling over his forehead, then took his free hand in both of hers. "I'm sorry."

"Sucks much, right? Christmas and everything. She was kind enough to wait until after I gave her her present. That's fifty bucks I'll never get back."

Presents.

Jacob didn't seem all that upset about splitting with Nicole, really. In fact, he seemed oddly cheerful. But the mention of presents sent another pang winging through Melinda's heart.

She'd spent so much time and effort planning out the

perfect presents for Mitch. Gifts that had sat, prettily wrapped and alone, underneath the tree all Christmas Day. Her mother had finally packed them away somewhere. She supposed she'd return them when they got back from Utah.

If she could stand the humiliation.

"You gave her a present?" she asked now, shutting Mitch away again. "I didn't think you guys were that serious."

She played idly with Jacob's fingers. He had such big hands.

Jacob shrugged. "We weren't. We had some laughs, you know, and she told me she was giving me something, so... Turns out a Starbuck's gift card and one of those stupid troll things she collects wasn't enough."

Melinda grimaced and squeezed his fingers.

Though she never tired of teasing him over the way girls fell at his feet these days—much to his still-astonished delight—sometimes she spied the sad, lonely teenager lurking behind his confident grin, the boy he'd successfully hidden from most people during their high-school days.

It hurt her heart.

After going through high school mostly dateless, then a couple months of pure wildness their first semester of college, Jacob was, in some ways, still learning to navigate the whole relationship thing. He wasn't always great at picking girls who wouldn't use him, ones he could trust and be himself with. He'd been screwed over more than once.

She'd never liked Nicole, or her predatory nature.

But then, what did she know? She'd had plenty of dates in high school once she came out of her shell, and look who she'd picked. Mitch. She and Jacob really were two peas in a pod.

Jacob mostly blew those experiences off, but once in a while he'd get that look in his eyes, and her heart would squeeze.

Out loud, she only said, "Her loss."

"You're damn right," he answered, and they both smiled.

"Still. Sorry, Jake."

Not for the first time, she wished she and Jacob had been meant to be together. That they didn't have such different goals. That he might see her as more than a friend. In so many ways, they were perfect for each other.

Except for the little problem of wanting totally different lives.

Jacob shrugged again. "More fish in the sea. We'll add 'freedom' to the good-mood-inducing list. When I'm a famous team doctor, traveling the country with all the hotshot athletes, giving interviews on all the sports channels, I'll have my pick."

And there it was.

He wanted the high life. The Hollywood lifestyle of pro sports, TV personalities, constant traveling, and mingling with the professional athlete's version of the glitterati. She wanted hearth and home in Pasodoro, a bunch of kids, her family and friends close by. She could never be happy with someone who was gone more than he was home or who expected her to join him on the loony, high-profile merry-go-round.

Get a grip, Mel.

Mitch had promised her the life she wanted and had claimed to want the same things. Only he was a liar and a fraud. At least with Jacob, she knew exactly how things stood, even if this rebounding thing was making her temporarily crazy, sending her heart and libido hungering after her best friend. She knew full well they wouldn't be able to make each other happy.

Friends forever, nothing more. That was their role. As it should be.

Except Jacob had looked at her when he said *my pick*, and that flash had gone off again. Something new in his eyes that had made an answering something twist deep inside her belly.

It's rebounding, she reminded herself. *It's just physical. Put it out of your mind.*

Jacob appeared deeply focused on their hands, idly fiddling with her fingers. His hands were so warm and comfortable. So big. Hers seemed pale and tiny by comparison.

"Thanks for the Lakers tickets, by the way," he said, looking up at her again. "Playing the Bulls. That'll be a great game. You always score a perfect ten on the gift-giving scale."

Melinda smiled. "Glad to hear it. Thanks for the watch." She rolled the left sleeve back on her sweatshirt to show the bright primary colors of the band and the watch face in the shape of Goofy, her favorite Disney character. "I love it."

"Of course you do. He looks just like you."

"Har har, funny man."

Jacob grinned cheekily. He lifted a finger to tweak her nose, but she batted it away.

"So," he said, " do you wanna go with me?"

Melinda raised her eyebrows, confused.

"To the game, woman. Lakers tickets? Ring a bell?"

"Oh. Um, sure. You don't want to take Rick or someone?"

Giving her an incredulous look, Jacob said, "Would you take Rick anywhere?"

"Good point," she said, then gave an elaborate shudder. "Not unless Aunt Pat pays me."

"Which I've told her repeatedly, no matter how many times she tries to make me take him out of the asylum for free. She's a cheapskate, your aunt."

They grinned at each other in complete agreement. Pretending to pick on Rick was a favorite pastime, whether her cousin was around to appreciate their humor or not.

Jacob gave a waggle of his fingers, bringing her back to his question. "So?"

"Yeah, that'll be fun."

"Cool." He took an audible breath. Then, "So about Mitch. Do you—no, never mind."

Her heart gave a little hitch. She'd hoped they were done with that topic. "Do I what?"

Jacob paused as if he wouldn't speak, but she squeezed his fingers again, and he met her eyes, a cautious look in his own.

"Do you think Mitch was seeing his ex—that he was with her while he was with you?"

"No," Melinda said, surprised.

A tiny, terrible pull on her heartstrings warbled suspiciously in her ears. What if...

"No, he wouldn't—" The denial was instinctive, but she broke off as the seed sprouted.

"I'm sorry," Jacob said, squeezing her hand in return. "Forget it."

"It's okay."

Yet the seed's seeking tendrils were on the move now,

winding their way into her heart.

Hadn't there been times when Mitch had seemed distant or evasive and she'd put it down to work stress or family issues? Times when he'd been mysteriously unavailable?

Yes, he'd always been careful to do the things he'd said he was going to do, to call when he said he would, but there had also been plenty of times when he'd told her upfront that he was busy. She'd appreciated his honesty, even through her disappointment over not getting to see him on those days.

What if he'd been playing her all along?

"Mel," Jacob said, a regretful note in his voice.

Pulling her unfocused gaze back to her friend, Melinda dredged up a smile. In the end, did it really matter? The result was the same.

"Really, it's okay," she said. "What's done is done, right? He's already proved he's a bastard."

"There are degrees, though."

This time it was Melinda who shrugged. "Not really. You either are or you're not. He is. It's only worse if I let it be worse. I won't."

Jacob's thumb rubbed across the back of her hand in soothing strokes. His tawny eyes stared deeply into hers. "It really is his loss, you know."

For a moment, a heartbeat of time as their eyes held. That something new flashed between them again. Something thrilling and unsettling. A tiny lightning bolt. Before she could grab hold of it, it was gone.

Just as well.

Her emotions were obviously still all over the place, tied up in knots by Mitch. Hopefully Jacob wouldn't notice anything off in her behavior. She'd die of embarrassment if he had any inkling of the direction of her thoughts tonight.

Deciding it was a good idea to get up and get busy, Melinda patted him on the head and went back to her closet, flipping determinedly through her clothes. It took another moment for the little spike in her pulse to level out.

That was weird. As weird as when she'd thought—hoped, let's be honest—for a moment, that he was about to kiss her. He had the sexiest mouth…

It was *not* that she suddenly wanted something to happen between them.

Of course not.

That would be a mistake of gargantuan proportions.

So she was attracted. So what. It was just hormones. She was attracted to Zac Efron, too, but it wasn't like she was going to act on it or anything.

Not that she had access to the movie star, but that was beside the point.

Her fingers landed on the hanger containing the slinky, siren-red dress she'd bought for the New Year's Eve party at the ski lodge, bringing her ex-jerkwad abruptly front and center again in her mind.

How many times had she imagined Mitch's hands caressing the bare parts of her back through the hot little dress's cutouts on either side of her spine? Or the way they'd fit together while they danced. And the kiss they'd share at midnight while looking forward to the start of a whole new year together, full of adventure and romance.

Her initial impulse screamed to leave the dress hanging in her closet and choose something else for New Year's—like her sweatpants and Cal State t-shirt. She squashed that notion almost instantly.

Nope.

She wasn't going to hide away in the condo while everyone else partied on New Year's Eve. She'd wear the damn dress, dance her ass off, and knock a few eyes out while she was at it.

Satisfied, Melinda grabbed her mile-high strappy heels in matching red, and her tiny, sparkly clutch, and tossed them next to her suitcase.

She and Jacob fell into casual chatter while she finished packing—the grades they were hoping for from the fall term at school, high school friends they'd seen over break—picking up the easy rhythm of their friendship as though those few electric moments had never happened.

Finally finished, Melinda sat on the suitcase to zip the bulging seams closed. Jacob rolled his eyes in amusement when she motioned him over to help. His heavier weight did the trick, and she was able to get it closed.

Jacob bounced up to grab her bag, but he pulled her in for a hard hug first, and a kiss on top of her head, which barely reached his shoulder. Warm fuzzies sprouted all over her body. Then he dug his fingers into her ribs and made her squeal.

"'Night, garlic breath," he said, flashing her a smirky grin when she looked indignant.

Tossing the garment bag with her New Year's dress in it over his shoulder, Jacob dragged her overflowing suitcase out of her room, listing dramatically to one side and hauling on it as though it weighed a thousand pounds.

Alone, Melinda showered and got ready for bed, then packed up as much as she could of her overnight kit, only leaving her toothbrush out for the next day. The less she had to do in the morning, the better.

Christian swung in with a half-rap of his knuckles on her doorframe to announce his presence.

"Hey, we're watching a movie if you want to come down," he said. *"Die Hard."*

At eighteen, baby-faced Christian was by far her sweetest cousin. He always made sure to include her in whatever was going on.

"Thanks," she said, "but I think I'll read for a bit and go to bed. I'm pretty tired."

"You sure?" he asked. "You're gonna miss the Bruce?"

When she nodded, he *tsk'd* reproachfully but gave her a hug and wished her goodnight.

After her cousin left—hollering *"Kowabunga!"* as he dashed down the hallway, to which he received an answering shout from the guys downstairs—Melinda stood indecisively, chewing the tip of her finger. She almost followed him after all. *Die Hard* was one of her favorite movies, and she'd be able to snuggle up with Jacob.

Her pulse gave an enthusiastic jump, which decided her against the idea instead. A jumping pulse wasn't something she should pursue, especially with her best friend.

Besides, she didn't relish the early start in the morning. Her bed and book called. She was exhausted from the emotional upheaval of the past few days.

5

Jacob helped Stan and Eddie's dad, Peter, cram Melinda's suitcase into the back of the SUV, one of three vehicles making the trip to Utah. Her bag weighed a freaking ton. If he hadn't watched her pack it up, he'd have sworn she'd added a layer of bricks to the bottom. It took all three of them to wrestle it into place.

Once they were done, Stan slammed the door, wiped his hands together, and patted him and Peter on the back.

"That's the last of it, boys," he said. "Thank God, because nothing else is going to fit."

Jacob left Stan and Peter discussing the weather conditions for the next day's drive and wound his way back to the family room where the rest of the guys, minus the adults, were about to start the first *Die Hard* movie.

"Classic," he said, and flopped into one of the recliners, pulling the lever to raise the footrest.

Eddie tossed him a beer, which he placed in the cup holder on the chair's armrest. He propped his hands behind his head and hunkered down to watch Bruce Willis kick some serious ass.

The guys called out encouragement as Bruce mucked up the bad guys' nefarious plans, or quoted their favorite lines from the film. Rick, who had a talent for mimicry, did his outstanding impression of Alan Rickman.

Jacob joined in by rote, but try as he might, he couldn't get his head into the flick. Instead, he kept reliving the moments in Melinda's room when their eyes had met. Something had happened. For an instant, his hands had actually tingled.

Tingled for God's sake.

And he'd wanted to touch her.

Her. Melinda.

His friend.

One of his best friends, a girl he'd known literally his entire life.

If he let them, his hands would tingle again right now, just thinking about her.

He wasn't that much of a pig, was he? To think about touching his best friend that way? He'd hoped all those random thoughts of her were just that—random thoughts, like changing the channel on the radio. Just his brain tossing out whatever stupid crap it landed on.

He'd mostly tuned it out. Had tried, for her sake, to be sorry the prick, Mitch, had broken up with her. Had tried, for their friendship's sake, to ignore the fact that he, Jacob, was unaccountably, unreasonably, undeniably happy knowing they were both single.

But tonight—oh, hell, if he was honest, it had been a lot of nights now. Something else had slid in there, had slid inside him, and he couldn't seem to change the freaking channel.

Sure, she was pretty. Beautiful, in fact. He'd always thought so, long before everyone else had caught on. It was only one of many facts about her, along with her intelligence, and her snarky sense of humor, and her nearly guy-like love of football. Even if she was a Packers fan.

A lot of guys had the hots for her, but it was his job to shut them the hell up if they talked about her in a way he didn't like. Because he was her friend. He watched out for her, and she watched out for him. They had each other's backs, always.

This was something else.

It freaked him out.

And had been for months.

Maybe even years, if he dared to look back that far.

But tonight, he'd swear she'd felt something, too.

And if she had...

Nope. Don't go there.

Reining himself in took effort, but it was the right thing to do. To protect the friendship. He tied it all down again, hoping this time the rope would hold.

Anyway, he'd only been screwing around. Right? Having fun. Being flirty. And she knew how to give as good as she got. That was all. It would be stupid to read anything more into it. Even if she had had that look in her eyes.

Jacob shook his head as if clearing water from his ears.

No, it had been a long day, and she was obviously still vulnerable, obviously still emotional over that dog turd, Mitch. Of course she was. It was to be expected.

Didn't he have things on his own mind, as well? Like the secrets he'd almost shared at dinner. Jacob blew out a breath. Eddie's dad's interruption had been well timed, cutting him off the way he had. It would be better to wait and spill those beans after the trip.

That was part of his problem—there were way too many loose strands crisscrossing all over his brain, tangling everything together, making a mess.

Hell, he'd been thinking about Nicole, too. That was all it was. Crossed wires and timing. He'd imagined it, whatever it was. It was nothing to worry about, had nothing to do with the fantasies that had been plaguing him for months before she'd even met her now ex-boyfriend.

He only had to look at his aunt and uncle to see what a bad idea it would be to even think about traveling down that path. Shelly and Victor had been best friends once. Now their divorce was tearing his whole family apart, hurting their kids, shredding relationships.

If there was one constant in his whole life he counted on, it was his friendship with Melinda. Crossed wires were no way in hell going to interfere with that friendship.

No way.

Satisfied, Jacob tuned back into the movie in time to cheer along with the rest of the guys as they all yelled out, "Yippy-ki-yay..."

Rubbing her eyes, Melinda put her book away, went through her nightly yoga routine, and set her alarm clock for the ungodly hour of four in the morning, yawning hugely. But once in bed, sleep eluded her, despite her fatigue.

The hands on her bedside clock seemed to move at half-speed. She brushed her cheek against her pillowcase, breathing in a faint wisp of Jacob's familiar scent.

An hour passed, then two.

Staring unseeing at her ceiling, she listened to the gradually decreasing noises in the house as everyone settled in for the night.

Three days ago, she'd been on top of the world, about to spend a romantic week with her boyfriend at a beautiful ski resort, including New Year's Eve and that all-important midnight kiss.

Now she was single once again, her heart broken, with no New Year's kiss in her future.

She'd thought she was so smart about Mitch. Smart and safe. She hadn't rushed it, hadn't pushed. He'd met all of her markers for a successful, genuine relationship. He'd called when he said he would. Did what he said he was going to do. She'd met his family and friends, he'd met hers.

Hadn't he said, "I love you," first? Hadn't he been the one to bring up marriage and long-term plans?

At twenty-seven, Mitch was older, accomplished, so

different from the high-school boys she'd dated, or even the college guys. A man. He'd made even casual dates into events, had turned the mundane into beautiful moments now etched in her memory.

In the end, he'd turned out to be just as big a jackass as any other guy she'd dated, and more than most. No one else had gotten beneath her skin the way he had, and looking back on it now, it all seemed so calculated, so deliberate. As though he'd had an agenda. As though he'd been proving something to himself about his own desirability as a boyfriend rather than being a great boyfriend for her sake.

The jerk.

Flipping over, she held one fingertip straight out toward her bay window, tracing the faint beams of moonlight streaming between the slats of her blinds and dancing through the air.

A not-so-tiny part of her was glad her parents were making her go on the ski trip, despite her earlier protests. Despite everything. Her messy bed—with its warm, white flannel sheets covered in bright yellow daisies, her blue, white, and yellow-striped down comforter, the veritable mountain of giant, squashy pillows, and the stuffed animals she'd collected since early childhood—was a comfortable haven, as was her sunny room.

She'd wallowed in that comfort for two solid days.

While a part of her wanted to keep right on wallowing, the rest of her knew it was time to get herself together and start getting over the rat bastard, no matter how much it hurt.

Somehow, after spending even a little time with Jacob, the ache had already eased to an almost-bearable level.

That moment with Jacob had sparked a different sort of ache. A heavy, drugging, delicious one. But she had a firm grip on the whole deal now. It was just rebounding from her ex.

Totally normal.

Melinda sniffed, but she was done crying over Mitch. The heartache would last for a while—damn it, she'd *loved* him, hadn't she?—but she was not about to let him ruin the ski trip or another single day of her life. Spending time with Jacob and her cousins, being out in the gorgeous scenery, working her muscles.

It would be great.

She was going to have the best time ever and prove to Mitch, herself, and anyone who cared to notice, that she didn't need him to be happy.

Reaching across her bedside table, she snagged her phone from its charging dock and brought up her photo album. She took a steadying breath, then before she could rethink it, went through and deleted every photo she had of Mitch and all the places they'd been together.

There. Step one. No more mooning over his image.

For the big finish, she deleted him from her contact list and blocked his number.

Feeling strong, feeling positive, Melinda drifted into sleep, her arms wrapped around her pillow.

She dreamed she was sitting on Jacob's lap in a ski lodge, his strong, sculpted arms around her while he nuzzled her neck with lips that were soft and warm and sent the most incredible longing crashing through her heated body, making her tremble. Braced against his chest, his hard-muscled thighs beneath her legs, she wanted to melt into him and run her hands all over his hot, smooth skin.

When Mitch walked in and stood over them, an angry frown creasing his brow, she turned away from him deliberately, placed her hands on either side of Jacob's handsome face, and pressed her lips to his, sinking into a deep, sensual kiss. Every neuron in her body lit up like a Fourth of July sparkler, and Mitch's presence faded away like the wisp of smoke from a dud firecracker.

Jacob's arms banded around her tightly, holding her pressed against his long, muscular length, and nothing about it felt wrong at all.

At five the next morning, Melinda sat shivering in the front passenger seat of the middle—and largest—SUV in their long, circular driveway, a thermos of hot chocolate in her cup holder. Though thoroughly bundled in a heavy blanket, mittens, a knit hat, and her red ski jacket, she could not get warm, or seem to wake up. She'd hit the snooze button on her alarm clock so many times, she'd only had time to brush her teeth, throw on her clothes, and dash to the car.

Eyes closed, she leaned back against the headrest, her iPod turned up loud enough to block out the noise of the last-minute preparations for leaving.

Brisk desert air flowed over her with the opening of the driver's side door, sending another shiver up her spine. She burrowed more deeply inside her blanket. The scent of sagebrush came in with the cold, fresh and clean.

Her cousin Danny, who was driving, climbed in beside her and turned on the engine to get the heater going. The oldest of the Carlisle boys, he was a natural leader and the most serious of the three. Or at least he seemed that way until people got to know his goofy side. He was studying to become a lawyer like his mother, and like Aunt Pat, he would make an excellent attorney someday.

Melinda peeled one eyelid up enough to peek at him, disgusted to find him looking rested and ready to go. It was five-freaking-a.m. The man was a machine.

"Morning, Princess," Danny said, patting her heartily on the knee through the layers she'd piled up.

She grunted at him and shoved his hand away, making him laugh.

"Nice to see you, too," he said.

"Shut up, Daniel," she said, her voice gravelly.

"Yes, Your Highness."

"Peasant."

Melinda turned her face to the window, shutting him out. The rest of the guys traveling in their car—Jacob, Christian, Gabe, and Wendell—climbed in back.

"Kumquat," Jacob said to her by way of morning greeting, patting her gently on top of her beanied cap as he plunked himself in the seat directly behind hers.

"Celery stalk," she answered, not opening her eyes. At least he sounded properly raspy and tired, as any normal human should so early in the morning.

Loud rustling filled the vehicle as the guys shifted around. Finally they settled and, from the sounds of it, went instantly back to sleep.

Her dad, who'd brought her the hot cocoa and a bear hug when she got in the SUV, would drive the lead car, along with her mother and Jacob's parents, Bill and Lois. The rear vehicle contained Aunt Pat and Uncle Allan, Nancy and Peter Thomas, along with their son, Eddie, and her cousin Rick.

Pulling out of the driveway, only twenty minutes late, they drove single-file over the bridge spanning the dry bed of the Mojave River. Skirting downtown Pasodoro, with its 1950s movie-set perfection, they passed the small cemetery where Seth was buried, then traveled along neighboring Hesperia's nearly empty Main Street through the cold, misty-gray morning air.

They only had to turn back once to make sure Stan had locked the front gate.

Some years, they flew to wherever they were going from the airport in Ontario—forty-five minutes south down the Cajon Pass. Since the Marshall's Peak Ski Resort in Utah was only a six-hour drive from Pasodoro, they'd opted for the road trip. It was easier to take all their gear that way.

In the past, they'd gone to Tahoe, Mammoth, Vail, Taos, and even some pricey resorts back east. They'd skied in most of the western states, too, as well as areas of Canada. Banff had been a group favorite.

In lean years, or ones with limited time, they went to their local resorts in Big Bear or on day trips to Mountain High in Wrightwood.

This was their first trip to Marshall's Peak.

Since the drive promised nothing but winter-dead, dirt-brown desert for a view, and maybe a few canyons in the tiny slice of Arizona they'd pass through, Melinda wasn't too worried about missing the scenery by sleeping the entire way.

It would take nearly half an hour just to reach the fifteen-freeway from their small town on the south-eastern edge of Hesperia's mesa.

Her mom, who'd grown up in Hesperia, sometimes talked about the old days when there had only been one stoplight on Main Street and no overpass for the railroad tracks, so people had had to wait for the trains to go by. Now there were stoplights on almost every corner.

In Melinda's opinion, even with the overpass and no traffic so early in the morning, getting to the freeway still took forever.

"In-N-Out!" Christian and Wendell chorused from the third row, evidently coming awake through some cosmic sixth sense of awareness as they passed the fast-food restaurant sitting at the corner of Main Street and the freeway entrance.

"Shut up, we're not stopping already," Gabe said from his seat behind Danny. "Go back to sleep."

"They're not even open yet, morons," Jacob grumbled.

Wedged in the middle row behind Melinda, Jacob had his long legs stretched through the space between her and Danny, resting his sock-covered feet on the center console, and sounded like he was less than half awake.

"Fifteen north and straight on 'til evening," Danny said, far too cheerfully, when they hit the onramp.

"Mmmph," was the most Melinda could manage, her face buried deep inside her blanket.

She already had a crick in her neck from leaning against the passenger window. Twisting to the other side, she laid her left arm across Jacob's legs, pillowed up her blanket on top of it to cushion her head, and shuffled around until she found the right spot.

By the time they'd wound through Victorville and out the other side, the car was quiet again, and Melinda happily drifted off.

Less than forty minutes later, she woke to the slowing of the SUV as they exited the freeway toward the McDonald's at Barstow Station.

"You've got to-*o-o* be kidding m-me," she yawned, stretching her legs as far as they'd reach. "We'll never get there at this rate."

"Grown-ups need coffee," Danny said, following the first car into the parking lot. "As long as we're here, children, anyone need to pee?"

Melinda dragged her blanket off and kicked out at him with her foot raised over the center console and Jacob's dangling legs, but he batted her away with ease.

Much grumbling and shifting around of big, male bodies came from the backseats before the driver's side passenger door opened. Gabe and Wendell practically fell out onto the asphalt before they gained their feet and loped into the nearly-empty restaurant, Wendell's red hair glistening like a halo in the light of the just-rising sun, a sharp contrast to Gabe's long, dark locks.

"Didn't they have a ton of coffee in their thermoses?" Melinda asked through another yawn, rotating her head left and right to work out kinks caused by sleeping scrunched over in the seat.

"A *ton*," Christian echoed grumpily from the back.

Jacob leaned over the top of Melinda's chair to rub her neck and shoulders, pressing expertly into the knots and melting them away. He'd always had a talent for backrubs. The firm touch of his strong, lean fingers made her *hmmmm* with pleasure, which brought her previous night's dream, and that—*wow*—kiss, strongly back to mind.

She shifted uncomfortably as her nerve endings sat up and purred.

Hot. That dream was very hot. And...

"God, I can't wait to get out of this freaking desert for good," Jacob said, and reminded her once again why they'd always be friends and nothing more.

Pasodoro and the high desert meant home for her. For Jacob, it was a no-man's land to escape as soon as possible.

Melinda rubbed a hand over her heart. Did Jacob realize how often he said those exact same words? He repeated that sentence almost every time they drove past the cemetery or visited Seth's grave. He said it almost every time they went out to the memorial garden to sit on their bench overlooking the riverbed, too.

She closed her eyes. He said it a lot, period.

And every time, the words stabbed a little harder into her heart.

She'd miss him so much when he finally left for good.

"According to your dad," Danny said through a wide stretch, dragging her attention back to him, "there's not enough coffee in the world to compensate for being on the road this early."

Honestly. Every year.

"He set the damn schedule," Melinda answered, getting her head back in the conversation with effort.

Her dad was as much a night owl as she usually was, yet every year he seemed to forget that fact when it came time to leave for the trip. Why it was so important for them to get to Marshall's Peak, or whatever ski resort they were going to in whatever year, by early afternoon was something she'd never understood. If they didn't get there in time to ski that first day, they certainly had enough time to make up for it the rest of the week.

"Don't shoot the messenger," Danny said, lolling his head against the seat rest with his eyes closed. "Uncle Stan wants coffee, Uncle Stan gets coffee."

Melinda gave a disdainful sniff, but let it go. It was too flipping early to be thinking—or speaking—so much.

"How'd you sleep?" Jacob asked her, yawning through the words and bringing the dream right back into her head.

"Okay," she said, glad he couldn't see her expression from his angle, or the reflection of that sizzling dream-kiss in her eyes.

Melinda sat up straight and patted his hands in a thanks-and-you-can-stop-now signal, then twitched the blanket back around her legs. He patted her head in return and flopped back in his seat, giving a dramatic, high-pitched screech as he stretched.

What was wrong with her that she could clearly see him in her mind's eye, all sleep-tousled and sexy, his chest and biceps sleek and tan and warm beneath his black jacket and t-shirt, which would rise up a bit with his stretching, exposing an inch or two of his flat, toned belly...

God.

She shook her head like a dog coming out of icy water. Jacob, sexy? She'd never, in all their lives, let herself truly consider him in that light, except as simple fact. He *was* sexy. But not in any way that related to her. Except maybe that one time when they'd both been drinking and—

And it didn't count. Jacob, she was pretty sure, didn't even remember that little event.

But she did.

Ohhhh, she did.

Melinda shivered, glad she could blame it on the chilly air.

Remembered or not, she knew what Jacob would say. They were just friends. One drunken make-out session wouldn't change his opinion.

Period.

Frowning out the passenger window, she wrangled her emotions. How could she even be thinking such things? She was still in mourning for Mitch. Mitch was the love of her life, not Jacob. Mitch had broken her heart. There was no way she could get over him that fast.

Only... Her heart didn't feel all that broken anymore.

Melinda chewed a fingernail. That worried her more than anything else. If she was already over Mitch, then clearly she must have no idea what true love really felt like in the first place. Was she that shallow, that coldhearted?

It had to be the rebound thing, right? It totally did.

She hoped.

The guys piled back in, their noisy chatter thankfully distracting her. The adults returned to their cars from their own bathroom breaks, fresh coffee cups in hand, and a kaleidoscope of memories flashed through Melinda's mind of all the times they'd stopped here over the years.

When she was little, the old railcars making up the dining section of the McDonald's restaurant had been magical places to play and run through, as often as not with her cousins and Jacob running right behind her, all of them clamoring for ice cream cones or candy from one of the gift shops.

As they'd gotten older, they'd stopped at the station many times with various school sports' teams traveling for games, or on family trips farther north.

Her heart gave a little twist for the kids they'd been, and she smiled out the passenger window as they pulled out of the parking lot, leaving the station behind.

Sleep still called to her as their mini-caravan headed north once more, but she was wide awake now, like it or not. She sipped her hot chocolate and listened to the guys with half an ear.

Danny and Gabe speculated about the double-black-diamond runs at Marshall's Peak and how the conditions might compare to other places they'd been. In the very back, Christian and Wendell played games on their hand-held devices, and Jacob egged them on halfheartedly, disparaging their skills and handing out insults in a routine sort of way.

They passed through the rest of Barstow, and the brown and gray desert took over the landscape again, only interrupted by random buildings, low-roofed houses, and the occasional tumbleweed.

"You guys hear from Zach recently?" Gabe asked. Along with Danny, Gabe was one of her brother's best friends.

"He called on Christmas and talked to everybody," Danny answered before Melinda could. "Still living the high life in Japan. You?"

"Nah. I talked to him before Thanksgiving, though. Said he was working his ass off and having a blast. Nearly fluent in Japanese, now, too."

"He had a head start with the Jitsukawas," Danny said.

Katsuo Jitsukawa and his wife, Manami, had helped manage the Honeywell's garden nursery since before Melinda was born. Her brother had learned Japanese and all about their culture alongside their daughter, Natsuko, who was only a few years older than Zach.

No one could have predicted back then how much that knowledge would come in handy for him as an adult, but he'd always loved the lessons—and the Jitsukawas—who were like family to them all.

"I hope he'll really be home in time for camping this summer," Melinda said, giving another stretch and hiding a yawn behind her hand. "He promised he would."

"Is it that hard to get time off?" Jacob wanted to know.

"The guy he's working with now is pretty intense about craft and business and the whole deal," Danny said. "I think Zach doesn't want to risk blowing the opportunity by whining about going home. The dude's going to make him famous by the time they're done."

The SUV overflowed with deep, masculine voices as the miles rolled past, but Melinda was used to being the only girl and found the guys' low timbres soothing. She was the only female in the kid generation in her entire family, including the cousins on her dad's side. Well, at least until her brother or one of her cousins married—though she could hardly imagine any of them settling down.

She was the only girl in most of their friends' extended families, as well.

Gabe had two sisters—his twin, Holly, who had a massive crush on Zach, though Melinda didn't think the guys were aware of that fact, and their older sister, Tessa—as well as two younger brothers. The boys and Tessa didn't come around that often, and Melinda hadn't seen much of Holly since Zach left for Japan.

Of the rest, Jacob was an only child. Eddie had no sisters, and his two older brothers weren't into skiing, though they usually came along on the summer camping trips. Wendell had two younger brothers and a sister, as flame-haired as himself, but his family had never taken part in their annual vacations. Seth had had a younger brother and sister, but they'd never been on any of the family trips, either, and she hadn't seen either of them very often since he'd died.

Which left Melinda surrounded by boys most of the time, even though the size of their group changed often.

Her dad's Honeywell relations always camped with them in the summer—adding another seven boys to the younger generation's mix—although they usually spent their winter vacations either at home or traveling the world, only rarely coming along on the ski trips.

Melinda did sometimes bring a girlfriend along, and a couple of the guys had brought girlfriends once or twice, too, at different times, including the one Jacob brought last year. But one or two extra females weren't enough to make a dent in all the testosterone.

It would be interesting to see how the dynamic changed once some of her cousins and friends started marrying and having kids of their own.

Most of the time she didn't mind being the only girl, and even enjoyed it. When the boys weren't ribbing her about something-or-other, they either treated her like a princess or like one of the guys, either of which suited her, depending on the circumstances—though when they got going with the guy humor, she often elected to join the women.

On the ski slopes, she got lonely sometimes, though. The guys were all expert-level skiers, and even the grown-ups skied the more difficult trails. While she was a competent athlete, her secret fear of heights kept her from attempting the tougher runs, which meant she spent most of her time skiing alone.

She'd hoped to spend those hours with Mitch this year. Holding hands, riding the lifts together, teasing each other down the runs. Being playful. Staring into each other's eyes or watching the stars overhead from the hot tub outside the lodge.

Melinda snorted to herself silently. So much for those romantic plans.

The SUV crested the small rise leading out of Barstow and started down the other side, a sea of frost-tipped brown undulating before them for miles.

Calico Ghost Town sat way off to the left, midway up another hill stretching from the desert floor, as it had for more than a hundred years. She hadn't been to the old mining-town-turned-tourist-attraction since the summer after high school when a bunch of them had camped on the grounds for a few days, Jacob included.

As though he'd heard her thoughts, Jacob piped up. "Hey, Calico. Mel, remember—"

"Yeah."

Jacob stretched forward and patted the top of her head again, and she smiled. It had been a good trip, despite the conditions. They'd been scoured raw with blowing sand and parched dry by the hot desert winds. Half of the plastic spikes that had come with their tents had shattered when they'd tried to drive them into the hard-packed earth. The ice in their coolers had melted so fast that by evening of the first day all of their drinks had gone lukewarm, necessitating many repeat trips to the local mini-mart for more and more ice.

And Sherise, one of her girlfriends, had surprised a huge rattlesnake in the restroom where it had gone to escape the heat, slithering its length across the marginally cooler concrete floor.

Melinda shuddered as they passed the Ghost Town Road exit and its giant cowboy signpost. She could still hear Sherise screaming her head off in the back of her mind, her piercing shrieks echoing off the bathroom's cinder-block walls, scaring them all half to death. Melinda's first thought had been axe-murderer.

She laughed quietly at the memory.

More than that, though, they'd all still been mourning Seth, and that trip had been the first time since his passing that they'd been able to make themselves let go and laugh again. Guiltily at first, but gradually it had expanded and loosened. Normalled out a bit, as Seth would have wanted. They'd toasted him liberally, sharing memories and tall tales, and though his loss was an always-present ache to this day, that trip had been the beginning of their healing.

It had also birthed the first ideas that had blossomed into positive ways to keep Seth's memory alive, to turn their sorrow over his tragic death into an affirmation of his life.

They'd started with the rodeo, now held annually over a summer weekend at Eddie's parents' ranch. Their fundraising endowed the scholarship they'd set up in Seth's name, and supported the nonprofit his parents had developed to raise awareness about the dangers of distracted driving. It also helped maintain the memorial garden nearly all of Pasodoro had pitched in to create.

Overlooking the Mojave River, the garden was situated on the favorite spot where Melinda, Jacob, and Seth had spent many afternoons whiling away the hours, solving the problems of the world over bottles of soda and Seth's mother's homemade cookies.

That one camping trip had become a turning point for many of them, full of fun, friendship, and a new sense of purpose for their lives.

Melinda turned to catch one more look of the old ghost town as it receded from view. They should go again sometime. Maybe next summer when they were on break from school. They could rustle up the same crowd and make a party of it, especially now that they were all over twenty-one.

Evidently following her train of thought along the same memory track, Jacob said, "We should do that again. Only don't invite Carl and Donna."

Snickering, Melinda nodded in full agreement.

On their second night of camping, Carl and Donna had retreated from the campfire, where everyone else sat roasting marshmallows, to go bounce on each other inside Carl's parents' borrowed trailer-tent. Only they'd bounced so enthusiastically that they'd torn away the rivets attaching the tent fabric to the sides of the trailer along the edge of the twin bed they'd been using and had tumbled out through the resulting hole, buck-naked.

"They sure knew how to put on a show," Melinda said, recalling the way the two had fallen all over themselves, giggling like loons, then stood, hand-in-hand, to take a bow before their startled friends.

"Yeah," Jacob said, "but let's book different entertainment next time. Donna's one thing, but naked Carl scarred me for life. Now if just the girls want to—*oof!*"

Jacob broke off, snickering when Melinda's water bottle hit him squarely in the forehead.

"They broke up, anyway," Melinda reminded him.

Tossing back her water bottle, Jacob said, "Yeah, but still."

The subdued note that had crept into his voice told her he wasn't happy to be reminded of the way their friends' relationship had ended.

Melinda sobered, too, as memories of Carl and Donna's breakup brought Mitch back to mind. She held his face there—so endearingly handsome with his puppy-dog brown eyes and slightly crooked nose, his wide smile with the dimple only on one side—and mentally drew a big red 'X' over him. The jackass.

Breaking up would have hurt badly enough. On Christmas Day, with no warning, and to go back to *Christina*...

No, Melinda scolded herself. Don't drag it up.

At least her breakup with Mitch hadn't affected anyone else. The thing with Carl and Donna had caused a rift in their entire group, since they'd all been friends. No one had wanted to pick sides, but even two-and-a-half-years later, it was still tough hanging out with either of them without the other. Their broken relationship was a big, unhappy elephant in any room, and a solid argument against friends getting involved.

Not that she needed an argument. Friendship wasn't the issue with her and Jacob, at least on her end. Her parents were great friends. So were Jacob's. So were all of her aunts and uncles. Friends could make great mates as long as they had similar goals.

She and Jacob didn't qualify.

Melinda shifted again, annoyed with herself. None of that mattered. She was not getting involved with any friends, certainly not Jacob. Just because she'd had a crazy dream...

And okay, yes, maybe her body tingled whenever he touched her or looked at her a certain way, and in her heart of hearts she feared she'd never find anyone as perfect for her as her best friend.

But she was not in love with Jacob. She once was in love with the rat, Mitch, and now her heart was broken and sending out all sorts of stupid mixed signals.

Shutting it away again, she stared sightlessly out the passenger window and allowed the desert speeding past to haze into a dull, blank wall of nothing. No thoughts, no emotions, only the soothing blur.

Now that everyone was truly awake, Danny turned on the music. Melinda brushed off the brief dip in her mood, and soon they were all singing along at the tops of their lungs to classic Eagles and *Hotel California*, followed by *Life In the Fast Lane*.

Unobserved from his spot behind her, Jacob followed the many expressions crossing Melinda's gorgeous face in the passenger-side mirror. Nostalgia to humor to sadness to a determined sort of grim acceptance.

Thinking about Mitch again, probably.

Asshole.

He'd like to plow his fist in the dude's face for hurting her, especially on Christmas.

Okay, he was glad they were through, he'd already admitted that to himself. For some reason he could never fully pin down, he hadn't liked the guy.

But man, he hated seeing Melinda unhappy.

His own feelings aside, Melinda sure had liked the dude. Jacob gave a mental grimace. She'd been gaga over him. Now she stared out the window, her big blue eyes deliberately blank, even as she sang along to the music.

She had the prettiest eyes he'd ever seen, a true, deep blue with even darker blue rings around the irises, and long, thick, dark lashes. When she smiled, they lit up like sparkly sapphires.

By the time they got back home from this trip, they'd be sparkling again. He'd make sure of it.

As her friend, making her smile was both his duty and his pleasure.

One hundred miles later, Melinda's throat had gone happily dust-dry from singing, and she'd successfully banished Mitch from her mind. They'd worked their way through half of the Eagle's canon and some of Foreigner's, ignoring Wendell and Christian's repeated calls for music from the current century.

They were into a rousing rendition of *Cold As Ice* by the time they reached Whiskey Pete's and Buffalo Bill's, the casino-resorts at the state line dividing California and Nevada, and their first hint of trouble.

Melinda turned down the music and answered her cell when her mom called from the front car. She frowned, her eyes tracking over the giant rollercoaster surrounding the casino on her right as Karen filled her in on the news.

"Okay," she said. "Bye."

Danny glanced at her once she'd hung up. "What's wrong?"

"There's some big accident outside Vegas. We might sit in traffic for a while."

"It's not even nine o'clock in the morning," Jacob complained.

"Great," Danny said, disregarding Jacob. "Alternate routes?"

"They're looking."

As it turned out, the accident was south of Jean, which was itself south of Las Vegas, and only a few miles from the state line. There were no good routes around it, nor freeway exits to access them in any case, just the long stretch of highway and miles of desert on either side. They hit the backup three miles after Karen's call and came to a dead stop.

"Great," Danny said again.

With a sigh, Melinda broke out the snacks, and Christian and Wendell wrestled the lid off the cooler in the very back to pass out drinks.

After twenty minutes without moving more than a few inches, the cars in front of them turned off their engines. Danny followed suit.

Karen, Stan, Lois, and Bill left their car and strolled to the SUV. Everyone got out to stretch and chat, stamping their feet against the cold and blowing plumes of white into the chilly morning air with every breath.

Melinda hopped down from her seat, her blanket wrapped around her body, and burrowed into her dad's arms. Stan rubbed his hands up and down her arms and back to warm her, tucking her beneath his chin and resting his cheek on her hair.

"Awake now, Sunshine?" he asked.

"Kinda," she said, stifling another yawn behind her mitten-covered hands.

Peter and Nancy Thomas wandered up from the third car in their caravan to announce that helicopters were on the way to airlift the injured from the scene of the accident. It was likely to be a while before the cars got moving again.

A small, birdlike woman with lively brown eyes and a sassy cap of Marilyn-Monroe-platinum-blond hair, Nancy barely topped five feet, but she could always be found in the middle of things with her sunny personality. Peter shared their son's brown hair, gray eyes, and studious demeanor, and had the perfect temperament for working with the many horses on their ranch.

Uncle Allan and Aunt Pat joined them next, hand in hand and well-bundled against the cold, then Rick and Eddie, who'd obviously just woken from naps.

Up ahead, a few cars made u-turns, four-bying over the bumpy desert median to head back to Primm and the state-line casinos.

"What do you think?" Stan asked, looking around the group. "Should we go back and sit it out in one of the hotels?"

They debated it for a while but eventually decided to stay in place and wait.

"We'll lose our shirts at the tables, and no one will want to ski," Peter said.

"Huh," said Bill, winking at Lois. "It's not the tables that worry me, my friend. It's my wife, bored, in a bunch of over-priced stores with designer names."

"Too right," Uncle Allan said, evading Aunt Pat's jabbing elbow with a hop, skip, and a girlish squeal that made everyone laugh.

Lois only smiled serenely at Bill. The glint in her eye said Jacob's dad would pay for that little comment later. Probably with a large credit card balance.

More and more people climbed out of the cars surrounding theirs, adding their voices to the mix, shaking hands and greeting each other like old friends, until it looked like they were having some weird highway-block party in the middle of the road.

With nothing to do but speculate about the cause of the accident, the extent of the "poor bastards" injuries, and wait, they milled about in small groups, leaned against the many vehicles, and shared whatever snacks and bottles of water or soda anyone had on hand, as first one hour, then the second, ticked slowly past.

By unspoken agreement, no one mentioned Seth or the accident that had taken his life. It wasn't the moment, though his memory shone in everyone's eyes.

They alternated napping and reading with calisthenics, or walked along the side of the highway and back to keep warm. The adults huddled over thermoses of coffee, and her parents took turns handling calls from the nursery, dealing with questions and calming Manami after a small inventory crisis.

With the car engines off, a light, frisky breeze cleared the industrial smell of exhaust away, leaving only the sharp, clean scent of fresh air, dry dirt, and desert sagebrush behind.

Word spread that clearing the accident was taking longer than expected. The backup now extended behind them, through Primm at the Nevada state line, and well back into California.

Melinda and Jacob slouched along the sandy shoulder of the highway for the third time, passing a car full of college-aged girls Rick, Christian, and Wendell were doing their best to impress with their manliness. Eddie had engaged a group of kids in an impromptu game of Capture the Flag, using the cars as obstacles, and looked to be having a great time.

Eddie had never been into the party scene, or the empty-headed arm-ornaments her cousins had favored when they were younger. He'd always been more serious-minded. He did date once in a while, but mostly he preferred to hang out with their group of friends or work on his parents' ranch, and he volunteered a lot. Melinda admired his work ethic and his convictions, but she wished he'd find someone. He deserved a girl who would recognize and appreciate the warrior's heart beating beneath his unassuming exterior.

Her cousin, Rick, by contrast, was a total ham, and always the center of attention with his movie-star looks and larger-than-life persona. Girls fell over themselves to get to his side.

Yet despite their surface differences, he and Eddie were inseparable, deeply committed to their mutual causes, and bound by their even deeper friendship.

Melinda and Jacob waved to the guys as they walked on by.

Now in the third hour of the standstill, they exchanged increasingly desultory greetings with their fellow stranded travelers. The initial air of camaraderie had finally begun to wear thin under mounting impatience.

Up ahead, a line made up mostly of women and girls snaked away from a motor-home parked in the fast lane.

"Look at that," Jacob said, jerking his chin at the motor-home as they passed it.

A sign in the window read 'Bathroom - $2.00' in big block print.

Melinda shook her head. "That's mercenary," she said with a small laugh. "Brilliant, but mercenary."

"And sexist," Jacob added. "Guys can go wherever."

He waved a hand over the expanse of desert to their right where, sure enough, in the distance a trail of men could be seen making their way to or from a low stand of weedy shrubs.

"Aww, Jakey," Melinda said, nudging him playfully with her shoulder, "look at you, all enlightened and everything. Who said that women's studies class wouldn't pay off?"

"Har-har," he said, nudging her back.

They continued in comfortable silence until they reached the big rig with the In-N-Out trailer that marked their turning point, more than a mile from where their own vehicles were parked, pivoted in unison, and headed back.

"Did you get the classes you wanted for next term?" Jacob asked.

"Yeah, except I had to take astronomy at eight in the freaking morning. You?"

"Yep, all of them. I told you not to wait on your gen-ed stuff. Those classes always fill up."

"I know, I know," she said, kicking at a rock. "I thought, being an upperclassman—"

Jacob scoffed. "Who do you think's filling them up? Everyone who waited."

With that, he was off on a tangent about internships, the classes he had left to take before graduation, and all of his grand future plans, which most emphatically did not include settling down in a small town like Pasodoro.

As they came back in sight of the bathroom-privilege-charging motor-home, a more immediate concern occupied Melinda's thoughts.

"Do you have any money?" she asked, interrupting him mid-sentence. She'd left her purse in the car.

Breaking off in confusion, Jacob looked her way. "What? Why?"

Slightly embarrassed, she gestured toward the motor-home and its long line. The heat climbed her cheeks in a wave when Jacob threw his head back and laughed. Still chortling, he nodded and took her elbow, gallantly escorting her toward the other women.

She'd grown up in the desert and had partied out in it plenty of times all through her high school years. In the high desert, if you wanted to get wasted with ten or twelve of your closest underage friends, driving off into the middle of nowhere was the safest way to do it without getting caught by the cops—or worse, someone's parents. She'd peed out there plenty of times, too. There wasn't a lot of choice that far out of town for a group of people drinking their weight in illegal alcohol.

And yet...

Somehow there seemed a vast difference between peeing beside two or three other drunken eighteen-year-old girls in the dark of night, with only the random jackrabbit for an audience, and trying it in broad daylight near the side of a road crammed full of cars and people as a twenty-one-year-old woman.

It occurred to her how nice it was to be beyond that party-girl phase. She'd never really enjoyed it, anyway, but there was something to be said for having a legal drink in a real bar with actual bathroom facilities on site.

Soon after they joined the line, the motor-home's door opened and Aunt Pat stepped down, nodding regal thanks like a Viking queen to an unseen occupant inside. She waved to Melinda and Jacob as she shuffle-jogged her way past, her blond hair streaming.

Jacob chuckled, but he gave Melinda the two dollars and

waited patiently with her. Once she'd had her turn, they fell back into step, making their way slowly toward their cars.

Melinda gradually became aware of a ripple of sound growing behind them as they walked.

"Hey," Jacob said just as she opened her mouth to speak. "Do you hear that?" They stopped and looked back the way they'd come. "People are starting their cars."

"Finally!" Melinda said.

They grinned at each other. A couple of guys leaning against the car next to them gave them both double high-fives and a loud *whoo-hoo!* before climbing back into their vehicle and turning its engine over.

Jacob and Melinda moved on, faster now, while all around them, engines began to rev and cars slowly crept forward. They shifted off the pavement to the side of the road, out of the way.

Everywhere they looked, people were diving back into their cars, celebratory whoops going up like it was the Fourth of July.

They were still a fair distance from their vehicles when Melinda spied Danny standing on the driver's side running board of the SUV and hailing them with his arms raised over his head, urging them to hurry up.

"Come on," Jacob said, and grabbed her hand.

Together, they sprinted toward the car, flashing past the many vehicles.

Laughing, Melinda gave his hand a squeeze, then disengaged and poured on the speed.

"Hey, slowpoke," she called, "last one there's a—ow!"

Her left foot landed in a hole, and she went down hard, scraping her hands and knees on the rough desert sand.

"Mel!" Jacob dropped to his knee beside her, one hand on her back as he peered at her face, tucking back the curtain of her hair. "Are you okay?"

Nodding, Melinda swiped the instant and instinctive rush of tears from her eyes. Stupid, girly reaction! She was more embarrassed than hurt, though her foot throbbed.

"Yeah," she said. "Just, you know—" She gestured with a wave of her hand to encompass herself, sprawled in the dirt.

She hoped he didn't hear the slight catch in her frustrated

sigh. She was not going to cry over a few scrapes. At least she hadn't torn a hole in the knees of her favorite jeans.

"Can you stand up?" he asked.

Without waiting for her response, Jacob grabbed her beneath her arms and hauled her up in one quick motion. When he set her back on her feet, she gasped in pain and lifted the left one up again.

"Damn it!" she said. It had better not be sprained and ruin what was already a half-ruined ski trip!

"Here, hop on," Jacob said, dropping down again with his back to her. He put his hands backward over his shoulders, reaching for hers so he could haul her up on his back. "We've got to get moving."

As if to underscore his statement, the car beside them rolled forward several feet.

Melinda grasped his hands and swung up, then wrapped her arms around his shoulders. His hands clamped her thighs securely as he took off at a jog for the SUV and the rest of their party.

"Is she all right?" Stan called across Karen through the open passenger window of their car as Jacob ran past with Melinda.

"I'm fine!" Melinda yelled back.

When they got to the SUV, Gabe held the passenger door open for Jacob to deposit her on the front seat, then the guys swung into the vehicle and Danny put it in drive, moving forward before she'd even buckled her seatbelt.

All around them, cars picked up speed, their drivers eager to move forward after their long wait.

Leaning over from the third row to pat her on the thigh, Christian asked, "Are you okay?"

"Fine," she said again, though embarrassed heat burned the tops of her cheekbones and the tips of her ears.

"You're lucky I'd just put my phone away," Danny said while Wendell snickered, "or that sucker'd already be on YouTube. You went down like a brick."

"Shut up, moron," Melinda said. Silently, she gave thanks the phone and its handy little video camera had indeed been put away.

"Yeah, don't they teach you kids etiquette anymore?" Gabe asked from his spot behind Danny, thwacking his friend on the top of his right ear. "You're supposed to say she went down like a *graceful* brick."

"Here, Mel," Jacob said, batting Gabe in the back of the head with one hand and giving her the first aid kit with the other, while the rest of the guys snorted laughter.

Melinda dug out the alcohol pads and swiped them over her stinging palms. The corners of her eyes still prickled, but she sniffed quietly, embarrassed, not wanting any of the guys to see. Her knees would probably be bruised tomorrow. Other than that, they seemed fine.

It was her left foot she was worried about, and she bit her lip as she tried rotating it. It hurt for sure, but she didn't think it was actually sprained.

Still, she dug back into the first aid kit for some anti-inflammatory medication to head off any swelling.

Just in case.

"Christian, grab some ice out of the cooler," Jacob said.

Christian made up a baggie full, frowning down any more comments on her gracelessness in the rearview mirror. Jacob handed the bag over the seat.

"Thanks, Jakey," she said coyly, batting her lashes to disguise their dampness and smiling teasingly at him over her shoulder. "You're going to make such a good team doctor."

"It's not the ice packs, baby," Jacob drawled. "It's the dimples. They have magic powers."

Next to Jacob, Gabe snorted. "Where'd you hear that bit of totally fallacious fantasy?"

"The cheerleaders told me."

"Really? I heard it from the football players," Melinda said, and the rest of the guys howled with laughter.

She flipped open the lighted mirror on the car's sun visor so she could see Jacob's reflection. He met her eyes and grinned, flashing his deep dimples.

"It's true," he said, mock sadly. "Day and night, they call begging for one little smile. They can't help themselves."

"I knew it," said Gabe. "Jakey McDimplekins, team mascot, that's you."

"That's Dr. Jakey McDimplekins to you, smart guy," Jacob said.

"Is that what you make the football players say when they call?" Gabe waggled his eyebrows suggestively.

"Shut up," Jacob said, popping him one on the arm.

It was true, though. Jacob would be a great doctor. He had the brains to be brilliant, but more importantly, he had the heart.

Melinda sometimes accompanied him when he volunteered at the local retirement homes or worked at the kids' summer camps with Rick and Eddie. He'd hang out for an afternoon, playing cards and shooting the breeze with the old timers, holding balls of yarn for the women while they knitted and trash-talked the men. Swimming and shooting hoops with the kids. He simply enjoyed their company, young and old, and had been volunteering since long before he'd decided on medicine for his future.

Jacob had been scouted for baseball in high school. Though he played for the university, he claimed he didn't have the drive to go pro. He loved intramurals and being in the thick of the action, being part of a team, but his first love was medicine and helping people.

Going into sports medicine and becoming a team doctor seemed like the ideal solution. He had the perfect personality to handle cranky sport-diva patients. He'd earn their trust because he genuinely cared about people, and it showed.

Plus, he wouldn't take any crap from the multi-millionaire players, so they'd respect him, too.

Whichever pro team he wound up with would be lucky to have him. She had no doubt he'd make it onto one of their medical rosters, though the field was fiercely competitive, but she'd miss him outrageously when he left.

At least that time was still years down the road.

Working her boot carefully off her tender foot, Melinda left her sock on and applied the ice pack over it. It didn't hurt as long as she didn't press on it too hard or rotate it too sharply.

"Hey," Danny said. "Look."

He pointed at the rear bumper of the car in front of them. It bore a bumper-sticker that read *Eat, drink, and be merry, for tomorrow you may be in Utah.*

"Great," Wendell said, "where the hell are they taking us?"

Although the SUV was once again in motion, it took another ten minutes before traffic fully opened up and they got back to normal speed.

By that time, they were passing the scene of the accident, where six police vehicles, two fire engines, a scatter of glass, and three absolutely totaled cars, each perched on its own tow-truck trailer, still marked the spot.

Abruptly, silence filled the SUV, and Seth's ghost seemed to settle inside with them, a powerful presence touching each of them with love, and sorrow, and regret.

Melinda shivered as they drove by the remains of the vehicles and said a quick prayer for the occupants who'd been inside the twisted shells of metal.

Karen called a few minutes later, and Melinda listened in silence while her mom gave her the oft-repeated lecture on safe driving, watching out for everyone else on the road, and reminded her why parents worried so much about their kids being behind the wheel.

As if they needed any reminders.

"Your mom freaking out?" Jacob asked when she hung up, his voice so deliberately casual, it hurt her heart.

"Totally." She blew out a breath, striving for the same tone. "And your mom says ditto everything my mom said."

"Got it," Jacob said.

She could hear the eye roll in his voice and knew exactly what it cost him—all of them—to respond playfully to the parental worry. The way any young adult would who'd never lost a close friend in a devastating accident.

"Mom and Nancy, too," Christian confirmed from the back seat as he hung up his cell phone. "I could hear Eddie getting his lecture through the phone while Mom gave hers to Rick and me at the same time." Putting on a passable imitation of Aunt Pat's voice, he added, "Daniel, you're to remember you hold all of our lives in your hands, son."

"Lest I forget," Danny said.

"Makes me glad my folks aren't here," Wendell commented.

"You said it, bro," said Gabe.

"Keep thinking that, dudes," Christian said with a smirk on his baby face. "My mom already called both of yours so they'd know you were safe in case they heard about the accident."

"Are you kidding?" Gabe asked.

Wendell groaned. "Oh, *man.*"

Right on cue, both of their phones went off, sending the rest of the car into a laughing fit that dispelled the gloom that had covered the group, while Gabe and Wendell tried to hear their mothers over the noise.

Melinda imagined a comforting brush of fingers over her shoulder as Seth's memory seemed to lift from the car.

Gabe, impatience ripe in his tone, said, "Mom, I'm a professional driver," into his phone, which was as far as he got before his mother's voice went audible to everyone in the car with reminders of all the *professional drivers* who'd died on various race courses *and* highways throughout history.

Not to mention friends.

"Okay, yes, I'm sorry," Gabe said, backpedaling as fast as he could when his mother stopped to take a breath. "I know you worry." Another pause. "Okay. I love you, too."

Hanging up, Gabe's level gaze and clenched jaw challenged his fellow passengers to make any snide comments. Wendell completed his own conversation, and silence rang in the car for two beats.

"Lectures delivered?" Melinda asked.

Gabe reached forward and tweaked her ear, and Wendell said, "Shut it, squirt."

"She's such a hypocrite," Gabe muttered.

His entire family, including his mother, raced cars either professionally, like Gabe, or as a hobby. But Mrs. McConnell was the only one allowed to voice words of advice or caution, and only with regard to everyone else. If anyone hinted at concern for *her* safety, she'd set them straight in a hot minute.

Since Seth's death, her lectures had trended toward the extreme end of the spectrum.

The guys continued to bitch and moan about the worrywart tendencies of their parental units for a few minutes, if only for form, though none of them had been surprised by the phone calls.

They'd managed to hold off the memories while waiting in the traffic backup, but they'd all been shaken by the sight of the crushed cars and the awful reminder of the bloodstained highway.

They stopped in Vegas for lunch—burgers at In-N-Out, to the delight of Christian and Wendell—and to gas up the cars, now more than three-and-a-half hours off schedule, according to the time-lord, her dad. He and Uncle Allan ate while huddled over the printouts Stan had made for the trip.

Melinda sat sideways, her legs dangling out the door of the SUV while she ate the meal her mom had brought her.

Her mother and Aunt Pat muttered and *tsk'd* over her foot, gently prodding her mildly puffy ankle, which showed some bruising.

"Jake said it was fine," she told them.

He'd also said to stay off it as much as possible for the rest of the day, just in case.

She didn't mention that bit.

He'd taken a look at it before grabbing his own lunch, his long, warm fingers rolling her bulky sock down and off. Then he'd carefully held onto her heel and rotated her foot to and fro, watching her face for any signs of pain.

Gooseflesh had raced up her legs and shivered along her

spine, but she'd put it down to the chilly breeze.

"Jakey's an expert now, is he?" asked Aunt Pat.

Melinda shrugged. "He's had enough sprains himself, and he does work in the student health center and volunteer at the hospital, so—"

"Which is all well and good," Karen interrupted, "and I tend to agree with him, but be careful for the next day or so. You don't want to make a minor injury worse by overdoing it."

Instead of arguing, Melinda leaned forward and hugged first her mom, then her aunt. She was used to their over-protectiveness, and even understood it most of the time. It was a loving—if occasionally annoying—by-product of being the only girl. Most of the time it didn't bother her at all, but she was not about to miss any time on the slopes this week. She didn't want to give herself time to mope.

She had something to prove.

Once her mom and Aunt Pat were occupied elsewhere, Melinda put her sock and shoe back on, lacing the boot loosely over her tender ankle. She got out of the SUV to test her foot, sliding carefully down from the high seat and stepping gingerly at first, braced for pain. Though it twinged, more than she wanted to admit, she was sure it wasn't injured enough to keep her off the slopes.

For his part, Jacob insisted on carrying her anywhere she wanted to go, and she mostly let him. It *did* still hurt, and she wanted to save her foot for skiing.

Plus, when he got in stubborn-mode, it was easier to simply play along.

If she was honest, she enjoyed being treated like a fragile flower sometimes, getting carried around by a big, handsome, muscular guy. She'd hate it as a regular thing—she was a girly-girl to her core, for sure, but she was also a strong, capable *woman* who could handle herself, thank you very much. But once in a while it was nice.

Jacob was really, really good at playing the rescuing knight.

Melinda absolutely would not think about why being touched or held by him, even in casual ways, had her pulse spiking and racing tingles shivering over her skin.

He was always picking her up and swinging her around or giving her piggyback rides. He'd done that their whole lives, even before he'd passed her up in height when they were twelve. Some of his college girlfriends had expressed... issues with how touchy-feely they were together, but it was how they'd always been.

It didn't mean anything. Even if she sometimes wished it did.

Like now.

Damn, this rebound process was a bitch.

Laying her cheek against his shoulder blade, she breathed in his scent.

Jacob would be a great catch for some lucky girl someday, anyone could see that. He was gorgeous, funny, smart, sweet. Loyal. And deep down, a truly good person. He'd had a few hiccups along the way—he wasn't perfect, after all. No one would forget his freshman year of college any time soon. Luckily, he'd straightened himself out.

Nowadays the girls wouldn't leave him alone, but they'd have to wait a while if they wanted him to get serious. At twenty-one, Jacob was far from ready to settle down.

Had that been the real problem with Nicole? Had she been angling for a commitment? Jacob had never given any indication he was looking for a serious relationship. He had a giant list of goals he wanted to achieve, including medical school and all the places he wanted to travel. All sorts of things to see and do and be before he'd even consider getting married or starting a family, which she, for one, respected.

Melinda had goals, too. Different than Jacob's, though they had the medical field in common. Studying to become a nurse-midwife made her incredibly happy. She could hardly wait to start serving the needs of the women and families in her community.

She didn't need a man—any man—to make her dreams come true.

But she still wanted to share her life with someone who loved her.

Mitch had swooped in, swept her off her feet, then sent wedding bells pealing through her stupid head, followed closely by a vision full of tiny feet. She'd believed her whole life was falling perfectly into place.

At least Jacob didn't mislead his girlfriends deliberately. He was honest about his goals.

He wasn't a liar like Mitch.

Though she still had several years of schooling and practical experience ahead of her before she could work on her own, once her training was complete, she'd move back to Pasodoro, as she'd always planned. She'd deliver babies in the hospital where she'd been born or assist in homebirths.

Yes, she wanted to get married and have babies of her own and raise them close to her family. But in the meantime, she'd be perfectly happy following her dream and living her life in her wonderful hometown.

Melinda sighed and held on to Jacob a little more tightly as he strode around the parking lot, stretching his legs, working off a small amount of his boundless energy—long car rides always made him twitchy—and taking her wherever she wanted to go.

Because he could never resist the opportunity to perform, Rick strode before them wherever they went, marching with his legs and arms locked in rigid lines, and intoning, "Make way for the queen! Here ye, here ye, make way, or lose your worthless heads!"

Jacob took to kicking him in the butt whenever he got close enough, so Rick changed tack and dropped low to the ground, imitating Dobby from *Harry Potter*.

"Master is angry? Master wishes Dobby to punish himself, Master, sir?"

"That's right," Jacob said, "and if you're not careful, I'll let my crazy, jailbird sister-in-law throw a knife your way, servant."

"Oh!" Melinda gasped, smacking Jacob on the back of the head. "Don't joke about Dobby's death scene! I love Dobby."

"Is that what they teach you at that fancy school?" Jacob asked.

Rick attended acting classes at CalArts in Valencia. He also had his eye on schools back east for his MFA program and dreamed of Broadway.

"Don't question the ways of The Force," Rick said, still in

Dobby's squeaky voice.

When Jacob deposited her back in the car and launched into a discussion about Marshall's Peak, the backcountry skiing, two tube parks, and four, count them *four*, parks for snowboarders, she broke out the map she'd downloaded from the resort's website. It showed the two main areas of the mountain making up the resort, crisscrossed by all the trails and lifts, as well as local points of interest.

With their heads bent close together, they traced the expert runs, where Jacob and the rest of the guys would spend most of their time. She studied the beginner trails.

"I love that they have one whole mountainside for beginners," she said.

"Waste of good ski space," was Jacob's opinion, "but at least it keeps them out of our way."

Melinda nudged his shoulder. "It *protects* the beginners from everyone else. Remember that time I got clipped by a boarder jumping where he wasn't supposed to? They've got it all separated out to keep everyone happy and safe. I like it."

"Whatever flips your skis," Jacob said, snagging her cap off and ruffling her hair.

"I'll probably start over there."

"Every year." He rolled his eyes. "Seriously?"

"I haven't been out yet this season."

"You've been skiing since you were four. You don't need another refresher lesson."

"I want to take it easy the first day, especially now with this stupid foot. Get my skis under me, get used to the area." Get used to the heights of the lifts again... "Besides, remember what Danny said about Marshall's Peak? It's the highest base elevation in the state. Headaches, bloody noses—"

"—which can happen just as easily on the bunny slopes as the expert ones." He gave her his soulful look. "Come on, string bean. You're a great skier. Come out with us. You'll love it, I swear."

Melinda huffed out a laugh and tugged a lock of his hair, shining like melted chocolate and caramel ribbons in the winter sunlight. "No way. I'm not skiing vertically down the side of a mountain."

"It's not that bad."

"I've seen the photos."

"It's not the same," Jacob said, waving his hand as if to say the steep slopes were nothing.

"I've seen the casts on your broken bones."

"One cast," Jacob countered, "don't exaggerate."

"And three for Christian, two for Danny, *four* for Gabe, one for—"

"Gabe's were from car crashes."

"Still."

"Okay, okay," he said. "But I feel bad you're on your own so much on these trips."

Well, she wasn't supposed to be this year, was she? Damn Mitch.

Because there was a strangely intense look in Jacob's eyes, she put a teasing note in her voice. "Are you kidding? It's the only time I get away from you stinky, disgusting boys."

"Well, there's that," he said, crossing his arms over his chest.

"It can't be discounted. Besides, I don't need to risk my life to prove my womanhood like you lunatics. We'll catch up at the lodge and stuff, like usual. And I'll be on the same side of the mountain by day two. It's fine."

"Yeah, but—" Jacob broke off when her dad called out to the group.

"Time to roll out, people," Stan said. He opened the passenger door of their car for her mom, and Karen climbed in as the rest of the party moved toward the vehicles.

Melinda and Jacob looked at each other for a moment, but whatever had been in Jacob's eyes before seemed to have faded. He kissed the top of her head, tucked her hat back in place, and hopped in the backseat. Melinda ignored the little flare of heat at the gesture. They were always hugging or kissing on each other. All the time.

It was totally normal.

Nothing to get excited over.

Shifting to get comfortable in her seat, she tugged on the

belt a little harder than necessary. It had to be the breakup with Mitch that had her emotions all twisted around and out of whack. She shoved the memory of that very sexy dream firmly into the back of her mind. Reboundtis. That had to be it.

By the time they left Las Vegas behind, the mammoth casinos nothing more than toy-sized structures in the side-view mirror, it was well after noon. They still had more than three hours to travel, and a black, roiling bank of clouds had appeared in the sky directly ahead.

"Great," Danny said, turning down the radio and peering through the windshield as the day got steadily darker.

Gabe, who'd been flipping through a sports magazine, leaned forward next to Danny's shoulder. "'Sup?"

"Weather," Danny said, turning on the headlights. "This could get nasty."

A group groan answered that prediction. Twenty minutes later, he was proved correct when the clouds opened wide and sent down a deluge of water mixed with ice, turning the road treacherous and slippery in minutes.

Danny slowed the SUV to a crawl behind Melinda's parents' car, and behind them Uncle Allan did the same. A few idiots flashed by in the next lane, sending sheets of water geysering over the hood and driver's side windows.

"I guess they didn't see the accident this morning," Jacob said.

"Man, we are never going to get to Utah," Wendell groused.

"You guys didn't actually want to, like, go skiing this week or anything, did you?" Christian asked from the backseat.

Jacob sighed loudly. Danny gripped the steering wheel and didn't respond.

Melinda ignored the guys and got on her cell phone to check out the weather information. This storm had not been predicted before they left, according to her dad, who had checked the reports repeatedly all during the previous week.

"It's not supposed to last long," she said after a quick scan.

"Good," Gabe snorted. "The rain's coming down so hard the sand doesn't have time to absorb it, look."

He pointed out her side window. The water was already standing in deep puddles all along the side of the road, as well as on the road itself. Soon they'd need a boat to go any farther. The windshield wipers swished on their highest setting but barely made a dent in the heavy splatter.

"Hey, maybe the drought's over," Christian said hopefully.

"It'll take more than one stupid storm, doofus," Gabe answered. "Anyway, we aren't in California anymore, it doesn't count."

Just when it seemed they'd have to pull over for a bit, the rain cut off like turning off a spout, and the winter sun sailed forth, glaring off the standing water in blinding swaths of light. A cheer went up inside the car.

After that, the weather dogged them intermittently, spitting snow, rain, ice, or a mixture of all three for long minutes at a time, with brief respites of sun. Melinda alternately napped and stared out the window. Whenever Mitch crept into her thoughts, she resolutely shut him right back out. A simmering anger for the way he'd treated her had overtaken the sadness. She welcomed its heat breaking the hold of the cold clutches of grief.

By the time they made it through the top northwest corner of Arizona and into Utah, the sky was darkening toward an early evening, hurried along by the low-lying clouds. As they started the climb up to Marshall's Peak at last, the rain mixture turned solidly to snow, adding new inches to the already white-covered landscape, and they slowed their speed once again.

Finally, they pulled into the parking lot of the condo's rental office. A collective sigh of relief wound through the vehicle.

They'd made it.

With all the delays, it was already past five o'clock. The trip had taken double the amount of time it was supposed to, but if they hustled through unpacking, Gabe informed them, they might still get in some night skiing.

They stayed in the car, waiting while the adults went inside to sign the paperwork and get the keys, and the snow continued to pile higher, snow on top of snow on top of snow.

"This powder is gonna *rock*," Christian said, rubbing his hands in glee.

"Dude," Wendell agreed, giving him a solid fist-bump.

"Man, I can't wait to get out of this tin can," Jacob said, laying his legs across Gabe's lap to stretch their length.

"Get off, peewee," Gabe said, shoving at him.

"Come on," Jacob invited after he sat up. He patted his hands on his own thighs. "Your turn, big guy."

Gabe waved him off, staring intently through the front windshield. "What's taking them so long?"

"Patience, Jedi," Christian said in a voice he evidently thought made him sound like a wise elder. He rubbed a hand on top of Wendell's red head as though for luck. "Skiing doth come to him who waits."

"Shut up," Wendell said, and shoved him, so of course Christian shoved him back.

Somehow Jacob and Gabe got pulled into it, too, so that all four of them were half-standing in the car, making it rock, and laughing wildly.

"Knock it off," Danny yelled suddenly, and everything stopped in mid-motion. He was staring at the rental office. "Something's wrong, look."

Sure enough, the grown-ups were exiting the building, hands waving, and speaking in a clearly aggravated manner.

"Oh, man, what now?" Jacob asked.

"Dude, this is the trip from hell," Christian put in, his former powder-euphoria draining instantly.

Danny rolled down the window as Karen stomped toward them through the driving snow, letting in a blast of freezing air.

Her mother, usually so calm and collected, had a fighting light in her eyes that Melinda knew meant trouble.

Uh-oh.

"So," Karen said, bracing her hands on the car door.

"There's a small problem."

Everyone seemed to hold their breaths waiting to see what the next issue would be.

"We're down one condo," she said.

"What?" Danny looked around at Melinda as if asking her if it was true.

"Evidently, a water line burst early this morning and flooded four of the condos. They've been shifting people around ever since, but they're sold out, so since we're all one big party—"

"Yeah, exactly," Gabe interrupted, "one big party. How are we all going to fit in two condos?"

"It's not that bad, actually. There're enough beds, it just requires some strategizing to get everyone settled. The bigger problem is we're also down two bathrooms and a third kitchen, which, with sixteen people, means we're going to have to be very cooperative with each other."

"Awesome," Melinda said, though not loudly enough for her mother to hear. She didn't want that battle light turned on *her*.

Jacob heard her and gave the back of her seat a warning kick.

"Why the hell didn't they call us to let us know?" Danny asked.

"They only had the house number for some reason—"

"What kind of—" Gabe began.

"Anyway," Karen continued, overriding him and handing a sheet of paper to Danny, "here's the map. We go up this way," she traced her finger along a curving blue line, "and park in this garage here beneath the condos. We'll figure out exactly where everyone is sleeping after we get unloaded. Melinda, since you're a bit gimpy, how about if you get dinner started while the rest of us unload?"

"Sure."

"Okay, then. Let's move."

Karen marched to her own car, the set of her shoulders the only evidence of her vexation. Silence descended inside the SUV as they followed Stan and Karen's car to the condo's indoor

parking garage.
 What a day.

The exterior of the multi-unit, two-story condo building wasn't particularly remarkable. Covered in charcoal-gray siding and white trim, with a steeply pitched roof to encourage the snow to slide off, it had regularly-spaced-but-smallish covered balconies along the upper floor. It reminded Melinda of the barracks-style housing found on a military base more than a luxury resort.

Not that it mattered. In the distance, trails of colored lights snaking down the mountainside had already captured the attention of everyone in the SUV. No one would care about the condo as long as the slopes lived up to their expectations.

As they drove down the hill, curving around the side of the condo to the parking garage underneath, she glimpsed a wide, covered walkway running along the front of the building. Doors to each condo opened into the porch-like structure, which was open at both ends of the building and plenty wide enough for people to juggle their gear and put on their skis. Guests could then ski right out of the building toward the loading area for the resort's shuttles, situated at the bottom of the far slope.

A group of people huddled there now, skis and snowboards

clasped in their hands, waiting on the next bus. The shuttles would ferry them to the lifts and back, or to the main lodge, the small market, and other local points of interest.

The parking garage, on the backside and underneath the condos, was as nondescript as the building itself. At the far end, yellow crime-scene-style tape barred four doors, and orange traffic cones sat around a wide, icy patch covering the parking spaces directly in front of them. The water had evidently leaked out the doors of the flooded condos and frozen into a solid sheet on the concrete.

Danny shook his head when Melinda pointed it out.

They parked in the assigned stalls, and Nancy unlocked the doors to their two adjacent condos. Melinda grabbed three bulging bags full of groceries and headed inside the first door, trying not to limp, while the rest of the group organized the unloading.

A narrow staircase led straight up from the garage door. She navigated the steps carefully, taking one at a time, as it hurt to push up on her injured foot, especially with the added weight of the groceries in her hands.

Once at the top, the stairway opened into the condo's laundry-slash-mudroom. That was a nice bonus feature—no having to truck loads of laundry to the main lodge if they needed to run a load, and it had room for muddy boots and for hanging wet snow gear to dry.

The laundry room sat directly across from a large, eat-in kitchen with a table big enough to seat eight. A breakfast bar fronting the kitchen would seat three more. Everyone else would have to spill into the family room to her right when the whole group got together.

The wood furnishings were simple but sturdy, the chairs covered in thick red cushions. The kitchen had a double oven, another plus with a group their size, a microwave, and an oversized fridge.

In the family room, the widescreen TV would keep the guys happy when they came in from the slopes, and the forest-green recliners and plushy couches looked comfortable with their massive pillows and mountain-cabin-themed upholstery in reds, browns, and greens.

Next to the front door, which would open onto the covered walkway she'd seen at the front of the building, a wooden, tightly spiraled staircase in the far corner led up to a loft area. It overlooked the high-ceilinged family room, where huge floor-to-ceiling windows opened toward the ski slopes, now blazing with light through the still-falling snow, ready for night skiing. From her vantage point in the kitchen, she could just make out the sliding-glass doors that opened onto their tiny outdoor balcony from the loft.

Melinda set the bags of groceries on the kitchen counter. Wandering the other direction, back past the laundry room, she headed down the short hallway toward the back of the condo.

On her left, a door opened onto the master bedroom. It had a king-size bed, a small private bath, and the same stunning view as the family room. It sat across from a storage closet big enough to house all their sporting gear.

The second bedroom, smaller than the master, and with the same incredible vista, was at the end of the hall across from the communal bathroom, which had dual-sinks and a glassed-in shower but not a lot of spare room.

She predicted fierce competition for shower time and hoped she wouldn't have to share a bathroom with Rick. He always took forever.

Originally, she was supposed to share the loft sleeping area, which had twin beds, with Mitch. Now, between the reduction in bedrooms and Mitch's absence, she had no clue where she'd be. Probably still in one of the lofts, since she doubted they'd have her share a larger bed with any of her cousins—they hadn't done that since they were little. But who would be in the second bed?

Oh, she'd had plans for that loft. Snuggling up with Mitch and watching the snow drift down late at night while everyone else slept. Sharing long, slow kisses. Holding hands and talking about their hopes and dreams, their future plans, how much they loved each other.

Damn him for ruining everything!

Scrubbing hard at the corners of her eyes to ward off the prickling tears, Melinda breathed deep and locked him back in the cell she'd created for him in her mind.

"I hope you're happy back with Captain Crazypants," she said out loud, thinking of Mitch with his ex, Christina. "You deserve each other."

She couldn't believe he'd gone back to *her*, of all people. Creepy, crazy Christina.

The one his parents hated.

The one who'd had an affair behind Mitch's back six months ago, then had thrown the news in his face like a weapon during yet another one of their endless, blazing arguments.

The one who'd deliberately crashed her car into his brand new one when he broke up with her, sending both of them to the hospital for stitches, plus a cast for Mitch's broken leg.

He'd gone back to the crazy one and dropped Melinda without a backward glance.

Bastard, bastard, bastard.

Shaking it off, Melinda went back to the kitchen to start putting the groceries away just as her mom came up the stairs with more bags.

"Here you go," Karen said in a sing-song voice. Then she frowned, looking at Melinda's face. "Are you okay?"

"Yep, fine," she said, putting as much cheer into her voice as she could manage. "Hungry. I was exploring a bit, but I'll get this rolling now."

Karen studied her for another moment, then nodded. "All righty. I've got Jake and Eddie bringing up the coolers."

Her mom went back for another armful, and Melinda got started on the dinner prep as the guys lugged in the heavy coolers.

With everyone helping, it didn't take long to get the cars unloaded. They piled all the gear into the second condo, awaiting dispersal once they had their sleeping assignments.

Once the rest of the foodstuffs they'd brought were delivered to the kitchen of the first condo, it became abundantly clear that food storage was going to be their biggest problem, at least initially. Luckily, it was a problem that would resolve itself as items were eaten, so they decided, all in all, they'd gotten off easy, despite the reduction in space.

Melinda put the finishing touches on their traditional first-night meal of submarine sandwiches, chips, drinks, and homemade chocolate-chip cookies. After she had everything arranged for people to make up their own plates, all she had to do was get out of the way.

For such a large group, they ate mostly in silence, a few grunts passing as answers to requests for condiments or napkins.

Fatigue settled over everyone like a blanket, and the falling snow outside further muted any sound. Melinda's eyelids were drooping by the time she'd finished her sandwich, and it wasn't even seven o'clock, despite the hour time difference between California and Utah.

Reaching for another potato chip, she saw Danny surreptitiously swallow a couple of pills and frowned at him. He sent her a look to keep her quiet. Danny had suffered from migraines since he was a kid, but usually if he took his meds early enough at onset, he could head them off.

She hoped he'd caught it in time.

By tradition, it fell to the guys to clean up after eating, so the women gathered around the large dining room table to work out the logistics of getting everyone into the right beds.

"Okay," Aunt Pat said, straightening from the table. "Here's how it's going to go. We retained the two biggest condos, three bedrooms each, including the lofts. The condo next door will sleep Allan and I in bedroom one, Nancy and Peter in bedroom two, Eddie and Gabe in the loft, and Danny and Rick on the pull-out couch in the family room."

Her two eldest sons erupted immediately, complaining over the arrangements. Pat stared down her nose at them both, despite their superior height, and raised an imperious hand, silencing them with one fierce glance.

"Every two nights," she continued, "we will rotate the pair on the couch with the pair in the loft on the twin beds. If you don't like your bedmates, switch it up."

"But—" Danny started.

"I didn't want to saddle Eddie with Rick," Pat interrupted. "He's your brother, you're used to him."

"Eddie's plenty used to him, too," Danny pointed out.

"Appreciate it, Aunt Pat," Eddie said, giving Danny a smirk.

Melinda had to laugh. As Rick's best friend, Eddie had had to bunk with Rick plenty of times in the past—as had they all at one point or another through childhood—and knew exactly what he was getting out of. Rick reached over to give her a pinch, but she evaded his grasping fingers.

"Fine," Danny said, though his voice was less than conciliatory. "If Rick kicks me all night long, I'm dumping his ass on the floor."

"He'll dump me whether I kick him or not, Mom, you know he will," Rick said. Pointing at his older brother, he added, "Watch the face, man. It's my livelihood."

Danny snorted. "Any lumps you pick up could only be an improvement."

"Daniel," Uncle Allan said.

"Just be glad none of you are paired up with The Cuddler," Wendell put in, jerking a thumb at Christian, who made a rude hand-gesture at his friend, out of sight of his mother's sharp eyes.

The other guys laughed, but Danny wasn't done bargaining.

"Why can't Rick stay in the loft bed by himself and the rest of us rotate?" Danny asked.

"Because I didn't think it was fair for everyone except him to have to share a bed," Aunt Pat said, "but if that's how you guys want to handle it, it's up to you."

"Score," Rick said, grinning.

Gabe placed a hand over Rick's face and shoved. "We haven't voted yet, numbnuts. Maybe we'll vote for you to sleep on the floor. Problem solved."

"Huh," Rick retorted. "Maybe Danny'll go on one of his nighttime wanderings, and I'll get the foldout to myself anyway."

"If I sleepwalk," Danny said pointedly, "it'll be in search of a weapon."

"Mom," Rick whined.

Ignoring them, Pat continued.

"In this condo, Karen and Stan are in bedroom one, Lois and Bill in bedroom two, Christian and Wendell are on the couch," she spoke right over Wendell's long-suffering sigh, "and

Melinda and Jacob are in the loft on the twin beds."

"We realize this isn't ideal," Nancy put in, smoothing a hand over her white-blond hair, "but we're not going to be in the condos that much, really, we never are."

"Exactly," Peter said. "As long as we can work out the shower schedules, the rest is just eating and sleeping. It shouldn't be too hard on anyone."

Bill gave a roguish growl and squeezed Lois around the waist. "The wife and I can shower together and save a rotation."

Lois batted at her husband's hands, a flush rising on her cheeks. "Bill!"

"Dad, gross," Jacob said, groaning into his hands and not looking at his parents.

"Now there's an idea," said Uncle Allan, waggling his eyebrows at Aunt Pat.

Drawing herself up to her full height, Aunt Pat said, "Don't even think about it," while all three of their sons clapped hands over their ears.

Gabe and Wendell kicked back on two of the dining-area chairs, ankles and arms crossed, obviously enjoying the fact that neither of their parents were present to get in on the act.

"My ears are bleeding," Rick moaned. "I think my ears are bleeding." He turned to Christian, his eyes wide and traumatized. "Are my ears bleeding?"

Eddie pointed at his parents and Melinda's, who were all giggling shiftily. "Grown-ups," he said. "Stop."

"You're no fun," Stan said, grinning at Eddie but winking lecherously at Melinda's mother.

Melinda blushed. Karen clicked her tongue with a tcha! sound and shook her head. Peter and Nancy exchanged a look no one had any trouble interpreting.

"I said stop!" Eddie repeated.

"All right, all right," Stan said, waving them all quiet, his eyes still twinkling, "everyone know where they're going? Grab what's yours and take it to your rooms. It's already after seven, so we'll deal with the rest tomorrow."

"Anyone who wants to shower here tonight, put your name on this list," Karen said, waving a sheet of lined paper. "We'll go in shifts. Pat will have the list for the other condo. Everyone else, once you have your stuff settled, meet in our family room and we'll unwind with a movie and some popcorn before bed, unless you're tired, in which case you can head to bed now. Understood? Let's move."

"No night skiing?" Gabe asked.

"That's up to you guys," Stan answered. "The grown-ups are waiting for tomorrow."

The guys stared at each other, considering, but they all seemed to come to the same conclusion.

"Nah," said Wendell. "tomorrow's good. I'm up for a movie and bed."

"So, roomie." Jacob loomed over the back of Melinda's chair, staring into her upturned face. "It's been a while since we've bunked together. You don't snore, do you?"

Jacob waggled his eyebrows playfully when Melinda scrunched her nose at him. She was so easy to rile.

"No worse than you, Foghorn Freakazoid," she said. Reaching up, she grabbed for the underside of his upper arm and pinched.

"Hey, watch it, you," he said, smacking her hand away. He dropped into the chair next to hers. "I bruise like a peach."

That made her laugh and sent the tiny golden stars in the deepest parts of her blue eyes sparkling. His chest hitched funny, and he couldn't look away from her.

She looked... different.

Jacob frowned. He'd noticed the midnight-blue rings around her irises many times before—so pretty—and the velvety smoothness of her skin, but tonight those things struck him like fresh discoveries.

"Bet you wish you'd brought a girlfriend along now, don'tcha, Mel?" Eddie asked as he walked past them, giving her a noogie on top of her head. "I pity you, rooming with this bozo."

Melinda laughed again, though Jacob saw a shadow cross behind her eyes—Mitch lurking there still, the bastard—and she said something in reply to Eddie. Jacob barely heard her words. She took a sip of her soda. Even watching her swallow, the delicate motion of her throat, made something inside him sizzle.

It was sort of amazing how beautiful she was, without even trying. She'd gone through the awkward stage like everyone else—eyes too big for her face behind some seriously thick glasses, mouth too wide over teeth covered in braces, first chubby and round, then all gangly limbs too long for her gangly body—but once she came out the other side, the consensus in the guys' junior-high locker room had been, *"Whoa."*

Not that he thought about her that way, he assured himself. Whatever his radio-station brain might say. To him, she was simply his good friend Mel.

Okay, she had a great body now, and she was seriously beautiful, but being beautiful was only one small part of who she was, inside and out. Something he usually took for granted.

Usually.

He'd had to school some jerkwads over the years—guys who hadn't known better than to make disgusting remarks about her and the things they'd like to do to her within his hearing. Their sophomore year of high school, one such *discussion* had gotten physical and landed both him and the mouthy asshat in the principal's office. It had been totally worth it. That was what friends were for, after all. To stand up for each other.

"Want some?"

Melinda's question pulled him back to the present. "Hmm?"

She waggled her soda bottle, her eyebrows raised. "Thirsty?"

"Oh. Um, yeah, thanks," he said, taking the uncapped bottle from her and trying not to think about whether he could taste her lips on the opening. They'd shared drinks and food their whole lives, for crying out loud.

Nothing new here, man.

Karen asked him and Melinda to make up the beds in the loft as she walked past on another errand. Jacob nodded and kicked back in his chair, not really listening.

To avoid staring too obviously at Melinda, he focused on observing the first-night ritual. The people moving about, the conversations. His mom and dad were talking to Nancy on the couch behind him, and he could hear Rick and Eddie out front in the covered walkway between the condos. It sounded like Rick had roped Eddie into helping him practice his lines again.

Next to him, Melinda held the soda bottle loosely and sat propped on one leg, her foot swinging idly while she read over the resort's pamphlet. The page was open to information about the New Year's Eve festivities.

All very normal. And yet...

He breathed deeply, taking in Melinda's scent. She smelled good. Always. Some mix of spicy and sweet, probably flowers and things he didn't know the names of, but the scent suited her. Her hair, a dark, chocolaty brown curling almost to her waist, shone glossy and rich in the bright kitchen lights. And her lips were—

Well, hell.

What was he doing thinking about Melinda's lips, for God's sake?

Something was definitely wrong with him. He shook his head, trying to get the image of her mouth out of his mind. So what if her lips were soft and pink? That was nothing to do with him. He shifted in the seat, uncomfortable.

Something had definitely changed in the past few months. She kept getting stuck in his mind where she didn't belong, messing him up. And when her Aunt Pat had read off the sleeping arrangements, putting him in the same room with Melinda, something deep in his belly had done a little shake, rattle, and roll.

His mental radio dial had gotten out of his control, returning to the same station all the time. The wrong one. And it played only one song, Melinda's name, wrapped around the sound of her laughter, over and over, though he somehow never got tired of hearing it or seeing her lush mouth and smiling eyes in his mind.

Not only did it affect his thoughts, sometimes it affected the words coming out of his stupid mouth.

He would never tell Melinda the real reason he and Nicole had broken up—because he'd called Nicole by Melinda's name, not once but twice in one week. Not during sex, thank God, but still.

It was beyond idiotic, and the two girls were nothing alike. There was no explanation for the mistake. His ears had rung painfully for days afterward, thanks to the volume of Nicole's shouting.

Of course, if he had committed that inexcusable blunder during sex, instead of worrying over potential hearing loss, he'd be walking around minus his favorite appendage.

So there was that, at least.

Still, it shamed him, made him feel no better than those bastards in high school. Melinda was his friend, she trusted him, and he was absolutely not going to betray that trust by thinking of her that way.

Besides which, they'd bunked together before.

Nothing new, he repeated to himself, even as his body twitched with denied desire.

Time to get over it.

Now.

"Hey," Melinda said, breaking into his thoughts. "Where'd you go?"

"What?"

"You seem a little out of it."

"Oh," he said, striving for normality. "Just tired. It's been a long day."

"That's for sure," she said.

Did her eyes always have to light up like that when she smiled?

Oh, God. Yeah. He was in trouble.

"Come on, roomie." Melinda poked his shoulder playfully. "Help me make up the beds so we can crash whenever."

Melinda jumped to her feet and held out her hand like she'd done a million times before, though he noted the slight wince when she put her weight on her left foot.

He was slow to take her hand, wondering for possibly the first time in his life what it would feel like to hold her slender fingers in his, as though he'd never held her hand before, and worrying his palm might turn sweaty, betraying the direction of his thoughts.

"Jake? You okay?"

He'd waited too long, staring at her fingers. Making it weird. It cost him some effort, but he flashed her a big everything's-great grin.

"Yeah, sorry," he said. "More out of it than I realized."

Taking her hand, Jacob let her pull him up, relief crashing over him when it felt completely normal.

Following her to the winding stairs leading to the loft, he started up after her, his eyes skimming her hair where it fell in waves over her slim back, and the sway of her—

Don't look at her ass, don't look at her ass, what the hell is wrong with you, don't look at her ass!

"What's the movie for tonight, do you know?" she asked.

Pulling his head out of the fog of lust that had momentarily swamped him, he cleared his throat. Then cleared it again.

"Uh, no. One of the *Bourne* movies, I think."

She reached the top of the staircase and stepped into the loft. Jacob stopped on the stairs, just for a moment, to catch his breath. He hung his head, letting the shame roll over him, and swiped away the tiny beads of sweat that had gathered along his upper lip. He renewed his vow to fix the situation and to keep her from seeing anything strange reflected in his eyes. She never needed to know he'd gone through this… thing.

When he reached the top, she was already airing the fitted sheet over the bed closest to the balcony door. He ignored the way her dark red sweater clung to her curves as she moved. She had a really small waist for a girl with such big—

"Which one do you want?" she asked.

"This one's fine," he said hoarsely, indicating the bed closest to the stairs. He gave himself a mental smack.

Get off it, man.

Jacob grabbed the other set of sheets and stared hard at the mattress while Melinda talked about a job she was hoping to get next term. He hoped he answered appropriately, because he had no idea what either of them actually said.

This was going to be a long week.

They'd just finished making the beds when a heavily panting Wendell topped the staircase dragging Melinda's suitcase.

"What did you pack in here," Wendell gasped, "an elephant?"

Shaking out his arms after he set it in place at the foot of her bed, he bent at the waist, then leaned on the bag trying to get his breath back.

Melinda rolled her eyes. "Boys. Honestly. Just because you can get through a week with one change of clothes doesn't mean the rest of us are so uncivilized."

"Whatever you say, Your Highness," Wendell said, ducking when she threw a pillow at him. He tugged her bag to the foot of her bed.

"You're supposed to kneel when you say that," she told him imperiously.

Wendell tossed her a grin and the pillow before heading for the stairs. "Movie in ten," he said.

"Where's my suitcase?" Jacob asked.

"Get it yourself, butt-munch," Wendell called back as his flaming red head rounded out of sight.

"You boys are so sweet to each other," Melinda said with a pretend sniffle, dabbing a fingertip near the corner of her lashes. "Truly. It brings a tear to my eye."

"Oh, shut up," Jacob said with a snort. "Come on, let's go watch the movie."

Melinda snuggled next to Jacob on the couch, as she usually did for movie nights when they were all together, a furry blanket wrapped around her and her purple slippers on her feet.

Though her left ankle continued to throb with a beat of its own, it had lessened steadily over the afternoon and evening. Climbing the stairs hurt the most. She'd had to take a few deep breaths on the way up to make the beds, and again coming back down, but the rest of the time she hardly noticed it. It should be fine by the next day.

Rick and Eddie sat on Jacob's other side, making the couch a bit of a crush and giving her an excuse to press more tightly against Jacob. Danny and most of the grown-ups had gone to bed after putting the two condos to rights, although her dad was camped out in one of the big recliners, his eyes half-lidded and fixed on the TV.

The rest of the guys sprawled over the room and furniture in heaps, tossing popcorn at each other and ragging on the bad guys while Matt Damon took them down one by one on the flickering screen.

Warm and comfy, she only paid half attention to the film. Jacob seemed okay now, but she was worried about him. He'd been acting off since they arrived at the condo.

Was he more upset about the breakup with Nicole than he'd let on? She hoped not. It didn't seem likely, but she hadn't spent a lot of time with them recently. Nicole had been obvious about her dislike for Melinda's relationship with Jacob, jealous of the easy familiarity between them, so Melinda had tried to give them some space, even though Jacob had said repeatedly not to worry about it, that it was Nicole's problem.

It was a problem that had come up before, whether from one of her boyfriends or another of Jacob's girlfriends. No one seemed to get the depth of their friendship, and several of their romantic relationships had soured out of that jealousy.

Their loss, as Jacob would say.

Neither of them were willing to give up their friendship for the sake of some guy or girl. The *right* guy or girl would get it, understand it, and it wouldn't be an issue.

Mitch had seemed okay with the two of them, although Jacob hadn't come around very often when Mitch was visiting.

Still, she hoped Jacob wasn't too hung up on Nicole. The girl had been bitchy and controlling about a lot of things, not just Melinda, and Jacob hadn't seemed very happy with her.

Not like Melinda had been with Mitch.

Resolutely closing that door for the hundredth time in three days, she tried to get back into the movie, only she'd seen it so many times that it couldn't hold her attention for long. Fatigue slid over her like sinking into a warm bath.

After her third jaw-cracking yawn in as many minutes, she finally gave up. Leaning over the recliner, she gave her sleepy dad a kiss on the cheek, waved to everyone else, and headed up to bed.

Melinda performed an abbreviated version of her nighttime yoga routine, adding a few rotations and stretches for her foot. It seemed flexible enough.

Outside, snow fell in big, heavy flakes, and the wind had picked up. Tuning out the movie noise from downstairs, she focused on the sound of the storm. It blew the snow against the giant windows in fitful spurts and howled down from the mountain peaks, but as she climbed beneath the covers, it seemed almost soothing.

She drifted with the soughing of the trees whispering in her ears and a comforting, familiar scent wrapped around her. Jacob's, she realized, as she nestled further into the blankets and fell asleep, a smile on her lips.

Jacob sat through the end of the movie, though he was bone tired by that point. If Wendell and Christian weren't bound for the couch, he might have slept there himself. Just to give his brain, and other... er, parts of his anatomy time to settle down.

Having Melinda squeezed tightly against him during the film had been an exercise in restraint he had not been prepared for. The urge to trace his lips over the downy-soft nape of her neck, or to bury his nose in the silky fullness of her hair and breathe her in had struck him like a hammer blow. Holding still with her head on his shoulder had required putting every muscle in his body on lockdown.

Though she'd gone to bed some time ago, his body still revved with unwanted energy.

Her scent still wrapped around him in invisible ribbons of temptation.

Closing his eyes, Jacob struggled for control while the rest of the guys stirred and rose, ready to call it a night.

Rick turned off the TV, and Melinda's dad pushed to his feet with a loud, screechy stretch. Ruffling Rick's hair, Stan shuffled down the hall to his room, yawning through a mumbled, "Goodnight."

"See you tomorrow, losers," Gabe said, grinning widely and casually flipping off the room at large, then following Rick and

Eddie toward the door. Friendly middle fingers popped up all over in response.

Wendell made a pithy comment Jacob didn't catch, but Gabe, Rick, and Eddie snickered appreciatively. Christian only rolled his eyes, though he shot a questioning look at Jacob.

He had too much Melinda on his mind to engage in their usual banter.

How many times had they snuggled up together without it bothering him? Too many to count. So why was it different now?

Jacob rolled his shoulders, trying to ease the muscle tension.

It was a mystery he didn't want to solve. It had to all be part of that radio-station-in-his-head thing. He sensed a dangerous revelation whispering along his mental airwaves, but if he refused to tune in, maybe it would go away.

He wanted it to go away.

Maybe it was the echo of Nicole's accusations ringing in his ears, and his brain had latched onto them for some reason. He frowned. Other girls had made similar claims and never created this reaction.

Whatever the cause, he was putting a stop to it.

"Dude, beat it," Wendell said, nudging him out of his seat so Wendell and Christian could pull out the sofa-bed.

"Yeah, yeah."

Taking his time, in no hurry to head to the loft, Jacob ambled into the kitchen. He rinsed out the mug of hot chocolate Eddie had left on the coffee table. Randomly straightened things that didn't need straightening.

Melinda—with her warm, curvy body, petal-soft skin, and sweet, enticing scent—wouldn't leave his head.

It had to stop. There was no point in risking their friendship. His aunt and uncle, and even Carl and Donna—his and Melinda's high school friends of pop-tent-peep-show fame—were perfect examples of the destruction friends-turned-lovers-turned-enemies could wreak on the people around them.

If he and Melinda got together, then broke up, it would tear like a cannon blast through both of their families and all of their friends, blowing apart loyalties and relationships all over the field.

Dousing the spark before it became a flame would be so much smarter.

If it wasn't already too late.

Leaning his elbows on the counter, Jacob dropped his head into his hands.

How the hell was he going to survive sleeping three feet away from her all week? In the semi-private dark, with only her pajamas for armor against his fertile imagination, and his emotions in an uproar.

Jacob cast one last look at the couch, but the guys were already piling into the hide-a-bed, pushing and shoving at each other like preschoolers.

Time to go up.

He'd just have to battle through. Once this week was over, once they weren't cocooned together in a warm, cozy loft, things were bound to level out again.

In any case, he'd be gone in six months. Maybe sooner, though no one except Eddie knew his plans. It had seemed only fair to give his friend plenty of advance warning, since Eddie would have to find a new roommate when Jacob moved out.

Afterward, he'd sworn Eddie to silence. Everyone else would have to wait to hear about it until the right moment.

Reaching the top of the spiral staircase, Jacob climbed into bed as quietly as he could, though it was a wasted effort with the guys still roughhousing downstairs, their voices getting louder by the second. If they didn't shut up, they were going to invite grown-up wrath to rain down on their hides.

Jacob smirked, rolling onto his back and clasping his hands behind his head as he stared at the ceiling. And waited.

Sure enough, two minutes later his mom opened her bedroom door and hissed, "Cool it, you two!"

Indistinct male voices mumbled, "Sorry," and, "Goodnight, Mama Lois," in contrite tones, somewhat spoiled by unrepentant snorts of laughter when his mom closed her door with a quiet but definite bang.

Evidently deeply asleep, Melinda hadn't budged through the noise. Jacob shifted to study her shape, lightly outlined in the near dark, and tried to come up with a good way to tell her he'd be leaving Cal State sooner rather than later.

He'd almost told her several times over the past four months. It was hell keeping secrets from his best friend when he was used to telling her absolutely everything. He'd wanted to tell her first, but now he was glad he'd waited. He could hold off a little longer—until she was fully over her breakup—before hitting her with his news.

She'd be happy for him.

Mostly.

Eventually.

He'd already had months to prepare for the coming changes to his daily life, including not seeing Melinda every day. It would take her a while to get used to the idea, too. There was no sense doubling up on her now, when she was already upset.

At least his leaving would solve his current problem where she was concerned, if he couldn't change the stupid radio dial himself. Once he embarked on his new adventure, he'd only see Melinda on visits home.

Which would suck, because he'd miss her.

A lot.

Still, preserving all their tightly twined relationships, not to mention their own friendship, was far more important. Putting some physical distance between them would smooth over any lingering weirdness on his part. His brain would finally reset to friends-as-usual.

It would all work out for the best.

If the thought of not seeing her all the time, of her meeting someone else—maybe even getting married, starting a family— caused his belly to clutch in pain, that was his problem.

In her sleep, Melinda shifted and sighed.

Wendell and Christian finally settled into bed downstairs, and the condo went quiet, though the wind whistled around the building. It was a cold, shivery sound, but the loft was warm, spiced with Melinda's scent. Her deep breathing, though hushed, reached his ears across the narrow space between their beds and soothed his jangled nerves.

Breathing deeply himself, he deliberately relaxed his muscles. The last of the curling restlessness in his belly eased.

It would be okay.

Better than okay, actually.

This was familiar, friendly, comfortable. Nothing to worry about. Just two friends, sharing a room, about to spend a great week skiing and playing in the snow.

Nothing could be better.

Yeah.

It would be good.

Jacob matched the rhythm of his own breathing to hers, tucked his body into the warm blankets—cursing the fool who'd created the so-called standard-length twin bed, as his feet hung off the end by a good six inches—and rolled onto his side.

He slid into sleep, wishing everything between himself and Melinda was as back to normal as he wanted to believe.

Morning brought the usual chaos, compounded by so many people trying to rotate their way through only two bathrooms. Somehow they managed without maiming each other, though according to Aunt Pat, Rick and Danny had gotten into an epic towel fight in the other condo.

Jacob eyed them warily—the brothers didn't get truly angry with each other often, but when they did it got serious fast. They seemed in good spirits, giving each other the usual smack talk and casual shoves. Jacob relaxed. No refereeing today.

Breakfast was hurried and loud, everyone dying to get out on the slopes, discussing their plans for the day at top volume. The rest of the week, except for New Year's Day, each condo's group would breakfast in their own kitchens. He always enjoyed the full-party meals.

Jacob caught Melinda's eye and stuck his tongue out behind his mother's back when Lois insisted the dishes be dealt with before they left, making Melinda giggle, and that was another tradition.

There was some jostling as everyone sorted out the items that hadn't gone in the right places the night before and generally got in each other's way.

Aunt Pat, he noted, had cornered Melinda off to one side for what looked like a serious conversation. Jacob frowned, wondering what was up. Then Melinda smiled at her aunt, the women hugged, and they melted seamlessly back into the horde to gather their gear.

Finally, everyone was dressed, skis or snowboards in hand, and they congregated in the hallway, double checking they had all their equipment before heading out into the bright morning sunshine.

"Don't forget your brain buckets," his dad called over all the racket, and everyone held their helmets in the air in acknowledgment. Bill gave them all the double thumbs up and moved forward.

The storm had blown itself out overnight, leaving a heavy new blanket of mostly undisturbed white over everything as far as the eye could see. It glistened like diamond dust in the sun, the scene so pure it hardly seemed real. A cloudless blue sky stretched overhead, though it was bitterly cold.

At least it wasn't windy. Jacob bounced lightly in place and pulled his hat more firmly over his ears.

The parking lot showed signs of recent activity—the various shuttles coming and going, taking fellow guests to the two main ski areas, the Bag Jump, the snowmobile rental office, and beyond.

A narrow path led from the edge of the wide exit out of the condo's covered walkway. It provided a clear, straight shot down to the waiting area for the next shuttle, evidence that they were not the first ones out this morning. Everything else remained pristine.

Filling his lungs with the sharp morning air, Jacob tilted his head back, eyes closed, face to the sun. Anticipation curled through his stomach. There was nothing better than fresh powder on challenging slopes and a gorgeous day.

Then he opened his eyes and saw Melinda directly in front of him, and the anticipation in his gut spiraled into a swooping sensation that left him dizzy. The voices all around him faded and he felt like he was looking down a long white tunnel. Everything vanished but Melinda.

She sparkled.

There was no other way to describe her, and looking at her in the mountain light shot a hard blow to his solar plexus.

He could not be falling for his friend.

No way.

But he couldn't take his eyes off her.

Melinda's ski jacket and pants were white and pale blue, making her eyes look even darker by comparison, and her hair gleamed in the sun, one thick, glossy braid falling down her back. Her cheeks were pink with cold. He knew her skin was every bit as soft as it looked, and his fingers itched to touch.

She stepped her boots into the bindings on her skis, preparing to ski down to the shuttle stop, and laughed at something Eddie said. The sound sent a delicious shiver down his spine. Jacob had to stop himself from calling for the attention of the rest of their group to note her perfection, though he did glance around, casual like, astounded that no one else seemed to notice the angel in their midst.

How could they not be as bowled over by her as he was?

Singly and in pairs, their group began the descent to the shuttle boarding area. Jacob stood rooted to the spot. This could not be happening. He—

"Earth to Jake," Rick said, clapping his gloved hands in front of Jacob's face. "You coming, man? I have a need to beat your ass on a slope. Repeatedly."

Jacob shook himself like a dog throwing off a pile of deep snow. "In your dreams, diva."

He pulled his tinted goggles down to cover his eyes and shoved off, following Melinda, who was already halfway to the bottom of the hill.

By the time he and Rick got to the lines for the shuttles, Melinda had already popped her skis back off and queued up for the bus going to the beginner's slopes. Jacob frowned. He was half tempted to go with her, to spend the day with her and goof off, enjoying each other's company. But he'd never hear the end of it from the guys.

"Come on, Mel," Jacob called instead, "come with us. We'll go slow today."

"The hell we will," Gabe said in disgust before she could answer. "If you wanna build snowmen and play Barbies with the girls, that's on you. The rest of us are skiing."

"Barbies!" Melinda huffed, crossing her eyes and sticking her tongue out at Gabe when he winked at her.

"Yeah, let her go to her baby hills," Rick chimed in, aiming a mock-patronizing look at Melinda. "We don't need no stinkin' girls getting in our way."

Danny opened his mouth to add his opinion to the mix, caught his mother's eye, and wisely subsided.

"Is that a fact, Richard?" Aunt Pat inquired sweetly of her middle son.

Rick mimed zipping and locking his lips, then throwing away the key, an angelic smile on his face.

Aunt Pat snorted. "That's what I thought."

"Dude, you are so whipped," Wendell said to Rick, though not loud enough for Aunt Pat to hear. Christian and Eddie only laughed.

"We'll see you at the lodge for lunch, Mel," Karen said as the first shuttle pulled in. "Call if you need anything, and if your ankle starts hurting again, go back to the condo and rest it for a while."

"I'll be fine, Mom," Melinda said. "See you later."

Jacob watched as Melinda climbed aboard the shuttle, along with two families with young children, and a couple of teenage girls who kept giving him and the other guys the eye, then giggling into their gloved hands.

Christian and Wendell gave the girls an eye back, and the giggling increased exponentially.

Rolling his own eyes, Jacob blew out a breath. Not only were the teen girls jailbait, they were giggly jailbait. He was so not interested. He searched out Melinda in her seat. She waved from her window as the shuttle pulled away.

Their shuttle pulled in right after hers departed, and Jacob put Melinda out of his head as best he could, focusing on the day ahead as they climbed aboard. He'd think about what all the craziness meant later.

Or never.

Never would be good.

The fifteen of them nearly filled the shuttle, and the trash talk flew. Most of the adults would stick to the intermediate or advanced slopes, but he and the rest of the guys, along with Peter Thomas and Melinda's Aunt Pat and Uncle Allan, would head straight to the expert runs.

Later in the week, they'd go to the snowboard parks and the Bag Jump—the best one in Utah, according to the pamphlet—to mix it up, or maybe rent some snowmobiles for a few hours, though most of their time would be spent on the slopes.

Jacob cracked his knuckles and rotated his neck to work out the kinks from sleeping on the tiny twin bed.

One of the perks of their annual ski trip was the utter exhaustion at the end of each day. It was a good exhaustion.

All-consuming.

With any luck, he'd be far too tired at night to think much about Melinda at all.

10

Melinda settled into her seat for the short ride to the beginner's side of the mountain, Aunt Pat's earlier words circling in her brain. Evidently, the rest of the women had agreed not to bring Mitch up at all during the course of their vacation, but her aunt had still wanted to speak her piece, and had pulled her aside right after breakfast.

Aunt Pat had had several choice words to say about the deceiver, also known as Mitch, and the way he'd betrayed not only Melinda but the whole family. Her aunt had assured her that, should it become necessary, Melinda's cousins would "deal" with Mitch in a way he'd understand, and Melinda was not to worry. They had his number now, and the two-timing, bottom-dwelling, rat bastard piece of filth would not bother her ever again.

Melinda couldn't help the grin that spread across her face. She had no doubt that if it came to a rumble between Mitch and her cousins, Aunt Pat would lead the charge.

Disembarking from the shuttle, and putting the matter firmly out of her mind, Melinda made her way over to check in for her first class, dodging fellow skiers left and right. Even this early—forty-minutes before the lifts opened—there were people everywhere.

The families she'd ridden with from the condos followed her to the rentals-and-reservations building, a squat no-nonsense space of white-painted wood and concrete blocks. The concrete floor was covered in thick black mesh to prevent slipping on the icy slush tracked in on everyone's boots.

Friendly employees processed guests quickly and smoothly, getting them onto the slopes to maximize the day.

At the check-in window beside hers, a young couple checked their children in for the kids' class. Their little boy, who was no more than four, ducked his head bashfully behind his father's legs when Melinda smiled at him as she stepped past.

"Have fun today," she said. He peeked at her and grinned, then hid again, giggling.

Back outside, she took in her surroundings fully for the first time. Melinda approved of what she saw.

Everyone's breath blew white in the chilly air, though the sun shone brilliantly, dazzling her eyes. The mountain thrust majestically upward into the bright blue sky like an offering to the gods of ski and board. Evergreens covered the slopes and smaller peaks, bits of color peeking through the heavy mantle of crystalline white. The trees gradually petered out as they climbed to the edge of the tree line where the rocky mountainside took over and soared to the highest peaks.

To her left, an enormous log-cabin-style lodge sat near the edge of the wide runout at the base of the ski runs. Fully decked out in Christmas lights and decorations, it overlooked the mountain with a comfortable air, inviting the winter enthusiasts into its warm interior for a hot drink, a quick meal, and a much-needed breather before heading back out onto the slopes. Frost rimmed the multi-paned windows, each with a large, red-ribboned wreath in its center, and red-and-orange flames from an impressive central fireplace glowed through the glass.

It looked like the perfect spot for a cozy break.

A huge rock-and-timber walled deck fronted the building, with clear plastic panels mounted on the low wall and plenty of outdoor heaters, tables, and chairs for guests. The panels would serve as protection for anyone enjoying the outdoor seating from the snow spray of passing skiers or the potential threat of a misfired snowball. Speakers mounted near the eaves piped Christmas music into the mix of voices and languages calling across the grounds.

Rows of snowboards, skis, and poles already lined the length of the wall, their ends jammed into tall mounds of snow to hold them upright while their owners took advantage of their early arrival at the lodge to get in one last cup of coffee.

"Brisk this morning," an older, magenta-haired woman said cheerily, clunking past in her unhooked ski boots and rubbing her gloved hands together as she made for the lodge steps.

Melinda smiled and *m-hmmm'd* in agreement.

The purity of the air was staggering, and she drank in deep lungfuls. Everywhere she looked, people in colorful ski clothes dealt with their gear or raced from one side of the wide, mostly flat base to the other, waiting for the lift operators to declare the slopes open.

The teen girls from the shuttle, who didn't have their own equipment, were lined up waiting to get fitted for their rental skis and actively scoping out the cute guys. They whispered to each other behind their hands.

Waving to the girls, Melinda secured her lift ticket on a ring through the front zipper on her jacket and skied to the meet-up area for the morning lesson, dodging fellow skiers as she went.

"Skier's left!" two guys hollered as they zipped past, going too fast for the crowds around them and nearly clipping the tips of her skis.

They should be on the other mountain. No way were they first-time skiers.

Well, neither was she, but she knew better than to race around the real beginners.

She had an adult beginner's class first thing, which would include anyone aged thirteen and up, then an intermediate class in the afternoon. She was looking forward to the beginner class the most. It was always fun to be surrounded by people on skis for the first time, especially the younger teens. They were so excited and enthusiastic, and she enjoyed cheering them on as they discovered their ski legs.

Plus, beginner classes usually used a surface lift—in this case a rope-tow—rather than the chair lifts, which helped her get her own ski legs back under her before attempting the elevated lifts and having to deal with her fear of heights.

No one knew the real reason for her insistence on starting every ski season with lessons, except her mother. She planned to keep it that way.

Melinda glanced at the chair lift off to her right and suppressed a shudder as she tracked an empty three-person seat moving up the cables, the mountain dropping away beneath it as it went flying above the tops of mammoth trees.

"Whew," she said under her breath, puffing out her cheeks.

And that was a beginner-mountain lift. The ones on the other side of the mountain, where she'd be the rest of the week, would be a lot higher and steeper.

The heights thing both embarrassed and irritated her, blindsiding her the way it had when she was thirteen. Prior to that summer, she'd never had a problem with heights, had in fact enjoyed them. She'd been a high diver for years.

But then...

Melinda had climbed the ladder to the top of the diving board at the rec center's public pool as she'd done hundreds of times. Maybe thousands. Had made her way to the edge, poised on the balls of her feet in preparation for making her first dive of the day. And some total idiot waiting his turn behind her had bounced the board.

Even now, the memory of that plummeting sensation swooping through her stomach could make her both nauseated and lightheaded.

She'd screamed as she fell, unable to help herself, unable to twist her body into any semblance of a dive or to recover from the sudden jolt off the board and out into space. She'd landed hard, a back-flop that had felt like smashing into concrete. The stunning shock of pain forced all the breath from her lungs.

In response, she'd tried to suck in a mouthful of air and had swallowed pool water instead, choking and flailing like an untrained swimmer. A sudden, visceral, and overwhelming certainty that she was about to drown had swamped her. She panicked.

Sam, the lifeguard—an oh-so-adorable nineteen-year-old boy she'd crushed on for ages—had subdued her wild struggles and pulled her from the water.

In her girlish daydreams, such an heroic rescue might have been thrilling and romantic. In reality, she'd been a blubbering, choking mess, her nose running watery snot all over her face and tears pouring from her eyes. Her swimsuit top had come down.

Even in her state of advanced terror, the humiliation had devastated her. An unbearable wave of it, totally eclipsing the fear and pain of the actual fall, even after she learned how close she'd come to cracking her head on the edge of the pool and possibly dying.

Inches. Mere inches.

They'd sent her home after they determined she wasn't seriously injured, and once she'd recovered physically, she'd purposefully blanked the incident out of her mind. Getting over the soul-crushing embarrassment was harder.

A lot harder.

Still, deep down, she knew Sam had no idea who she was. She was barely a teenager, covered in bad skin, braces, and the kind of shyness that pulsed around her like an electric fence. He was already out of high school, handsome, popular, and outgoing, and he had a gorgeous girlfriend. It wasn't likely Melinda's little episode had influenced his opinion of her one way or the other, because he hadn't had an opinion to influence in the first place. He was simply doing his job.

So she put on her big-girl panties and, an avid swimmer, she was back at the pool a few days later, like usual.

But she never went near the high dive again.

It wasn't until the beginning of the following school year that she discovered her avoidance of the high dive was only a minor symptom in a full-blown case of acrophobia.

Her junior-high-school band had gone to their annual, enormous music competition at a university near Los Angeles that October. While the honor band warmed up, she and her fellow flute players had dashed to the top of the steep—and exceptionally high—bleachers in the school's gymnasium to await their turn to play.

She'd reached the top, turned to sit down, and frozen in place like a flash-formed ice sculpture.

The tug on her center of gravity seemed like a physical pull, one she felt still, any time she ventured too close to a ledge, even one as innocuous as the second-floor railing at the mall in San Bernardino, or the top step of a downward escalator, never mind the soaring ski lifts. It was an invisible, relentless force seemingly determined to cast her out and away, to propel her into space where she'd free-fall to the deadly ground, impossibly far below.

That day in the university gym, her vision had wavered, and she'd collapsed, flailing backward onto the steps in reaction against that incessant pull, shuddering beneath an avalanche of unreasoning terror. Heart thundering in her ears, breath stalled, and tears running down her face, her friends had gathered around her in bewildered concern.

She'd needed an embarrassingly long time to pull herself even marginally back together.

It had taken a friend's threat to call their band director for assistance to jerk Melinda out of her spiraling panic. She'd had to scoot down the steps on her butt, her friends surrounding her for protection against the wrenching gravitational tow, her legs trembling the whole way.

Later, she'd made a not-entirely successful joke out of the whole event, brushing it off as a weird fluke, not wanting anyone to realize the full extent of her fear.

Since then, she'd fought the consuming dread at every turn, unwilling to let her phobia control her life.

For the most part she managed not to let it interfere with her activities, except for that time in New York City when she'd gone to the top of the Empire State Building with her family. They'd badgered and teased her into it—kindly, not understanding the real depth of her fear. She'd been unwilling to give a good reason for not going.

She'd been sick for three days afterward.

If her hands tingled and sprang with fear-sweat when

reading books or watching movie scenes involving heights, only she knew. She'd developed strategies to deal with the anxiety and told no one, not even Jacob, only confiding in her mother.

And Mitch.

She'd told Mitch her greatest fear and embarrassment, had trusted enough to share that vulnerable part of herself with him. He'd seemed so supportive and understanding, too, making her love him even more. Now she knew it had been another part of his good-boyfriend act. He hadn't really cared at all.

"Stop." Melinda said the word out loud, then pretended not to notice the odd looks tossed her way by the three very hot ski instructors gliding toward the lifts.

She refused to spend the day shackled by the intensity of Mitch's absence, feeling him, missing him in the empty space at her side. Her phobia was enough of a challenge for one morning. Mitch was a liar and a jerk. She had no time for him today.

Or ever again.

She wished Jacob had decided to come with her. By now, he'd be on his way to the backcountry with the others, ready to challenge himself against the sheer rock face of a nearly perpendicular drop.

She shuddered.

Lunatics, all of them.

"Nine-thirty class," a deep, masculine voice called across the snow. "Where are my newbs? Gather up."

Melinda gave the ski lift one last glance, then turned toward her morning instructor, who had both hands raised in the air, waving the oncoming class in his direction.

Yes, she had her strategies. She took bunny-slope lessons the first time out skiing every year so that she could work her way up to getting on the regular lifts. After the first ride or two each year, usually she was okay for the rest of the season.

Sometimes, especially if the winds caused more-than-usual swaying on the seats, she had to push herself extra hard to keep going, and push she did. She would never go near the black-diamond or expert runs the guys all thrived on, but overall, this particular little strategy worked for her.

Every year, she re-conquered her fear. It was a small victory, but a victory nonetheless.

While it did get lonely spending so much time on the tamer slopes by herself, it was either that or not ski at all, and she wouldn't let that be an option.

And sometimes, she thought, scanning the smiling ski instructor in his red-and-black ski pants and jacket, sometimes the lessons gave her a little gift, too. Like a morning spent with a totally hot guy on the slopes.

Melinda smiled to herself. Perfect! He'd be a welcome distraction from her love-life woes and the ski lifts all rolled into one.

As the rest of the class gathered around, slipping and sliding a bit while trying to control their skis, the instructor performed a couple of quick warm-up moves, getting ready to lead the class.

What she could see of his face—a strong jaw line, carved cheekbones, and a ready smile—looked more than promising. It was impossible to see his eyes through his goggles, and his forehead was covered by his ski cap, but his hair was a shaggy golden-blond. The ends brushed the collar of his jacket. He was nowhere near as tall as her cousins or Jacob, maybe five-ten-or-eleven like Eddie, and it was hard to tell much about his physique through the ski garb, other than that he was fit. He struck her as more obviously muscle bound, as though he had the body of a weightlifter or a boxer.

"Okay, everyone. Welcome to the beginner's class," he began.

She detected a slight accent in his voice. Scandinavian, maybe? He pushed his goggles back on his head, revealing pale green eyes with thick, short blond eyelashes. Cute, Melinda decided. Definitely cute.

"My name's Dane Olsen, and I'll be your instructor today. Why don't you introduce yourselves, tell us where you're from, and also if you've had any experience on skis before."

They went around in a loose circle while Dane checked them off on his clipboard. There was a newly-wed couple from Kansas, who were on their honeymoon, and a brother and sister in their early teens from Arizona, plus their grandfather, who had to be fast approaching his seventies. None of them had skied before.

Melinda smiled a greeting when it was her turn and opened her mouth to speak, but Dane spoke first.

"You must be Melinda," he said, putting a checkmark beside another entry on his list.

He swept his gaze over her and smiled, showing small, white teeth with crooked incisors. Adorable. When his green eyes met hers, Melinda smiled back.

He said, "No way you're a first-timer."

"I like a refresher now and then," she said with a shrug.

"Wait, Melinda Honeywell, right?" Dane said, consulting his clipboard again. "Don't I have you this afternoon, too?"

"You're teaching the intermediate class?"

Now his smile widened even further. "A glutton for punishment, I see," he said with a wink. "I'll make sure you get a good workout."

The look in his eyes had pleasant heat crawling up her cheeks, but thankfully he returned his attention to the rest of the class before anyone noticed, and they began the lesson.

"You guys are in luck today with all this fresh powder," Dane told them. "Great conditions."

For the first hour, they went over the basics again and again, from safety rules, to using their poles, to the herringbone step for walking up a hill on skis without sliding backward. Once the class had mostly mastered staying on their feet while moving forward, and the critical skill of stopping when desired instead of by accident, Dane got them going on the rope-tow.

It felt good to be on skis again, even at this slow pace. Melinda enjoyed taking her time with the maneuvers, testing out her still-sore ankle and finding it steady, reveling in the gorgeous day. She pulled a tube of lip balm out of her pocket and smoothed it over her lips to keep them moist, smiling to herself when she caught Dane watching.

The teenagers took to it right away and were soon racing each other down the beginner slope, their grandfather on their heels, all three giggling maniacally. The honeymooners had considerably more trouble, but didn't seem to care in the least. Melinda suspected the wife was putting on a bit of a damsel-in-distress show for her new husband, who played the rescuing hero with equal flair.

"Keep your knees over your toes, Cheryl," Dane called to the wife, "not so far forward."

Cheryl waved an acknowledgement and continued on her way with her hubby in hot pursuit. That left Dane with a little extra time for Melinda, and he took advantage of it, teasing and flirting with her all over the slope. He came on a little strong a few times, but after everything that had happened with Mitch, it soothed her damaged heart to know a hot ski instructor found her attractive.

She wasn't full of false modesty. She'd gone through an extended fugly stage when she was younger, but she knew she was pretty now, and she gave her thanks and the credit for her looks where it was due—to God, good fortune, and her parents' combined DNA. Mitch's leaving her had had nothing to do with her, and everything to do with his own screwed up psyche.

Who else would willingly go back to someone as unstable as Christina?

Melinda had plenty of confidence in herself and her accomplishments. She wanted a man who would appreciate who she was as a person, not just how she looked.

Still... She had to admit, as Dane flashed past her with another wolfish smile, it was nice to get a little ego-boosting validation.

Dane swooshed to a stop at the bottom of the hill, spraying an arc of snow, and blew his whistle to catch everyone's attention.

"Okay, guys," he said, "great job. You've done really well with the basics and the rope-tow. We've got about twenty more minutes, so it's time to try the regular lifts and get off the bunny slope. You ready?"

Everyone nodded, the honeymooners a bit nervously, and Melinda concentrated on deep-breathing to settle the skittish jump in her pulse.

It's like riding a bike, she reminded herself. *You've done it a million times. No big deal.*

Taking another deep breath, she pushed off and followed

the rest of the class to the lift line. Dane stood at the front of their group, giving instructions and having them watch other skiers approach and get onto the swinging seats.

Melinda barely heard him. She knew how to do it, of course, but that didn't stop the buzzing in her ears.

The lift seated three per bench. They were going to go up in pairs the first time to make it easier to disembark at the top without getting tangled in each other's skis.

Dane got the teens going, letting them know there'd be help at the top for getting off the lift and instructing them to wait before heading down the hill.

Next were the honeymooners, who needed two tries, then whooped like lottery winners when they managed to take their seat. Dane paired Melinda with the kids' grandfather, who got it in one, then followed them up on his own bench.

Melinda kept her left hand in a vise-grip on the handle and stared straight ahead, above the trees, making sure to keep her eyes from the earth falling away below her skis. Her pulse beat a hard staccato in her ears, and her breaths got shorter and shorter.

She needed a distraction.

Refocusing her attention on the next bench with the honeymooners helped. They were making out like mad, not paying the least attention to the lift, the heights, the view, or the approaching top of the line where they'd need to get off.

She'd planned to make out with Mitch plenty on this trip, and to have a few hot-and-heavy kissing sessions to take her mind off riding the lifts, as the honeymooners were doing.

Oh, well. The best laid plans.

More disturbing was the vision of making out with Jacob that intruded on her thoughts, replacing Mitch's face. Heat spiraled through her veins in crazy loops.

That was... interesting.

And sort of crazily thrilling.

And, oh God, it had to stop.

Luckily, after the first few minutes of riding, the grandfather, whose name was Barney, proved to be a chatty bench mate. His cheerful conversation helped distract her enough that by the time they reached the top, her breathing had almost returned to normal, even if her hands remained tightly clenched.

The honeymooners, predictably, fell in a heap trying to get off the lift. They bounced back up, mile-wide grins on their faces, and eyes for only each other. Hand in hand, they shuffle-stepped awkwardly out of the way in time for Melinda and Barney to disembark.

Dane sped off the lift, saluting the pretty female operator monitoring everyone's progress off the seats, but the girl cut her eyes sideways, ignoring him. Dane continued on as if he hadn't noticed and gathered the class in a circle again, out of the way of the lift.

"Okay, we're going to take the slope slowly the first time," he said. "You guys follow me, and stay in a loose vee formation as best you can. We're going to traverse the hill in wide, level lines to keep our speed down. If you get going too fast, remember your snowplow—make a pizza-slice shape with your skis and dig in a bit, and you'll slow right down. Try not to cross your skis. When it's time to turn, push out with your downhill ski to carve, and shift your weight like this."

He gave a few quick demonstrations to make sure they all remembered, then they were off.

The new hill was considerably longer than the bunny slope. They started off well enough, though everyone but Dane and Melinda fell at least once on the way down.

She concentrated on perfecting her form, making sure her ankle held solid on the turns, and staying out of the way of the other skiers, who avoided the class and their slow speeds as much as possible.

There were plenty of calls of, "Skier's right!" and "Skier's left!" as they flashed past the class, and some called out encouragement or hailed Dane.

Although the top of the run was high up the mountain, the grade was mild and didn't bother Melinda the way the lifts did. Something about being on her own two feet—or skis—made a difference, especially with no steep drop-offs or cliffs to worry about, so she was able to enjoy the exercise and the day.

The tremors caused by riding the lift had vanished as soon

as she left the bench. They'd come back for the next ride, of course, though each round would get easier. Pride kept her chin lifted. What mattered was that she controlled her phobia. Day after day, year after year, she didn't let it stop her. Someday, maybe the lifts wouldn't bother her at all anymore. Until then, she'd keep fighting the fear and keep doing what she loved.

"Looking good, Miss Honeywell," Dane called, looking her up and down with an obvious approval that had nothing to do with her athletic skills.

Melinda smiled her thanks, though she didn't take the flattery to heart. Ski instructors were notoriously flirty.

When they reached the bottom, Melinda grinned at the exhilarated faces of her fellow classmates. They'd made it, and everyone was pumped up and ready to do it again.

She'd been skiing for too many years to remember what it had felt like the first time she'd made it down a real run, but it didn't matter. She shared their delight in the accomplishment, if for different reasons, and now that the annual first-lift hurdle was behind her, she was ready to tackle the slopes, too.

The intermediate class later that afternoon would be more about working on her skill level, not worrying about the lifts.

She glanced at Dane, who had waved them back into their class circle. It wouldn't be a hardship to spend another couple hours in his company, either. He caught her eye, and she smiled.

"Awesome!" Dane said. "Really great job, everyone. Before I turn you loose on the slopes, I'd like to thank you on behalf of myself and the lodge for taking my class." He pulled a handful of paper slips from his breast pocket and passed them around. "Here's a coupon for ten-percent off your next purchase in any of the resort restaurants. Now let's go up together one more time, then when you reach the bottom, you're free to go enjoy the rest of your day. Have fun, and remember to stay safe."

The newlyweds got on the lift first this time—two tries, again—then the teens rode up with their grandfather, leaving Melinda to ride with Dane.

After they took their seat, Dane transferred his poles to his outside hand and laid his left arm across the back of the chair around Melinda's shoulders. She held on tight to the bar on her side and tried to ignore the way he kicked his legs back and forth, making the seat swing more than she liked.

"So, Melinda Honeywell," he said, big smile in place, blindingly-white teeth flashing in the sun. "California, right? What part?"

"Southern. The high desert." She bit her lip. Did he really have to move around so much?

"The high desert. Where's that, like Palm Springs?"

"No, Palm Springs is low desert. The high desert is north, up the Cajon Pass. If you've ever driven from here through Vegas and on toward LA, you've gone right through it. What about you?"

"Denmark," he said, puffing out his chest.

"Dane from Denmark?" she said, chuckling a bit through her teeth and squeezing her fingers ever tighter around the handle as he continued to swing his legs.

He grinned. "Yeah, my parents lacked imagination. Are you okay?"

"What? Oh, yeah, I just—"

"Is this bothering you?" he asked, kicking his legs out harder.

Swallowing a squeak, she nodded. "A little. Would you mind—"

"I bet you don't want me to do this, huh?" Dane bounced and rocked side to side, chortling.

The seat shimmied and swayed, and all the blood seemed to drain out of her head.

"Please don't do that," she managed, her voice coming out high and thin.

Seeming to realize she was serious, Dane stopped the motion, patting her on the shoulder.

"Okay, okay, sorry," he said, still grinning.

Was he really that much of a jerk, or had he only been playing around? She looked at him out of the corner of her eye, hoping he'd only been showing off. They rode in silence for a moment, Melinda trying desperately to come up with a new topic.

"So, Denmark," she said finally. "Wow. What brought you

out here?"

"Work," he stated, as though that should be obvious.

He brought his hand from around her shoulder and skimmed it down her cheek, then snagged a lock of her hair and fanned the ends between his gloved fingers.

"Do you work here every year?" Melinda asked, trying to ignore his hand. "What do you do in the off-season?"

"I teach skiing all over the world, a different place every year," he answered with a shrug. "Summers I teach surfing, same thing. Last year I was in Hawaii, next summer I've got a gig lined up in Australia."

"That's incredible," Melinda said, impressed. "You must get to see some amazing places."

"It doesn't suck," he said. "When the lesson season's slow, I travel. Thailand, Peru, South Africa, Russia. All over."

They reached the end of the lift and hopped off. The rest of the class had already gone down the slope, so they started off together. Dane kept the pace slow so they could talk.

"Have you been anywhere?" he asked.

"Some. Not like you, but I've been all over the States and into Canada. Mexico. I'm still in college, but when I graduate I want to go to Europe."

He scoffed. "College. The best education's getting out and seeing the world."

Maybe, but she wanted her traditional education, too, and her home-sweet-home waiting for her at the end of the day. Or the vacation.

"Do you go by yourself?" she asked.

"Mostly," he said with another shrug. "Sometimes I go with friends, or I hook up with people there. There's always someone new and something different to see."

Melinda considered him as they made their way down the slope. It sounded like an amazing lifestyle, and she definitely wanted to travel, but she wanted to share it with someone. One of her girlfriends, maybe. Or Jacob. He'd be great to travel with. He was fun, easy going, and he'd keep her safe at the same time that he'd push her to try new things she might otherwise miss. He wouldn't go for the beaten path all the time.

"What's been your favorite—"

"Watch out!" Dane shouted, and lunged at her, knocking her off her feet.

11

Melinda gasped as Dane's body slammed her into the snow, jolting the air from her lungs. He might not be as tall as her cousins, but he was very muscular, and his body felt enormous. Powerful and heavy. He covered her from head to toe. She couldn't draw a breath.

"Damn bombers!" Dane was yelling. "Take that shit to the other mountain, assholes!"

A whole bunch of what she assumed was Danish flew from his mouth after that. Squirming in panic to get free, Melinda elbowed him in the ribs to get him to move. She needed air!

"Hey, sorry," he said, shifting off her and helping her back to her feet, brushing the snow from her legs and back. "Jerk-offs came flying down and almost hit you, acting all crazy. They know better than to do that over here. If I catch 'em, they're getting the boot."

"Thanks," she said, still winded, and more than a little unnerved by how powerless she'd felt with him pinning her down that way.

She swiped the snow from her face, suddenly freezing. The other skiers were nowhere to be seen. They must have been seriously speeding to get to the bottom of the hill and out of sight so fast.

Both of their skis had popped off. Dane gave her a hand while she stepped back into her bindings, then he dropped into his. Melinda hoped he couldn't feel her trembling.

"Damn, hang on," he said just as they were about to continue down the slope.

Melinda watched quizzically as he shoved his goggles to his forehead and dug in his pockets, then dragged out a tissue.

"Here," he said, moving closer and using it to dab beneath her nose and onto her top lip. It came away bloody.

"Oh, God," she said, taking the tissue from him and holding it to her nose herself, embarrassed now. "Sorry. Thanks. My face is so cold, I didn't even feel it."

"Oh, yeah?" he said, staring fixedly at her lips and licking his own. His voice deepened. "I could fix that for you."

"Ah," she said. "Hmm."

Melinda huffed out a small, awkward laugh, not sure what to say to that. She suddenly felt like a tiny minnow facing a very hungry shark.

He stared a moment longer, his green eyes uncomfortably intent. Then he smiled and swept his hand out before her with a flourish.

"Come on," he said. "Let me at least buy you lunch for knocking you into the snow and giving you a bloody nose."

"Oh, um. That's nice of you, but it's really not necessary." *A second ago I thought you wanted me to be your lunch, so...* "You saved me from a hit, and the altitude probably caused the nosebleed."

"I want to make it up to you." He put on a pleading look.

"I'm supposed to meet my family—"

"Please?"

"I—" Oh, crap. He obviously felt badly, and she didn't want to argue. "Okay. I'll call them when we get to the bottom."

"Great," he said, smiling again, more warmly now. "Let's go."

Lunch turned out to be fun, even though he seemed oddly intense sometimes. Dane entertained her with stories of his travels and the people he'd met. The little frisson of unease she'd noticed earlier disappeared, and she found herself enjoying his company.

They sat by the fireplace after they ate and talked some more, and Dane waited patiently while she bought a postcard in the lodge's gift shop to send to Zach in Japan, including the postage necessary to mail it.

She scrawled *I miss you, wish you were here! Love, Mel* across the card and deposited it in the little mailbox at the front desk, then she and Dane headed back out onto the slopes together.

Once or twice, he looked at her sort of oddly. Maybe it was a Danish thing. He definitely acted differently than the guys she was used to—more formal in some ways, a little pushy—but that was probably because he'd traveled so much and dealt with so many people from all walks of life.

He didn't mess around with the lift chairs again, and he didn't make any more weird comments about her lips, so by the time their afternoon class began, she was relaxed and ready to enjoy the afternoon.

The intermediate class was a lot more crowded. Dane kept busy handling the varying levels of competency and working through the skills everyone wanted to practice. Despite the nice lunch and afternoon, Melinda was glad for the reprieve.

After a few runs, a girl Melinda's age, named Hannah, struck up a conversation in the lift line. She had light brown hair, pale gray eyes, and a sweet smile. The two of them shared the lift a few times and skied together down the slopes.

"Do you know that guy?" Hannah asked when Dane went by with another student and waved at Melinda. "The instructor?"

"Dane? Not really. We met this morning when I took his first class."

"He's pretty cute," Hannah said, eyes twinkling. "I think he likes you."

Melinda shrugged. "Oh, I don't know. I'm only here for a week, and he's sort of a nomad, so..."

"Star-crossed lovers," Hannah said with a dramatic sigh, fluttering her fingers in front of her face—which, in the bulky ski gloves, looked more like wiggling a couple of dark blue sausages—making Melinda laugh. "How romantic."

Dane was called away at the end of class after giving out

another round of coupon cards to everyone. Melinda waved when he did, a little relieved he hadn't asked for her phone number. She'd pretended not to notice that his number was on the back of the card he'd given her. Overall, he seemed harmless enough, but he was still a bit of a creep.

She said goodbye to Hannah, who was meeting the rest of her group in the lodge, and skied slowly toward the shuttle. It was near the end of the ski day by then, and her ankle had started throbbing about an hour before.

She was ready for a break.

Popping off her skis to wait for the bus, Melinda studied the mountains in the distance, wondering where her friends and family were. Now that her first day was over, at least she'd be on the same mountain tomorrow, with a chance to cross paths with them once in a while.

Maybe she could convince Jacob to spend some time with her on the intermediate slopes. The ski trip always brought home to her how much she hated spending the whole day without his company.

Luckily, during the rest of the year, she didn't have to.

Melinda got back to the condo before anyone else and took advantage of the solitude by getting her shower out of the way. There would be more skiing later, but once she took her boots off, her foot hurt badly enough that she decided to call it quits for the evening.

Normally the resort only offered night skiing on the weekends. During the Christmas and New Year's holidays, the lights stayed on until ten every evening except Sundays. She'd go back out with everyone tomorrow night instead.

Wrapping a towel around her wet hair, Melinda bundled

into her warm, comfy pjs, her fluffy robe, and ancient slippers, and grabbed an apple from the kitchen.

She flopped on the family-room couch, munching the tart, juicy fruit, and turned on the TV for some white noise, then sat staring west out the windows toward the mountains.

The wind had started kicking up again just as she'd climbed off the shuttle, instantly lowering the temperature. Now the trees swayed heavily in the strengthening breeze. Snow blew off their branches in lacy wisps or fell in giant clumps, depending on the gust.

Maybe another storm was coming in.

Puffs of white blew off the tops of the mountain peaks, too, glowing orange with the last bit of light from the setting sun behind them. It looked mind-numbingly cold, almost arctic, but astoundingly beautiful.

She should grab her camera...

Eyes drifting shut, Melinda snuggled back into the sofa and dragged a blanket over herself. Her muscles ached pleasantly from the exertion of the day, though her foot still twinged. Fatigue dragged at her eyelids.

Where was everyone, though? She'd thought they'd be back by now. Patting the pockets of her robe, Melinda frowned. Damn, she'd left her phone in her ski jacket.

Unable to summon the energy to go check for a message, she squinted at the clock on the DVD player above the TV. Five-fifteen. She'd give them until five-thirty then go grab her phone.

Closing her eyes again, she was on the verge of dropping off to sleep when the door to the condo banged open.

A horde of ice-covered people spilled in from the covered walkway, along with a blast of frigid air, pulling off clothes and gear willy-nilly and talking at full volume about the killer slopes, the air they'd caught beneath their skis on the jumps, the way that one section had given way under Uncle Allan's feet. On and on.

Melinda resisted clapping her hands over her ears, but it was a near thing.

"Hi, honey," her dad said, waving his hand as he headed

straight for the master bedroom and presumably the shower.

"Wendell, Christian, wipe up that water there, please," Karen said, tossing them a towel. "Hi, sweetie," she added to Melinda. "Did you have fun?"

"Kumquat!" Jacob yelled, and flopped next to her on the couch, still in his ski pants. "How goes it?"

"Get off, you're all wet!" Melinda cried, whipping the edge of her blanket away from him.

"Jacob Robert Tanner!" Lois scolded, wagging her finger at her son. "Strip."

"Yeah, yeah. Hey," he grunted when Melinda shoved at him, "nice to see you, too."

Melinda flapped her hands, brushing him back. "Off, off, off."

"Okay, okay, jeez," he said, standing and working off his outerwear pants right there. "It's just a little water."

"Freezing water," Melinda countered. "I'm all nice and dry."

"Good, you can warm me up," Jacob said, clapping his icy hands to her cheeks and laughing when she squealed and kicked him away.

"Jacob," Lois said warningly from the kitchen. "Behave."

With his back to his mother, Jacob looked at Melinda and rolled his eyes. She grinned saucily up at him, but he only said, "Yes, mother," in a tone that had Lois blowing out an amused *tcha* of exasperation.

Melinda tried to ignore the way Jacob's two thinner base layers highlighted the muscles of his thighs and calves as he finished stripping off his outerwear, and the way his thermal undershirt caressed his abs and the muscles in his arms.

She really did.

But they were *right there* in her face, for God's sake. How could she not stare a little?

Jacob bounded down the short hallway and handed his ski pants to someone in the laundry room to toss in the dryer, then bounded back and onto the couch again.

"Better?" he asked.

"Better. So, how was it?"

Jacob casually pulled her legs across his lap and rubbed her ankles and feet as he launched into an enthusiastic account of the day, which had included some backcountry skiing, as well as the diamond runs.

His fingers were strong and gentle. Warmth spread up her calves, her thighs, and all the way into her belly. The soreness she'd experienced toward the last half of the day melted smoothly away as Jacob chattered about everything he and the rest of the group had seen and done.

The powder was awesome, the views were awesome, the wildlife they'd seen was awesome, the air they'd caught was awesome—

"So basically everything was awesome?" Melinda asked extra sweetly when he finally took a breath. She batted her lashes and gave him a big, innocent smile.

Jacob put his hand over her face and pushed. "Smart ass," he said with a chuckle.

He snagged the half-eaten apple out of her hand and took a healthy bite before handing it back, continuing with his mouth full and juice dripping down his chin.

"Yeah, it was pretty great," he said. "We're going back out for a couple hours after dinner. Why are you ready for bed?"

"I'm beat. I want dinner and mindless TV and sleep, in that order."

"Boring. Okay, well how was your day? How come you didn't come over for lunch?"

Hoping he couldn't see the blush climbing into her cheeks, Melinda strove for casual.

"I sort of hit it off with my ski instructor, so we went to lunch together. Didn't Mom tell you? I called."

"We didn't see the rest of the group 'til later 'cuz they stayed on the main trails," Jacob said. "So your ski instructor, huh? Is he hot?"

"How do you know it was a he?"

"I can see it on your face, you hussy. So, tell me all about him."

Melinda crossed her arms over her chest and scowled. "I don't know, he's just a guy. His name's Dane, and he's from Denmark—"

"*Dane* from Denmark? Seriously? Who does that to a kid? That's like naming an American *American.*"

"We went to school with a guy named Dane," Melinda reminded him, despite the fact that she'd teased Dane about the same thing.

"Yeah, but he wasn't from Denmark," Jacob said.

"What difference does it make?"

"I don't know. It just does."

"Anyway—"

"Hey, Mel," Christian said, interrupting her as he came down the hallway. "Jake, your dad wants you."

Jacob patted Melinda's knee and slid out from under her legs, bouncing up to find Bill. Christian fell into Jacob's place with a loud groan.

"Tired?" Melinda asked.

"Nah, not too bad. Need food, then we're going back. Aren't you coming?"

"Tomorrow," she said.

Christian nodded and started to say something else, but Wendell called to him from the kitchen and he hopped up again.

Melinda watched the casual chaos while Lois and her mother tried to get dinner rolling with everyone coming and going through the space, snagging drinks, grabbing bags of chips, tossing gear into corners, and generally making a nuisance of themselves.

The front door opened and everyone from the second condo trooped in, too, doubling the size of the group, yet somehow—mostly thanks to Rick—quintupling the amount of noise.

Smiling, Melinda settled back into her spot on the couch. It was good to be home for the night, surrounded by family and friends, with the yummy scent of Lois's famous chicken beginning to waft through the condo.

Comforted and comfortable, she barely noticed when Gabe shoved her legs over and he and Eddie sat on the couch beside her. They changed the channel to an all-sports station and turned the volume of the TV way up.

Best of all, she'd hardly thought of Mitch—or her

inconvenient, but undeniable, attraction to Jacob—all day.

They had to wake her for dinner.

Groggy but starving, she managed to plow her way through the baked chicken, mashed potatoes, and salad almost as well as the guys.

Though her level of tiredness had reached epic proportions by the time they finished the meal, she stuck around to help Karen, Lois, and Nancy with the clean up. Aunt Pat and the men, minus her dad who, like Melinda, was ready for bed, got back into their gear and took off for the last few hours of night skiing.

Once the dishes were done, her dad joined her at the dinner table for a round of Spite and Malice. They chatted about spring plantings for the nursery and the new sales associate they'd hired in November, about her schooling, and about their plans for the summer.

"Zach said he'll be home for camping," her dad said, giving a face-splitting yawn. "Did he tell you?"

"Yeah," she said, stealing a sip from Stan's cup of hot tea. "I hope it's true."

"Me, too. It's been a long time since he was home."

They smiled at each other a bit sadly, both missing her older brother. He'd only been home twice for short visits in the three years since he'd moved to Japan. It wasn't enough.

Melinda beat her dad soundly at the card game, as usual.

"I taught you too well," he said mournfully. "I should've held back some tricks."

"Ha," Melinda said. "I need no tricks. It's all strategy and skill."

They shared matching grins, then he kissed her forehead

and wandered off to bed after kissing her mom goodnight, too.

The women had settled in front of the TV, and Nancy had put in the DVD of *Friends With Benefits*. Melinda joined them, trying not to blush in front of the grown-ups when Mila Kunis and Justin Timberlake got busy on screen, but wow, some of those scenes were steamy!

The blush burned hotter when an image of herself and Jacob experimenting with that sort of arrangement—complete with the movie's happily-ever-after ending—popped into her head.

A bit wistful, but supremely glad her father had already gone to bed, Melinda covered her eyes for the next super-sexy scene and dragged up a picture of Dane in her mind to replace Jacob's handsome face.

Dane was cute enough, in an overbearing sort of way, and plenty strong, but she liked her guys taller. Darker. Sweeter. More like Jacob.

Damn it!

Mentally smacking herself, Melinda tuned back into the movie. She had to stop doing that. Jacob did not belong in her head that way. At all. If this was rebounding, it sucked. There was no earthly reason that getting over Mitch should have to involve Jacob.

Yet somehow, the hurt over Mitch had faded a great deal from the moment Jacob showed up at the house, and had continued to improve ever since.

What did that say about her? She'd loved the lying Mitch-weasel, hadn't she? So how could she feel so much better after only a few days? Surely she should grieve the end of their relationship longer than that. It seemed so shallow otherwise.

Then again, Mitch certainly wasn't grieving. If their time together had all been an illusion, a stage production, then maybe her heart didn't need to bleed over its end.

She was in charge of her emotions. She could decide where to invest them. Not that they needed to shift to Jacob. Daydreams aside, nothing would change the fact that they wanted very different lives after college.

Though if she could clone a Jacob—an exact replica, but

one who wanted to stay with her in Pasodoro—she'd do it in a heartbeat.

Melinda sighed.

Damn.

When the DVD ended, Melinda said goodnight, though it was still shy of ten o'clock. The guys would probably be back soon, but fatigue urged her toward her warm bed and sleep. She kissed her mom on the cheek, then Jacob's mom, then Eddie's, grabbed her cell phone out of her ski jacket, and climbed the spiral stairs to the loft.

Hopping into bed, she snagged the book she'd brought along—a Christmas gift she'd been dying to dive into—and read for a while. The low murmur of the women's voices drifted to her from downstairs, a soothing backdrop. They put on some quiet music while they talked, and someone popped popcorn, half-tempting her to go back down for a bowl, but she was too tired and too comfortable all wrapped up in her blankets.

Later, she roused from her book to Nancy's chirpy voice saying goodnight and the closing of the front door as Nancy headed to her own room in the other condo. Melinda squinted at the bedside clock, surprised they'd lasted so long as tired as everyone had been after their first full day of skiing.

Her mom and Jacob's, talking quietly, flicked off the downstairs lights one at a time. Lois said something that made her mom laugh, then came the muffled thumps of their two doors closing in the hallway, and all went silent.

Marking her spot in her book with a yawn, Melinda grabbed her phone and scrolled through her messages and email, answering or deleting as needed, wondering where the guys were. It was getting pretty late.

She was about to turn her phone off when she realized she had a missed call and a voice message. Touching the screen to bring it up, she frowned at the unfamiliar phone number. She pressed play to hear the message, then instantly wished she hadn't.

Mitch's voice flowed from the speaker.

Warm.

Familiar.

Her heart gave a painful squeeze.

Damn him!

Hot tears came, but they were more for herself than for the loss of him, and she blinked them back.

"Melly," he said, his deep voice achingly low and tender, full of regret. "It's me. I miss you, babe. Listen, I'm sorry about everything. I wish—"

But Melinda didn't hear what he wished. She pushed delete, then tossed her phone on the bedside table, her emotions somersaulting through her heart.

Not because she hurt, but because she didn't hurt as much as she thought she should.

Self-loathing filled her. She was shallow, careless, heartless. She'd been in love with him. She was so sure. All that time together, all those memories. Yet in a mere four days, she'd gotten over him almost entirely?

That couldn't be real love.

Which meant she had no idea what real love felt like. Jacob's image winding around her heart and mind only made her more confused.

Miserable, Melinda buried her face in her pillow and cried.

Jacob sprayed a face full of snow onto Danny, Gabe, and Wendell as he swooshed to a stop next to them at the bottom of the run. The last of the night.

Wendell said, "Dude."

Danny and Gabe just grunted.

It was a testament to everyone's fatigue that they barely registered the onslaught and didn't bother to retaliate, merely wiping the snow from their goggles and blowing into their cupped hands, hoping to warm the scant amounts of skin exposed to the frigid temperature.

Moonlight beamed from a clear, diamond-hard night sky, though it was no match for the glaring yellow glow of the floodlights or the colorful rows of Christmas bulbs strung along the three ski slopes the resort kept open for night runs.

Jacob could hardly remember the last few hours, despite the constant competition and trash talk he knew had gone on. It was tradition with this crew, as much as the trip itself. No one had looked at him oddly, though, so he must have held his own.

Not hard, since he could take them on in his sleep,

especially the old timers who pretty much sucked at talking smack.

But still.

It was damned annoying having his brain invaded by images of Melinda and some jockstrap ski instructor when he should have been all about the powder.

Staring blindly back up the brightly-lit slope, he wondered if Melinda had given the guy her phone number, then wondered why he should care. There were about a billion reasons why nothing was ever going to happen between the two of them, starting with their long friendship and moving down the list from there. Even if he wanted something to happen.

Which he didn't.

Did he?

Okay, maybe he did.

Maybe he even daydreamed about it sometimes. That didn't mean he was going to act on it, and never mind how sweet and warm and sexily gorgeous she'd looked all bundled up and sleeping on the couch earlier. Risking their friendship would put them on a path straight to hell, along with all his other good intentions.

Friends getting together was so not a good idea.

Jacob sighed.

Of course friendships could develop into solid relationships. He was surrounded by couples who'd done exactly that, including his own parents. That wasn't the problem. It was what happened to everyone involved if the romance didn't work out.

The specter of his aunt and uncle and their ruined relationship flashed through his mind. Would Victor even be his uncle anymore, once the divorce was final? Who would get the kids? Would he still get to see his cousins? Not as often, that was for sure.

His Aunt Shelly had met Victor in high school. They'd been the best of friends, had lived together for years before getting married. He'd never even seen them argue. Now they were done, his two cousins were suffering more than anyone. Their breakup was tearing a hole through his entire family.

"Take that, sucka!" Aunt Pat yelled, coming in for a fast landing and catching him distracted, spraying him head to toe with the same treatment he'd given to the guys.

Those three had managed to duck out of the way this time and were now leaning on each other for support as they laughed their asses off for his benefit.

"Woman," Jacob spluttered through his mouthful of snow, "I am so spiking your coffee with laxatives."

"Ha," Pat said, beaming at him unrepentantly. "You have to catch me first, scooter-bug."

"You think you're fast now, wait 'til that special blend hits your system, and you're miles away from a bathroom."

"Dude, that's evil," Gabe said, unholy glee in his eyes.

"Genius," said Danny, grinning madly at his mother. He rubbed his hands together in anticipation. "Pure genius."

"Now, boys," Pat said, still chortling. A warrior secure in her imperviousness to boyish pranks. "No ganging up on the ladies."

"Don't start whatcha can't finish, Aunt Pittypat." Jacob waggled his eyebrows at her meaningfully. "I learned that lesson at your knee."

Pale blue eyes lasered him, and her mouth quirked upward on one side, half humor, half dare.

"Best remember what you learned about paybacks, too, sonny boy." She lifted a blond eyebrow to answer his. "Remember last time."

Danny sobered instantly. Jacob snorted, admitting nothing.

"What happened last time?" Gabe wanted to know.

"Yeah, Jake, spill," Wendell coaxed. "What'd we miss? We need a good laugh."

Angling his chin, Jacob ignored them.

"Come on, Jakey," Pat said, her voice singsong now, her eyes dancing. "You know it. Who's your daddy?"

Giving in with a laugh and an eye roll, Jacob leaned forward on his skis and kissed her on her chilly cheek. "You are, Aunt Pat. You are."

By the time they'd gathered the rest of their group and returned, the first condo was quiet and mostly dark. Only a few low lights left on in the kitchen illuminated the entry area so they could see to deal with their gear. Stan and the women had all gone to bed, and Jacob had every intention of following immediately.

Wendell and Christian shuffled inside, already half stripped and half asleep on their feet.

Rick sketched a silent, elaborate bow, then slung an arm around Eddie's shoulders, who refrained from bowing but gave a two-fingered tap to his brow for a goodnight. They moved down the hall, too tired for the usual catcalls, Gabe and Danny in their wake. Jacob saluted the rest of the group as they, too, tromped off to the second condo.

Aunt Pat brought up the rear, herding her lowly subjects. She dug a finger into his ribs as she passed and made him snort out a laugh.

He made to follow his dad inside after Wendell and Christian, but Bill held him back with a lifted hand, pulling the condo door partially closed. Jacob raised questioning brows at the man he matched almost exactly in height, though his father had filled out a bit more broadly in recent years.

Bill waited until the second condo's door closed, leaving them alone in the wide, cold walkway, before facing Jacob. Their breath puffed white in the dimly lit corridor. His dad's eyes, the same golden brown as his own, swept over Jacob's face, and a frown pulled his father's brows together over the bridge of his nose.

"Everything all right with you, son?" Bill asked.

Surprised, Jacob frowned in answer. "Yeah," he said. "Of course. Why?"

His dad studied him intently and didn't respond right away. Jacob fought a sudden, irrational need to squirm the way he had as a kid whenever one or both of his parents had cornered him for A Talk, no matter the topic.

"You seem a bit subdued," Bill said finally. "On edge."

Jacob stilled, settling his face into what he hoped were noncommittal lines. Maybe he hadn't been as good at hiding the upheaval inside him as he'd believed.

Maybe he should take acting lessons from Rick.

He thought of the secret he was keeping from everyone first, a secret both exciting and stressful, and something he wasn't sure how his parents would handle. But it was Melinda's laughing face that danced in his brain, and he swallowed thickly.

"I'm fine," Jacob said, making his voice extra hearty. "Great, actually. Vacation, right? Food, fun, fresh powder. What's not to like?"

His dad studied him another long, uncomfortable moment, then clapped a big, warm hand onto Jacob's shoulder and squeezed.

"Good," Bill said, his voice equally energetic and possibly as false. "I thought maybe the divorce…"

Jacob shifted, sobering. The destruction of his aunt and uncle's marriage was a painful topic for his whole family, tearing them apart much like Carl and Donna's breakup had torn through his and Melinda's group of friends nearly three years ago.

How much worse would it be if he and Melinda tangled up romantically, and then it fell apart? It would destroy not only their families, not only their friends, but all of them. Not only would they lose each other, they'd lose everything, one of the best things in their lives.

It was a nightmare waiting to happen.

As much as part of him wanted to test those waters, he couldn't risk the potential tsunami of devastation.

Although he was a pretty good swimmer…

Just stop now. Stop.

To his dad, Jacob only shook his head. His aunt and uncle, his cousins, they were all on his mind, but he didn't want to talk about their situation. Nor did he in any way want to discuss whatever was going on between him and Melinda.

If something was going on between him and Melinda.

Which it wasn't.

Exactly.

"Is it school?" Bill asked. "I know your last semester was tough, but you worked your ass off. You deserve some down time."

Latching on to the handy excuse, relieved, Jacob said, "Sure. You know school, it's always something."

If his dad wanted to talk about school, he could go with that, although last semester hadn't been the real problem, and they both knew it. Jacob didn't even care that the ghost of his less-than-stellar freshman year flickered between them for a beat or two. School problems were easy scapegoats for any weirdness his dad might have detected in his behavior.

"Are you worried about next year?" Bill asked.

"Nope," Jacob said, grinning now.

He was worried—a bit—though not in the way his dad might think. They'd see after he spilled his secret, but he wanted to get them all through the ski trip and into the new year before putting everyone in an uproar. Especially Melinda.

"I'm set."

"Good," Bill repeated, nodding, a half-smile on his face, though his eyes were still intense. "That's good."

Bill cleared his throat and his eyes seemed to go even deeper, beaming light inside all of Jacob's darkest corners the way only a dad who knows his son well can do.

"And your friends?" Bill continued. "Everything good there?"

His friends? There was only one friend on his mind at the moment—a sweet, sexy, gorgeous friend who was driving him more than a little crazy—but his dad couldn't possibly know that. Could he?

Umm...

"Yeah." Really not going there. "All good."

Jacob shifted again, getting twitchier by the second beneath that knowing stare. The weight of his dad's hand on his shoulder took on more and more gravity the longer it sat there.

"So..." Jacob inclined his head toward the condo, an

everything's-cool-so-let's-go-in gesture.

Still, Bill pinned him in place with his fatherly gaze and the kindly but firm pressure of his hand. Jacob had the sensation of being questioned by a caring but relentless examiner, as though entire conversations were taking place between his subconscious and his dad's, all without his meaning to say a word. Brown eyes drilled patiently into brown, making him wonder just what his dad could see inside his head and what secrets his eyes betrayed.

Where did all the air go?

Emotions he didn't want to look at too closely backed up in his throat. The first stirring of panic flicked along his nerve-endings. He definitely wasn't ready to divulge his secret, and his mixed up feelings for Melinda were not meant for the light of day, nor a father-son powwow.

Just when Jacob thought he'd have to throw off his dad's restraining hand and run screaming into the snow to escape that deep, all-seeing parental scrutiny, Bill dialed back the intensity.

Not by so much as a twitchy eyelid did Jacob give away his utter relief.

"Okay, Jakey," Bill said. He gave one more gentle squeeze on Jacob's shoulder before dropping his hand. "You know I'm here for you if you need to talk. About anything."

Horrified by the sudden rise of a lump in his throat, Jacob pounded on his chest and coughed to clear it, as though he'd only swallowed wrong. He worried his tight, raspy voice might have revealed more than he'd wanted when he nodded and said, "I know, Dad."

Eyes gentle now, Bill smiled and nodded back. He preceded Jacob into the condo at last, moving in his steady, unhurried way toward the laundry room to unload his gear before heading to bed.

That was his dad in a nutshell. Steady, unhurried, and capable of wearing away the bullshit like water wearing down rock.

Closing and locking the condo's door, Jacob leaned his head back, resting against the solid wood. Eyes closed, he breathed deeply. His mind shuddered, exhausted, as though he and his dad had engaged in a mental sword fight instead of a friendly, mostly meaningless conversation.

Meaningless on the top layers, at least.

Somehow, although Melinda's name had never been mentioned, or even girls in general, the sensation in Jacob's gut told him she'd been front and center through the whole thing. There were currents underneath the words, ripples he didn't understand, and a persistent suspicion that his dad knew way more than he'd let on.

More than Jacob would be comfortable with, or was ready to admit, even to himself.

When he opened his eyes again, they tracked to the top of the curved staircase along with his thoughts.

Crap.

He waited until he heard his dad enter his own room, then took his turn in the laundry room, followed by a quick shower. He hadn't brought any clean clothes down with him earlier, so he wrapped a towel around his waist and made his way through the silent condo, up the curving stairs, and into the loft.

Eyeing Melinda's motionless shape on the other bed, Jacob grabbed his flannel pajama bottoms and the thermal shirt he'd slept in last night from the foot of his bed. She was facing the window, away from him. As quietly as possible, he dragged the shirt over his head, then dropped the damp towel, stepped into the pajama pants, and yanked them up. He breathed a sigh of relief. She hadn't turned.

Jacob grabbed the towel from the floor and flung it over the loft railing to dry, silencing his mother's chiding voice in his head.

Climbing beneath the covers, he settled himself as comfortably as he could with his feet hanging off the end of the damn toy-sized bed. At school, he had an extra-long twin in his dorm room, and even that often seemed too short. He was used to the California-king-sized bed he had at home. This one was like sleeping in a toddler bed.

Drawing his knees up, Jacob flopped to his side with a groan, seeking comfort. Fatigue dragged at him, and he yawned widely. He closed his eyes, but his brain didn't want to turn off, his thoughts spinning on the giant hamster wheel in his head, chasing each other around in no particular order.

It wasn't until he deliberately slowed and deepened his breathing in preparation for quieting his mind that he heard the soft sniffles coming from the bed three feet from his own.

Uh-oh.

Jacob stilled, listening harder. Another quiet sniffle, and a hitching breath. He knew what that meant.

His heart squeezed.

Melinda was crying.

Trying hard to keep it to herself, too, but there was no quiet like snow-covered-mountain quiet for amplifying every little sound.

Tossing aside his covers, Jacob swung his legs over the side of the bed facing hers, his elbows on his knees. Contemplating.

"Mel," he whispered. "Hey."

She curled on her side, still facing away from him. He stretched out one hand and ran it from her shoulder down to her wrist, leaving his hand over hers. She sniffed, louder this time.

"Melinda," he said.

"Sorry." The whispered word sounded rough, as though her throat hurt from holding back the tears.

"Talk to me."

"Can't," she said, hiccoughing. Then, "I'm so stupid."

Screw that.

Jacob stood and nudged her up with one hand, pulling gently with the other against her mild resistance. He swung his left leg around her back until he was sitting against the headboard of her bed, dragging her up between his legs and onto his chest.

She was warm and soft and sweet-smelling, and he wanted to nuzzle. He wrapped his arms around her instead, and held her securely, one hand stroking her hair where her head settled against his shoulder, silent for now.

Waiting.

Melinda held herself stiffly for a moment, no more than that, before she melted into him, curving her body and snuggling her face into the side of his neck. She wrapped her arms around him in turn and shuddered as the tears finally escaped. They came in a hot flood, soaking his shirt.

Resting his chin on the top of her head, Jacob smoothed his hands over her back, her arms, her hair. There would be time for words later. For now, he'd provide the shoulder she needed.

He'd seen her cry before, loads of times over the years. When they were four and she skinned her knee on the playground. Hiding in her closet after school on the day Evan Wagner had called her fatty-fatty-fatterson in front of the whole class.

Then in sixth grade, after they'd had a huge fight—their first ever—over something stupid he couldn't even remember now. And that time in college when he'd held her hair while she hurled after drinking way too much at a friend's party.

Worst of all, through the awful days of their senior year of high school after Seth Mazer, their best friend, died in a terrible car accident.

Holding each other up through the horror and grief, the absolute wrongness of a teenager's funeral. Of knowing they would never again see his freckled face, or answer his gap-toothed smile, or tease him over his crazy hand-painted t-shirts.

Shirts his mother had given out to his closest friends, and which they all wore in Seth's memory, though they were starting to fade with time and many washings.

Jacob sucked in a breath, blew it out quietly, waiting for the ache to settle again, though it never faded completely. They'd cried together then. Their friend had left a constant hole in all their lives.

Even now, nearly three years later, a voice or a laugh or a song on the radio would trigger a memory, a moment out of a too-short life shared with Seth, and choke him up. But if Melinda was there, and they shared that look—the one that said, *I know. I heard it, too. I remember*—then he could smile with the memory, and the ache would ache a little less.

Tears had been shed more times than he could count in a lifetime of memories spent together, both sad and happy.

Yet something about the sobs shaking her small shoulders tonight, with her warm, curvy body held tight against his, and her sugar-and-spice scent surrounding him in her narrow bed, tugged on a different part of his heart.

The part that clearly saw the tsunami wave coming, and didn't give a damn.

Slowly, Melinda's tears subsided. She rubbed her cheek against the roughness of his thermal shirt, her right hand brushing absently at the shoulder seam.

"Sorry," she said again.

"Don't be stupid." Jacob squeezed her in his arms to take any sting from the words. "You wanna talk about it?"

Her shoulder raised in a tiny shrug.

"Mitch called," she said, her voice trembling a bit, obviously struggling in the aftermath of tears.

Jacob mentally flicked aside the desire to smash that guy like the cockroach he was. That wasn't what she needed now.

"He left a message."

"What'd he say?" Jacob shifted her closer, proud of the evenness of his tone.

"I don't know. I erased it."

Inside, Jacob gave a little cheer.

Good girl.

He hugged her again, dropping a kiss on top of her head.

"I know he's an ass," she said. "Or I do now. But I believed in him for a while."

"It's only been a couple of days," Jacob said, deliberately relaxing his hands. The urge to smash was growing stronger with her words. "Give it time."

"Yeah. I just… I thought he really wanted the same things. That he wanted them with me because he loved me. You know? Now… He was nothing but a liar."

Jacob told himself not to ask, to let it go, but listening to her, thinking of the future she'd believed she was planning with Mitch, he had to know.

Clearing his throat, he said, "Did you really want to get married now? So young?"

"It wasn't only that. I mean, no, I didn't want marriage right now, but…"

He swallowed the instinctive sigh of relief and tried to stay focused. "What, then?"

"I don't know, all of it. I don't want to get married now, but I don't want to wait too long, either. I want to stay in Pasodoro. I want to build a life there with my family and friends, and have a bunch of kids. I want to raise them where we grew up. Sunday dinners, family trips like this one. You know. All the stuff we always do. I think he just parroted back the things I'd told him I wanted."

"Is staying in Paso that important?"

Melinda rubbed her cheek against his chest again. "It is to me."

Her hair twined around his fingers, and he played with the strands idly while he considered her words, a nagging pain growing inside his chest.

He loved his family, their friends, the familiarity of the home and town he'd grown up in, the traditions. But there were other memories there now.

Painful ones.

And he had dreams to pursue.

The thought of living out his life in Pasodoro…

"Do you ever think about going somewhere else?" he asked.

"Sure," she answered, though he could hear the frown in her voice. "I mean, we did, didn't we? For school. And I want to travel and stuff, you know that."

"Yeah," he persisted, "but to live."

"Oh. No, never. I always want to live in Paso. I love it there. It's home."

Jacob wanted to groan with frustration. "Home is who you're with, isn't it? I mean, you wouldn't want to stay there if everyone else moved, would you? Or what if you meet your dream guy and his job is in New York? What then?"

What about me? he wanted to ask, but held the words back. He was so not going there. Why was he even pursuing this?

He should just stop.

"I guess I don't know," she said, and Jacob could feel the frown pulling at her brow. "I don't know how I could really be happy that far from home. From everyone."

"Yeah," he said, blowing out a breath that stirred the hair on top of her head.

Drop it, man. Just drop it now.

They lay silent for a while. Melinda drew random shapes on his shoulder with her fingernail. He played with her hair. Somehow, it all seemed very natural, even though a voice in the back of his mind insisted this was the sort of thing couples did and he should go back to his own bed. Before the tsunami wave hit, and he drowned.

He was very aware of her body resting on his, but strangely, in comforting her, Jacob found himself comforted, too, rather than aroused.

The warm, solid weight of her resting between his legs and curled onto his chest heated him inside and out like a favorite blanket, quieting his mind and soothing the nerves the talk with his father had jumbled. Her hair was a river of silk beneath his stroking hand, as soft and smooth as the delicate skin of her forehead tucked beneath his chin.

This was right.

All his denials and rationalizations and skirting around the truth vanished in a puff of air.

This, Melinda, was everything he wanted.

He'd have to think about what that would mean, what to do about it, and how, and when, but he knew one thing already.

It was too late to turn back the tide. He'd have to surf the wave and hope they both survived.

He never wanted to move.

"Jake?" Melinda whispered sometime later.

Too relaxed for words, he hummed in response, his lips vibrating against the top of her head.

"Thanks."

Jacob tightened his arms around her in answer, glad when she burrowed even more snuggly into his body. He became aware of their breathing, slow and synchronized, deepening toward sleep. Recognized the moment Melinda tumbled smoothly off that soft edge into dreams and, smiling in contentment, followed.

Melinda came awake slowly, her limbs drugged and heavy with warmth, and an impression of security she couldn't name.

It took a solid effort to peel her eyes open and another long moment for her brain to wake enough to understand the picture her eyes and senses painted.

She was in her bed in the loft, where she belonged. The room held a touch of morning chill in the air. It stung the tip of her nose, though she was cozy as could be, and the quiet sounds of movement and tantalizing scents floating from downstairs indicated people were up and making breakfast.

But that was where normal ended.

Raising her head from the warm, homey spot where she'd nested, Melinda stared into Jacob's sleeping face, not two inches from her own. As her senses caught up with her, her breathing increased.

She thought, *Oh, my God*. And fought an insane urge to giggle.

Melinda lay sprawled, head to toe, facedown over Jacob's body, one hand curled into the burnished bronze hair at the nape of his neck, the other wrapped around his side. Her hair slid over him on either side of his body, a chocolate curtain. One lock wound its way over his left shoulder and curled beneath him, trapping her in place.

Her breasts flattened firmly against his muscular chest, and the rest of their bodies lined up in... interesting ways.

She sucked in a breath and let it out slowly, trying to ignore the tingling heat beginning to spread from every point of contact.

Jacob held her tightly on top of him with one arm, the other flung to the side and hanging off the bed. The blankets covered them to the level of her waist, but it was his large hand, fingers splayed across her lower back, that burned.

He breathed deeply, sound asleep, as though they slept together this way every night.

Sheer shock kept her in place.

She remembered him coming into the loft. Remembered trying to hush her crying, not wanting him to hear. Jacob climbing into bed with her to give comfort.

And then... and then, they must have fallen asleep.

Now, here they were, wrapped around each other like kittens.

Well, not exactly like kittens. Her mind traveled a not-so-innocent, very un-kittenish path of discovery, cataloguing the full-body contact sending very inappropriate sensations zinging along her nerve ends. Like bolts of electricity.

She almost expected her hair to stand on end.

Thank God no one had come upstairs looking for them yet. Being caught together this way would be extremely difficult to explain to their parents, even if it had been innocent enough to begin with.

It was only now, with those little zapping electrical flashes zipping along her pulse points, and arcing between every sensitive nerve until they formed one continuous loop of molten heat, that it occurred to her it had stopped being entirely innocent the moment she'd opened her eyes.

His body felt so good beneath her own, so right somehow.

He'd been such a scrawny, nerdy minnow, despite his height, until well after high school. A boy, both in looks and in personality.

Though he was still playful, and plenty geeky, there was very little of the boy left in him these days, and his body was all man.

Hard and muscular, tall and strong.

A hum of pleasure vibrated in her throat, surprising her. She had to stop herself from running her hands down his arms. Or nuzzling the velvety hollow of his throat, where he smelled, oh, *God*, so good.

This was *Jacob*, for heaven's sake.

But...

His skin, warm and smooth and spicy, called out for her touch, and his heart beat comfortably against her own. He tantalized her senses like melted caramel sliding over her tongue.

Only two *very* thin clothing layers separated their naked bodies.

Hardly any barrier at all.

As soon as the thought popped into her head, the heat increased exponentially, until it seemed fire would flare between them, a spontaneous combustion of breasts, bellies, hips, thighs. And other places she decided not to name.

A silent snicker shook her body.

Jacob's eyes slid halfway open, their brilliant topaz depths blurred with sleep, and suddenly she was holding her breath. He groaned low in his throat and brought his free arm up, rubbing a hand over his face and the prickly shadow of stubble darkening his cheeks.

Melinda held still as a statue, exquisitely aware of the rasp of his arm sliding across the bed's bottom sheet. Of the flexing of his biceps beneath the dark blue fabric of his long-sleeved thermal shirt. Of the hard stretch of his chest and abdomen, and his heavily-muscled thighs beneath her own.

Squeezing his eyes shut, Jacob scrunched his face up, then opened his eyes wide until they watered, their pale golden brown clearer now. A half-smile warmed his mouth as he focused on her with his still-drowsy gaze.

"Hey, potato chip," he said sleepily, his voice extra deep and—*confound it*—sexily rough with morning.

Melinda opened her mouth to respond, but only a croak

reached her lips. He stroked his fingers from the top of her head slowly down the length of her hair, as though from long habit, as though he woke with her in his arms every day.

Halfway down her back, his hand stopped.

With her eyes locked on his, she saw the moment he came fully awake and realization dawned. His sleepy gaze went sharp, his breath halted along with his stroking hand, and every muscle in his body flexed hard.

He said, "Ah," the single syllable cautious now.

Pressed together as they were, Melinda couldn't miss another muscle growing firm and hard beneath her, nor the answering heat spiraling deep in her belly.

A red flush spread across the planes of Jacob's sculptured cheekbones, and he closed his eyes again in obvious mortification, but neither of them moved.

Melinda didn't think she *could* move, not even if her life depended on it. Which it very well could, if one of their fathers came to the top of the spiral staircase and saw them wrapped together in her bed.

After a moment, Jacob reopened his eyes, folding his full lips together as he studied her. She studied him right back, the silence dragging out as they weighed each other and the curious position they'd found themselves in. It put her in mind of the dream she'd had before leaving on the trip.

"So, good morning," Jacob said finally.

Melinda cleared her throat. "Morning."

"Do you—" he began.

His mother's shout from downstairs cut him off.

"Jakey, Mel, are you two up?" Lois called as they both gasped and jerked upright, only Melinda didn't move high enough, and they cracked foreheads with mutually pained groans. "Breakfast is ready in five!"

For a startled heartbeat, they stared into each other's widened eyes. Blowing out a breath, Jacob placed a protective hand over Melinda's ear and shifted to call over her shoulder. "Be right down!"

He flopped back on the bed, and his eyes met hers again as he dissolved in quiet mirth. The sound rumbled through her body, tickling and bouncing her against him until she joined in.

And just like that, they were back to normal.

"Oh, my God," she whispered, still giggling.

"I know. That could have been..." He couldn't seem to finish, and their laughing vibrated the bed.

"Yeah."

Realizing her fingers still clutched Jacob's hair at the back of his neck, Melinda moved her hand to rub the reddened spot above his left eyebrow while he rubbed the matching redness on hers where they'd whacked bone onto bone.

When their eyes met now, they grinned. The golden flecks in his topaz gaze danced. Jacob quirked his eyebrow and slapped her on her flannel-covered butt.

"Come on, bacon bits," he said. "I'm starved."

Breakfast was rowdy, and no one seemed to notice that she and Jacob couldn't look at each other without breaking into giggles.

Even though she'd still spend the greatest portion of her day alone, Melinda was glad it was day two of the trip, her first day on the same side of the mountain—if not the same trails—as everyone else. They'd cross paths once in a while, at least, or wave from a different lift line, and they'd all meet for lunch in the main lodge.

It was another crisp, clear day, every bit as cold as the one before, though the overnight winds had died down.

They got a bit of a late start, so by the time the rest of the group joined them and they made it to the mountain, the lifts were already running, the lines long, and the day in full swing.

As Melinda stepped into her bindings, her eyes automatically sought Jacob in the midst of the rest of the guys. He had his head thrown back, laughing over something Gabe had said, and his dark hair and coppery highlights shone in the bright sun.

Jacob's dad, Bill, added a comment that had the whole group guffawing, practically bent double with it, Uncle Allan wiping tears from his eyes.

Melinda smiled. She loved them all so much, it made her heart ache just a little. There were no better people on earth, in her estimation, than her family and their friends.

"Where are you headed first, honey?" Karen asked as she skied to a stop next to Melinda. She tossed back her short cap of dark hair and fitted her knit hat snuggly over her ears.

"Over there, I think," Melinda said, pointing to one of the intermediate slope's lifts. "You?"

"I thought I'd tag along for a while, if you want some company."

Pleasure lit inside her. "Sure," Melinda said with a surprised smile. "That'd be great. But what about Nancy and Lois?"

Aunt Pat would be off in the backcountry with the guys again, but her mom usually stuck with the other two women.

"I'll catch up with them at lunch. Maybe by then you'll be ready to move up a level."

Melinda didn't say anything to answer her mom's gentle prodding. She told herself she was perfectly fine sticking to the intermediate slopes, even if she did wonder every once in a while exactly how much steeper the expert lifts and runs might be. Was it time to push herself to the next level after all these years?

The idea made her hands and feet tingle with anxiety.

Still, the seed had planted, and she was tired of spending so much time alone. She'd think about it later.

For now, the day beckoned.

Following Karen toward the lift she'd indicated earlier, Melinda glanced back toward their guys in time to see them skiing en masse toward a black diamond lift, Aunt Pat in the lead.

Melinda scanned the rest of the group. Jacob must have been watching her. Their gazes met, and he grinned and waved before trailing after the rest of his group, leaving her with a smile on her face and a glowing warmth deep in her belly.

She joined her mother in line for their lift and tilted her face to the sky, soaking in the beauty of the day. They spoke comfortably about the resort, the weather, the New Year's Eve party planned for the following night in the main lodge. Easy topics for an easy, relaxing day.

Once safely ensconced on the lift seat, her mother twisted slightly to face Melinda. "How are the heights for you this year?" she asked.

Consciously relaxing her death-grip on the bar beside her, Melinda shrugged casually. "Not bad."

"That's good," Karen said, smiling supportively. "I'm proud of you, you know."

Melinda looked at her mother in question.

"For sticking with it and pushing yourself to do the things you love despite the phobia. A lot of people wouldn't."

Pondering that, Melinda merely said, "Thanks," but the planted seed sprouted a little higher.

She'd been doing essentially the same thing for years, starting with the bunny slopes and moving only as high as the intermediate. Even that had been a battle the first few years after her fall, but since then, she'd stopped pushing herself to improve any further.

If she truly wanted to conquer her fear, maybe it was time to push to that next level after all. Not for her mother or anyone else. She knew that wasn't what her mom was suggesting. She didn't have anything to prove to anyone but herself.

Yet for the first time in a long time, she acknowledged she'd let herself coast on her mid-level victory.

Melinda turned her gaze to the left and the expert lifts soaring even higher than her own, which already felt incredibly far from the ground, wondering if Jacob and the rest of the group were already at the top or still in line. Inside her warm ski gloves, her hands went suddenly sweaty and weak, as though she'd lost control of her muscles.

Karen remained quiet, humming under her breath while Melinda examined her feelings.

She *could* do it, if she made herself, but did she really want to? And if so, why? She had no desire to go hurtling down a snow-covered rock cliff face the way her cousins and Jacob did, after all. Though it would be nice to have company more often on the tougher runs.

Jacob bounced through her mental vision, a smile flashing against the tan of his skin. If she moved up, she'd have more time with him, and that sounded like an excellent reason all on its own.

Everything was more fun in Jacob's company.

Flexing her fingers and scrunching her toes inside her stiff ski boots, Melinda tried to work out the nervous tingles scurrying through her bloodstream.

The expert lifts were so *high*.

They reached the top and hopped off their lift chair, Melinda grateful to put aside her line of thinking. She didn't want to examine her sudden urge to spend extra time with Jacob. Not yet. That path seemed even more dangerous than the double-black-diamond slopes.

"Race you!" Karen yelled and took off down the run with a gleeful cackle.

Grinning, Melinda followed at her own pace. Her mother was a daredevil, not even bothering to turn on the slope, simply heading straight down at breakneck speed, her body tucked into a crouch, face forward, her poles lifted behind her. Snow flew beneath her skis, sending a delicate spray in twin lacy plumes at her back. She'd reach the bottom long before Melinda would at her more sedate pace, but Melinda was well used to coming in last on the ski slopes.

In the water it was another story. She could challenge just about anyone to a race and come out lengths ahead, even against Jacob or the other guys and their longer reaches.

The air was sharp enough to sting, but Melinda reveled in the beauty surrounding her. There was nothing like swooshing down a powder-covered slope through a winter wonderland, the sun and wind on her face, her muscles flexing.

The sheer joy of it filled her like song.

At the bottom, she and her mother changed courses to another intermediate run and hopped on the lift. This one soared steeper than the first and felt faster, as though they were hurtling through the bright blue sky at a reckless pace.

Melinda breathed in through her nose and out through her mouth, studiously ignoring the ground as it fell away in a rush below her skis, reminding herself the lifts were simply the price she had to pay to engage in one of her favorite activities, and well worth the effort.

Cold bit through her protective layers like piercing needles now that she was stationary for the length of the lift. Beside her, Karen rubbed her hands together vigorously to warm them. Melinda hoped the weather would stay clear, at least. A storm could drop the temperatures to unbearable levels.

"Tell me about this ski instructor," Karen said out of the blue. "We didn't have a chance to talk last night."

"Oh," Melinda said with a small laugh, unsure why she suddenly felt uncomfortable. She gave what she hoped looked like a careless shrug. "He's from Denmark, and he travels all over the world teaching skiing and surfing. His life's been pretty incredible, I think."

Karen tilted her head to the sun. "That sounds amazing. Getting to see so many places, meeting people, experiencing so much. He must have been interesting to talk to."

"He was. He's only five years older than me, and he's been practically everywhere. I'm a little jealous."

"Traveling is a wonderful gift," her mom agreed. "You should do more, especially once you get out of school. See the world a bit before you settle down."

"Mm-hmm," Melinda murmured, thinking of her conversation with Jacob the night before.

He had lots of travel plans, not to mention the traveling he'd do for work once he got on with a professional sports team like he wanted.

She wanted to see more of the world, for sure, but she was a homebody at her core. She'd never be happy without a solid home base to go back to after every journey, no matter how long or short. And that home base meant *home*—Pasodoro, where the great majority of her family and friends were never more than a short drive away—not some soulless apartment in New York City or Podunk Wherever.

"Is he cute?" Karen asked, pulling Melinda's attention back

to the present.

Melinda couldn't see them beneath Karen's knit cap, but she was sure her mother's eyebrows were wiggling up and down.

"Yes, cute," Melinda answered, blowing out an amused breath. "But—" She broke off, not sure what she'd intended to say.

Karen didn't let her stop there. "But?"

"I don't know," Melinda answered. "He's just not..."

She trailed off again, flailing her free hand around, searching for words.

"Not like Jacob," Karen supplied, her voice supremely casual.

"Now why do you say that?" Melinda asked, frowning. Was she giving off some sort of Jacob-vibe she wasn't even aware of somehow?

"You've always held him up as a sort of ideal," her mother said innocently.

"I have?"

"Sure, ever since you decided to marry him."

"What?" Melinda gasped, choking on a laugh, even as her heart gave a little lurch. "I was four!"

"Well, you always were a wise little thing," Karen said, her tone comfortable. "He's a good ideal to hold."

Melinda shook her head as though her mother had hit her flat in the face with a frying pan, trying to re-gather her scattered wits.

"What I was going to say is it's not like Dane has any potential, so it doesn't really matter if he's cute or interesting."

"Of course not," Karen said, surprise in her voice now. "I didn't ask if you were going to marry him, sweetheart. You've just met, and it's unlikely you'll see him again once we leave. That doesn't mean you can't enjoy your time with a cute, interesting boy while we're here."

"Well, right." Back on track, Melinda nodded her head decisively. "We're only here for a week, and he's a world traveler, probably with the clichéd woman in every port. Besides, I'm still getting over Mitch—" she broke off in exasperation at Karen's indignant snort "—and Dane's not really my type, anyway. And not because he's not like Jake!" she added when her mother opened her mouth to make another comment.

Folding her arms across her body in agitation, Melinda momentarily forgot all about holding onto the bar, frowning over the tops of the trees as the end of the lift rushed toward them.

"Good to know," Karen said, her voice once again as mellow as could be. "I'd hate to see you pining after someone who's rarely around. Long-distance relationships are tough. Lots of extra work. They're only worth the effort for someone truly special."

With that, they skied off the bench, and Melinda followed her mother down the next slope, traversing each curve slowly, her thoughts a jumble.

Her mother's last comment seemed sort of double-edged. Was she warning Melinda off getting involved with anyone long distance, or intimating that Jacob would be worth the trouble if they got involved, given his future plans?

Or was she reading too much into an innocent statement?

Why did it seem like everywhere she turned the last few days, Jacob was there?

Her cheeks heated as a vision of waking snuggled on top of him that morning wove before her eyes. The absolute rightness of that moment had staggered her before she'd managed to wake herself up fully and tried to bury those unwelcome emotions. Jacob's obvious reaction to her had sent more than embarrassment and an uncontrollable answering heat winging through her body.

Of course, she understood about guys and mornings and all that stuff. She'd taken sex ed, after all, and had spent the night with Mitch plenty of times. It didn't necessarily mean anything beyond basic biology.

Except for the look in Jacob's eyes.

Nope, not going there.

It was all too soon after Mitch, and too dangerous with a friend as close as Jacob. It didn't matter if he'd found his way into her fantasies more times than she wanted to admit, it didn't matter that she admired him above any guy she could name except for her dad, or that she loved spending time with him more than any of her other friends.

It didn't matter that he knew her inside out and could make her laugh even when her heart was breaking, or that he'd stuck by her through even her ugliest phases, both the physical and the emotional ones.

He could very well be the most perfect guy on earth for her, but traveling that path was a journey to nowhere. He wanted to light the world on fire, living the glamorous life. If they got involved, she'd be lonely all the time, not just on the slopes. The consequences would be disastrous to her heart.

Speeding up to catch her mother, Melinda determinedly left those thoughts behind like so much powder flying away beneath her skis.

"So, Jake," Christian said, holding out his ski pole to stop Jacob from screaming down the next slope after the rest of their rapidly vanishing group. "Hold up a sec."

"Yeah?" Jacob asked, following Christian to the side and out of the way of any other skiers, though the steep, mogul-covered trail stood empty as far back as he could see.

Christian settled himself in a small open space between two soaring pine trees, and Jacob matched his comfortable stance, sitting back a bit on his skis.

When the younger man lifted his goggles to the top of his forehead, Jacob did that, too, so they could see each other's eyes.

Rocking slightly, Christian scrutinized him with uncharacteristic solemnity. Jacob had the sudden urge to fidget the way he did when his parents lasered him with remarkably similar stares.

The silence stretched out until Jacob finally opened his mouth to speak, but Christian dove into the breech.

"What's going on with you and my cousin?" he asked, knocking Jacob completely off stride.

Of all the topics he might have suspected Christian wanted to discuss, that one would not even have made the list.

"Uh," he said, and actually felt his brain grind to a halt.

"You think no one's noticed?" Christian asked, his pale blond eyebrows raised in superior disbelief.

"Uh," Jacob said again, trying to kick start his brain like one of Gabe's pre-rehabbed motorcycles. "Hmm."

"Because we've noticed."

Twin spots of bright red color, the curse of the pale-skinned, splotched Christian's cheeks, but his eyes, nearly as deep a blue as Melinda's, never wavered.

Stalling, still kicking over his brain, Jacob asked, "What? What have you noticed?"

That was possibly a stupid question. Did he really want Christian to spell it out? Jacob blamed his faulty mental wires for tossing words out of his mouth before he'd fully considered the consequences.

"You can't keep your eyes off her, man," Christian said, sternness riding his baby face. "It's obvious. And she's… I don't know. Something's changed. I want to know what it is and what you're gonna do about it."

Jacob stared at the ground, suddenly very aware of the stinging cold, though waves of heat rolled through his body on the inside. He blew out a breath that puffed white on the crystalline air and wondered how to answer his life-long friend. His thoughts were a tangle, his words locked in his chest.

Christian sighed. "Look, Jake," he said, "you're a good guy. You're my friend, practically another brother, and I like you a lot. Fact is, you guys could be good together, but…"

Looking up when Christian broke off, Jacob said, "But?"

Awkward now, Christian shifted on his skis, his eyes staring over the stunning vista spread out below the mountain, and Jacob followed his gaze. White as far as the eye could see, so pure it almost hurt.

"We've talked about it." Christian faced him again, his eyes piercing.

"We who?" Jacob asked, admitting nothing.

"Dan and Rick and me."

The idea of the brothers holding a powwow about him and Melinda had squirmy eels writhing through his belly. It hadn't occurred to him to worry about their approval.

In hindsight, that seemed incredibly stupid.

They were more than family to her, more than friends to him. A relationship with Melinda would impact all of them, both of their families, all of their friends. They were too tightly entwined for it to be any other way.

He'd considered the extended family as potential collateral damage in the event of a breakup, but he hadn't given any thought to seeking their pre-approval for him and Melinda to get together in the first place. The only approval he'd been thinking about stemmed from their parents.

Now that Christian had confronted him, he silently admitted he needed to cast a much wider net.

How did it all get so freaking complicated?

"They're worried about it," Christian continued, and Jacob's stomach sank to the tips of his skis. "We've all been friends a long time. So there's that."

"Yeah," Jacob murmured. "There's that."

"And she got dumped like four days ago by a guy we all thought she'd marry someday."

The squirmy eels writhed some more. He'd known it was too fast, hadn't he? Too soon. But damn it, he couldn't help the way he felt, and that wasn't a new thing, as much as he might have tried to ignore it for months and months.

If the timing sucked, so be it, but…

"Have you thought about what you'd have to give up?" Christian asked.

Jacob looked at him, not understanding.

"I'm just saying, you better think this through, dude. Do you want this big, famous lifestyle, or do you want Melinda? You won't get both, at least not if you really want to make her happy, which you'd better."

His conversation with Melinda on that very topic confirmed Christian's words. But they were young still, years of schooling still ahead of them. And internships…

He shied away from thinking about what the rest of the

group didn't know. His future plans were the least of his worries at the moment.

Surely, once she got out of school and had some freedom, Melinda would realize there was way more to life than hiding away in Pasodoro forever.

Christian was still speaking. With the thoughts whirling around his head, Jacob almost missed his friend's words.

"But if we're honest," Christian said, "there's no one else we'd rather see her with. Definitely not that Mitch bastard."

"You—what?" Jacob asked, surprise almost stealing his tongue.

"Yeah. The friendship angle's tricky, though. So be sure. 'Cuz if you're just screwing around, if you hurt her, we'll take you out. Clear?"

Jacob studied his young friend in return. He had half a mind to deny it, to deny the whole thing and keep it private for at least a while longer, but there was a spark inside him that wouldn't let him get away with such an obvious—and ultimately pointless—deception.

There *was* something different going on.

He might not know what to do about it all yet, or what would happen, but he could at least be honest about that much.

"I—" he said, then broke off, unsure what he wanted to say.

Christian simply raised his brows again.

"Hell," Jacob muttered. "Yeah. Yes. We're clear."

"Okay, then," Christian said, his normally cheerful smile back in place as though the last uncomfortable moments had never happened.

He clapped Jacob on the shoulder, dug his poles into the soft powder, and pushed off, quickly careening out of sight down the next steep section of slope.

Jacob stared after him, his brain as twisted up as when the conversation had first started, but for one gleaming light shining through the rest of the chaos.

Had Christian, in playing Head Of The Family, just given Jacob not only permission, but outright approval, to date Melinda?

Head in the clouds, an uncontrollable grin stretching across his face, Jacob pushed his goggles back in place and glided forward, tipping his skis over the edge of the steep incline, hardly watching where he was going.

Dating Melinda.

That was the trick, wasn't it, the crux of the whole matter.

A relationship, for them, could never be as casual as dating. They had too much history, both between themselves and between their families, too many events and memories and life-long traditions shared to ever allow such a complicated thing as the two of them dating to be simple.

Complicated meant serious, and serious shot his personal timeline all to hell. The nerves in his belly woke up. He wasn't ready for serious now. He had plans, a schedule, goals.

But...

Hadn't his mother always told him that the best things in life were worth working for, worth the risks, worth the complications? And hadn't he, on some level, compared every girl he'd ever dated to Melinda?

And they'd all fallen well short of her perfection.

Everything seemed so serious all of a sudden. Was she really the one for him? Forever? The idea put a hitch in his breath, shot shivers down his spine, but no one could possibly mean more to him than she did. Of that, he had no doubts.

An image of waking with her that morning made his smile stretch even wider.

It was a big leap from that morning to happily-ever-after, though.

They'd go slow. They had time. Time to work things out, talk about it all, decide what they really wanted. No reason to rush into anything.

Timing would be crucial, but the fact that they were such great friends could, instead of portending potential disaster, make their relationship even deeper and more special than either of them could ever imagine.

His aunt and uncle's divorce, and even Carl and Donna's ruined relationship, flashed in his mind. He shoved them aside.

Sometimes relationships failed.

That didn't mean they all failed, and it was stupid to compare himself and Melinda to anyone else.

It was time to go for it—cautiously, for her sake—but full out, the way he did everything. If he wanted her, and he did, full out was the only way to go.

She'd come around once she understood his plans. Twenty-one was way too young for her to decide to bury herself in Pasodoro forever. Life waited for them beyond the boundaries of their small hometown, and together, that life would be amazing.

Suddenly cheerful, Jacob gave himself over to the slope, exhilarating in the speed and challenge of the terrain. His laughter floated behind him like ancient gonfalons proclaiming a victorious knight, one who'd successfully scaled the castle walls and won the hand of his fair princess.

Okay, so maybe he'd watched *Shrek* with his young cousins a few too many times over Christmas break, but something about a knight, a small-town castle, and a princess Melinda in need of rescue seemed fitting.

Zooming around a sharp, steep curve with that fanciful notion painting pictures in his mind, Jacob flew off the jump.

He soared flat-out, his joyful whoop ringing in his ears and echoing across the mountain. He tucked, preparing to land, and never saw the small shape hurtling straight toward him from the far side of the trail.

The collision knocked him out of his skis, and he plummeted down the slope, end over end off a second jump, finally tumbling to a stop a good sixty feet past the point of impact.

Dazed, Jacob flopped onto his back, spitting snow and filling his lungs to get his breath back, taking stock, aware of a dull throbbing in his left wrist.

"Crap," he mumbled, using his right hand to push himself to a sitting position, cradling his left in his lap.

Icy snow trickled down the back of his neck and inside his layered clothing.

Great.

He shook his head to rid his ears of a persistent ringing,

unsure exactly what had happened. Had he hit a deer?

Another trickle—this one from his nose—caught his attention, and he threw his head back to keep the blood from dripping on his jacket.

"What the hell."

Fumbling in his front pocket, Jacob tugged off his right glove, snagged a small packet, and ripped it open, staunching his bloody nose with several tissues.

Looking back the way he'd come, he identified his poles, wide-flung across the trail, and the swath his body had cut through the deep powder as he'd slid down the mountain. Nothing else was visible from his vantage point below the second jump.

As yet, no one else approached down the run. He needed to gather up his gear before another skier flew around that hairpin turn and tripped over his equipment.

Jacob stood, surprised to find his legs a bit wobbly, and started climbing up the hill, sinking to the knees in the drifts of still-pristine white along the sides of the path. Not many people aside from his group of friends had attempted this run since the last snowfall.

He had to stop twice to catch his breath, cradling his arm against his side. Evidently the fall had knocked more air out of him than he'd realized. His head swam, oddly light.

Grabbing the first pole, Jacob tracked across the trail to snatch the second, grumbling to himself and using the first pole to prop himself up.

Stupid deer.

Glancing up to the next level, he blew out another breath.

Damn.

It was a steep incline up to his skis. Usually not a problem, but he was very aware of his heavy breathing and less-than-steady legs, and the drop from the jump was nearly vertical.

He ended up moving into the tree line and finding hand-and-footholds to climb beneath their sheltering branches where the snow wasn't so deep and the incline was more manageable.

His left wrist continued to throb.

It wasn't until he stepped back onto the run to pick up his

first ski that he finally saw the motionless body in the middle of the path, and his heart plummeted to his toes as dread and panic filled the spot it left behind.

Melinda and Karen spent the rest of the morning getting in as many runs as possible and conversing on safe topics, the bright air shimmering with their happy chatter.

It was an exhilarating day, and Melinda found herself surprised when the time for lunch arrived.

"Already?" she asked.

Karen double checked her watch. "I said we'd meet them at one. It's quarter-to now. We'll barely have time to get this last slope in."

They took off down the hill, Melinda trailing in Karen's speed-demon wake, as usual. Her belly rumbled, making its opinion on the upcoming break known. She hoped Jacob would order extra fries with his usual burger so she could snag a few.

Once she reached the bottom and rejoined her mother, they made their way to the lodge, jammed their poles and skis into the towering piles of snow lining the enclosed patio—a patio nearly double the size of the deck at the lodge on the beginner's side of the mountain—and trekked to their lockers to exchange their clunky ski boots for warm and comfy after-ski shoes.

Most people didn't bother changing, they simply stumped around in their ski boots, ate as fast as possible, and went right back out to the lifts. Melinda and her mother both preferred to eat in comfort.

Melinda unsnapped her helmet and tossed it into the locker along with her boots. Her braid needed redoing, and the hair that had escaped was a crackling, static-filled halo around her head. She fixed it as quickly as possible, while Karen, who'd exchanged her helmet for a knit ski cap and solved her own static-haired issues in three seconds, tapped her foot and stared pointedly at her watch.

"No one cares what you look like coming off the slopes, Princess Perfect. I'm hungry."

"They may not care, but I do. Two seconds."

"That's what you always say," Karen mock-complained. "You're almost as bad as Rick." Putting her hands together in a prayerful manner beneath her chin, she begged, "Feed. Me." She moved her hands to her belly and clutched. "Must. Eat. Must. Drink."

Melinda snorted. "Now who's as bad as Rick?"

"Hmph," Karen huffed, crossing her arms over her chest and tapping her foot even harder. "Let's go before they run out of food."

Winking at her glowering mother in the mirror, Melinda gave her hair a final pat. She sang out, "Coming, coming," beaming a smile, then gave her mother a smacking kiss on the cheek, all innocence and sunshine.

She swiped lip balm across her mouth, still grinning, as she followed her mother toward the lodge restaurant.

They waved to the other members of their party, spread unevenly across four lined-up tables, and hustled to place their meal orders at the counter.

Melinda decided on a grilled-cheese sandwich made with havarti and bacon, a cup of tomato soup, and hot tea, while Karen ordered a double-bacon-cheeseburger, extra-large chili-cheese fries, and a hot chocolate mounded with whipped cream, an *I-dare-you-to-say-anything* look on her face. Her mother might be the size of a faerie, but she could match the boys for appetite.

Luckily for her, she also matched their metabolisms.

Approaching their tables, Melinda scanned the group. Uncle Allan and Eddie's dad, Peter, stood with their arms slung around each other's shoulders at the head of the farthest table, regaling everyone with a story involving a family of squirrels, a moose, a pinecone, and a pair of snowshoes, that had them all in stitches.

"The best part is," Peter said, wiping his streaming eyes with his free hand, "it's all true!"

"I don't believe a word," Bill said, snorting a laugh, while Eddie and Wendell rolled against each other, holding their bellies, and Christian pounded his hand on the tabletop, howling.

Melinda sat beside her mother and waited until the laughter had died down before leaning forward to ask, "Where's Jake?"

Danny and Rick gave her odd looks, and the last of his smile left Christian's face, but it was Nancy who answered.

"Oh, dear," she said, fluttering her hands in her birdlike way as Karen added a questioning glance to Melinda's, "didn't you hear? I thought sure someone had told you."

"Told us what?" Melinda and her mother said in unison.

Wendell, his red hair standing up in spikes all over his head, spoke around a bite of burger. "He's in the ER."

"Not again," Karen said, concern ripe in her voice.

The blood seemed to drop right out of Melinda's head.

"Is he all right?" she demanded, half rising from her seat, worry shooting her pounding heart uncomfortably high into her throat. "What happened?"

Karen placed a soothing hand on her shoulder, urging her back down.

"Sweetie, he's fine, or everyone wouldn't be here enjoying their lunches." Karen turned her gaze on Bill and Lois. "What did happen?"

Before either of them could speak, Gabe shifted in his seat at a middle table and said, "He took out some poor old lady on a slope and went with her to make sure she was okay." He shoved fries in his mouth. "She's fine. So is he."

"Well, he's mostly fine," Aunt Pat put in, a bit defensively, Melinda thought, as her aunt glared at Gabe. "He hurt his wrist, and he's banged up a little."

"Like I said," Gabe repeated, as though it was no big deal.

Maybe after all the collisions Gabe had been in on various race courses across the country, a little skiing mishap seemed like no big deal to him, but panic hovered like bile midway up Melinda's throat.

"Gabriel," Karen said in her admonishing-mom voice. He merely shrugged and chomped down on another handful of fries.

Melinda turned to Jacob's parents, only now realizing that

they seemed perfectly relaxed. Her heart slowed to an almost-normal rhythm, but she wanted verbal reassurance from the two people who'd know the full extent of his injuries the best.

"You're sure he's okay?" she asked.

Lois reached across the table to pat the back of her hand. "He's fine, sweetie. Banged up, as Pat said, but nothing that will keep him off the slopes for even an hour. Gabe's right. Jakey was mostly shaken up over hitting someone else, especially an elderly person."

Freshman year hung unspoken above the tables, the memories stark and painful, though everyone seemed determined to ignore ancient history. As though there were no similarities at all.

Not again, not again! rang through Melinda's head at ear-numbing decibels.

She shuddered, her eyes searching Lois's face.

Jacob's mother gazed serenely back. "He'd be here already," she said, "except that he insisted on staying with the woman while she got treated. They're being extra cautious due to her age, but overall she seemed fine. Just a little dazed when it first happened, and it freaked poor Jakey out."

Melinda could only imagine. Poor Jacob. But okay. That all made sense. She took in a deep breath, blowing out the spike of fear and the worry for Jacob.

Conversation resumed around her, and she took another deep breath and allowed her stomach to settle. She exchanged a relieved glance with Bill, who, despite their age difference, looked so like his son. Shared memories were silently sent and received, more vivid in Bill's eyes than they'd been in Lois's, who seemed to have those early college months locked down tight.

As an athlete and an active guy, Jacob had visited emergency rooms on numerous occasions over his lifetime. Luckily, most of those visits had been for minor injuries. Except for that time in their freshman year of college, during what friends and family referred to as his "dark period," though not in his hearing.

Melinda shuddered again, remembering that year, those few terrible months, and that last awful trip to the ER.

The seeds of that time had sprouted after Seth's death. There'd been a new wildness in Jacob, a recklessness he'd never displayed before. Leaving home and starting college had only exacerbated it and had given him opportunities to act out in ways he never would have back in Pasodoro.

But Jacob had come out of that time even stronger than before. More, in every way—more dedicated, more determined, more joyful, more thoughtful, more loving.

More a man.

He'd turned his life back around after his brief foray down a dangerous path, and it had not been easy. He'd worked hard to earn back the trust he'd lost from so many people, had taken responsibility for his actions, had made restitution where necessary—and in some areas where it wasn't necessary, too—and he became an even better person for it in the end.

People didn't only trust him again, they respected him, too.

Pride grew a painful lump in Melinda's throat and had tears pricking the corners of her eyes—pride in him and in all he'd accomplished since then. No one had ever stopped loving him, of course. Love was a gift. But the rest... the rest, he'd earned.

Swallowing her emotions along with a brief prayer of thanks that he and the elderly woman were okay, Melinda finally bit into her sandwich as the others' conversations continued. Now that she was sure nothing serious had happened to Jacob, her mind wandered, free to look forward to the rest of the day again.

Still, no matter what anyone said, the incident had to have dredged up painful memories for him, not only of freshman year, but of Seth, too. She made a mental note to make sure he was as okay inside as he apparently was on the outside.

The women lingered over the meal, though the guys, along with Aunt Pat, headed back out to the lifts as soon as they finished. They didn't expect to return until the sun went down.

Christian, who'd been oddly quiet during the meal, squeezed Melinda's shoulder on his way out.

Karen decided to spend the afternoon with Nancy and Lois and only cajoled Melinda to join them a little bit. She took Melinda's, "Not yet," with good grace, hugged her tightly, and followed the other two to the locker room to suit back up.

Melinda sat a while longer, enjoying the heat of the fireplace at her back and the crystalline, snow-covered views through the lodge's enormous windows, and hoping for a sight of Jacob.

Despite his parents' reassurances, she wanted to see him for herself.

Though she waited over half-an-hour, he never appeared.

Finally, she gave up, deciding she'd have to catch him at the condo later. Or maybe she'd just head over there now and see if he was back.

She swallowed the last of her tea, though it had gone cold some time ago, and stood to retrieve her ski boots just as someone called her name across the length of the crowded restaurant.

15

"Hi, Dane," Melinda said, concealing her disappointment that he wasn't Jacob with a warm smile as he strode to her side.

"How's it going? You changed mountains."

He looked her over with an answering smile that had color rising to her cheeks. Admiration gleamed in his pale green gaze, yet his words, though innocent enough, held a strange wisp of accusation.

"Um," she said, slightly taken aback. "Yeah. Well, I always do on the second day. Are you teaching over here today?"

Dane's stance shifted, relaxing a bit. "No, I'm off," he said. "I've been looking for you. I thought maybe you were avoiding me."

"Why would I do that?"

"You didn't call last night. Didn't you see my number on the card I gave you?"

"Sorry," she said, flushing hotter.

She resisted expanding on what she considered a good, noncommittal answer. He wouldn't want to hear that she'd seen his number but hadn't wanted to call.

Guilt twinged lightly along her shoulders. She hoped she hadn't hurt his feelings.

"Now that I've found you, want to hit the slopes with me?" he asked. He smiled again. "I can show you some spots the tourists always miss."

"Um…"

It wasn't as if she didn't like him, exactly, though she wasn't eager to spend the afternoon with him, either. Besides, she was worried about Jacob.

"Come on," he urged. "It'll be fun."

Melinda waffled, the part of her that didn't want to be rude fighting with the part of her that wanted to check on her friend.

Of course, for all she knew, Jacob was already back out on the slopes.

"Come on," Dane said again, and sent her a charming smile.

Frustrated, she ground her teeth. What would Jacob want her to do?

Well, that was easy.

If he really was fine, as everyone insisted, he'd want her to go ski and not waste the day. And he'd be out there somewhere himself. If he wasn't fine, he wouldn't want her hovering over him while he licked his wounds.

Damn it.

Fine. She'd compromise. She'd go ski with Dane for a while, but she'd text Jacob first, and she'd go back a little early, too, in case he wanted to talk. Or needed a hug.

To Dane, she said, "Okay, but I stick to the intermediate slopes. I'll understand if that's too tame for you."

Dane shrugged. "No big. I can catch the diamonds any time. Where's your gear?"

He escorted her to the locker room, then waited outside the lodge while she got ready.

When she came back out—after sending several super-cheerful, emoticon-heavy texts to Jacob and waiting what seemed an eternity for a response that didn't come—she found Dane leaning negligently against a mounded pile of snow as though he was posing for a fashion shoot.

Amused, Melinda hid her smile. He did have a great body

and a handsome face, yet he seemed both overconfident in some areas and almost insecure in others, always trying a bit too hard. He probably thought he came across as masculine and charming instead of domineering and arrogant.

Poor guy.

She'd heard her brother, her cousins, and their friends talk often enough about how hard it was for guys to approach girls they liked. Did Dane like her? Maybe that was his problem. He was intimidated and trying not to show it, though why he should find her intimidating she couldn't guess.

Melinda vowed to be extra nice to him all afternoon to make up for it.

As they moved toward the first lift, Dane told her a couple of jokes, and she made sure to laugh enthusiastically. His appreciative grin dazzled in the afternoon sunlight.

Good God, what a day.

Jacob swiped his bandage-wrapped left hand over his face as he trudged from the shuttle stop toward the lodge. The fine powder of the day before had turned to slushy muck in the parking lot after so many cars and feet and skis had traversed the grounds.

At least the runs were still fresh, and the powder-like conditions would last even longer in the backcountry where a lot fewer people dared to go. But visions of the skiing to be had failed to raise his spirits much.

Head down, he followed the path behind a rowdy group of teens.

Relief that the woman he'd struck, Neta Smalls, was okay was tempered by the stress of the whole experience. When he'd first seen her crumpled body in the middle of the ski slope, he'd feared she might be dead.

He would never forget the breath-and-strength-stealing impact of that moment, as though a sadistic giant had reached through the back of his neck and pulled his spine straight out, and all his muscles and organs with it, leaving him an enormous, quivering, oxygen-starved blob of pure terror.

Neta was a tiny spitfire of a woman, and tough as nails, as he'd learned in the intervening hours, much to his relieved amusement.

But still.

She was seventy-eight years old, and he'd clipped her a good one, even if technically she had run into him. He hadn't been paying close attention. His mind had been caught up in daydreams of Melinda, and Neta had paid the price.

She had a hell of a bruise running across her left hip and another on her arm, with his ski's name on each one.

Jacob sighed, deliberately closing his mind against images of another elderly woman, pale and shaking thanks to him. And a young woman with bruises all over her body. Bruises he'd put there with his carelessness. Even after all this time, memories of the early months of his freshman year of college could drag him down into a dark pit lined with sticky guilt.

That final night. The crash, the destruction, the fear and pain.

Thank God he'd turned his life around after that, with no lasting damage to anyone, but he'd never forget the moments that had changed him forever.

Worst of all, there was Seth.

Remembering his first year of college always led him unavoidably to thoughts of Seth, his best friend aside from Melinda. And the night he died. The most painful topic of all. The worst moment of his entire life.

Hearing the words for the first time, not understanding how it could be true.

Awful.
Unbelievable.
Final.
God, he missed his friend.

It could still rise up and choke him by the throat. As though it had all just happened. The pain would stab, as fresh and sharp as in the first minutes and days after Seth had died.

Worst of all were the trips home, when he had to face the constant reminders of his friend's too-short life everywhere he looked.

All because some stupid, careless woman couldn't wait to send a fucking text until she got off the road. So she'd orphaned her children and killed his best friend.

Thinking about it could make him crazy. The rage that had burned through him had been nearly as bad as the grief, and harder to control. For a while, he'd gone every bit as stupid as Seth's killer. Worse in some ways, because his actions had been deliberately wild, deliberately reckless.

Thank God he'd never killed anyone.

If anything positive had come out of that whole time period, that whole awful mess, it was the focus and direction he'd finally found for his life, as though Seth still sat beside him, guiding him along.

Seth never got his chance to really live, to finish growing up and get out of Pasodoro, to travel and explore, to meet new people, to do all the things he'd dreamed about when they were kids.

So Jacob would, for both of them.

Becoming a team doctor had seemed the smartest, most expedient way to accomplish those goals, since he'd always planned to go into medicine anyway. He'd be the best damn doctor he could possibly be, and he'd have the money and the opportunity to live the sort of life his friend had always envisioned.

It was the best way he knew to honor Seth's memory.

He'd never stop missing his friend, or suffering the guilt when something happened to remind him of his freshman year. But he would do everything in his power to give back, to care for his patients, his family, and his friends, and to make sure he never took his life, or anyone else's, for granted.

Today, Jacob had sat with Neta Smalls and her twinkly-eyed husband, Clyde, for hours, fresh guilt heavy on his shoulders.

While they waited and went through all the tedium of a trip to the ER, he'd answered their questions as best he could and helped them answer more questions for the medical staff, some of whom had treated them like young children unable to speak for themselves.

He'd run into that attitude before, when visiting the retirement home in Pasodoro and other places, and it always made him mad. There were some elderly people who did have trouble expressing themselves, but most were perfectly capable, if the nurses and orderlies would be patient and give them an extra second to answer.

Clyde and Neta had entertained him, amused him, and touched him with stories from their life together, holding hands the entire time. Jacob hadn't left until he'd realized the two of them were spending more time reassuring *him* than allowing Neta to rest.

Guilt still rode his shoulders, but they'd parted friends.

Now he just wanted to grab his gear and get back out on the slopes to salvage what he could of the afternoon, working off the lingering pangs of remorse on the steep, unforgiving face of the mountain.

The ER doctor had wanted him to take the rest of the day off, which sounded like the worst possible idea. He had no intention of wasting time lazing around the condo by himself with only his miserable thoughts for company.

Jacob rounded the corner of the lodge in time to see Melinda skiing toward one of the chair lines. Heart lifting, he raised his hand, on the verge of hailing her before he realized she wasn't alone.

The guy had his back to Jacob, though he was too short to be any of their friends or her cousins, despite the pale blond strands of hair sticking out beneath his ski cap.

He had to be the ski instructor.

A sensation he didn't care for clutched in Jacob's belly. One he wasn't familiar with, yet had no trouble identifying.

Jealousy.

Terrific.

Unwelcome awareness crept over him.

Earlier, he'd been so caught up in the idea of himself and Melinda together, he hadn't stopped to think the whole thing over from her point of view. He'd worried a little about their families' reactions, but he realized he hadn't really considered her feelings at all.

Like the fact that she was still getting over that asshole, Mitch, as Christian had reminded him. Or worse, that she might not feel the way he did in the first place. And even if she did, she might not be willing to give up her own dreams and desires to follow his. Could he ask her to? Could he give up his own dreams to make her happy?

Either way, it seemed one of them would have to give up a lot for the other. That sounded like a poor recipe for starting any sort of relationship.

Worst of all, he'd never considered she might already be interested in someone else.

Slowing to a stop in the middle of the path, Jacob frowned. He'd decided he wanted her, that she was the one for him, but what did that really mean? All that intellectualizing about complications and his plans and timelines. What did he really feel?

Other skiers brushed past him, but he hardly noticed, his eyes trained on Melinda and the ski instructor.

He'd been ready to risk their friendship for the sake of... of what, exactly? His newly awakened lust? Love? The possibility of love? He wasn't ready to say the big L-word, was he?

Sure he loved her, he'd loved her his whole life, and told her so all the damn time, but that was friendship love.

Was this capital 'L' love?

If it wasn't, then he shouldn't even bring it up, because anything less than L-O-V-E love wouldn't be worth the risk. He certainly wasn't going to risk their friendship over sex, no matter how hot she made him. Which was *hot*. But if he did capital 'L' love her, then that...

Well, that was just fucking scary.

Head spinning, Jacob fumbled his way to the outdoor patio and slumped into a chair. What the hell was he doing?

Jacob scrubbed his hands over his face and groaned, barely

registering the soreness in his wrist.

He hadn't even told her his news yet. He couldn't toss a relationship in her lap and then tell her, oh, by the way, I'm also leaving for months, see ya later.

God.

He was losing his edge on that tsunami wave, heading for a wipeout. He needed to think. Last night he'd decided she was it for him. In the bright light of day, what did that really mean? He had to figure that out before he moved forward.

In the meantime...

Jacob flicked his gaze toward Melinda and the Danish pastry puff, now boarding the lift chair.

Yeah.

In the meantime, he wasn't going to become That Guy, the jealous caveman idiot who couldn't stand to see his woman in the company of another male.

No way.

Melinda had a lot of guy friends, possibly more guy friends than girlfriends, and he'd never had a problem with it before. Not really.

Was this what it had felt like to his past girlfriends when they'd seen him hanging out with Melinda?

Huh.

That was a new consideration.

Jacob frowned. He'd always dismissed their jealousy of his relationship with Melinda as the girl's problem, but maybe they'd had a small point. It put him in a weird position. For the first time, he was truly able to understand what those girls had complained about.

At least to a degree.

However, Melinda wasn't dating the Denmarkian donut hole. She would most likely never see him again, and he refused to succumb to the whole green-eyed-monster routine.

By God, he was not going to become That Guy.

Rubbing a hand over his still-clutching belly, Jacob pulled his determination up from around his ankles. He was not going to get his skivvies in a twist over some ski-slope strudel she'd just met and would never see again, just because he had ideas of romance running around the rabbit warren in his brain.

That much settled, Jacob shoved out of the chair and headed for the locker room and his gear, ignoring the aches and pains from the accident. Maybe he was better off skiing alone for a while.

He had some thinking to do, and a bitch of an attitude to lose.

Waving goodbye to Dane at the end of the afternoon, Melinda rejoined her mom, Lois, and Nancy, who had waited for her at the shuttle stop to ride back to the condos together. Dinner that night would be held in the second condo, cooked by the men, so the women were going back early to take advantage of the quiet and four empty bathrooms for some nice, long, hot showers before the guys returned.

Nancy hung up her cell phone in frustration after trying unsuccessfully to reach Eddie.

"Phone's dead *again*," she muttered.

Melinda exchanged wryly amused glances with her mother and her aunt, but wisely stayed silent.

Eddie was a smart guy, and ruthlessly organized about every other aspect of his life, yet he had a serious mental block when it came to charging his phone. It drove everyone batty, especially his mother.

Settling into her seat on the shuttle, Melinda stared out the window.

True to his word, Dane had shown her some breathtaking views mere steps off the main trails, vistas most visitors to the resort missed. Though she'd stayed well away from the edges, Dane hadn't tried to force her closer or made any snide remarks about her hanging back.

The valley had stretched below them in a miracle of untouched white surrounded by the soaring mountain peaks, rocky ledges, and ancient trees. It looked like a fantasy land. She couldn't wait to show Jacob.

Back at the condo, Lois and her mom offered to take turns in the master bath for their showers, so Melinda headed straight to the hall bathroom and poured half a bottle of the resort's bubble bath in the tub. She settled back with a lusty moan of pure bliss in the steamy-hot water.

Her mind floating, Melinda's thoughts drifted over the day. Near perfection.

Except for the incident with Jacob.

A frown pulled at her brows. She hoped he'd taken it easy after his accident that morning, but she knew her friend. He'd probably gone right back out and skied harder than ever, if only to prove he could. He hadn't answered any of the texts she'd sent, but he often forgot to check his phone when out on the slopes, which frustrated her almost as much as dead-cell-Eddie frustrated Nancy.

She'd check Jacob over during dinner to satisfy herself he really was okay.

Melinda frothed her fingers through the lacy bubbles. Maybe she could convince him to make it a hot-tub night instead of going back for more skiing. Force him to rest. She could claim her own soreness and a desire for company. Besides, none of them had made use of the resort's multiple Jacuzzis yet, despite the pie chart the guys had made for chasing after the snow bunnies.

It was the same every year. She chuckled quietly to herself. The guys always talked big and made grand plans for collecting all the female hearts in the land, but each year, they spent every available moment on the slopes, or eating, or sleeping, which left precious little time for chasing women.

They had better luck on the summer camping trips, which seemed custom-designed for casual flings. Skiing was all about the thrill of conquering mountains, not hearts.

She dribbled hot water over her arms, glossing over thoughts of her own heart.

The pain of Mitch's desertion had definitely faded, maybe even faster than she would have liked, since it made her call her true feelings into question. Had she really loved him if she could get over him so quickly, while the mere idea of losing Jacob made her soul shudder with despair? She had no answer for that question, only more doubts.

Not wanting to let that mess back into her head, Melinda took stock of the rest of her body instead. She felt good. Pleasantly exerted. Her foot hadn't hurt at all today, thankfully, though her muscles reveled in the warmth of the bath after two full days of skiing in frigid temperatures.

Poor Jacob had to be sore after his accident, even if it wasn't serious. It wouldn't be a hardship to spend time in the heated whirlpool tonight instead of on the slopes, and it would do Jacob good, too. They could relax and tip their heads back to stare at the stars. Maybe have some wine, listen to music, talk.

She closed her eyes and let herself drift.

A sharp knock on the door bolted Melinda out of her nap, and she sloshed upright in water gone lukewarm.

"Wha-hmm?" she mumbled, her head groggy and disoriented.

"Mel?" Karen called through the door. "Lois and I are going next door to open some wine with Nancy. The guys should be back soon to start dinner. Are you coming?"

"'Kay," she answered, yawning widely. "I need to rinse off, then I'll be over."

"Hustle up," her mother said. "Oh, and bring the big salad bowl, will you? Your dad will forget, and I have my hands full with the wine bottles."

"Sure thing."

Stretching, Melinda sank low in the water for a few more minutes, trying to chase the fog from her brain. She'd really zonked. Finally, knowing she was on the verge of falling back to sleep, she forced herself upright and turned the showerhead on full blast.

Despite the big lunch she'd had, sharp hunger pangs gnawed inside her belly, and a glass of wine sounded excellent for warming up her insides. She needed to get next door before the guys returned and ate and drank everything in sight.

16

Jake, toss all that stuff in the dryer," Bill said as the two of them and Melinda's dad, Stan, stripped their outer layers off just inside the door of their condo. "And grab a towel, or your mother will skin us for leaving water all over the floor."

"Your dad and I are heading over now to get the steaks started," Stan added, as he headed down the hall in search of his slippers. "Bring the roll pans with you, okay?"

"Dryer, towel, rolls, check," Jacob answered, rubbing a hand briskly over his hair and scattering water droplets. "I'm gonna rinse off real fast first."

"Make it snappy, son," Bill advised, giving Jacob a wink, "you know how your mother gets when she's hungry."

"Yes, sir, double check on the dragon."

"All right then, see you in a few."

Stan came back through the kitchen and grabbed trays of marinated steaks and two large pre-cooked potato casseroles that only needed reheating. He jerked his chin at Bill to indicate he should grab the pies sitting on the counter.

Thus encumbered, they waited while Jacob opened the door

for them, then headed to the other condo. Wendell and Christian had already gone over in search of food.

Jacob grabbed the gear and threw it in the dryer, then snagged a towel and mopped up the entryway. He tossed that in the laundry room, too, then popped open the door to the bathroom.

A wave of steam and a female shriek greeted him, but he hardly heard her startled scream over the sudden pounding in his ears. His blood pressure shot into the stratosphere like a rocket blast.

Holy crap, she's a goddess.

Melinda stood, one foot in the shower, dripping wet, a washcloth in hand. Shocked blue eyes met his equally stunned brown, and everything froze for an endless beat. Then—

"Get out, Jacob!"

The soaking-wet washcloth slapped him straight in the face, snapping him out of his lust-fueled trance, and he finally jerked the door closed.

But not before his eyes had taken the full measure of a completely naked Melinda.

Another outraged scream rattled the door panel and told him she'd caught the appreciative—and wholly uncontrollable—grin that had spread across his face before the door slammed shut.

He leaned, weak-kneed, against the opposite wall.

"Sorry!" he managed, the word choking out through a guilty spurt of stupefied laughter, half-strangling him. Jacob clasped both hands around his constricted throat and wisely kept the reverent, "Wow," to himself.

He should have closed his eyes. He should have slammed the door immediately or turned his back like a gentleman. But his muscles had frozen every bit as much as hers had, and he hadn't been able to help the sweep of his eyes.

God knew he should have. But he was only human.

Rubbing a hand over his belly, Jacob blinked his eyes clear. He hadn't seen her totally nude since they were little kids, innocently skinny dipping in the lake while camping with their families.

Things had definitely changed.

Tripping over his own feet on his journey back down the short hallway, Jacob collapsed on the couch, one hand on his belly, still dazed, still chuckling, and still slightly breathless.

She'd changed, all right.

Wow, wow, wow. And again, wow.

It was one thing to see her in her clothes every day and know an amazing body existed beneath the layers of fabric. It was one thing to hold her or hug her and feel those curves, that heat, against his own body. It was one thing to see her in her skimpy bathing suits, or once in a while when she whipped off a top to change and he sometimes caught sight of her in a lacy bra.

It was something completely else to see her in all her majestically bare glory.

Melinda. Oh, God.

He closed his eyes again, and there she was, the way he would see her every time he closed his eyes from now on, until the end of his life.

Her velvety-smooth ivory skin dewed with water droplets from her shower and blushed pink from the heat. Her river of hair, nearly black from the wet, sliding down her slender back almost to her waist, and her dazzling blue eyes, thickly lashed and wide with surprise. Her rosy lips parted and moist, as though she'd just licked them with her small, pink tongue.

And the darker rose of her nipples—her *nipples*—tipping her full, round breasts.

Jacob licked his own lips and tried not to think of putting his mouth on her. Right there. Of touching and suckling her the way he desperately wanted at that moment. His belly tightened like a fist, his whole body zinging.

It was something completely else to trace the deep curve of her waist with his eyes, following along the flare of her hips. To skim the slope of her belly down to the darkly shadowed vee between her legs and to feel the answering surge between his own. He'd gone straight from limp to full mast in zero-point-zero-one seconds, all the blood dumping out of his brain to his groin in a rushing flood.

He was still lightheaded.

Not that he'd had any doubts about his physical attraction to her, but if he had, that brief glimpse would certainly have answered the question.

He wanted her.

Bad.

Frowning now, leveling his breathing with a concerted effort, Jacob studied his hands in his lap.

That wasn't all it was, though.

All the craziness that had been going on in his head the last several months—the physical stuff absolutely had a part in it.

A big part.

Yet so much more filled in the center, the deep, important stuff.

Not just history, not just friendship.

Why couldn't he articulate the words, even to himself?

Earlier, with Christian, he'd been certain, ready to stake his claim on her. Then he'd seen her with the Norwegian biscuit, and his first instinct had been an immediate *me-Tarzan-her-mine* response. That was all physical reaction. Possessive, he-man bullshit.

Sex was important—duh—but it wasn't the most important thing.

What did he *feel?*

Jacob closed his eyes and tried to delve inside his heart.

Holding Melinda in his mind's eye—a fully clothed Melinda, for now, to keep him focused—Jacob studied her. Not only her beautiful face or rocking body.

Her.

The real Melinda.

The person inside.

One of his best friends, one of the few people on earth he could be completely himself with. He could picture her easily in a thousand moods and scenarios, in a million memories.

Their childhood and school years.

Holidays and vacations.

Family events.

All the regular, generic days they took for granted, just living life.

Swimming, skiing, laughing, crying, studying, watching a movie. Dancing, eating, sleeping. Thoughtful and serious, giddy and giggling, happy, sad, and every shade in between.

And he felt...

What?

Concentrating harder than he ever had, seeking truth, Jacob let his emotions swarm free, and the answer rolled through him with the power of a tsunami capped by a category-five hurricane.

L-O-V-E.

Oh, shit.

Oh, joy.

Oh, crap.

Love.

For real.

Capital L love.

Love like he'd never felt, never experienced. Jacob scrubbed his hands over his face again, digging hard into his cheekbones, the corners of his eyes.

Love.

The hurricane kept blowing, swirling over him, taking him under.

Down in the gut love, way down deep in the heart love.

Oh, God.

He felt everything, and too much. Elation, serenity, comfort, arousal. Fear. A fierce need to protect, and the purest form of happiness he could imagine.

It overwhelmed him, stopped his breath. He fought against the flood, but it filled him up, overflowed every boundary, and wrung him out.

And then...

Everything settled.

Like attaining a higher state of consciousness. A transcendence. He felt, keenly, he was not the same man who'd fallen onto the couch mere minutes ago. A continental shift had rearranged every atom in his body, every priority, every sense, and tipped his emotional balance onto a new, elevated plane.

Whoa.

Grasping his hair, Jacob tugged violently. Was he still

himself, a whole person? Or some new half-man who couldn't survive without his woman, whose every breath revolved around the wellbeing of another? Could he live that way, survive for long inside that level of intensity?

The depth of love he had for Melinda, freshly discovered, had burst inside his chest like a new sun, burning away old hurts and insecurities. Vaporizing the tsunami wave. It would take time to get used to. And that sort of fire could soon use up all the oxygen. He needed to know it was sustainable.

Survivable.

More cautiously this time, he took stock. That sense of everything settling into place stayed with him, and the nuclear fire banked to a steady, warming glow. He'd traveled light years in seconds, and it might take the rest of himself a little more time to catch up, but the rightness of it relaxed inside him, a new, confident strength.

Jacob had his answer now, and his purpose. His reason to risk. Those risks might be enormous, but the rewards would be staggering.

He loved her.

Now it would be up to him to convince Melinda.

They'd Friend Zoned each other their whole lives. Was that design or habit?

Even with his new confidence in his own feelings, Jacob discovered room for fear remained.

Sometimes, like waking with her this morning, he believed something deeper than friendship shone in her eyes.

But what if he was wrong?

Melinda stayed in the bathroom as long as she dared, trying to regain her equilibrium, a towel now wrapped firmly around her body. She needed a strategy, a wisecrack, something.

Anything.

A way to play it the next time she had to look Jacob in the eye, which could be within seconds of opening the bathroom door.

Crap.

Crap-crap-crap.

Groaning, she leaned against the wall beside the shower and lightly banged her forehead on it. There was no pretending he hadn't gotten an eyeful. And there was no pretending it wasn't much different than seeing her in her bikini.

It was *totally* different.

She knew it.

He knew it.

And it would be there between them every time they looked at each other from now into the foreseeable future unless she figured out a way to diffuse the situation.

The problem was, her mind was a complete and utter blank. Why hadn't she locked the freaking door?

Forget that, why hadn't he freaking *knocked?*

Melinda sighed. Loudly.

Not that it mattered. What was done was done.

Those few seconds had seemed to last an eternity as Jacob's eyes had first met hers, then lowered, inch by slow inch, all the way down to her toes. And back up. Not missing a thing. Raising the heat of a scorching blush along the path of his devouring gaze.

And that *smile*... Holy God.

Well, at least he'd appreciated the view.

There was no mistaking that fact. His eyes had glowed with lust, his smile turned positively wolfish, and try as she might, Melinda couldn't quite squelch the curls of excitement twisting through her belly.

A turned-on Jacob was a very hot, sexily appealing Jacob.

Who knew?

Well, she did. Between that morning and this moment, there was no doubt about it. None at all. Jacob Tanner was a sexy-as-hell beast of a man.

Lord Almighty.

Fanning her heated cheeks, Melinda rolled sideways until her back leaned against the wall instead. She'd fallen in and out of girlish crushes on Jacob many times over their shared lifetime. It was hard not to when he was so sweet.

And smart.

And funny.

He was the only person who could make her laugh, no matter her mood. He was the only person she regularly confided in aside from her mother, the one guy she could trust with all of her deepest, darkest secrets.

Then he'd gone and grown into a seriously good-looking man. Who wouldn't crush once in a while on a guy like that? Nothing serious, and nothing worth risking their friendship over, of course.

At least, not in the past.

And there was no future in it. Absolutely none. He wanted his life, she wanted hers. But suddenly things seemed different, and not only because her relationship with Mitch was done.

Waking snuggled with Jacob that morning had been an experience. At once arousing and comforting and somehow very right. He looked at her differently these days, too, and not just when she was standing in front of him bare-assed naked.

That might bear some thinking on, but for now...

"Get yourself together, Mel," she told her reflection. "No more stalling."

No ideas for handling the awkwardness had come to her yet, but putting off the inevitable would only make it worse. Better to face him now than dread it any longer.

One thing was certain. Night skiing was in. The sexy, scantily-clad, intimate hot tub idea was out of the question. Completely out.

When Melinda finally poked her head out the bathroom door, the condo was quiet and empty. Jacob must have already gone next door.

Good. That gave her a few extra seconds to tighten her hold on her dignity.

Stepping into the chilly hallway between condos, Melinda sucked in a deep breath, blew it out, squared her shoulders, and strode the few steps to the second, identical, condo. She opened the door without bothering to knock and walked into a wall of boisterous noise and the rich, enticing scents of dinner cooking.

"*Hola*, my foxy fajita!" Jacob hollered from the other side of the kitchen, and winked at her, a wide, totally normal smile on his face. "Catch!"

He tossed her a small, squishy football in a perfect spiral, narrowly missing beaning Gabe in the head. She caught the neon-green ball one-handed.

"Watch it, bro," Gabe said, swatting lazily at Jacob and missing him by a wide margin.

"Jacob Robert, no football in the house," Lois said, taking the rolls out of the oven. "Move it."

Melinda's eyes met Jacob's, and just like that, once again, they were fine. The red-faced image of her nakedness holding court in her mind faded away. She dropped her gaze to the ball, rolling it between her hands.

How did he do that?

No matter how awkward or embarrassed she ever felt, he could make it right with a few silly words and a saucy wink.

Moving to her side, Jacob tugged the football from her grasp and lobbed it into the family room, where Wendell snagged it out of the air by rote, not missing a beat in his conversation with Christian. Jacob slung his arm around her shoulders, squeezed her in, and kissed the top of her head.

"Enjoy your shower?" he asked innocently, though his eyes danced into hers. He waggled his eyebrows suggestively.

Melinda laughed. She couldn't help it. Elbowing him in the stomach, she shook her head and went to see if the grown-ups needed help with dinner.

On the slopes later, Jacob surprised her by sticking with her for the evening. The toughest runs were closed for the night anyway, but he claimed he didn't want to overstress his wrist on a more challenging hill. Melinda didn't question him, or the warm glow suffusing her heart.

It was a gorgeous night, though bitterly cold. The sky shone with millions of stars on a velvety-black background, and the air was so pure it almost hurt to breathe.

After two full days of crowded skiing, the fresh powder from their arrival had started to pack down, making for faster conditions. Thin sheets of ice had crackled beneath their boots upon disembarking from the shuttle.

Jacob kept up a running commentary the whole night, discussing everything from the conditions to his hopes for the new year, to the Angels' shot at the World Series in the fall.

Wrinkling her nose, Melinda said, "No baseball talk, it's still football season! What about the playoffs? I think the Packers' front line is in trouble."

"You always think their front line is in trouble."

"Well, they have been ever since—"

"Yeah, yeah," Jacob said, waving his hand at her. "You and your Packers. They're not even a California team! I'll tell you whose front line's in trouble—"

They argued the point, as they had a thousand times before, neither giving an inch.

Whenever he wasn't looking, she watched him from beneath her lashes.

The shower incident had put his earlier accident, and her determination to make sure he was all right, out of her mind for a while, but other than very slightly favoring his injured left wrist and a few angry red scrapes on his face, she couldn't see anything wrong with him physically.

Inside was another matter, but he didn't bring it up, and she was loathe to broach the subject when they were having so much fun.

He challenged her to races—which she lost—and trivia contests, which she won. He told jokes and one-liners the whole time they were on the lifts, including one about a leprechaun and two tiny green balls that made her throw her head back and howl with laughter. His delivery was such that even jokes she'd heard plenty of times before seemed freshly hilarious. Melinda's eyes streamed, and her sides ached.

Wendell and Christian joined them for a couple of runs and a short, fierce snowball fight, and the night flew by.

Through it all, Jacob seemed to make a special point of touching her in some way, either holding her hand, or putting his hand to her back to guide her, or slinging an arm around her shoulders.

Despite the frigid air, Melinda existed in a warm bubble of happiness.

She wasn't ready for the night to come to an end, but all too soon, it was time to return to the condos.

Back on the shuttle, Melinda rested her head on Jacob's shoulder with a deeply contented sigh. What a perfect night.

"Hey," Jacob said, his voice low in her ear, "you've got snowmobiles tomorrow, right?"

Stifling a yawn behind her hand, Melinda nodded. "Yeah, why?"

Man, she was tired. She would have no trouble getting to sleep tonight.

"Want some company?"

Surprised, Melinda sat up to consider him. Jacob looked back at her with studied innocence, his eyebrows raised, awaiting her answer.

"You're going to give up a whole day of skiing," she said. "To ride a snowmobile. With me."

Jacob shrugged, eminently casual. "Sure, why not? They're fun."

"For the whole day? I'm not planning to come back in early."

"Yeah," he said with another shrug. "A change of pace sounds good."

Something was definitely up. He hadn't traded more than a half-day of skiing for snowmobiling since they were twelve, riding on the backs of their parents' vehicles.

"What about your wrist? Won't the handling be hard on you?"

"It's fine," he said, brushing off his injury. He studied her closely in turn. "Unless you want time to yourself?"

Technically, she'd have company, since her dad was going with her. Since she was under twenty-five, she wasn't old enough to rent a snowmobile on her own, but Stan would let her meander as she chose.

She'd planned to take her new camera—a Christmas gift she'd not devoted proper time to yet, with all the drama over Mitch and then getting ready for the trip—and go for a leisurely ride, seeing what photographic opportunities she could scare up.

Her dad, who shared her passion for photography, took a snowmobile day for that reason every year, but he always got so engrossed in what he was doing that he wouldn't miss her company.

A day with Jacob suddenly sounded far more fun than lugging around her camera alone.

"No, that would be awesome," she said, her smile blossoming.

This was Jacob, making an obvious and unusual change in his plans in order to spend extra time with her.

For no other reason except that he wanted to.

Her heartbeat kicked against her ribs, and the heat of a blush flushed her cheeks with pleasure.

Friends they might be, even best friends, but he'd never given up a whole day on the slopes specifically to hang out with her before. Not when he could hang out with her any time he wanted, without having to give up one of his favorite activities on earth.

Melinda ignored the little thrill zipping through her bloodstream, hoping he couldn't detect her emotions in her eyes. They were simply two friends who were going to spend the day together.

Nearly alone.

Like they had more times than she could count. She shouldn't read anything more into it.

But there was that zippy thrill...

Jacob smiled in response, and the rest of the short drive passed in silence. Melinda stared out the window, chewing her lower lip and wondering what the hell she was thinking and why the hell her whole body tingled now every time Jacob touched her in even the most casual way.

When he'd asked her if she would change her plans to stay in Pasodoro to follow the right guy somewhere else, had he meant himself?

She had to be reading too much into it all. It seemed too much to hope that Jacob could truly view her as more than a friend. He'd never indicated otherwise.

But if...

If he did, if they fell in love, if he wanted her to go with him, would she?

17

Pressing a hand to her belly, Melinda breathed deeply to calm the jumping frogs that had suddenly invaded her stomach.

Jacob, Jacob, Jacob.

No one else on earth could even make her think twice about her decision to stay in Pasodoro. It was what she'd always wanted.

But...

Was staying another security blanket? Another way to not be brave, like sticking to the intermediate ski slopes, another way not to push herself?

Maybe she was more of a coward than she'd ever realized.

Was it cowardly to want to stay in the place she loved, with the people she loved? As a nurse-midwife, she'd most likely find work wherever she wanted, but she wanted to serve the needs in her hometown.

And it wasn't only that.

There was also her work for Seth's nonprofit and the fundraising for the scholarship in his name. Maintaining the memorial garden, the annual rodeo.

Things that were deeply, personally important to her, and to Pasodoro.

Low-grade anxiety tightened her throat. Even the idea of leaving made her scared and sad, but there was no point in getting wound up about it now. It was nothing but pointless speculation.

Unless and until something happened between herself and Jacob, she didn't need to stress out over making such a monumental decision.

Comforted, Melinda relaxed again, and the rest of the short ride passed in soothing silence.

They disembarked and trudged up the incline to the condo building, the rest of their group as boisterous as ever. Gabe and Danny had met a couple of girls on the slopes and stayed behind to hang out with them in the lodge bar. Rick, Christian, Wendell, and Eddie grumbled good-naturedly over their lack of female companionship, tossing the traditional insults amongst themselves and calling each other's manhood into question.

Behind their backs, Melinda snickered at Jacob's dramatic eye-rolling and beating on his chest in a great me-Tarzan imitation.

Once inside the first condo, Melinda dealt with her gear and sat for a few minutes with her mom and Jacob's, talking over the day and the plans for the next morning. As soon as she could, she made her excuses and called goodnight to everyone.

Escaping upstairs, Melinda hustled through a few quick yoga poses and into her pajamas while the downstairs was still in an uproar.

One by one, people called out their own goodnights, and the condo quieted, though Wendell and Christian had thrown *The Avengers* into the DVD player—a relatively current movie, for once, they were quick to point out—and had the volume tuned to a dull rumble.

Through it all, she thought of Jacob.

"So," Jacob said as he climbed to the top of the twisting staircase. He lowered his voice so the guys downstairs wouldn't hear him, but his words sparked through Melinda like firecrackers. "Whose bed should we sleep in tonight?"

"Jake!" she said with a giggling gasp. "Be quiet!"

Eyes wide, Melinda sprang from her bed and peered over the rail into the family room. Wendell and Christian were engrossed in their film. She resisted pressing a hand to her pitching belly, or admitting, even to herself, how good the suggestion sounded.

To be held all night in his arms again, breathing the same air, breathing *him*, his scent.

Heaven.

Jacob chuckled. He looked sexily warm and snuggle-able in his pajamas. Melinda licked her lips.

Flicking off the overhead light and throwing the room into partial shadow, he tossed the covers back on his own bed and climbed in, his long, long legs hanging off the end of the too-short mattress.

"Spoilsport," he admonished her. He waggled his eyebrows at her the way he had in the kitchen earlier.

"Oh, shut up," she said, and flounced into her own bed, pulling the covers beneath her chin.

He only laughed again and tucked his hands beneath his head, elbows splayed, to stare at the ceiling.

"Goodnight, Mel."

Sighing, Melinda clicked off the bedside lamp and turned on her side to face the window, staring at the stars hanging above the shadow of the mountains. "Goodnight, Jake."

The next morning dawned in white and gray, with giant flakes of snow swirling lazily from the overcast sky. It wasn't yet heavy enough to cut their visibility on the snowmobiles, though her dad would have checked conditions several times since rising, just in case.

"Happy New Year's Eve, sweetie," her mother greeted her once she reached the kitchen.

Bill and Lois, still on their first cups of coffee, mumbled their acknowledgements, their eyes half-lidded. Her dad's hair stuck up in every direction.

"Apple fritter," Jacob said, coming down the stairs behind her and giving her shoulders a quick rub.

"Bear claw," Melinda answered.

She took the offered cup of hot chocolate from her mother and sipped, her eyes closing in pleasure.

Breakfast was hurried, the rest of the guys whooping over the new fall of fresh powder and eager to be off. Rick and Eddie didn't even bother coming in, only threw the condo door open with salutes to the elders and catcalls to Wendell and Christian to get their butts in gear, the day was wasting.

"Are you sure you don't want to go with them, Jake?" Melinda asked, noticing his eyes following the others out the door.

"No way, pork chop, you're not getting rid of me that easy."

"They're going to the bag jump," she said warningly.

Jacob shrugged. "I'm not feeling it today."

Melinda peered at him, still having trouble believing he really wanted to spend the day on a snowmobile, but she let it go. He was a big boy, capable of making his own decisions, and she would enjoy his company.

Her dad rinsed his mug in the sink and set it on the sideboard, then gathered up the cooler containing their picnic lunch.

"Ready?" he asked.

By the time they reached the rental office, the snow was swirling down with a bit more attitude, frosting their eyelashes and forming an icy scrum on the ridged seams of their winter gear.

Melinda and Stan had reservations for their own vehicles, since they'd planned for their outing well in advance, but the lot behind the rental building was already almost empty. Jacob lucked out and claimed the last sled available for the whole day.

"You folks in'erested in a guided tour?" the rental agent

asked, his head bent over a small stack of paperwork he filled out with a barely legible scrawl. He smelled faintly of cinnamon and pipe tobacco and reminded Melinda of her grandfather.

Stan raised his brows questioningly at Melinda and Jacob, who both shook their heads.

Addressing the mountain of a man, who was decked out in red-and-green Christmas-patterned flannel and ancient jeans held up by snappy reindeer-covered red suspenders, Stan said, "Thanks, but we're good."

The man, whose name was Clay, shrugged his massive shoulders, his muscles lifting heavily and straining the seams of his festive shirt.

"Alrighty, then," he said, and launched into an obviously much-rehearsed spiel on sledding operations and safety. "Got it?" he asked, finally winding down and peering at them with stern gray eyes.

Three heads nodded in answer, and he continued.

"Trails're posted. Stay clear o' ledges and away from the ski slopes. Folks in the backcountry go where they please, never mind no trails, so watch fer 'em. Vehicles're due back half-hour before closing at four." Pausing for breath, the agent returned to his papers to finish the final sheet and handed the stack and his pen to Stan. "Sign here, here, 'n here, initial in them four spots on each sheet. That's for the young'uns."

Stan followed his instructions, signing the last initial with a flourish.

"You sled before?" Clay asked with another piercing stare for each of them in turn. When they said yes, he gave a satisfied jerk of his chin. He held a closed fist out to Stan and said, "Here's your keys."

They fell into her dad's waiting hand with a dull clink.

They left through the rear of the shop and headed for the last three snowmobiles. Melinda turned back to see that Clay had followed them out. He stood on the back step, arms akimbo, his dark, wooly beard collecting a wreath of white as he watched their progress across the snowy lot.

The sleds were old two-seaters with two-stroke engines only, instead of four like newer models had, but they seemed in good condition. Only the bumpers showed the wear, where they'd run into trees or boulders, and the windshield on her dad's had taken some abuse but was clear enough to see through.

Stan tossed a key each to Melinda and Jacob, used a couple of bungee cords to strap their cooler to the rack on the rear of his sled, then climbed aboard.

Once they were all seated, engines revving, Clay lifted a hand in farewell and disappeared into the warmth of his shop, slamming the door at his back.

"Follow me to the trailhead," her dad shouted over the low roar of their engines. "It splits three ways after about a hundred yards, so you two can decide which way you want to go or stick with me. You have your map, Mel?"

"Yeah!" she yelled back.

"If we split up, meet me at the top of trail three for lunch at twelve-thirty," Stan said. "Call if you're going to be late. Ready?"

In answer, she and Jacob raised into kneeling positions mimicking her dad's, one foot firmly planted on the running board, the other knee on the seat for easier maneuvering while they rode across the road to the top of the trail.

Squeezing the throttle lightly to keep her speed down, Melinda sledded after her dad, Jacob bringing up the rear. Snow continued to fall in a steady rush, but visibility wasn't too bad. Once they reached the triple-tined fork in the path, Stan lifted his hand in farewell, opened up the throttle, and took off for a long open stretch down the left-hand side in a plume of white.

Melinda and Jacob exchanged identical grins.

To the right, the trail led to the base of a steep hill and nearly straight up. Melinda tilted her head in that direction, and Jacob nodded in agreement.

At the same time, they squeezed hard on the throttle and raced side by side down the straightaway, standing upright on the boards for better visibility, and giggling maniacally.

Hitting the slope at speed, Melinda bore down on the throttle for even more juice, leaned forward over her handlebars, and shot up, ahead of Jacob.

Riders at the top preparing to descend yielded the hill, whooping and hollering to egg them on as she and Jacob flew.

He nearly caught her, but with a last burst of speed, Melinda crested the slope, shot past the cheering sledders, and jetted down the path cutting across the mountain.

She tossed a victorious grin over her shoulder, then squealed when she saw how close he was. Face forward once more, she whispered and coaxed her ride for yet more speed as though encouraging a race horse.

"Anyone ever tell you you ride like a maniac?" Jacob yelled as he pulled alongside.

"Every time I ride with you, little girl," Melinda shouted back, laughter ringing.

Maybe Jacob hadn't gone snowmobiling with her in a long time, but they raced ATVs every summer, and Gabe had been one of her personal driving instructors long before she turned sixteen. He'd taught her almost everything he knew about driving—and racing—all sorts of vehicles.

Behind a wheel or gripping handlebars, heights or no heights, she knew no fear.

Secretly, she loved it when Jacob referred to her as a psycho Mario Andretti on crack.

"Race you to that tree," Melinda hollered, pointing into the distance at a massive evergreen towering over the edge of a wide clearing.

Seeming to consider it, Jacob gave her a look. "I don't know…"

"What's wrong, you chicken?"

"Of course I am," he said with a loud snort. "The last time I beat you at anything, you bit me."

"I was five. And you bit me back!"

"Still."

"Come on, don't be a baby, Jakey," she wheedled. "Besides, you won't beat me, anyway. Then I won't have to bite you."

Jacob huffed when she blew a saucy kiss at him. "We'll see about that, pipsqueak. Let's go!"

He took off on a shout, catching her by surprise. With a wild laugh, she flew after him, pouring on the speed.

And she beat him.

The scenery blew past with exhilarating speed, as did the

time. They raced over all sorts of terrains, alternately standing, kneeling, or posting, shifting their weight on the sleds to account for the bumps and falls, the heights of the hills, and the depth of the snow.

Before they knew it, it was time to meet her dad for lunch.

They circled back and lightened up on the throttles, chatting about the ride, the continuing snow, the rest of the week, and the New Year's Eve party scheduled in the lodge that night.

Stan hailed them as they approached, and they ate sitting comfortably on their rides. Her dad showed off some of the photos he'd taken, making Melinda wish she'd brought her camera on the expedition after all. She'd opted to leave it behind since Jacob was joining her, but her dad had gotten a slew of great shots, including one of an enormous buck half-hidden in the white-plumed trees and staring out over the basin.

"Don't be late getting back," Stan said as they were wrapping up. "The torchlight parade and fireworks are at dusk, and we need time for dinner before getting ready for the lodge party. Are you guys going for any night skiing first?"

Melinda said no, but Jacob nodded.

"I think all the guys are," he said. "You're not coming, Mel?"

"Nope, I'm going to do my nails and be girly before the party starts. I'll see you guys when you get there. And don't come in straight from the slopes! I know you brought nice clothes, so go back and change first."

"Yes, ma'am," Jacob said, saluting smartly.

Tucking their trash into a sack and packing it in the cooler, Melinda handed it back to her dad to strap to his vehicle and swiped the fresh snow off her goggles.

"Will they be able to have the fireworks in all this snow?" she asked.

"Sure," Stan said, clearing the covering of white frost from his own goggles and putting them back in place. "As long as the winds don't get too strong."

"That's good, I'd hate to miss them." Leaning over, Melinda pressed a kiss to her father's chilly cheek. "Have fun with the photos."

"See you at the rental office by three-thirty," her dad said before motoring off.

Melinda sat for another moment, taking in the purity of the view, the quiet of the steadily falling snow, and the comfortable companionship of Jacob beside her.

The scent of icy pine, sharp and clean, filled her lungs.

She might have missed out on some photography for the day, but she wouldn't trade it for the chance to spend extra time with him, laughing and talking and racing their hearts out.

"Ready?" he asked.

Nodding, Melinda swung her right leg over the seat and started up her sled, following him down the next trail.

She'd planned to ask him about yesterday's accident, but Jacob seemed so cheerful, she couldn't see any benefit in dragging up bad memories. She let it go, at least for now.

Full bellies made them mellow. They kept their speed down to enjoy the view, staying far to the right and out of the way of the other snowmobilers and occasional cross-country skiers or snowshoers.

"Hey, Mel," Jacob called, "what do you call a penguin in the desert?"

"I don't know."

"Lost."

"Har-har," she said with an exaggerated eye roll, though she couldn't stop the giggle that went with it. He was so silly sometimes.

The snow began to fall more heavily toward the end of the day, making Melinda wonder if they were in for another big storm that night, and if the fireworks would be canceled after all. So far, they'd lucked out with the winds, but that could change any time.

Melinda led the way down a steep incline, zigzagging her sled and thinking about the party that night.

What would Jacob think when he saw her in her slinky red party dress?

She was toeing a dangerous line, and she knew it. There was a fire in her, a need to poke a sleeping dragon and see if an answering blaze burned inside his belly.

And if it did—

Jacob shouted behind her, the tone of his voice alerting her, and she whipped her head around in time to see him dive off the back of his sled as it began a slow-motion roll straight toward her.

Stifling a scream, she hauled on her handlebars to move her vehicle to the left out of the way and slowed carefully to a stop.

After making sure no one was in the path of danger from the tumbling snowmobile, Melinda twisted in her seat and called back to Jacob.

"Are you all right?"

He waved a hand to indicate he was okay, and clawed his way up, his eyes trained on his sled and its thud-thud-thudding path to the bottom of the hill. Shaking his head, Jacob worked his way diagonally down the mountain to her and climbed on the back of her snowmobile.

"What happened?" she asked as Jacob grabbed the passenger strap with one hand, wrapping his other arm around her waist.

"Snow gave way under the right ski and I overbalanced," he said with disgust. "These old machines don't recover very well. I couldn't pull it back."

"At least you're not hurt."

"I don't think the same can be said for my sled," Jacob answered. He blew out a frustrated breath.

"We have insurance. Don't worry about it. Did you hurt your wrist again?"

"It's fine."

Melinda made her way cautiously down the rest of the slope, stopping once so Jacob could pick up the belly pan that had popped off the snowmobile on one of its rotations.

"Definitely not riding it back with this thing detached," he said, looking it over.

When they reached the bottom and the crashed sled, she and Jacob pushed it off the trail out of the way of other riders, left the belly pan on the seat, and Jacob climbed back on with her for the rest of the ride to the rental office.

"Lucky we were headed back anyway," he said.

Melinda nodded in agreement and focused on the trail. The snow poured down, harder by the minute now, and even the lightly stirring wind whipped cold through every layer of clothing, but she hardly noticed the frigid temperature with Jacob tucked tightly against her back.

Logically she knew they had on too many thick, insulating layers to actually feel his body warming her head to toe, or his heart beating steadily against her back. It was nothing like being all snuggled up together in her bed with only thin cotton between them, their bodies putting off a furnace-worth of burning heat.

And yet, with his arm securely around her, Melinda's skin hummed, hyper aware of her body plastered to his, basically sitting in his lap.

Sensation overwhelmed her, like being burned from the inside out.

The urge to throw the snowmobile's stop switch, flip around on the seat, and burrow into Jacob's chest both stunned her and flooded her body with a tingling pleasure she could hardly wrap her mind around.

And it sucked.

Even if she could throw away her own dreams to follow him around the country, even if she could talk her way past their lifelong friendship, Jacob never would.

Hadn't she been in this exact situation before, longing for some sign from him, reading too much into innocent glances, only to have it all fizzle away into nothing once again?

Maybe he looked at her in that certain way sometimes, and maybe he'd wanted to spend the day with her instead of skiing, but when it came right down to it, he'd never given her any serious indication that he saw her as more than a friend.

Melinda sighed.

Her emotions had been all over the place since Mitch dumped her. Clearly she wasn't thinking straight. Yet there was something about Jacob, she couldn't deny it. Something that, if she were honest, she would admit had been there long before Mitch or any other guy had ever caught her fancy.

The question was, what could a best friend do about any of it without risking the friendship, and still stay true to herself at the same time?

Jacob held tight to Melinda, his chest pressed against her back, breathing in the ice-laced scent of her glossy hair where wispy strands had escaped the braid tucked into her helmet.

It sucked that his sled was toast, but at least he hadn't hit anybody, and since its temporary death gave him a chance to ride wrapped around his best girl, he planned to take advantage of every minute.

He'd woken with one thought in his head that morning. It was New Year's Eve. There was a big party happening at the lodge that night.

And at midnight, there would be a perfect excuse to kiss Melinda's lush, rosy mouth.

Grinning to himself, Jacob tightened his arms around her in a fierce hug.

"Okay?" she asked over her shoulder.

"Great!" he said, a little louder than he'd intended, but he could blame that on the noise of the engine.

He had a hazy memory of kissing Melinda once before. Kissing her senseless, the way he wanted to do again.

In his memory, they'd both been more than a little drunk, more than a little giggly, and very enthusiastic. He wasn't sure if it was a real memory or a wishful dream, but he couldn't wait to repeat the experience in the here and now.

Finally, the rental office came into view.

Melinda's dad stood out front waiting for them. When he saw that they were doubled up on one sled, he jumped down the front steps and started toward them, but Melinda waved to him one-handed to indicate all was well.

After they explained what had happened, and where they'd left his sled, they repeated the story for the rental agent. Clay seemed less than happy. Despite the insurance coverage, he was out a sled until the money came through to replace it, and it was peak season.

"I'm sorry, sir," Jacob said.

Clay shrugged, then bowed his head regretfully and stomped inside, muttering under his breath.

"You're sure you're all right, Jake?" Stan asked, a hand clamped to his shoulder.

"Never better," he answered, silently acknowledging that while he was sorry about the sled, overall his mood was pretty damn cheerful.

Midnight was coming.

By the time they sorted out the details and filled out the necessary paperwork, it was after four. They needed to get back for the parade and early fireworks.

The shuttle dropped them at the lodge for the opening festivities, where they met up with the rest of their group. They ranged along the edge of the deck surrounding the lodge, the massive overhead heaters on full and everyone's attention focused on the top of the closest slope.

The snow lightened just in time for the parade, as though it had only been awaiting the entertainment.

On the pretext of helping to keep her warm, Jacob scooted as close to Melinda as he could manage, not quite brave enough to reach for her hand in front of everyone. Not yet. But putting his arm around her shoulders—for warmth, of course—was totally normal.

The main lights all over the resort went out, and the Christmas lights strung across the ski slope flickered on in cheerful holiday colors.

At the top of the run, torches flared to life, and as the skiers holding them aloft began their descent, fireworks sparked across the sky in the background, drawing cheers and whoops from the crowd.

More fireworks would go off at midnight, but the lodge didn't stint on the early display.

Jacob sat with his arm draped casually around Melinda, her head resting against his chest. She clapped along with everyone else, a smile lighting her face as she watched the show.

He watched Melinda instead, and found her more beautiful than any light in any sky ever created or imagined.

After the torchlight parade ended, Melinda headed back to the condos with the grown-ups, while the guys grabbed a quick meal at the lodge and went out for some night skiing.

She turned once on the trek to the shuttle, feeling eyes on the back of her head. Her gaze met the intensity of Jacob's as he stared at her over Danny's shoulder, making her shiver with an emotion that had nothing to do with the cold.

Jacob's dad had brought his gear from the condo for him that morning and stored it in a locker, so Jacob didn't have to waste time going back to grab it.

A pity, since they could have snuggled up on the shuttle.

Melinda climbed aboard with the others and stared out the dark window. Night had already fallen, and the slopes blazed with colorful strings of Christmas bulbs and the bright glow of the overhead lights guiding night skiers down the trails through the steadily falling snow.

Once back at the condo, Melinda ate hurriedly, then showered and took special care with her hair and makeup.

She'd discovered another message on her cell from the unknown phone number Mitch had called her from before, but she'd deleted it without listening, blocked it, and washed the memory of the call away along with her shampoo suds.

He was not going to intrude on her New Year's Eve.

Wrapped in a robe, she sat at the kitchen table and did her nails, painting them a pretty shell pink to offset the siren-red of her slinky dress. She was going to dance her ass off and enjoy every minute of the party, which was scheduled to go until two in the morning.

Her mom twirled into the room in a sparkly midnight-blue dress that showed off her youthful figure and glowing skin, and Lois swept in behind her in a gorgeous knee-length sheath of deep apricot.

"You both look stunning," Melinda said, for some reason finding herself tearing up.

"Aren't you sweet," Lois said, beaming. "We won't hold a candle to you, but I think we cleaned up pretty well."

"I'll say," her dad said, walking down the short hallway while he shot his cuffs and scanning his wife from top to bottom and back up again, making her mother giggle like a young girl. He kissed her cheek, then took her hand and gave her a whirl. "As beautiful as the day we met."

"Oh, stop," Karen said, but she smiled and kissed him back. She brushed away imaginary lint from his suit collar. "You clean up pretty well yourself."

"We can't let the kids have all the fun," Bill said, coming to a stop beside Lois and giving her the same once-over Stan had given Karen. He waggled his brows at her and said in a stage whisper, "On the other hand, maybe you and I should stay in tonight."

"Aren't you ready, honey?" Karen asked Melinda, noting her fuzzy robe and slippers.

"Give me five minutes," she said, and whisked upstairs.

It took her ten, but when she descended the spiral stairs and saw the expression on her parents' faces—glowing pride on her mom's and wary protectiveness on her dad's—she decided it had been worth the extra fussing.

Her smile spread ear to ear. Jacob was going to notice her as a woman tonight.

Not just a friend.

Maybe, if he saw her in that light, something more might spark between them.

The idea both terrified and excited her, yet the more she thought about it, the more she wanted to explore the possibilities. The more her emotions expanded, the less important their different life goals seemed.

Anyway, with time, she was sure he'd change his mind about settling in Pasodoro. Why wouldn't he? Most of their friends and families lived there. It was perfect.

So she'd explore those feelings.

Cautiously.

Being careful of their friendship, of course. Always.

Yet something was happening inside her, and it seemed, every once in a while, like an answering something might be happening inside Jacob.

She needed to know if this was only another—stronger—crush phase, or rebounding from Mitch, or something more.

A tiny voice whispered this was a dangerous path to tread, even as Jacob's eyes danced in her mind and her pulse scrambled with a nervous sort of hunger.

But for now...

Melinda raised the camera in her hand. "Stand over by the window, you guys, I want a picture of you all decked out."

Her parents and Jacob's complied, their arms around each other and bright smiles on their faces. Melinda's heart swelled as she studied them. They made such a striking pair of friends, and she loved them all so deeply.

For a moment, doubt assailed her, and her own smile wobbled.

Would they be unhappy if she and Jacob started dating? Would it destroy their friendships, too, if it went badly? How could she risk it?

Straightening her spine, she reminded herself of one of the

key lessons her parents had taught her growing up—not to live her life worrying about what-ifs. Life was meant to be lived, and love was meant to be loved.

She almost bobbled the camera.

Love?

Holy crap.

Her heart leapt forward like a horse charging out of the gate, racing so fast her head swam with the speed. She couldn't deny the truth. She'd used Mitch and her mixed up feelings as an excuse long enough. He was but a distant memory now, a faint echo of pain.

She couldn't—wouldn't—deny her own heart any longer.

This was real.

Somehow, some way, some time, she'd fallen in love with Jacob. This was not a crush, not a passing fancy, not a childish dream or a teenage fantasy.

It was love. Pure and true and all-consuming.

A sigh trembled from her lips. She squeezed her eyes shut, half in fear of the unknown, half in the first full, excited flush of her secret admission.

Love.

It was at once new yet familiar, breathtaking yet reassuring, astounding yet completely normal.

She was deeply, achingly, madly in love.

With Jacob.

Her best friend.

Now what was she going to do?

Melinda's eyes popped open. Oh, God. She couldn't tell him. She couldn't tell anyone. That much was certain. He'd run for the hills faster than any horse in Nancy and Peter's stable.

"Sunshine, you okay?" her dad asked, snapping her back.

She realized she'd been standing and staring at her parents, slack jawed, for nearly a minute.

Was she okay?

No. She was wonderful, and terrified, and happier than she'd ever been, and a nervous wreck. She couldn't lay claim to anything as simple as okay.

"I'm great," she said, and meant it, though her voice

wavered. "Say 'champagne and strawberries.'"

"Champagne and strawberries!" the four of them chorused as she raised her camera.

Whatever happened, she'd answered one all-important question. She knew what love was, without a shadow of a doubt, and it had nothing to do with what she'd imagined for Mitch. Her feelings for Jacob transcended anything she'd ever known or even allowed herself to feel before.

She was light years beyond okay.

Melinda held that love firmly in mind, a full-wattage smile covering her face from ear to ear. She imagined it was bright enough to dispense with the flash on her camera.

She snapped several photos. Her parents and Jacob's were laughing and talking in each one, unstudied and natural, and each picture was wonderful in its own way, but Melinda already knew the first photo would be her favorite.

All four of them had their heads thrown back, mouths wide open with raucous laughter, arms around each other and the women's hands on their husband's chests. With the snow swirling outside the glass behind them and the warmth of the lights highlighting their party clothes, Melinda thought it was the most beautiful shot she'd ever taken.

The women carried their heels and clutches in plastic bags to protect them from the snow and wore their after-ski boots down to the shuttle stop. They stood in a tight huddle, covered in thick coats, and still froze, even with Bill and Stan blocking the worst of the wind.

Sparkly party dresses and bare legs were no match for a Utah winter.

Hopping gratefully aboard the heated shuttle, they sighed

with relief and settled into their seats, rubbing their chilled hands and legs. Melinda listened to the older couples' chatter with half an ear, wondering where the guys were and how long it would be before they showed up to the party.

Aunt Pat and Uncle Allan, along with Nancy and Peter, had headed over earlier for drinks in the bar. Now it was already eight-thirty, though night skiing would run until ten o'clock. If the guys stayed the whole time, went back to the condos to change, and then came over to the lodge, they might not get to the party until close to midnight.

A little of the evening's shine seemed to dim.

If they arrived that late, the party would practically be over. Melinda pursed her lips into a brief pout. She wanted time with all of them. Especially Jacob. But she was determined to have an amazing night, and plenty of people her age would flood the lodge for the party. She would not sit in a corner waiting for someone to notice her and ask her to dance.

Not tonight.

If she wanted to dance, and she did, she'd be perfectly happy doing the asking, even if she had to approach a few strangers. She felt lit up inside, like a rocket set to go off, her freshly admitted love for Jacob burning her up with excitement. If she didn't dance, she'd explode.

As it turned out, her pumped-up courage wasn't necessary.

Hannah, the girl she'd met in her intermediate ski class on their first day, hailed her as soon as she walked through the door from the heavily festooned foyer and into the enormous ballroom. The lodge employees had decked the whole place out for the festivities.

"Melinda! Wow, you're glowing. Awesome dress, too!" Hannah shouted over the roar of the music, grabbing Melinda by the hand and turning with her to scan the glittering crowd. Hannah's dress, an equally slinky, deep, sunset orange, sparkled in the low lighting. "Great party, isn't it?"

The room looked amazing.

Multi-colored balloons covered every inch of the ceiling, trailing curlicued ribbons in matching hues above the party-goers' heads, and confetti already fluttered in shallow waves across the floor, kicked up and swirled by dancing feet. A banquet table by the doors held rows of party hats for guests to wear, as well as a selection of noisemakers, and piles of colorful, beaded necklaces with the new year hanging off of them in giant plastic numbers.

Across the far wall, a long section had been cordoned off to keep the alcohol service separate from the main room and away from the under-aged partiers, the security presence thick and obvious. A busy bar with multiple lines five people deep served glasses of wine or champagne or bottles of beer.

Outside the roped-off area, rows of small, cloth-covered tables held warming trays full of finger foods or decorative glasses containing petite desserts. The round fireplace in the middle of the room crackled with cheerful flames.

"Incredible," Melinda agreed, nearly vibrating with excitement on her spindly heels.

"Come on!" Hannah tugged on her hand excitedly, bouncing in her strappy sandals.

Waving to her parents and Jacob's as the older couples wandered toward the other grown-ups, Melinda followed Hannah to the party-favor table, grinning as Hannah draped five or six necklaces around her own neck and held out a like number to Melinda.

Melinda passed on the necklaces, selecting a sparkly-silver New Year's tiara instead. She placed it carefully, trying not to destroy the curls she'd so painstakingly arranged on top of her head earlier. The rest of her hair fell in springy spirals down her partially-bare back.

Thus accessorized, Melinda followed Hannah to the group of people the other girl was hanging out with. They included a few instructors and ski patrol people Melinda had seen around, though not actually spoken to, and a couple of college kids Hannah had met who, like Hannah, were staying in the lodge itself rather than the condos or cabins.

Someone shoved a glass of cider into Melinda's hand with a shouted, "If you want something stronger, you'll have to get a wrist band and wait in line."

The girl pointed toward the bar area and the security guard

checking arm bands before letting people through the rope. Melinda noticed her parents were already in line.

The group welcomed her as one of their own. They danced and talked and laughed, the shine firmly back in place on the night, and Melinda whirled around the floor feeling flirty and full of fun.

It seemed only natural when Dane strode in around ten o'clock and joined their boisterous group.

Dressed in a black suit with a dark raspberry shirt and a heavily patterned tie, his hair slicked back and his grin wide and gleaming, he made a handsome sight. Melinda greeted him with a genuine smile.

Grabbing her by the hand, he swung her around and twirled her into a deep dip in the middle of the dance floor, then pulled her up and into his muscular arms.

He danced well, which in her experience was unusual, since only Rick and Jacob of her personal circle enjoyed dancing and were actually good at it. Her brother, all of their cousins, their friends, and most of the guys she'd known in her life stuck to the hold-tight-and-sway-slowly-in-one-spot school of dance when they weren't deliberately hamming it up with moves like some obscure wild animal's terrifying mating ritual.

"You look amazing," Dane said, whispering the words into her ear, his mouth close to her skin, making her shiver.

In her heels, Melinda nearly matched his height, though his tightly corded arms and wide chest made her very aware of his size and strength. She pulled his right hand back in place at her waist, as it tended to wander downward if she wasn't careful, but she smiled her thanks for the compliment.

"Red is perfect for you," he continued, and his hand snuck around her side so that his warm fingers brushed her bare skin where the cutouts in the dress left her back exposed.

"Thank you," Melinda said, shifting a bit to remove the skin-to-skin contact.

Scanning the crowded room, she wondered what was keeping her guys. It was fortunate for Dane that they hadn't shown up yet, as more than one of them would likely take exception to his roving hands.

Just then, her cousins and their friends descended on the party, and Melinda's heart skipped a beat in pride. They looked so handsome in their dressy clothes.

Her cousins had already shed their suit jackets, though Rick sported a charcoal vest, and they all three looked camera-ready in their jewel-toned dress shirts and black slacks.

Gabe scanned the crowd, dark and dangerous in all black, which made his eyes glow like emeralds even from across the crowded room. Eddie, too, was striking in a dark gray suit and teal shirt. Wendell, as usual on dressy occasions, had gone for wild. He wore a crazily patterned vest in a swirl of vivid colors that clashed marvelously with his red hair, and pants almost the same blue-green shade as Eddie's shirt.

But it was Jacob who took her breath away.

He stood shoulder-to-shoulder with her Viking-god cousins, his sable, bronze-tipped hair glinting beneath the crystal chandeliers. Like the others, he'd dispensed with his suit jacket, and his dark-copper silk shirt set off the width of his shoulders, his muscular arms, and his perennially tanned skin. The fabric smoothed over his body, skimming down to his tapered waist, and his charcoal dress slacks accentuated the length of his legs.

He grinned at something Rick said, strong white teeth flashing between his sensual lips and deep dimples popping beneath his carved cheekbones.

Something inside her went liquidy and hot, and she shivered deliciously.

He looked amazing.

"Cold?" Dane asked.

"Hmm?" Melinda answered absently, pulling her attention back to her dance partner with effort. Her eyes kept straying to Jacob. He hadn't seen her yet.

"Melinda?" Dane repeated, grasping her chin with one hand to pull her gaze back to his. "I asked if you were cold."

Delicately removing herself from his too-firm hold, Melinda said, "No, I'm fine, thanks, but my friends have arrived. Excuse me."

A frustrated frown creased Dane's brow as he followed the direction of her gaze, but he dipped his head in a sort of awkward bow. "I'll find you later for another dance."

At that moment, Jacob's eyes found her, and the bolt that sizzled across the space between them lit her up inside in ways that made her needy and weak. She was amazed the arc of energy had not been clearly visible.

"Melinda," Dane said again, impatience biting through the loudness of the music.

Not really listening, Melinda said, "All right," over her shoulder, and continued moving toward the door.

By the time she reached the entryway, the other guys had already tossed waves her way and moved off in the direction of a group of twenty-something girls in high heels and tiny skirts, but Jacob tracked every step of her progress to his side.

"Melinda," he said, his eyes dark and smoldering as they took her in from head to toe, "you're spectacular."

When Jacob looked at her in that hungry, devouring way, her insides writhed with an anticipatory sort of thrill. And there was something about the way Jacob said her full name, something he rarely did, that stroked across her senses like a caress, making her shiver with pleasure.

"You look pretty spectacular yourself," she said. She smiled into his sparkling eyes, taking in his tall, striking form in turn, and every bit as appreciatively. He had to be the handsomest man in the room. "All the girls are drooling."

Jacob's eyes never left her face.

"What girls?" he said as if there were no other women in the world, let alone in the room, and she laughed to cover the sharp up-tick in her pulse rate.

"What took you guys so long?" she asked, wondering if he could see her heart dancing in her eyes. "It's almost eleven already."

Jacob snorted, seeming to shake himself out of the trance he'd fallen into as he'd stared at her. "One guess," he said.

"Rick?"

"Got it in one." Jacob shook his head. "I don't know how he ever makes a curtain call. We were going to come ahead without him, but he kept saying he was almost ready. Moron."

"You all should know better than to fall for that by now,"

Melinda said, chuckling. Rick was notorious.

"I know it." Jacob blew out an exasperated breath. "What did we miss?"

"Not a lot. Everyone's just dancing and hanging out."

Jerking his chin in the direction of the bar, Jacob asked, "Is that your little Belgian waffle?"

Following his line of sight, Melinda made out Dane's blond head amidst the crowd. She shrugged, having already dismissed the ski instructor from mind.

"He's not my little anything," she said, "he's just a guy. Anyway, he sort of creeps me out."

Melinda regretted the words the instant they left her mouth. Jacob's gaze arrowed back to hers, his eyes slitted and glinting dangerously.

"In what way?"

His voice, terse and hard, made her wrinkle her nose, wishing she'd been less forthcoming. Jacob—all the guys in their group, really—had a protective streak a mile wide.

Which wasn't a problem, but she didn't want anything to mar the night, least of all anything to do with Dane.

"Nothing, never mind," she said. "He's just not my type."

"Mel," Jacob said, a warning in his tone.

"Honestly," she answered, and tugged on his arm. "Forget it. Come on, let's dance."

Jacob allowed her to tow him onto the floor, though his gaze strayed frequently to Dane's side of the room.

One of their favorite rock songs came on, and soon enough Jacob seemed to forget about the other man, refocusing all his attention on her. He was such a good dancer. Melinda loved twirling around the floor with him. Her laughter bubbled over every time he grabbed her hand and spun her around.

She was gasping for breath by the time the song ended, a wide smile on her lips as the next one started.

A slow song.

Without missing a beat, Jacob moved his body into hers, pulling her tightly against him and holding her to his chest. His heart beat rapidly beneath her ear, and his scent—spicy, woodsy, all male—filled her senses.

Closing her eyes, Melinda gave herself up to the sensations surrounding her, Jacob's strong arms around her, his wide chest cushioning her head. Everywhere their bodies touched seemed to sizzle. His big, warm palm seared her bare back, like a pleasure burn on her skin.

Even her scalp tingled.

He moved with her effortlessly. In Melinda's mind, the melody wrapped around them and seemed to transport them to an island of their own in the midst of the crowded room.

Midnight was coming, and with it the time for a New Year's kiss.

Jacob, Jacob, Jacob.

Her friend.

Her best friend, but she no longer feared the something more beating within her heart. Love, strong and sure, powerful and uplifting.

Earth-shattering.

A feeling she'd been fighting for far too long.

How could she have ever doubted her love for him? At one time, she'd worried perhaps it was only that lowest relationship denominator—sexual attraction. Mixed with friendship and history, of course, but… Attraction didn't equal love.

Yet it was definitely part of it, and desire for him fairly screamed through her system.

Did he know? Would he guess if he stared too long into her eyes? She'd have to be careful until the time was right for them to talk. To convince him they were meant to be together.

Friends and lovers, forever.

It would be smarter—safer—to be cautious. She couldn't risk scaring him off or letting herself get carried away too soon, not with so much unsaid, and uncertain, between them. She certainly couldn't risk their friendship unless she was a thousand percent positive of his feelings.

If he didn't love her the same way, she would die a little inside, but she wouldn't give up their friendship for anything. Even the safety of her own heart.

Melinda rubbed her cheek over Jacob's chest, tightening her arms around him. She wished she could kiss him right there in

the middle of the dance floor in front of everyone.
	Instead, she sighed.
	All those tingles and daydreams of New Year's kisses would simply have to wait.

19

The song came to an end.

Avoiding the sparkly tiara she'd perched amid her curls, Jacob pressed a kiss to the top of Melinda's head where she rested against him, his heart beating painfully.

He wanted... so much.

Too much, probably, too soon, but he wished more than anything that they could find somewhere quiet—and private—to talk.

Another song started, a faster one, but she didn't pull away immediately. When she did, her eyes were dazed, unfocused, an emotion swimming in their blue depths that he couldn't read.

Her lips parted, sweet and soft, as she stared up at him. Their eyes held for a beat, then another, and she tilted her chin ever so slightly upward, almost as though asking for a kiss.

Jacob lowered his head, staring into her eyes all the while, asking, testing, unsure, until their noses brushed and their mouths were only a whisper apart.

They held immobile in the midst of the other dancers swirling around them, staring into each other's eyes. The party lights glinted in the depths of Melinda's bottomless blue.

Her lids lowered, and her body, trembling lightly, melted into him like heated caramel. Her breasts pressed, full, enticing, incredible, against his chest.

One more centimeter...

"Melinda!"

A too-hearty masculine voice sliced the moment in two, and Jacob snapped alert, the effect of the voice no less jarring than if he'd rammed himself head-first into one of the enormous snow banks outside.

"There you are," the voice continued, pitched above the loud music, and Jacob turned to observe the Danish pancake pushing his way through the dancers around them to get to Melinda's side. "I've been looking everywhere for you."

Melinda's eyes opened gradually, seeming slow to return to reality.

Finally, the fog left the stunning blue, and she straightened.

"What? Oh, Dane. Um. Hi."

She broke off with a half-laugh and stepped awkwardly out of Jacob's arms.

Jacob let his hands fall to his sides, wishing she still pressed against him. The blood pounded painfully in his temples and at every pulse point.

He wanted her so bad he could hardly breathe.

"Dane, this is Jacob." Melinda waved a hand between them by way of introduction. "Jake, my ski instructor, Dane."

The three of them formed an uncomfortable circle, the only ones standing motionless on the dance floor, as the shorter man took his measure.

Jacob returned the perusal, knowing one side of his mouth had lifted slightly in a sneer he couldn't control. He didn't like what he saw. The man was a wolf in dog's clothing if he'd ever seen one.

"Nice to meet you," Jacob lied.

Dane nodded, his expression equally insincere. Turning sideways to block Jacob, Dane put his hand on Melinda's arm.

"Ready for that next dance?" he asked, seeming to pretend Jacob had ceased to exist.

Melinda looked into Jacob's eyes as though searching for something, and he opened his mouth to object, to drag her away to a dark corner where he could have her all to himself, but at that moment Rick and Eddie materialized at his side.

"Dude, where've you been?" Rick asked. He cut his eyes at his cousin. "Hey, Mel." Facing Jacob again, he said, "Come on, we've got a table on the other side. First round's on me!"

Turning, fully expecting Jacob to follow, Rick and Eddie led the way back across the room, never looking back. Dane had already moved in the opposite direction, his hand clasping Melinda's arm so that it stretched away from her body, but she stood looking at Jacob.

"I'll meet you guys in a minute, okay?" she said, her tone apologetic. "I said I'd dance with him again."

"No problem, tamale sauce," Jacob said, trying to smile as Melinda moved off with the Scandinavian bonbon, still smiling over her shoulder at Jacob.

He would not do the caveman thing, Jacob reminded himself.

Not.

Deliberately, he loosened his hands out of the fists they'd formed at his sides. Neither was he going to leave Melinda in that douche bag's company for very long.

He and Melinda might not have had the all-important conversation he'd only half-formed in his mind, but it was beyond clear to him now that she felt something for him, too, and he wasn't going to let that opportunity slip away.

New Year's Eve was the perfect time to start fresh.

As he followed Rick and Eddie toward the rest of their party, Jacob knew one thing for certain. He'd never looked forward to a new year, or a new year's kiss, more than the one set to begin at the stroke of midnight.

Melinda followed Dane across the smooth, dark wood floor, as far away from Jacob as the guy could drag her and technically remain on the large square designated for dancing.

If her senses hadn't been so drenched in Jacob, so overwhelmed with the emotions storming through her body, she might have surfaced from that intense, incredible almost-kiss fast enough to successfully blow Dane off instead of winding up stuck with him for another dance.

She'd never been so turned on from *not* kissing someone in her life.

As it was, she resisted tugging her arm out of Dane's grasp, not wanting to cause a scene since Jacob continued to watch them, but if Dane grabbed her that way again, she was going to give him serious hell. He held on to her so tightly, she'd probably have bruises.

Dane finally released her arm and turned to dance with her, although it was clear his focus wasn't on the music or his stiff, jerky steps. He positively glowered, and his eyes kept sweeping the enormous room as though searching the crowd for an impending attack.

Over Dane's shoulder, Melinda spotted Jacob bowing to a tiny, elderly couple, then taking the woman on his arm to the dance floor. The woman beamed at him, chattering a mile a minute, and something she said made Jacob throw his head back, both of them laughing heartily before he swept her into the dance, going for a ballroom style to the thumping beat of the thoroughly modern music.

Despite her diminutive size, the woman had no trouble keeping up with Jacob's long, energetic steps, and the two of them moved speedily around the edges of the dance floor. Melinda grinned. Was it any wonder she loved him?

Loved him.

Oh, God.

Something slammed hard against her ribcage. It took a moment to realize it was her heart knocking in fear.

She'd gone and fallen in love with Jacob. And it was possibly the stupidest thing she'd ever done.

Oxygen seemed suddenly in short supply. Would the

surprise of her feelings ever normalize, ever not steal her breath? She couldn't take them in, nor escape the sense of impending doom.

How could she have opened herself up to the potential for such a devastating heartache?

If she'd thought Mitch had broken her heart, Jacob could obliterate it.

If only he could feel the same. If he'd be willing to settle down with her in Pasodoro.

Not yet, of course, not so soon. They were still so young. He had to finish his schooling. So did she. But eventually.

If it were a possibility, and if he loved her, too…

It was such a long shot. If something more truly lurked between them, uncovering it would require a long, slow, cautious exploration. Not a wild jump. Maybe if she repeated that reminder enough, her brain would get the message.

And her heart.

The tiny, annoying voice in her head jeered scornfully, a whispered, *Yeah, right,* echoing through her mind. Melinda focused on not stumbling over her dance steps. Her heart was already a goner.

How could she have been so stupid?

Yet even as her mind said one thing, her heart rolled around in glee on a private carpet of rose petals, and her eyes sought Jacob through the crowd.

The yearning inside threatened to swallow her whole.

The song, which had been almost half over before she and Dane started dancing, seemed to last forever as she counted down the seconds before she could return to Jacob. When the music finally came to an end, she almost couldn't disguise her relief.

Melinda moved to leave the floor as another slow song came on. Dane pulled her back into his arms. Across from them, Jacob slowed to the new tempo with his tiny partner, the two of them keeping up a non-stop conversation. The elderly woman's fluffy white hair didn't even reach the middle of his chest, much less the top of Jacob's broad shoulders, as Melinda did.

For some reason, watching them together brought

sentimental tears to her eyes. Jacob really was one in a million.

To Dane, she said, "I should go," and pulled away from his grasping hands, intending to find her cousins and wait for Jacob to finish his dance.

Dane cut her off.

"One more," he said, making an obvious effort to put his charm back in place while holding her firmly at his side.

"No, really," she tried again, casting around for an excuse. "I'm overheated. I think I'll take a short walk outside."

Dane's eyes flared, a sudden searing heat and something else. Like a dog going on alert. His fingers clutched at her back, then spread wide as though he made a conscious effort to relax his grip.

"Me, too," he said, and something in his voice sent a shiver down her spine. "I'll come with you."

Melinda opened her mouth to refuse his company, but he added, "I want to show you the northern lights."

"We can't see them from here, can we?" she asked, momentarily distracted from leaving, despite herself.

"Only at certain times," Dane said. "We're lucky tonight."

"Even in this weather?"

"Of course."

"That's nice of you," she said, regrouping, "but—"

"I insist."

Oh, really? Enough was enough.

"No, thanks," she said. She spoke politely but firmly, determined to get the message across. Something about him set off alarm bells in her head, and it was past time to listen to their pealing. "I'd rather go alone."

For a moment, it seemed he would continue to argue the point. His eyes burned hotter and his mouth thinned to a hard line, making him suddenly ugly. She tensed. Their eyes clashed as the crowd flowed around them. Melinda held firm, refusing to drop his gaze.

Finally, Dane put his hands up in a gesture of bad-tempered surrender, looking her over with a derogatory sneer.

He said, "Fine," his voice a frozen bullet, then called her something undoubtedly filthy in his native tongue.

Spinning on his heel, he left her standing alone at the edge of the dance floor.

Creepazoid.

Melinda watched him fade back into the crowd without regret. Jacob still whirled around the floor with his elderly partner, and she really did need some air. She'd take a moment while he was occupied, before rejoining their group, to get her heart and mind back under control, or Jacob would surely see her feelings in her eyes.

She wasn't ready for that conversation. Not quite yet.

Making her way through the doors into the empty lobby, she headed out toward the lodge's main entrance. Snow poured down in buckets through the glass doors.

She debated going back for her coat and her snow boots to protect her shoes, but she didn't want to cross Dane's field of vision to do it. Thanks to the coldness of the air, the snow would be more dry than wet, and she *was* hot, thanks to the dancing and the surge of annoyance Dane had brought out in her. She'd only go out for a minute, to cool her temper, then she'd find Jacob and her cousins and get back to the party.

Dane wouldn't come near her again once she was with her guys.

Satisfied with her plan, Melinda pushed the annoying ski instructor to the back of her mind and stepped through the front doors, sucking in a quick breath at the frigid blast of air. It was seriously cold! But it felt good, too. Refreshing.

Bolstering.

She moved out onto the main part of the deserted patio looking over the bottom of the ski runs, empty now, though still cheerfully lit with Christmas lights.

Goose bumps raced over her exposed skin. She wouldn't stay out long at all, or she'd wind up a bright red Popsicle on real ice-pick heels. She huffed out a laugh at the image. Thank goodness her dress wasn't satin, because she was already covered in snowflakes.

At least the winds that had risen after the earlier fireworks had died down again. The midnight fireworks would hopefully go off on schedule, despite the snow and bitter cold.

Wrapping her arms around herself for warmth, Melinda moved forward, her thoughts returning to that moment on the dance floor when Jacob's lips had almost, almost touched hers in a kiss that would have been nothing like the friendly ones they habitually exchanged.

Shivers that had nothing to do with the cold racing over her skin now, though heat spiraled into her belly.

What would it have been like to feel his lips on hers? *Damn* Dane for interrupting them and keeping her from finding out.

"Jerk," she muttered.

Though the flagstones had been cleared before the party, new-fallen drifts had covered them again, and they glowed in the lights from the windows at her back.

The stones were icy underneath the fresh layer of white. Melinda slid a little in her heels as she walked toward the far end of the patio, hoping the white stuff wouldn't destroy the pretty rhinestone-studded red leather.

Rubbing her bare arms, she scanned the sky overhead, looking for the northern lights and trying to remember everything she'd ever heard about them. She was next to positive they weren't visible this far south.

Why would Dane lie about such a thing?

Even if they could be seen in southern Utah, the sky was a solid blanket of white. No colors broke through the thick snow.

"Looking for the lights?" a deep voice said behind her, and Melinda whirled to see Dane leaning against the side of the lodge, staring at her from beneath lowered brows.

Heart caught in her throat, Melinda stared back, wondering how long he'd been behind her. He must have followed right after her, but she'd been caught up in her own thoughts. She hadn't heard him.

Berating herself for giving him an opportunity to find her alone, she began to edge around him toward the doors at his back.

Dane stepped into her path.

"Sorry," he said, though he didn't look it. "I didn't mean to startle you."

"Move," she said, injecting some force into the word and

drawing herself up to her full height, staring him down. She wasn't going to mess around with being polite. Not now.

He grinned.

"Make me," he said, and stepped forward.

She stepped back.

"Stop it, Dane," Melinda said, as he continued to stalk her.

"Come on, Melinda," he said cajolingly, "don't be like that. I came out to keep you company. Keep you warm."

"I'm warm enough."

"You're shivering. Come here."

Dane held out a hand, which she pointedly ignored. He was too close. She moved backward again and bumped hard against the deck railing.

Damn it!

The only opening was to her left, around the side of the building.

She took it, edging away from him and hoping for a door to escape through or a window to bang on, all the while trying not to let him see he was making her nervous.

He matched her step for step.

Once around the corner, the south side of the lodge sheltered them somewhat from the driving snow, but it was not well lit.

One glance was enough to realize her mistake.

There were no windows along its length on the ground level at all, and only one huge gray roll-up door she'd never be able to lift herself, if it was even unlocked. The long, solid wall made up the back of the lodge's storage rooms.

Perfect.

Just perfect.

The only way out was down an equally long, railed walkway and all the way around the building, or through Dane, who continued to maneuver her farther and farther down the side of the lodge, one step at a time.

Firming her chin, she planted her feet in the slippery snow and glared into his smiling face. "I said stop."

"Stop what?" Dane said, obviously taunting her now, an edge in his voice. "I came out to show you the lights."

"I don't want to see them anymore," she said. "I'm going back in. Move aside."

"Oh, you don't mean that," he said, smiling wider.

He took another step.

"Man, what is wrong with you tonight?" Rick asked, jerking Jacob's attention to him and away from his fourth scan of the dance floor.

Where the hell was Melinda? He'd lost sight of her after delivering Neta Smalls back to her husband at the end of their second dance.

"What d'you mean?" he asked, confused.

Rick pointed at his legs, and Jacob realized he'd been bouncing them in agitation, his hands slapping his knees.

Making a deliberate effort to calm himself, he shook his head and said, "Nothing. It's New Year's, I'm just keyed up."

"Right." Rick rolled his eyes. "It has nothing to do with my cousin or the fact that you haven't been able to keep your eyes off her all week."

Jacob gave a quick scan around the table to make sure no one had heard Rick's words, then frowned at his friend. "Keep it down, will you?"

"So you don't deny it? I thought Christian was off his meds when he said you were gaga for her. Is it true?"

Huffing out a breath, Jacob stared hard at Rick, his mind a whirl.

No time like the present.

"It's true," he bit out, and endured Rick's howl of laughter.

"Oh, man," Rick said, still chuckling. "Wait 'til everyone hears. You and Mel—"

"Shut up and tell me if you see her."

Rick wiped his streaming eyes and scanned the room, craning his neck around the dancers and wait staff circulating to refill drinks.

"Nope, sorry," he said, taking a swig of his beer. "Why? Lose her already?"

"She was with that ski instructor she met the other day. I don't like the guy's looks."

"Of course you don't," Rick scoffed.

"No, I mean it. Something's off about him."

"Off about who?" Eddie asked, taking the empty seat next to Rick.

Ignoring his question, Jacob asked his own instead. "Have you seen Mel?"

"Sure," Eddie said, tilting his beer bottle to his mouth.

"Recently?" Jacob gritted between clenched teeth, gripping his knees tightly to keep from lashing out in frustration.

"Yeah," Eddie answered with a who-cares shrug, frowning at Jacob. "She went outside with that dude she was dancing with."

"Damn it!" Jacob shot to his feet, nearly upending his own drink in the process. "When?"

"I don't know," Eddie said, surprised, his eyes darting between Jacob and a now-scowling Rick. "Ten, fifteen minutes ago?"

Rick said, "Want us to come?" But he was speaking to Jacob's back, as Jacob had already pushed away from the table.

"I got it," Jacob answered over his shoulder, knowing his voice had descended to a dangerous growl and not caring when several people shifted warily out of his way.

Something wasn't right about that Danish guy, and the hell if he was going to let him be alone with Melinda.

With that decision propelling him across the floor, Jacob hit the lobby, then the front doors, and shoved through them, his gaze sweeping the empty patio and beyond for Melinda's red dress.

20

Dane stood only a foot away now, his breath puffing white and warm over her, his body blocking her from getting by him on the narrow walkway. She couldn't vault the railing in her snug party dress. Even if she did, if she tore the seams and went for it, she'd wind up stuck in a huge mound of snow.

She dared not turn her back on him, and there was no way she could outrun him in her heels.

Panic licked the edges of her thoughts.

Mind spinning, Melinda gauged him, weighing her options.

Would he really attack her if she tried to slip past him? She could hardly believe he might, but he seemed so… intense.

She gathered herself to risk it, but without warning, he lunged forward, pushing her back until her body pressed flat against the wall, caging her between his muscular arms.

"Hey!" she squeaked.

"I thought you were different," he said, rage seeming to spring from nowhere as he growled the words in her face. "Ha. You're just like all the other bimbos in every resort on earth. Bitch."

"What do you—"

He leaned his body heavily against hers, trapping her in place. Her ribs creaked painfully beneath the pressure. She couldn't take a deep breath.

"Hey," she said again, squirming against him, disgust replacing fear. She stopped moving abruptly when she recognized the bulge grinding against her pelvis. Anger simmered. This was so not happening. "Knock it off."

"You think you're so beautiful," he said nastily in his accented English, his voice as hard as the rest of his body, ramming himself against her again. "Too good for me, right? I'll show you."

"Dane," she said, her voice sharp, fear rising up again and twisting with the anger, breathless from lack of air. "You're hurting—stop it," she gasped as he pressed even harder against her, cutting her off.

He looked at her for one long moment while she glared back at him and struggled to breathe, to draw enough air to shout at him and make him back off, but he swooped his mouth down, claiming her lips in a bruising kiss, cutting off her words. He thrust his tongue roughly between her teeth and halfway down her throat, making her gag. His hands crushed her arms.

"Dane! Stop it!" she said again, or tried to. The words stayed locked inside, blocked by his battering mouth.

Instinctively, she tried to bite down hard on his tongue. She only caught the tip. He howled in her ear, but he didn't let go. Fury contorted his face, and he slapped her hard, knocking her into the unyielding wall at her back.

Lights exploded behind her eyes.

Stunned shock and lack of oxygen held her immobile for two heartbeats too long before she began to struggle in earnest, but the delay gave him the upper hand.

He was so *strong!*

She couldn't budge him, couldn't breathe against the pain and his renewed invasion of her mouth. Panic beat powerful wings inside her ribcage, and her stomach lurched.

Anger gave way to primitive terror.

Shoving at him with all her might did less than nothing. He

even let go of her arms, as though her strength was no concern to him, though she struck him with her fists as hard as she could.

He wrapped one hand around her throat, his thumb pressing hard beneath her jaw.

Melinda scrabbled her fingers over his face, going for his eyes, but he increased the pressure, squeezing her neck until everything started to go black.

Tears fell and froze on her cheeks.

When she sucked in another shallow breath to scream, he hauled back and slapped her across the face again, so hard her opposite cheek whipped into the wall at her back, scraping against the wood.

He pulled at her skirt, exposing more of her bare legs, but it was snug on her body and only rose so far as she fought him.

Melinda bucked and twisted, evading him as best she could, and she screamed again, screamed and screamed.

The sound went nowhere, devoured by his mouth.

Her vision wanted to go dark. How long could she hold him off?

No-no-no-nonononoooooo!

The sound of her screams echoed in her head, but only sobbed through her lips.

She tried to bite him again, but the force of his teeth and tongue, his grinding mouth, kept her jaw open wide to his invasion.

The violation nauseated her. The disgust of his groping hands made her head spin.

Melinda wrenched and squirmed and hammered her fists against his head. It was as though he didn't even feel her blows.

Black dots and flashing lights swam before her eyes. She fought against the pull to slide under that darkness, away from the pain.

If she succumbed, he'd win, and she refused to go down easy.

Her mind screamed, *Jacob!* but she was alone. Even if he came looking for her, it would be too late. Dane could rape her right here, standing in the driving snow, pinned against the outside of the building where her friends and family danced.

No.

No. I will not be a victim.

With that thought crystal clear in her mind, a strange calm descended out of the fear.

She wasn't helpless. At least not yet.

He had the advantage, true, but for now, she was still standing, she could still fight. Dane had caught her by surprise. She needed to *think*.

By God, she would save herself, and this scum would never touch her again.

Blocking out the cruelty of his hands on her body, Melinda forced her right leg to the side, out from under him. Drawing it up as high as she could manage in her snug party dress, she stomped down hard with her spiked heel directly on top of his foot.

Dane cried out and jerked against her as her shoe's heel snapped off from the force of her strike.

Instead of releasing her, he grabbed her shoulders and slammed her back into the wall, striking her head against the wood a third time.

Red stars flared behind her lids, and the pain rolled nausea through her belly. She cried out, but when he pulled back to smash her against the wall again, he gave her the split-second opening she needed.

As though she'd practiced the move a thousand times before, Melinda gathered every bit of strength she owned and rammed her knee directly into the bastard's crotch, a warrior's roar punching the wind.

Without a sound, Dane dropped at her feet like a stone.

Adrenaline hit when Jacob finally noted the heel prints in the snow leading away from the lodge's entrance. They could only be Melinda's, and were followed closely by male dress-shoe tracks heading around the far side of the building.

She and Dane were nowhere to be seen.

What the hell did they go that way for? There was nothing over there.

Jacob had been irritated before, feeling possessive, and yeah, a little worried. Now instinct, a primal foreboding, stabbed into his stomach like an icy dagger.

Melinda was in danger. He knew it.

Charging across the patio, Jacob skidded around the icy corner at full speed.

His eyes landed immediately on the struggling couple outlined against the building in the dim lamplight and thick, swirling snow.

At that exact moment, Melinda screamed, a sound he would never forget, full of pain and fear and rage.

It echoed out into the night. It shattered him, stole his breath, stopped his heart.

Mindless with dread, Jacob sprinted down the nightmare walkway, never seeming to reach any closer, ready to kill the bloody bastard.

Three steps from Melinda's side, she gave an all-mighty shriek, drove her knee into the man's balls, and took him down like a pro.

Pride swelled Jacob's chest for half-a-second—*thatta girl!*—before he focused on her face.

The same fierce pride, coupled with determination and a healthy dose of triumph, had already winked out of her blazing blue eyes, reaction setting in as she stared blankly back at Jacob, then at the writhing, retching man at her feet.

Melinda's face, chalk white but for the blood-red handprints on both cheeks, gleamed whiter than the swirling snow, her skin drawn tight across her cheekbones. Her swollen mouth pulled into a grimace. Breaths shallow and panting, her chest jerked with each respiration as she gulped for air. Her whole body trembled. A high keening sound whistled through her lips.

He took in the rest in one swift glance—the hiked skirt, the tear in the right shoulder seam of her pretty dress, the snapped heel on her shoe. Her New Year's tiara sparkled wetly at her feet where it had fallen off her head, and her hair whirled loose and tangled around her body.

Even in the low lighting, the scarlet marks on her face and bare arms showed clearly, bruises already blooming where the son of a bitch had put his hands on her.

Had hurt her.

A killing rage exploded inside Jacob's head, turning everything to red mist in front of his eyes. He battled it back with every ounce of strength he possessed.

His priority—Melinda, always—needed him to stay in control.

For now.

Cautious, Jacob stepped nearer to her slowly, his hands up at his sides where she could see them, wanting her to know she was safe, that no one would grab her or hurt her, not ever again, but she wasn't looking at him. She didn't seem to know he was even there.

"Mel," Jacob said softly.

She didn't respond.

He'd never seen her so strong—strong enough to take down a beast who outweighed her by at least sixty pounds of pure, hard muscle—and yet so delicate. So fragile. Like spun sugar, she seemed ready to dissolve into the storm with the slightest breath.

Reaching toward her carefully—*friend, calm, safe*—elevating his voice gently over the groans of the man on the ground, he said again, "Melinda."

This time, her eyes jerked to his, and they were wet, drenched with silent tears. The dilation of her pupils made them look enormous in her small, pale face, shock turning the lovely blue almost black.

"JJ?" she whimpered, the childhood nickname barely audible, and it was that small thing, the use of a name she hadn't called him by in more than a decade, that destroyed him.

All restraint fled.

Scooping her into his arms, he lifted her up, relieved

beyond all measure when she didn't stiffen against him but instead fused her body to his. Jacob held her as tightly as he dared.

Her arms clamped forcefully around his neck, and she burrowed into him as though trying to climb inside his skin, to merge them into one being. Hard, wracking sobs shook her from head to foot.

Jacob buried his face in her hair, his own emotions swarming through him in a storm he couldn't fight.

He rocked her, soothing them both with the whisper of her name, over and over, a chant and a prayer, gratitude for her safety winging out into the universe on those three quiet syllables.

Long minutes later, Melinda gave a final shudder and loosened her hold, sliding down his body to stand on her own two feet once more.

Jacob struggled against his own needs and let her go reluctantly. She rested her flooded cheek against his chest.

Tremors still rocked her slender body, but her breathing had returned almost to normal, and she swiped the last of her tears away with the back of her hand.

"I'm okay," she said, her voice almost believable.

"Thank God."

On the ground beside them, her attacker started to move again, low moans still issuing from his mouth. Slithering away.

How appropriate.

Jacob straightened, his every motion slow and controlled to avoid startling Melinda. Handling her as carefully as he would the finest china teacup in his mother's prized collection, he placed his hands lightly on top of her shoulders, away from the bruises on her arms, and leaned her gently against the wall for support. With one finger, he lifted her chin, raising her eyes to meet his own.

"Steady?" he asked. When she nodded jerkily, he brushed her forehead with a barely-there kiss. "Okay. Give me one minute."

Eyes plumbing hers, he waited until the spark of fighting spirit rekindled in the deep, dark blue. Nodding in satisfaction, he gave her shoulders a gentle squeeze.

"Good," he said. "Wait right here for me. I just have to—"

Breaking off, Jacob stood away, one hand still on her shoulder until he was certain she'd hold.

Then, in one swift motion, he stepped over, kicked the crawling, sneaking, scum-sucking-pervert bastard onto his back and hauled him up by his shirtfront, leaning down until they were nose to nose.

At his back, Melinda said not a word.

In a low voice vibrating with deadly intent, Jacob spoke directly into the older man's pain-whitened face.

"If you ever touch her again, if you come within five-hundred miles of her, I will kill you." He shook him once, the way a dog might shake a dead snake. "Understood?"

Dane's pale green eyes slitted with pain and fury, his mouth a tight line, but he nodded once, a hard jerk of his square chin.

Far from satisfied, Jacob leaned in even closer.

He said, "Good."

Then drew back his arm and cocked the son of a bitch right in the nose.

The bone crunched beneath his fist and blood spurted as Dane howled, both of his hands now clutching his face instead of his balls. Jacob shook him once more, then tossed him back to the ground where he rolled around like a stranded turtle.

That's better.

Turning his back on the pile of shit, Jacob stepped back to Melinda, slightly worried over what he'd find in her eyes.

He wasn't sorry for punching the slimy scumbag.

At all.

But he didn't want the violence raging through him to upset Melinda more than she already was, even though the bastard deserved it.

He waited, breath held.

When her eyes met his, he saw no condemnation or reproach. In fact, she looked like she might want another shot at the guy herself.

Jacob smothered the smile that wanted to crease his face. She'd been through hell, no doubt, but his Melinda was still in there.

He cupped her cheek lightly in his hand and said, "Okay?"
"Okay."

Her smile wobbled, wan and small, but it was a smile. He'd take it.

Pulling her back into his chest with one arm securely around her back, he stepped firmly on Dane's pant leg to hold him in place, but otherwise ignored the man rolling from side to side in agony at his feet.

Jacob pulled his cell phone out of his pocket with his free hand, speed dialing and hoping Gabe would hear his phone inside all the noise of the party.

Of the younger generation's part of their group, Gabe was the man everyone wanted as first-responder in a crisis, and Jacob didn't want to explain the situation to Melinda's father over the phone in any case. Gabe had an ability to drill down to the essentials and mobilize like no one else.

Jacob sometimes wondered if Gabe had been a war general in another life.

Or a master assassin.

"Hey, where'd you disappear to?" Gabe's humor-filled voice shouted through the phone over the raucous noise of New Year's Eve blaring in the background. "You're missing all the fun."

Jacob got straight to the point. "I'm outside, on the south side of the building. I've got Mel. We need security out here. Now."

"Is she all right?"

It was not a casual question. All levity had deserted Gabe's voice. Jacob could almost see him going still and deadly quiet in the midst of the party, every cell in his body on alert. A warrior called to battle.

"Mel's been attacked." Jacob continued speaking over the sharp hiss of Gabe's breath. "She's okay, but we need to get this fucker locked up." Glancing down at the top of Melinda's dark head, snuggled against his chest, he added, "Get Stan and Karen. And her coat. She's cold." He rubbed a hand up and down her back, wishing he had his to offer, but he'd taken it off inside.

"Hurry."

The phone went dead, Gabe clicking off without acknowledging the order. Not that it mattered. The other man would find them in seconds, his mission carried out to the letter and ready to help hold—or demolish—Dane.

In the meantime, Jacob held Melinda and waited.

Sure enough, mere moments later, Gabe ran around the corner, barreling straight for them.

On his heels followed not only the security team and Melinda's parents, but her cousins, aunt, uncle, Jacob's own parents, Eddie's parents, Eddie, and Wendell, every one of them prepared to slay dragons with their bare hands.

Melinda heard the rumble of friends and family approaching. It was time to release her grip on Jacob, but she clutched him tighter instead, just for another moment.

She might have taken the attacking scumbag out herself, but having Jacob arrive when he did, providing her with both his shoulder to lean on and his solid presence as backup, had been an immeasurable relief.

Though the revulsion had lessened as soon as Dane stopped touching her, her legs still trembled, and her emotions were all over the place.

The one thing she knew for certain was that she was exactly where she wanted to be. In Jacob's strong, protective arms.

"Mel," Jacob murmured into her hair, giving her a gentle nudge. "Your family needs to know you're okay."

Nodding against his chest, Melinda took a deep breath and steeled herself for the next part of the ordeal.

Resolutely avoiding looking directly at Dane, who was already handcuffed and in security's custody, blood dripping from his smashed nose, she straightened her spine and stepped back a half-foot from the safety of Jacob's embrace. Her knees wobbled, but she stood on her own two feet.

Strong. She was strong. And she was lucky. She'd protected herself. So many women never even got the chance, or if they did, they were unable to overcome their attackers.

And if she'd failed, her knight had shown up in the nick of time.

Melinda lifted her chin to meet her family's gazes. She couldn't help the flinch when she heard her mother's and Lois's mutual gasps as they caught sight of her face, the curses from the men. Tears ran down Nancy's cheeks. Everyone froze in place for a heartbeat of time. Melinda's eyes were all for her father.

Stan took one step forward, his shaking hand held out toward her, then he seemed to stumble uncertainly as he took in her condition. His face was a white mask, his eyes filled with grief, and fear, and fury for the one who had battered her, though like Melinda, he ignored the man.

Over it all hung the powerless pain of a parent whose child has been hurt.

Stumbling a bit herself as she stepped toward her father in her heelless shoe, Melinda said, "Daddy," in a voice that broke, unable to stop the return of the tears cascading down her cheeks.

Then she was in his arms, and it was like being a child again, after suffering a hurt, seeking comfort from the first, best man in her life.

Safe, safe, safe.

With her family and friends all around her, with Jacob at her back, the last dregs of fear vanished. Her head still swam unsteadily on her shoulders, her body still shuddered, but no one could hurt her now.

Nancy stepped forward to wrap Melinda's coat around her shoulders, and her mother's hand landed gently on her back, stroking in a slow circle as she leaned into the embrace. Stan's left arm encircled Karen, too, making them into a three-way hug, Melinda between them, protected inside the wider caring circle of their family and friends.

Finally, she disengaged gently from her parents' grasp,

holding both of their hands with her own and looking from one to the other, making sure they could read her eyes.

"I'm okay," she said. "Really."

"Your face," Karen whispered, running a delicate finger over the bruises on Melinda's cheeks and at the sides of her mouth. Her mother's eyes filled with tears, but she didn't let them fall.

"It looks worse than it is," Melinda said, trying to reassure her mother, though her lips—and many places besides—ached and stung. "I promise."

And she was. She was so, so lucky.

Her father's eyes gleamed suspiciously. He sniffed himself back to composure and pressed a kiss to Melinda's snow-covered forehead before lifting his gaze to Jacob, who stood watching just beyond their small circle, flanked by his own parents and the rest of their group. Jacob's mother's arms held around him, and his dad's hand gripped his shoulder.

"You saved her," Stan said, and his voice wavered with emotion as Melinda leaned against his side. "Thank you."

"No," Jacob said, his eyes meeting Melinda's. She read pride in his gaze, and it boosted her spirits every bit as much as his words. "She saved herself. I only got my two bits in at the end."

"Looks like more than two, if you ask me," said Aunt Pat, ferocious satisfaction in her voice, "and thank you for it. Our girl can handle herself, make no mistake, but it doesn't hurt to have a cleanup hitter on standby."

After that, everyone surged forward, each one needing a hug and a word to reassure themselves Melinda was all right.

When she wound up back in Jacob's arms at the end, no one questioned why she was there or wondered over the possessive way he held her in his arms.

The police arrived, having been contacted by security, as the midnight fireworks erupted overhead. The rest of the guests had been kept inside the lodge due to the circumstances, so the fiery lights seemed to burst solely for her family and friends.

Melinda tilted her head to the sky to watch the colors dance and fade amidst the heavy fall of snow.

She'd forgotten it was New Year's Eve and a party raged on

in the building behind them. It seemed like a lifetime ago that she had walked out the lodge's front doors, Dane unknowingly in pursuit.

Melinda shivered. They all had to be freezing, even in their coats and huddled together, but no one seemed to want to go back into the lodge. She was glad. The last thing she wanted was to give the party-goers a good look at her face.

"I'm sorry I ruined the party for everyone," she said, raising her eyes to Jacob. She'd had quite a different night in mind for this evening.

"Don't be stupid," he said, frowning back at her. "You didn't ruin anything. He did."

Jacob jerked his chin in Dane's direction, where the police had taken him and were deep in conversation with the security team. Her cousins and their friends, along with all four dads, formed a semi-circle around the officers, as though offering them backup.

"Indeed," Aunt Pat sniffed, having overheard them. Nancy, Lois, and Karen joined her. "You know better than to think something so foolish, Melinda."

"It's not the way I wanted to start off the year," Melinda said. "Not for any of you, either."

"We're not the ones who were nearly—" Nancy paused, collecting her composure. "Who were nearly—"

"But I wasn't," Melinda broke in, taking Nancy's free hand while the tiny woman dabbed at her teary eyes with the other. "I wasn't." She squeezed Nancy's small hand, and she made sure to meet her mother's and her aunt's gazes squarely. "I won't say it was nothing, but truly, I'm fine. No serious harm done."

"And thank the Lord for that," her mom said, injecting a note of bright briskness into her voice. "New Year's is just a day like any other, and a party is just a party. What matters is you're safe."

"Absolutely right," Lois said. "We can celebrate tomorrow." Looking up at the continuing fireworks, she corrected herself. "Or rather, later today. In fact—"

"Excuse me, ma'am, everyone," one of the officers interrupted. "We need to take statements."

"She needs a doctor," Karen protested.

"Mom, I'm fine. Just bruised."

"You'll go anyway, I don't—"

"We'll get her to one," the policeman interrupted, scanning Melinda. "Soon, I promise."

21

The rest of the night passed by in a blur. Melinda knew she'd have to give a statement. That was bad enough, but she hadn't counted on having to go to the clinic for an exam, followed by the most humiliating photographs of her life.

The others had returned to the condo by then, except for her parents and Jacob, though Jacob and her father stayed out in the waiting room during the exam.

"I don't think she's concussed," Mae, the nurse said, after they investigated the blood matting Melinda's hair on the back of her head. Her hair was so dark that no one had noticed it until she got to the clinic. "But you'll want to keep an eye on her."

"Of course," Karen murmured, rubbing Melinda's hand between both of hers. "Of course. Should she have an MRI?"

"She's not showing any of the signs that would indicate a need for one, but we'll talk with the doctor to make sure."

After the exam, and after the policewoman left, Mae treated the rest of Melinda's injuries. They were thankfully minor, but the medical process was starting to make her feel more like a victim than she had with her back pressed against that building.

She wanted to go back to the condo and climb into bed.

A doctor came in to talk to her in his supposed-to-be-soothing voice. He prescribed pain medication. He offered anti-anxiety meds, too, in case she might need them. He gave her samples of both for the night, since the pharmacy was long closed, plus a couple of sleeping pills for good measure, tucking them into her hand. She heard his words only as indistinct noise, rumbling from far away, down a long tunnel.

God, she hated hospitals.

Although the little clinic couldn't quite claim hospital status, it had all the same smells, and reminded her of times she'd rather forget. Multiple visits to see Gabe or members of his family after racing accidents. Jacob's freshman year. Seth.

She sniffled. A dragging fatigue set in, so that it took an effort to keep her eyes open.

Still beside her, still holding onto her, Karen answered the doctor's words with words of her own, equally nonsensical to Melinda. It was like listening to people talk underwater, and she wanted to stay down there in the cool, dark depths, with the muted sounds and blurred colors and soft, blunted edges.

The doctor finally left.

She sat on the edge of the exam table, dressed in an enormous pair of sweats the clinic had provided to help warm her up, and her own snow boots, retrieved by one of her cousins. She'd lost her clutch somewhere. It only had a few dollars, her ID, a lipstick, and her phone in it, but she'd have to deal with that later. And damn it, she'd really liked that little purse.

Her damaged dress and ruined shoes sat in the bottom of a trashcan. She never wanted to see them again. She'd broken six of her fingernails in her struggle with Dane, too, though she hadn't noticed the torn and jagged edges until she'd arrived at the clinic.

Melinda stared blankly at the medicine packets in her hands.

For some reason, the state of her nails made tears want to flood back into her eyes, which in turn made her weak and trembly all over again. She didn't want to feel weak. She'd kicked the sucker in the balls and laid him out flat. She was a victor.

Where was her strength?

Her mom wrapped her arms around her shoulders and hugged her tightly. "Do you want to go home, sweetie?"

"Yes! I want to shower and go to bed."

"No, honey, I mean *home.*"

Sniffing away the looming crying jag, Melinda leaned back to see her mother's face. "What do you mean?"

"We don't have to stay the rest of the week. The others can if they want, or they could come home, too. No one would blame you. And you could sleep in your own bed." Karen brushed the hair out of Melinda's face, then cupped her bruised cheek in her palm. "Or you could sleep with Dad and me, if you want."

That last bit startled a small laugh from Melinda, and she was able to give her mother a genuine smile, though it wobbled at the edges. "I haven't done that since I was little."

"Not so little," Karen disagreed, a slight teasing note in her voice now. Her words ended with a waver. "I think you were fourteen the last time."

"There was a serial killer on the loose!"

"In New York," Karen said, grinning in a way that almost reached her eyes.

"Still."

Serious again, her mother placed both hands on Melinda's cheeks and looked into her eyes, searching, yes, but also sending, her message of love and support strong and clear.

"Yes," Karen said, her voice soft. "Still."

Melinda dropped her forehead against her mother's. They wrapped their arms around each other and stayed that way for a time, simply giving and receiving comfort, breathing the same air.

"I really am fine, you know. I promise. I'm just tired and sore, and it's making me weepy."

"I know, honey. That's to be expected."

"I don't want to go home," Melinda said finally.

She knew how lucky she was to have escaped a very different outcome to the night. Dane might have raped her if he'd had the chance. But she'd stopped him, and she wanted everyone to stop treating her as though something much worse had happened. The only way to make that happen was to get back to normal as quickly as possible.

But she needed, and gave thanks for, her mother's comfort.

"Okay." Karen brushed a hand down the length of Melinda's hair. "As long as you're sure. If you change your mind, just say so. Whatever you need, honey, okay?"

Melinda nodded, the gratitude for her mom—for both her parents—filling her up.

Every hurt she'd ever suffered in her life, no matter how serious or trivial, had been soothed and shared in exactly this way. Her mother's arms were her safe haven, her refuge and her solace. Her father was her rock, her anchor, no matter how turbulent the sea. The two of them together were as constant and sure as the sun's daily rising in the east.

And then there was Jacob.

Her friend.

Her knight.

And just maybe something more. If he could see her as a woman, not simply a friend. She wanted, so much, for him to love her back.

But she couldn't think about that now. Not right now, with the feel of Dane's hurting hands imprinted on her skin.

She shuddered once, hard, but pushed the almost-horror away. That was over. She'd survived, mostly intact. She needed a shower and sleep and her family and friends around her.

She needed normal.

"Will I have to come back here?" Melinda asked after a while.

"Come back?"

"F-for court."

"Oh," Karen said, a frown pulling at her brows. "I don't know, sweetie. I don't think so. As much as I'd like to string him up and have him horse-whipped, unless he's been in trouble before, I'm sorry to say he'll probably get a slap on the wrist without ever going to court."

Melinda stared at the far wall. It seemed incredible that a man could attack a woman and not go to jail, but she wasn't so naïve as to believe it wasn't true. It happened all the time. Only, before, it had happened to other people.

The injustice of the system had horrified her, always, but she'd never really understood how it *felt* until tonight.

She sent another *thank you* out into the universe for the secure, protected world she inhabited most of the time, and a prayer of safety for those less fortunate.

Her mom brushed loose hair back from Melinda's forehead and stroked a hand down her arm, careful to avoid the bruises.

"At the very least," Karen said, "I can guarantee he'll lose his job. He won't come near you again or hurt anyone else here."

Knowing her mom needed it as much as she herself did, Melinda put on a brave face and smiled, nodding her agreement.

"Okay," Melinda said, and saying the word, felt braver.

She'd beaten the bastard. That mattered.

It would be all right.

"My baby girl," Karen said, a small break in her voice. "I love you so very much."

"I love you, too, Mom."

It seemed like more than mere hours had passed, like days and days had gone by while Jacob had been sitting on the hard plastic chair next to Melinda's father.

Waiting.

Worrying.

Talking little, but communing somehow, in their mutual concern for Melinda.

Waiting longer.

Worrying some more.

Staring, mesmerized, at the colorful Christmas twinkle lights outlining the doors up and down the drab hallway, their cheerfulness unsettling in the hospital atmosphere.

They'd watched in stony silence as Dane had been marched

past, still cuffed, to have his nose tended to. Jacob was glad Melinda didn't know the man was in the same building.

Not long after that, a representative from the resort had hustled down the hallway and escorted Stan into an office. The man had apologized profusely for "the unfortunate incident" and had comped their whole group's entire week at the resort.

He'd obviously feared the Honeywells would sue, or at least generate some really nasty publicity. Melinda's family would never do something like that—punish an entire company for one person's actions—but the flustered rep didn't know any better. He'd been alternately relieved and confused by Stan's calm acceptance of the official apology and the refund of their week's fees.

Since then, the clinic had remained quiet.

What was taking so long?

Dropping his head into his hands, Jacob scrubbed at his gritty eyes, trying not to think of all the reasons they could be keeping Melinda in the tiny room across the hall. A lot of people had been in and out of there over the past hours, yet he'd never managed to catch even a glimpse of her when the door swished open or closed.

Usually, in this sort of environment, he was on the other side of those doors, busy helping, taking notes, learning his future trade. His experience on this side of the doors was limited. The moments of chaos at the hospital after Seth's accident, though horrible, had not lasted very long, as Seth had quickly succumbed to his injuries.

Prior to this trip—waiting to hear about Neta, now waiting for Melinda—Jacob had never fully appreciated just how awful it was to be the one waiting.

Beside him, Stan reached his arms over his head and stretched and groaned.

"I'm sure it won't be much longer," he said, raking his fingers through hair that was already standing up on end and pointing in every direction. "They probably—"

He broke off when the door across from them opened once again, and Karen stepped into view.

Jacob leapt to his feet in relief as Melinda and her mom

finally exited the exam room. Karen kept a steadying arm around Melinda's shoulders, leading her to them across the narrow hallway. He scanned Melinda's face and had to suck back a curse, and worse, emotions that clogged his throat and made his eyes tingle at their corners.

Stan said, "Hey, sweetheart," in a quiet voice that sounded as choked up as Jacob felt.

She looked... Well, she looked like hell.

Purple-black circles ringed her eyes, and she was far too pale, her cheeks sunken with fatigue. The dark red marks on her cheeks and around her mouth stood out harshly against her skin, like a macabre clown's smeared face paint. The hospital-supplied sweatshirt and pants hung on her, making her seem even smaller, more fragile.

Jacob didn't think he would ever forget, would ever get over the sight of the fingerprint-shaped bruises ringing her neck.

His heart squeezed painfully, but he caught Karen's warning eye and straightened his shoulders. Now was not the time for coddling, her glance said, and looking Melinda over again, he silently agreed. Too much comforting right now and she'd shatter into a million tiny pieces.

Instead, he beamed the brightest smile he could manage.

"Hey, angel-food cake," he said, hoping he hadn't overdone the heartiness of his tone. At his side, Stan gripped his shoulder and squeezed in silent approval.

Melinda's sad, tired gaze lightened a tiny fraction. "Shishkebab," she said.

Her voice was rough, sandpapery, though the sudden twinkle in her too-dark eyes let him know she'd been saving that one up for a while.

And wow, it was appropriate.

More so than she could possibly know.

Shishkebab described precisely the way he felt. Skewered equally with worry and with love for her, roasted over the twin emotional flames. It was time to stick the proverbial fork in him. He was done.

Stan moved to intercept her, taking Melinda carefully in his arms, hugging her close while Karen stood by, one hand on her daughter's back. Melinda closed her eyes for a moment, seeming to soak in her father's love and support. Jacob rubbed his own eyes while she wasn't looking.

But when she opened them—the blue still too dark but coming back finally, not so black with fear and reaction—when she opened them, they looked right into his. And held.

And held.

She stretched out her hand to him, and her parents stepped aside, letting her go. He met her halfway, and then she was in his arms, plastered against him.

Strong and real.

In his arms, where he always wanted her. Where he wanted her to stay and never go.

He leaned down, pressing his face into her messy, beautiful hair. Taking in the scents that were not all her own. Scents he was used to from his work in various emergency rooms and doctor's offices and clinics, scents that should never have touched Melinda. Odors of medicine and antiseptic and crap-quality cafeteria food and distant sickness, and even the bitter cold from outside.

His stomach clenched, recoiled, but he shook it off because underneath it all was still Melinda, and he hadn't realized how much he'd needed that reassurance, the warmth and the true underneath-it-all smell of her, until she was back in his arms.

Thank God, thank God.

For one awful minute, he worried he was going to lose it right there, right in front of her and her parents and the nurse at the end of the hallway, but he sucked it up, bolted it down, put it away.

It was done, the night was over, and she was okay. Would *be* okay, he'd make sure of it. No one would ever hurt her again.

She said, "Jakey," in a small voice, and he hugged her even tighter.

"Ready, green bean?" he asked, and she nodded against his chest.

He caught her parents eyes and nodded toward the exit, then swept Melinda right off her feet into his arms, carrying her toward the door.

"I can walk," she protested in her still-gritty voice.

"I know," he said, brushing a kiss over the top of her head. "This is for me."

From the corner of his eye, he could see her rolling hers. But with a tired little groan, she settled trustingly against him, her body going slack and her eyes drifting closed as she pressed her head to his shoulder.

That feeling in his heart flopped right over, made him dopey with relief, like a big, stupid dog having its belly scratched by his favorite human.

Love was a funny, powerful thing, one moment choking him up, the next making him want to sing and dance like a fool.

He carried her through the thick, swirling snow across the small parking lot, her parents speaking in low voices behind him, then waited while Stan unlocked the door to the car he'd fetched while they'd been waiting in the clinic. The wind had come back, rising and falling around them. The snow came down harder than ever.

Settling Melinda in the backseat, Jacob scooted around the other side of the car and climbed in to sit beside her, taking her hand gently in his. Silence reigned in the little car, the quiet of extreme fatigue. It was nearly three in the morning. Melinda laid her head on his shoulder and closed her eyes while Stan drove them back to the condo.

Over her token protest, Jacob carried her up the flight of stairs into their unit, the four of them keeping as quiet as possible to avoid waking the others. Dim lights shone in the kitchen to light their way.

Christian and Wendell, who'd both been snoring lightly from the depths of the family room sofa-bed, popped their heads up with mutual grunts, blinking blearily as they came in. Tufts of blond and red hair stuck up wildly from their respective heads.

Rubbing his eyes with both fists, Christian said, "M-kay?" through a jaw-cracking yawn, and Wendell bobbed his head, birdlike, lending his silent support to the query.

"Okay," Melinda answered.

"'Kay," they said together, yawning in unison now. Wendell added a mumbled, "G'night," and they both flopped back onto the bed, where they appeared to slip immediately back into sleep.

Jacob's parents' bedroom door was closed, though Lois had left a note on the counter that read, *Thinking of you, sweetie. Hugs and love, Bill and Lois.* Melinda's sparkly handbag sat beside it.

Jacob set Melinda on her feet by the kitchen table. She hugged him around the waist and simply hung on.

He wished, fervently, that they were alone, but when Stan and Karen came forward, he gave Melinda one more squeeze and stepped aside. He said goodnight, then left them to talk. He mounted the stairs and was about to change into his pajamas when Melinda's mother surprised him by entering the loft.

"She needs to shower," Karen said by way of explanation, her voice a whisper.

Moving to Melinda's suitcase, she selected her daughter's pajamas, robe, and slippers, then turned to face him, the clothing clutched to her chest. She stood still, tears gathering at the corners of her eyes, which she blinked furiously back.

"Are you okay?" Jacob asked, knowing it was a stupid question, but not knowing what else to say. Her daughter had almost been raped, *had* been abused.

Of course she wasn't okay.

Karen seemed to gather herself together. Still whispering, she said, "I wanted to thank you. For what you did. For being there when—" She cleared her throat. "For being there for her."

Ducking his head, Jacob waved her thanks away. "I didn't do anything."

"Of course you—"

"No," he interrupted her, needing her to see. "I punched him when he was already down, and that was for me as much as her."

Wanting to make his point, he looked the woman who was like a second mother to him dead in the eye.

"You need to know this, Karen, and really believe it. She took care of herself. You raised her strong, and smart. She's going to be okay. I'll always be there for her, and so will you, and Stan, and the rest of the family, and she knows that. But she needs to know you believe she can handle herself, too. That she's not a victim."

Karen stared at him, an odd look on her face. She set Melinda's clothing down on the end of his bed, then stepped to him and took him in her arms for a fierce hug.

"You're right, and I do know that," she said, holding tight. "You're such a wise man, Jacob. I'm so proud of the person you've become. And you're a good friend."

She leaned back and cupped his cheeks in her hands the way she often did to Melinda, her eyes searching his deeply.

"But you're wrong about one thing," she continued. "You did a lot tonight. You stood up for her, even if she handled herself. You comforted her, and you made her know she was safe again. That is a priceless gift. As her mother, and someone who loves you both, I won't ever forget it. Thank you."

Karen kissed him on both cheeks, hugged him once more, then scooped up Melinda's sleep clothes and was gone, leaving him standing there staring after her, so many emotions rioting through his system that he couldn't identify them all.

22

With nothing else to do, Jacob changed into his pajamas, then sat at the end of his bed, staring at his feet. He heard the shower turn on downstairs, and a long while later, shut off again. Time dragged slowly. Tired as he was, he couldn't make himself climb into bed. Not until he knew where Melinda would settle for the night.

Maybe then he could relax.

The memory of her bruised face, damp eyes, and trembling chin haunted him, hurt his heart, and he rubbed his own eyes, trying to scrub the vision out. Every time he blinked, the scene was right there, waiting to replay in his mind. Melinda struggling against Dane. Melinda screaming.

Jacob's knuckles were bruised from punching Dane, though he'd washed the blood away at the clinic. He flexed his stiff fingers, enjoying the ache and sting, wishing he'd hit the bastard again. And harder.

Wishing even more that it had never been necessary in the first place.

Later, the faint whir of Melinda's hair dryer sounded down

the quiet hallway. Almost done, then. The bathroom door opened, and Jacob peeked over the loft railing to watch as she went back to the kitchen and her parents, who had waited for her to return to the table.

Still he sat.

The night was supposed to have gone so differently. Dancing, laughing, New Year's Eve kissing.

Now he wasn't sure how to broach all the things he wanted—needed—to say to Melinda, or when the time would be right again.

The question was how to go from everything that had happened tonight back to where they'd been headed a few hours before.

He didn't know.

Jacob stared hard at his fingers. His feelings would have to wait. Now that he knew for certain that Melinda was The One, he wanted to act on those feelings as fast as possible, but hers had to come first. It was far more important for her to recover and get back to normal before he sprang his hopes on her out of the blue.

Patience had never been his strong suit. But for her, he would wait.

She would be okay. He'd meant it when he said those words to Karen. As delicate as Melinda might look, she was made of tougher stuff on the inside. She would be okay.

So he would wait.

Listening to the low murmur of Stan and Karen's voices, the slightly lighter notes of Melinda's, Jacob wondered if Melinda would come up soon or maybe sleep in her parents' room.

If she came up, would it be better for her if he pretended to be asleep, so she didn't feel she had to make conversation or talk about the night? Or would she want him to be waiting up for her?

He stayed on the edge of his bed, indecisive.

Before he could choose which path to take, he heard Melinda's parents say goodnight and head to their room. Their bedroom door closed quietly. Silence settled over the condo, though outside the windows, the snow continued to whirl and the wind had picked up to howl.

Jacob waited, bouncing his heels, expecting Melinda to top the stairs any moment, but she didn't come and didn't come, and finally he stepped stealthily to the loft railing to look down into the kitchen.

She sat at the table with her back to him, not moving, a steaming red mug cupped in her hands.

Now what should he do?

Jacob scratched his fingers through his hair. She probably needed some time to herself. But she looked so small and alone, it pulled at his heart.

Remembering he hadn't brushed his teeth yet gave him the excuse he needed, and Jacob made his way quietly down the curving stairs. Melinda looked over her shoulder when he reached the bottom.

"Hey," she said, a wan smile on her tired face.

"Hey," he whispered back.

Forcing his face into neutral lines to keep from reacting again to the sight of the ugly bruises splayed across her mouth and cheekbones, Jacob smiled in return.

His fists had clenched instinctively, wanting to pound on the sorry excuse for a man who had dared to hurt his woman, but he continued walking, striving for casual. He stretched and relaxed his hands.

As he passed behind her seat, he reached out and lightly squeezed her shoulder, then ran his fingers over her freshly-washed hair, careful to avoid the tender area where Dane had bashed her head against a jagged piece of wall hard enough to draw blood.

"Have to brush my teeth," Jacob said, explaining his presence downstairs.

Melinda nodded and took a sip of her tea, the scents of cinnamon and honey swirling from the hot mug.

She was still far too pale, which was saying something. With her Irish coloring, she was always pale, despite living in the California desert. Now her skin looked practically translucent. Her dark hair shone in the low kitchen lighting, and she was well-bundled in her thick, shaggy robe and furry purple slippers.

Continuing down the hall, Jacob dealt with his teeth, then stood, hands braced on the bathroom counter, staring at himself in the mirror. He took a breath, needing another moment to get himself back under control before facing Melinda.

Every time he caught sight of her face, the violence rose up inside him again, and it was all he could do to keep the murderous look out of his eyes. He hoped he'd broken Dane's nose badly enough that it would never look the same. He hoped the bloody coward would wear the mark of his fist on his face for the rest of the man's miserable life.

Maybe it would serve as a warning sign to other women that the bastard was not to be trusted.

Of course, the scumbag would probably use it as proof of some invented heroic tale and rope the unsuspecting women in even more.

Jacob sighed.

Nothing he could do about that.

If there was any justice in the world, Dane would at least serve some jail time for attacking Melinda, but he knew better than to expect that to be the case. Nope, the bastard would get a little talking to, a wagging finger in his face, and be back out preying on some other unsuspecting female in no time flat.

It could have ended so much worse. He knew that. But the slime had bruised her, hit her. It didn't take broken bones, or worse, to leave lasting scars. Thank God Melinda was strong and had an equally strong support network.

But he wished it had never happened.

Damn it all to hell.

Standing straight again, Jacob jiggled his hands and arms, rolled his head back and forth, and jumped lightly in place, trying to rid himself of the bloodlust the thoughts of Dane brought out in him. He was not, by nature, a violent person. But if someone threatened Melinda, whether by word—as had happened in high school—or by deed...

Well, they'd just better watch out.

Satisfied he had himself back under control, he returned to the kitchen. Melinda still sat at the table, staring into her mug of tea, her brow furrowed.

"Okay, chili bowl?" he asked, taking a seat next to her and putting his palm out, offering the connection instead of simply taking her hand the way he usually would, so that it was her choice.

Relief spread through him in a warm glow when she reached over and grasped his fingers.

Melinda raised her gaze and smiled, though her mouth winced a little at the pulling on her lips.

She said, "Okay, French dip."

Jacob twirled an imaginary mustache and said, "French, ooh-la-la," in a terrible accent and made her smile again, though it still didn't quite reach her eyes.

On the couch, Christian gave a loud snort and flipped over, shoving his blankets off and throwing one leg across both of Wendell's. Now Jacob grinned, a genuine smile.

Rick was well known for fighting in his sleep, Danny for walking and talking, but Christian wasn't nicknamed The Cuddler for nothing.

On any other occasion, Jacob would have whipped out his cell phone and Facebooked that photo with all due haste, but tonight wasn't the moment.

He blew out a breath. Nope, not tonight.

When Melinda glanced his way with questioning brows raised, he indicated the sofa bed with a nod. Melinda looked, and her dark blue eyes lit up with humor.

"Every time," she whispered with a quiet giggle. "Poor Wendell."

Jacob shrugged, though inside he did a happy dance to see the mirth back in her expression. "He's used to it," he said.

Melinda snorted and said, "That just makes it worse."

They smiled at each other in mutual amusement.

When her grin faded, Jacob squeezed her fingers lightly.

"Ready to head up?" he asked after a minute, wanting to offer her a little more time on her own if she needed it, but more than willing to stay if she wanted company. "It's after four."

She nodded. "I'll just finish my tea," she said, and he took that as his cue to give her some space.

"Okay. See you up there."

Rising from the table, Jacob pressed a kiss onto the top of her head.

"Jake?"

"Yeah?"

"It looks worse than it is. Truly. Don't keep looking at me like I'm about to break."

He breathed in hard, one long sniff to suck back the emotion that wanted to pour out of him. "I'll try, cream puff. Okay?"

"'K. Goodnight, Jake," Melinda said, her voice lowering back down to a whisper. She reached for his hand again and squeezed his fingers, holding him by her side. "And thank you. For before. I—"

"Don't thank me."

Oh, God, he didn't want to lose it in front of her. He struggled against the words hanging on the tip of his tongue, words that would spew more violence and hate all over Dane and not do Melinda any good.

Clearing his throat, he said, "I wish I'd gotten there sooner."

"You got there in time. That's what matters."

Strapping on his humor like an iron shield, he scoffed lightly and ruffled her hair—carefully, far from her head injury—pulling back his regrets. They were for him to bear. He wouldn't burden her with them.

"In time to see you drop his ass like a champ," he said. "I was just the clean-up crew."

"You were—*are*—more than that to me," she said, and wrapped her arms around his waist for a hard hug.

Jacob hugged her back. He had to force himself to let go, to give her the time she needed.

"Get some rest," he said, and climbed the stairs back to the loft, hoping against hope that her words meant what he wanted her to mean.

He peeled back the covers and flopped into bed facing the window, watching the snow swirl and dive, thrown in every direction by the roaring wind. It seemed even louder now than it had downstairs. If the storm worsened too much more, they might close the ski lifts tomorrow. Or rather, later today.

Not that he cared.

He doubted Melinda would be up to skiing, and he didn't plan to leave her side. They could hang out in the condo and watch movies or go for a drive or something if the weather lightened up. But he hoped the mountains stayed open so the others could go ski and give them time alone, just to be together.

Melinda topped the loft stairs a few moments later. She gave his toes her habitual friendly waggle where they hung off the end of the too-short bed as she walked past and climbed into her own bed. Her silhouette was barely visible in the nearly pitch-dark loft, the faint glow of the nightlight left on in the kitchen downstairs only reaching so far. Any moonlight beyond the windows was totally obliterated by the storm.

He listened to her shuffle around to get comfortable, then silence descended, except for the unrelenting winds and the low creaking of the building.

More able to relax himself now that she was safely snugged in for the night, Jacob let his eyes drift closed, conscious of his own breathing deepening toward sleep.

What a freaking day.

Exhaustion settled over him like an extra blanket, muffling all sound.

Then...

From the other bed, he heard, "Jake?"

Just his name, low and hesitant, nearly inaudible over the sound of the storm, more a feeling than an actual word.

Opening his eyes, he could hardly make out her slender hand stretched across the space between their beds. He dug his arm out of his blanket cocoon and reached for her fingers, wrapping them inside his own.

"What's up?" he whispered.

Melinda held his hand, silent for so long he wondered if she'd fallen asleep.

Then she said, "Would you—" She took a deep breath. "Would you—No, never mind."

"What?"

"It's silly."

"Mel. What."

"I just—I wondered if you... if you would sleep with me again."

Jacob's hand twitched involuntarily, and his heart swelled with the strength of the emotions coursing through him at her request.

Striving to keep his voice in check, not wanting to scare her with the force of his response, he said, "Of course," and nearly sprang out of bed, tripping over his own two feet on the single step to her side.

She turned and scooted over, and he slid in behind her, wrapping her in his arms as he did so and pulling her securely back against his chest.

Spooning her as he'd dreamed of doing.

He tucked his long legs beneath her bent knees, her bottom seated snuggly in his lap, and breathed deeply of her scent—the shampooed freshness of her hair, her soap smell, and the sweet, spicy scent that was only Melinda.

The bed was patently too small for the two of them, but he'd never been happier or more comfortable in his life.

Except maybe the other night, when she'd slept splayed full-out on top of his body.

Melinda's arms entwined with his, her skin velvety soft and smooth. Her low hum of contentment purred in his ears.

He shivered.

The firm, rounded undersides of her breasts resting against his forearms through her pajama top made him ache. She stroked the backs of his hands with delicate fingertips and sent electricity sizzling through his system.

"Is this okay?" she asked.

"Totally."

She obviously had no idea what she was doing to him.

Jacob sucked air silently through his teeth—one breath, then two, then three—and tightened the reins on his body's response to hers. Of all nights, now was not the time.

Running baseball stats in his head didn't really help, but it was better than nothing. She needed comfort and security, and by God, he was going to provide it if it killed him. He could control himself for her sake.

He wasn't a monster like that asshole, Dane, nor would he take advantage of her when she was so vulnerable.

No matter how much he yearned for her. Or how much he wanted to banish even the ghost of another man's hands from her body. Especially the hands of a man who had caused her pain.

His body tensed at the unnecessary reminder of all she'd been through. It sent the need to pound the other man into microscopic particles of dust raging, a flashflood in his veins.

Deliberately, he relaxed his muscles, not wanting Melinda to notice his sudden rigidity. If things went the way he hoped, if she accepted him, there would be plenty of time—years and years ahead of them—to enjoy each other physically.

Years and years.

Jacob took another deep, hushed breath. The idea of their future together supplied the last bit of calming strength he needed to settle himself down. To be the friend and protector she needed.

The lover could wait.

"Thank you, Jakey," Melinda murmured sleepily, and nestled against him with a contented sigh. She was sound asleep before he could find any words to reply.

Jacob lay quietly, soaking in the simple pleasure of holding her, her scent and warmth surrounding him. He bent his left arm up with his hand under his head, and Melinda shifted with him so that her head rested on the inside of his upper arm.

Eyes wide open, he stared above her head and out the window, watching the whirling snow. Enjoying Melinda's slow, even breathing against his chest, barely heard even with no space at all between them.

His awareness of her spun through every throbbing cell and tingling fiber of his being, even the few places where their bodies didn't actually touch. It was a deeper awareness than the merely physical. There was a purity to it, a beauty that eclipsed anything he'd ever known or suspected.

A lump formed in his throat, surprising him, the intensity of his emotions filling all the nooks and crannies in his soul, all the dark, lonely places, with light. His heart seemed to beat in time with hers. Their breaths synchronized.

If he could hold her this way for the rest of his life, he would never want to move again.

Seven days ago, he would never have dared imagine he'd find himself holding Melinda through the night, not once but twice in one week. He would never have imagined, at twenty-one, discovering such a depth of feeling, or even wanting it.

Now he couldn't imagine going back to the way he'd been a few days before, couldn't imagine putting the blinders back on and denying the truth of his love for her.

Melinda was it for him. Preserving their friendship was of paramount importance, yet it all seemed so simple now. So right. Still terrifying in some ways, but the rightness overshadowed all other considerations.

Filled with a comfort of his own, Jacob followed her down into slumber.

The next time Jacob opened his eyes, a shadow loomed over him between the bed and the window, which resolved itself slowly into the person of Melinda's mother.

His sleep-hazed brain and blurred eyes took another few moments to focus.

When they did, he suddenly became unnervingly, alarmingly conscious of the warm, solid weight of Karen's only daughter—her twenty-one-year-old *unmarried* daughter—snuggled tightly against him in sleep, his arms firmly around her curvy body and the two of them tucked oh-so-cozily beneath the covers.

Oh, *shit*.

He said, "Ah."

"Good morning," Karen answered, keeping her voice low

so as not to wake Melinda.

And she smiled at them both.

Smiled!

Jacob blinked several times, rapidly, waiting for all the blood that had dumped out of his head at the first sight of Karen to find its way back to at least a couple of his malfunctioning brain cells.

A smile.

That was not the reaction he'd expected to having a parent find the two of them in bed together. He kept silent, staring at her in confusion.

"I didn't mean to startle you," she said. "I wanted to let you know the rest of us are clearing out so Melinda can rest. Call us if you need anything."

Karen leaned over and pressed a kiss to his forehead and then to Melinda's, sending his bemusement skyrocketing. Then she smiled again, and made her way out of the loft.

Bizarre.

Jacob's whole body wanted to twitch in reaction, but he kept it to a light shudder so he didn't risk disturbing Melinda. His heart hammered as though he'd been running up a long, steep hill ahead of an invading army, only to turn and find the warriors with their hands held out to him, offering a feast.

The sleeping girl in his arms shifted slightly and murmured something unintelligible. Jacob settled in, expecting to lie awake and hold her until she woke. No way could he get back to sleep with his pulse pounding so hard and fast, the worry over Karen finding them this way frothing in his brain.

Not that it would be a hardship to stay where he was, Melinda all but fused to his body, but...

Karen had *smiled*.

What did that mean? He half expected her to come back, the rest of their parents in tow, to gesture at the two of them with a fond expression on her face, as if to say, "Look, aren't they adorable?"

That was certainly the vibe he'd gotten from her. Indulgent affection.

It was weird.

Very weird.

And jeez, if he'd known she'd be fine with it, he might have climbed into Melinda's bed long before now, he thought, then had to swallow the nervous snicker that wanted to escape his mouth.

Instead, he leaned forward half-an-inch to take a deeper breath of Melinda's sweet-smelling hair. Calm settled over him again, and he tightened his arms around her more securely.

His thoughts drifted toward dreaming, to a bigger bed and a cool, cushy room that belonged only to the two of them, with the pieces of their clothing tossed together in an intimate pile, and glistening sunlight dusting Melinda's bare skin with gold as his hands glided smoothly over her velvety warmth...

Appalled, Jacob jerked his right arm back up, wrapping his hand safely around her waist again. His wandering mind had encouraged wandering fingers, their stroking drawn onward by Melinda's satin curves. He'd been a breath away from delving between her legs to find her heat, cupping her softness, arousing her slowly until she'd turn toward him, open for him. Welcome his body with hers...

Sinking back into pleasurable daydreams, Jacob's eyelids grew heavy, then closed.

He smiled drowsily at the images scrolling slowly through his mind, hardly conscious enough to be surprised when he slid comfortably back into sleep.

Confusion clouded Melinda's mind when she woke. Everything seemed slightly off kilter, though she couldn't identify exactly why.

Sunlight beamed into her eyes through a window heavily frosted with snow.

Rubbing the sleep from her lashes, she realized the loft was far quieter than it had been the night before. The wind had died. The storm must have blown itself out sometime during the early morning hours.

She hummed to herself, more comfortable than she could ever remember being. Safe and secure and warm, yet simultaneously her body sank into the thin mattress, heavy and sore, as though she'd been beaten with a baseball bat.

And it clicked.

Memories of the night past slammed into her head with painful clarity. Every muscle tensed, and anxiety crawled up her throat, stealing her breath for a moment, before the awareness of where she was and whose arms held her so securely rose above the panic.

Letting out a shaky breath, Melinda hugged Jacob's strong arms even more tightly, closing her eyes and rubbing her cheek against the back of his hand in thanks for his presence. For not waking alone.

"Mel?" he asked, groggy with sleep. The warmth of his raspy morning voice ruffled the hair on top of her head where he'd buried his face to sleep. "Okay?"

"Yeah," she said, taking careful breaths while her heart settled back to normal.

She was with Jacob. She was okay.

"Happy New Year," he mumbled, nuzzling into the back of her neck.

"Happy New Year," she said, and wondered what the next year had in store for them. She sent up a quick prayer for a safe and happy year for everyone, and hoped this new one would end better than the last one.

They stayed quiet for a while, comfortable just holding each other and breathing. Outside, the sun sparkled the frosted windows like diamonds.

"Did you sleep all right?" Jacob asked.

She *mm-hmm'd* in answer and hugged his arms again.

"Thanks to you," she said, even as a blush shot up from the tips of her toes.

"My pleasure," he said, and there was a note in his voice that had her ears pricking up with hope and caution mixed.

"Jake," she said, but before she could finish, her stomach rumbled loudly in the quiet room.

Melinda started to giggle, embarrassed, but then Jacob's belly growled even louder and sent her into gales of laughter. His answering chuckles shook against her body and made her laugh harder yet.

"I guess we're hungry," he said.

"I guess so," she agreed.

Jacob squeezed his arms around her, then lightly slapped his hand on the curve of her hip. "Come on, then," he said. "I'll make breakfast."

"Deal." She shifted over so he could pull his arm out from beneath her body.

He climbed from the bed, and Melinda rolled onto her back to look at him. His hair stood out in tufts all over his head, and the smile he gave her, all sleepy and warm, melted her heart. He stretched his arms over his head and bent side to side to ease the stiffness from his limbs.

Melinda couldn't tear her eyes away from the sight of his powerful body, from the muscles bunching and lengthening beneath his pjs, or from the sliver of tanned skin briefly visible above the waistband of his pajama bottoms.

All she could think was, *Wow*.

After rubbing the sleep from his eyes, Jacob smiled at her again and held both large hands out to help her up from the bed.

They stood only a hair's breadth apart, staring into each other's eyes, his hands still grasping hers, their fingers now entwined. She took a deep breath, and her breasts brushed his chest.

They both twitched from the contact.

Time spun out, and the silence lengthened. Neither of them looked away.

Jacob said, "Mel—" and she said, "Jake—" at the same time, but they didn't laugh now, only smiled a little while their eyes continued to delve into each other's.

Searching.

Finally, Jacob leaned forward and kissed her forehead. "Come on. I'll feed you."

Suddenly aware of the deep silence in the rest of the condo, Melinda said, "Where is everyone?"

"They left," he answered over his shoulder as he led the way downstairs and into the kitchen. "Your mom thought they should clear out so you could rest."

"Oh," she said, frowning at his back and nibbling the tip of one finger.

She didn't want everyone treating her like an invalid. Then again, she wasn't really up to a day on the slopes, either, so maybe it was better this way.

Besides, it would give her unexpected—but welcome—time alone with Jacob.

Then the significance of his words sank in.

"Wait." She stopped, one foot out in space, the other on the bottom tread of the staircase. "When did you talk to my mom?"

With his head in the fridge, Jacob's body stiffened.

He said, "Ah," and straightened to face her, his arms full of ingredients for pancakes. "She, uh, came upstairs. Earlier."

Melinda blanched. "She saw us?"

A strangely watchful look crossed his face as he studied her in return. "Yeah. She did."

"Oh, my God."

Moving forward as though underwater, she sank into one of the chairs at the kitchen table and put her head in her hands.

"She didn't seem to mind, Mel," he said, caution in every syllable.

When she peeked up at him, he was watching her, his expression guarded.

"She didn't?" Melinda could hardly believe that.

"She smiled."

"She smiled?" Melinda repeated, mentally smacking herself for parroting everything he said, but shock held her firmly in its grip.

Her mother might have known she'd slept with Mitch, but that didn't mean was okay with finding her daughter in bed with a guy. Any guy, no matter who he was, no matter how chaste the occasion. Even Jacob.

It seemed unreal to think her mother could have caught them in bed together and not blown a gasket.

"It's not like anything happened," Jacob said now, putting the pancake ingredients down on the counter. "It was totally innocent, and we were both still dressed. After what happened, I think she knew you needed a friend. That's all."

"I guess," she said, her brain wrangling with the issue.

It seemed so out of character for her mother, but it was Jacob, after all. Maybe that made the difference.

Would it still, if her mom discovered they were romantically involved? That might put a different spin on it. But—

Her thoughts broke off as Jacob spoke, and she looked up at the strange, hesitant tone in his voice.

"Do *you* mind?" he asked, not looking at her.

"Me?"

"That she saw us together?"

"Oh. Um…" Did she? Melinda searched her heart. It had seemed like a big deal a moment ago…

He came to the table and took the chair next to hers, turning it to face her and grasping her hand. The muscles in his shoulders and upper arms rippled with tension beneath the fabric of his shirt.

"Because, Mel—" He broke off and cleared his throat. She didn't think she'd ever seen him look so nervous, and her own heartbeat sped up in response. "I have to—I need to say something to you, and maybe this isn't the right time, but—"

Jacob sucked in a deep, deep breath, and prepared to put everything on the line.

It wasn't the right time, damn it. He knew it wasn't. He still needed to tell her his news, she still needed time after the night before, after Mitch, time to come around to his point of view.

Yet all of a sudden he couldn't stand not telling her, not knowing, and Melinda's eyes, huge and deeply blue, were glued to his face, nerves and questions dancing in their depths.

"Jake?" she said, as he lifted their joined fingers and kissed the back of her hand.

He said, "I—" But he shook his head and stopped, blowing out a breath.

Get it together, Jake.

This was harder than he'd imagined.

Scooting his chair closer to hers, he leaned slowly toward her, watching her all the while, oxygen already backing up in his lungs.

Ever-so-gently, he placed his big hands on either side of her bruised, delicate face. Touching lightly so as not to hurt. He held there for a moment, hardly daring to breathe at all, absorbing the silk of her skin, the look in her wide, wide eyes.

She stayed perfectly motionless, though her lips parted, and her breaths came faster.

Now was the moment.

Grabbing hold of his courage, shutting off the voices circling through his mind full of worries and doubts and what-ifs, he closed his eyes, and moved forward another inch.

Another inch.

Then half-an-inch more.

And pressed his lips, whisper-soft, to hers.

Even that super-gentle contact sent jolt after jolt through his body.

Her lips… Ah, amazing. So soft, so warm.

But he held himself motionless, waiting.

And waiting.

He seemed to wait through eons, though only a moment passed before the barely-there return pressure of her sweet, full mouth on his shot his pulse through the snow-covered roof.

Eureka!

He tried to stay cool, and he tried not to over-think, but *Oh, my God, Melinda, I'm kissing Melinda, and her mouth tastes like sugar cookies, even with morning breath and everything, and I don't even care, because wow...*

It was all he could do not to jump up in the air and whoop like a fool all over the condo. She'd kissed him back! After all this time, all their years together.

She'd kissed him back.

How could he have known everything he'd ever wanted was right there beside him his entire life?

Jacob kept himself together through sheer dint of will, hardly moving, though fireworks snap-sizzle-popped behind his lids, and finally, finally he broke their most delicate of connections. He leaned backward slightly, opening his eyes to look into hers.

Now he would see the beginning or the end of everything. The fear he'd denied before slammed into his gut. What if—

Melinda raised a hand to her lips, staring back at him, a small 'o' of surprise on her plush mouth and his hands still on her heated cheeks.

He said, "Mel—" but she placed her hand against his lips to shush him, and her gaze followed the motion, staring at her fingertips against his mouth, then back to his eyes.

When her other hand came up between his arms and both of her hands slid over his cheekbones to hold his face the way he held hers, his belly tightened, jittered, jumped.

The warmth of her creamy skin seemed hot enough to scorch.

His heart rate accelerated even more, pounding in his veins. He'd never felt more turned on or more nervous, as though this kiss, right here, right now, was the very first of his life. In a way it was, because it was his first kiss with *Melinda*.

All others paled into insignificance.

Her gaze dropped to his lips again, then rose, very slowly this time, back to his eyes, the blue dark and sparkling, and when she leaned forward, his breath stopped altogether.

Like the faintest brush of dandelion fluff, her lips teased his mouth. She pressed tiny little kisses across his lips and one to each corner, and he held statue-still, unable to breathe, only feel, and the feeling…

Holy God.

Then she came back to the center and sank against him, pressing her luscious mouth more fully to his, igniting a fire in his belly.

But she was injured.

"I don't want to hurt you," he said, leaning away only slightly, regret heavy in his stomach, touching her bruised lips with a shaking fingertip.

"I don't even feel it." She breathed the words against him, everything, everything so soft and sweet and gentle, he could hardly bear it.

"I—" he began, but awkwardness clutched his tongue.

They should wait.

They should talk.

This was Melinda. But…

"What is it?" she asked, her words whispering over his skin, raising all the tiny hairs on his arms and the back of his neck.

Where was his courage now?

Hesitant, he kept his eyes on hers, hoping she could read the truth there, the needs. The emotions. The hopes.

"I want to—" He moved his hands awkwardly.

"I know," she whispered, not looking away from him, and there was his courage, wrapped in trust and shining from the depths of her shimmering eyes. "Me, too."

Schooling himself to stay careful, Jacob slid his hands under her arms, slowly pulling her from her chair, their gazes locked. He drew her across the brief space separating them and onto his lap.

Melinda's legs straddled him, smooth, warm muscles gripping him through her thin pajama bottoms, and their bodies pressed together. Chest to belly to lap to thighs. Her buttocks rested on top of his legs, firm and erotic and mind-blowing, and their heartbeats slammed against each other's.

Oh, God.

Their mouths held, only a breath apart.

Then she winced slightly, and he went motionless immediately, holding her still.

He said, "Wait—" but she shook her head no, said, "Don't stop," in a low, throaty voice as she wrapped her arms around his neck and pressed her cheek against his, her breasts crushing like heaven against his chest.

"Mel—" he said, her name a groan as his own arms came more fully around her body, pressing her even closer.

He was hard as a rock, his body beyond listening or caring that this moment wasn't going to go that far.

Not yet.

"Melinda—"

"Jake," she whispered into his ear. "Shut up and kiss me again. Please."

Nothing could have held him back.

Mindful of her bruises, he kept the pressure soft, attentive to her every sound, every flicker of emotion or mood as he nibbled her scrumptious mouth and the smooth, sweet line of her jaw.

She hummed in her throat, a sound of pleasure, and he thought the top of his head might blow off. She nipped his earlobe playfully, making him jump, and sent his senses scrambling.

Jacob stroked his hands gently over her slender back, along the curves of her waist and hips, soaking up the heat pumping off her body through the thinness of the fabric separating his hands from her bare skin.

Scant millimeters, but he wanted the barrier gone.

Wanted bare skin.

Wanted her.

His body begged him to hurry, to throw caution aside and dive deep, but he recognized the importance of timing. Of savoring. And—God help him—of waiting.

They explored each other's lips, nuzzling, testing, tasting, everything sweet and slow and mellow, all wrapped together with a silken ribbon of surprise and discovery. His body wept with need.

But inside, his heart soared.

Melinda's mind had tumbled like an out of control thrill ride when Jacob first pressed his lips to hers.

Soft as it was, and as many kisses as they'd shared as friends over their lifetime together—on the head, the forehead, the cheek, even friendly pecks on the lips often enough—this kiss had instantly registered on an exciting, unfamiliar level, new and different and wonderful.

A first kiss.

A real kiss, not simply a peck between friends.

Now her head swam, intoxicated by the feel of his muscles

bunching beneath her seeking fingers, his hard, strong body melded to hers, an inferno of heat fusing them together as he stroked her back.

This was a mistake. A wonderful, incredible, amazing mistake. They hadn't talked yet. Their friendship hung in the balance… She couldn't stop.

She could hardly believe she was in Jacob's lap, with his hardness, the raw evidence of his desire, pressing firmly against her.

Unmistakable.

Unbearably arousing.

She could hardly believe she was kissing him, their arms around each other like they'd never let go. It was so very *right,* so exactly where she wanted to be, wanted to *stay,* she felt a fool for not realizing her love for him years sooner.

The dream she'd had the night before they left for Utah flitted through her mind. It almost seemed prophetic somehow. Had she known, even then, what this could be like?

No. She might have wondered, guessed, dreamed, but nothing compared to the reality.

Her best friend Jacob had suddenly become so much more.

He was everything.

The thrill of it screamed through her system, both exciting and terrifying, and everything in between, but in this moment, all she knew was she never wanted him to stop kissing her. Never wanted him to stop touching her.

Not ever.

When the tip of his tongue met hers, the thrill shot even higher. She didn't care that her mouth hurt, or her cheeks, or any of a hundred other places. She only wanted to kiss Jacob and keep on kissing him. The glide of his tongue gently stroking hers, of his hands caressing her body, softly, slowly, made her bones sigh with pleasure, made her muscles go all melty and weak.

She sagged against him, unable to hold herself upright against the sensations swamping her body.

All that, from only a kiss.

A long time later, they finally surfaced, both breathing heavily. When they pulled back to look at each other, Melinda found herself suddenly shy of meeting his gaze. Part giggly, part terrified. Her whole body seemed to vibrate, full of tingles and needs, desires she couldn't yet voice.

All for Jacob.

Everything had changed since yesterday, and again in the time since they'd come downstairs. Changed and intensified. He must feel more than friendship for her, too, or he would never have kissed her that way.

Her mind begged for caution. *Don't jump in, don't jump in,* echoed in her ears.

And yet…

Jacob tipped a finger beneath her chin to lift her gaze to his, his eyes searching. Could he read her every emotion, did he know the fears pounding in her heart, her veins? As well as they knew each other, this was fresh territory for them both.

Unexplored.

Potentially dangerous.

The gigglyness faded away, leaving the half-terrified part of her cowering alone, with no euphoric buffer against reality.

What were they doing?

24

The longer they sat staring at each other, the more reality started to creep back in at the edges of Melinda's awareness.

All the reasons she'd resisted loving him this way to begin with. All the dreams they each held, dreams hung from goal posts on opposite ends of a long, long field. All the changes a relationship between them would bring to their lives, and to the lives of their friends and families.

The multi-dimensional disaster if it didn't work out.

But she wanted.

Oh, she wanted.

And the look in his topaz eyes said he wanted, too, and what was life without a little risk...

Jacob exhaled as though he'd been holding his breath.

He said, "Melinda."

She said, "I know."

He said, " But..."

And she whispered, "Yeah..."

His finger still held beneath her chin, but now he slid his whole hand along her cheek again, cupping her face. The look in his eyes melted her heart.

He said, "Wow—"

And she said, "Jake," and kissed him again, for all she was worth.

It was magical, the way the nerves smoothed out again.

They'd have to talk about their relationship—what this all meant, what they were going to do. How they each felt.

Yet the moment their lips touched, the rightness of it descended once more, blocking out everything except his mouth on hers, his body strong and hot beneath her hands, and all those worries flitted away into trivialities.

Details would get handled. For now...

Mmmmmm.

Melinda hummed against his mouth, a deep purr of pure pleasure. If only they could stay this way, locked together forever, it would be perfect.

No sooner did she have that thought than Jacob's stomach rumbled, and hers answered, loud and insistent.

Instead of ruining the moment, it made everything normal, comfortable and real and friendly, and they broke apart laughing.

Jacob squeezed her tightly, one hard hug, before settling her gently back onto her own chair.

"I guess we better eat," he said.

Their eyes met, and they grinned. A bit nervously, true, but still.

He kissed her forehead, like always, then hopped up and moved around the kitchen counter to the pile of ingredients he'd left there. He grabbed a bowl from a low cupboard and mixed and stirred, tossing her cute, dimpled little grins every time their eyes met, then he got the pancakes cooking on a small griddle.

They didn't say much, and she was glad. She wanted to savor the memory of that amazing kiss, not ruin it with a lot of thinking and rationalizing and discussing.

That would come later.

She'd always enjoyed watching him cook, so she focused on his motions for now and set the rest aside. He was a surprisingly good cook, as his mother had insisted on him learning to feed himself from a young age.

Jacob poured milk for each of them when the pancakes were ready, then joined her at the table with plates piled high. They held hands while they ate, playing with each other's fingers and giggling a bit whenever they caught each other's gaze.

When they were finished, they washed and dried the dishes side by side.

Hand in hand, they flopped on the couch in the family room, Melinda snugged between Jacob's legs and stretched across his chest. They turned the TV on low and found a channel showing reruns of the Rose Parade from earlier that morning, though they were too caught up in each other to pay much attention to the floats or commentary.

His busy hands and mouth kept her in a constant state of need, her pulse thrumming heavily, and her mind blessedly quiet except for his name.

Jacob-Jacob-Jacob…

The novelty of his fingers stroking across her highly sensitized skin left her breathless. His lips and teeth nibbling the sides of her neck, or the tender spots below her ears, then down along her collar bones, his hands creeping ever closer to areas crying out for his touch sent her heart racing with joy and fear, desire rampaging wildly in her belly.

Panting for air, they finally broke the kiss.

Melinda sank onto his chest, nuzzling beneath his chin, reveling in the drumming beat of his heart beneath her cheek and the hard, heavy bulge pressing against her lower abdomen. She wasn't the only one breathing like a winded racehorse.

Or the only one so turned on she was about to combust.

Good, she thought with a private snicker. It was only fair.

Jacob bowed up in a long stretch, lifting her along with his body, then settled back again with his arms wrapped around her, his fingers running through the strands of her hair curling loose to her waist.

With a sigh, he placed his cheek on the top of her head and rested there, rubbing his face slowly over her hair.

"I want to be with you, Mel," he said, his voice low and a little trembly. With nerves? That made two of them. "I want us to be together."

Melinda froze, though her heart did a weird sort of vault, like shooting straight to the top of a mile-high rollercoaster, freefalling into a series of wild loop-de-loops all the way down to the ground, then shooting straight up again. Then repeating the entire maneuver a thousand times between one second and the next.

It made her dizzy and scared and exhilarated all at once. Could he possibly mean what she hoped he did?

She waited what felt like an eternity, struggling for calm. With one fingertip, she drew inconsequential designs across the right side of his chest while she kept her cheek pressed to the left, her eyes tracking the motion.

When he didn't say anything else, she finally shifted to prop herself up on his chest and looked into his eyes.

Eyes, she saw now, dancing with nerves and emotions, brightening the gold flakes in their depths to wavering flames. She realized he'd been practically holding his breath since he'd spoken. Waiting for her to answer.

Lowering her gaze to his mouth, she ran her fingers lightly over his lips. He had such a sensual mouth. How often had she noticed how very kissable he was over the years? How often had she wanted to find out for herself exactly how his lips tasted? But that was part of the problem, wasn't it?

No one was supposed to think about their friends that way.

"What does that mean?" she asked softly, the only words she could get past her suddenly dry throat. *Don't jump in, don't jump in...* She kept her eyes on his mouth.

Jacob huffed out a breath.

"It means everything," he said, his lips moving against her stroking fingers, and she could hear the light frown in his voice, even without looking. "It means I want this. Us."

"Sex?" she asked, even as she cringed at the harsh sound of the single syllable in the quiet room. But she had to know.

"No, not *sex,*" he said, putting a strange emphasis on the word.

Shifting beneath her to a more upright position, Jacob hauled her up with him, then raised her chin so she had no choice but to meet his gaze. The look on his face was more serious than she'd ever seen him.

A tangled knot of emotion lodged itself in her throat.

With his free hand, he brushed her hair back, tucking a strand behind her ear.

"I don't want to date you just for fun. This isn't a whim, even if it seems fast, and I know it does, but I feel…" He paused, swallowed hard. "I feel… for you. I have feelings for you. Can you kiss me the way you did and say it's just friendship or just sex, or do you feel something more, too?"

"Jake—"

"Because it's not just friendship, and it's not just sex. Yes, I want to make love with you," he said, and sent her heart on another fast loop around the rollercoaster. "But that's not all. I just want to be with you. Be together." He stared deeply into her eyes. Breathed. "I'm in love with you, Mel. I love you."

Her whole body clutched, and tears sprang to her eyes unbidden.

"You-you do?"

His gaze locked on hers, he nodded. She blew out a breath, shock, joy, fear, hope rocketing around her heart.

Oh, God.

She didn't know what to say, what to do. What to feel. This was what she'd wanted in her secret heart, what she'd been afraid to hope for, what she'd given up on so many times over the years.

It was what she wanted now, more than anything, but…

Don't jump in!

"Oh, Jacob," she said, her voice barely a whisper, everything in her aching.

She wanted to say it too, to shout it from the highest mountain peak outside their window, only the words got lost on the way to her lips, tripped up by worry.

Instead of *I love you, too,* she said, "Are you sure?"

He went still as stone for the space of three heartbeats.

"I am," he said, his voice sounding a little hoarse now. "I'm sure."

"But…" Melinda struggled to find the right words, knowing she was already screwing it up, watching the light fade from his eyes. "How?" she whispered. "When?"

The ache inside increased every second.

"It's been coming on for a while," he said slowly. A flush had risen into his tanned cheeks, tipped his ears with red. "Then... It just—" He tapped a fist over his heart. "Hit."

The wrecked expression on his face said it had hit him like a Mack truck.

She knew the feeling.

"Jake, I—"

"It's okay, Mel," he said, scooting up straighter. "You don't have to say anything. I didn't plan this, didn't want this. I didn't mean for it to happen."

He moved to set her aside. She grabbed hold of him. Held on.

He said, "I don't—"

"No, Jacob, wait, please. Wait."

He stopped moving, collapsed back on the couch as though all the strength had drained from his muscles. She tucked herself into his chest, holding him there with her. Tears wanted to fall, but she held them back. If she fell apart, she'd never get through what she needed to say.

I love you trembled on her lips, begging to be proclaimed, though he wouldn't believe her now. How could she have screwed this up so fast, when he was giving her the very thing she wanted most on earth?

His love.

Now he'd shuttered himself away from her again, and she would have to wait for the right moment to come back around, a moment when he would believe her.

But first...

Sitting up, she straddled his legs so they could look into each other's eyes, so he could see her expression. Couldn't he read the truth in her eyes, couldn't he see the love and the fear tearing her apart?

Her hands splayed across his chest. Seeking his strength. She needed it, needed him around her, supporting her, holding her heart.

"I-I've been feeling—something—too," she started, not

knowing why she was backpedaling from her own emotions, hating herself for hurting him, for hurting herself, unable to stop. "I have. But there are so many other considerations, so many obstacles—"

"Obstacles don't matter," Jacob interrupted, the flames rekindling in his sherry eyes. "Not if we're together. Love conquers all, haven't you heard? And I love you, Mel. I do."

"I love you, too, you know I do," she said, pleading with him to hear the words she couldn't say. She knew by the look in his eyes that he understood she still hadn't said *I love you,* not the way he wanted. "I always have—"

"But?"

There was so much caution in that one, flat word, in the tone of his voice. Melinda's heart constricted.

"What we're talking about now, this is different," she said, panic egging her on the more his expression darkened, grasping wildly at straws. "I don't want to risk our friendship when nothing else has changed. What about our future? We want such different things. And what if this is all just rebounding? You just broke up with Nicole, too, and—"

"Rebounding?" He looked at her, and there was temper there now. "Rebounding."

"I—"

With no warning, Jacob surged upward, swooped in, his mouth on hers like a fever, and she could only hold on and hope for more.

He kissed her like he'd never stop, and that was fine with her. She clung to him, met his lips, his tongue stroke for stroke, and demanded more, took more, and still he gave.

More, and more, and more.

When he tore his mouth away, she could only stare back at him, dazed and off balanced.

"Did that feel like rebounding to you?"

Weak, unable to speak, Melinda shook her head. Her mind stumbled around in her skull, drunk with lust, and her body quivered with need.

Relaxing again, Jacob placed his hands gently on either side of her face. He tugged her down until her forehead rested against his. He opened his mouth to speak, but she pressed her hand to his lips once more.

"What I feel for you is different," she murmured, her voice low and heavy. "It's so much more than I've ever felt for anyone, ever, it's more everything. Friendship is only the beginning. It's powerful, Jacob. And scary. You toss away the idea of obstacles like they're nothing, but if we start this, if we change everything, what will happen? Will you stay with me in Paso, give up all your plans and dreams?"

Something secretive moved in his eyes, down in their dark-gold depths. He wouldn't meet her gaze. Nerves shot to high alert, though she couldn't name the cause. He was hiding something. She felt it in the sudden pitching of her belly.

Oh, God.

She wanted to scream at him. *What? What is it?*

"Jake?"

He only shook his head, his lips clamped shut.

Determined to remain outwardly calm, Melinda rested her palm against his cheek.

"If you stayed," she said, "if I asked you to give up everything you've been working toward, I couldn't live with myself. Don't you see? And you'd hate me for it eventually. That's no way to start a relationship."

"Do we have to know now?" he asked, his eyes suddenly fierce. Burning. "We're not even out of school. Do we have to have our entire futures mapped out right this second? I love you, Mel. If we're together, we'll figure it out. Maybe later you'll decide you're okay with leaving Paso. You might want to come with me, did you ever think of that? You've never given any other options a chance."

"Neither have you," she protested, sitting up again. "And you're basically saying you won't stay in Paso, so—"

"Being a team doctor means I have to travel. It's part of the package. They need nurse-midwives everywhere. If you're worried about finding a job—"

"It's not that, Jacob. You know it isn't."

Frowning now, he grabbed her hands with both of his, his expression intent.

"The point is we'd be together," he said. "Whatever happens down the road, we'll handle it. This is right. Can't you feel it?"

Raising her hands to his chest, he pressed them both over his heart, its thundering beat galloping beneath her palms.

She stared at their clasped hands, but in her mind's eye, Melinda saw the sweet little house she'd always imagined sharing with her one true love, with its pretty garden, a dog or two rolling on the grass, a swing set full of giggling children. She knew it inside and out, knew it sat just a few blocks from her parents' home, in the town of her birth, where most of her family and friends all lived. Every birthday and holiday would be shared with those same people, as they had been every year of her life.

Her kids would grow up with her cousin's children and the children of her friends. They'd go to school together, at the same school she and Jacob had gone to, and on Sundays they'd go to the same little church she'd always attended. They'd go to their senior proms at the local resort, as she had. She'd work in the hospital where she'd been born, and she'd go home at the end of each day knowing and loving her place in the world.

Safe, content, and happy.

It was everything she'd always wanted.

Except Jacob wouldn't be part of it.

"Jake," she said softly, her heart aching, pulling hard in opposite directions, "it isn't only us we have to worry about. It's our families and friends, too. We shouldn't do this if we know it will end badly."

"We don't know that," he argued, frustration whitening the edges of his lush mouth.

She wanted to press gentle kisses there, to ease the tension, but he was asking so much. To give up everything she'd hoped for. Could she do it, even for him?

"We don't, Mel," he said again when she stayed silent. "Anyway, there are no guarantees, you know that. Look at Carl and Donna, look at my aunt and uncle. But we have something special, even more special than I'd realized until now."

"I know, but—"

"I'm asking you to trust me. I'm asking you to be brave. I'm asking you to be with me."

She couldn't tear her eyes from his, yet even as he argued with her, that unknown shadow shifted in his gaze again, a secret unshared.

What was he hiding?

"Jake—"

"Look, I know I sprang this on you. I'm sorry. I meant to wait, but I couldn't stop after that kiss, and…" He broke off, sighed. "Don't say any more now, okay? I love you. That's not going to change. We'll work it out. I promise."

"You're sure? Because I can't lose you, Jake." Melinda sniffed, hard.

"You never will. We never will."

"But—"

"What?"

"Can we wait…" She trailed off, unsure how to say what she wanted to say.

This was Jacob, the one person she could say anything to, but this…

Her stomach clenched, both in need and worry.

"Can we wait for the physical stuff? Just until, you know—I don't want to risk—"

"Shhh," Jacob whispered, putting a gentle finger over her lips. "We'll wait. I don't want sex confusing the issue, either. You're so important to me, Mel. You have to know that. I don't want to rush anything about this. When the time's right, when it's perfect and we both agree, we'll be together. Not a second before. Okay?"

Nodding, relieved, she smiled more fully.

She wanted him like nothing she'd ever experienced, but it was like he'd said. Making love would only confuse things. She wanted her head and heart clear before traveling with him down that all-new road.

"Okay," she said. But the needs rioting through her system wouldn't quite let it go at that. "We can still, you know, kiss, though. Right?"

"Hell, yes," he said, chuckling now, and kissed her to prove it. "Just promise you'll be thinking."

How could she think of anything else?

Studying him, she wished with all her heart that she'd simply told him she loved him, the consequences be damned. Because she did love him, painfully. But they had to be smart.

When the time was right, she'd make sure he believed it and never had reason to doubt her again.

Ever.

"I promise," she said, a smile beginning to bloom across her lips.

He smiled back, a smile full of sweetness and patience and relief.

And love.

He loved her. And she loved him.

The knowledge was heady, euphoric, and she slid down, even more tightly against him, wanting to be part of him, wanting to communicate the strength of her feelings to him on a deep, almost spiritual level.

When he kissed her again, she poured herself into the meeting of lips and tongues and breaths, reveling in the sensations, the emotions.

The miracle.

He loved her.

It was amazing.

And it was terrifying.

25

Perfection.

She was perfection, he couldn't get enough. Couldn't get close enough, touch enough, feel enough. He wanted to breathe her in until she became a part of him, until every disparate particle of themselves fused together into a new whole.

She might not be sure it would work yet, but he was. He loved her. And she loved him. He didn't doubt it for a second.

So he'd be patient.

Well, he'd try.

He'd be her friend, like always, and kiss her brainless besides.

Jacob stroked his hands up, up, up beneath her pajama top, his fingers flexing and smoothing over her bare skin, her silky back, tracing her delicate shoulder blades and the length of her spine, driving himself crazy.

Her thighs grasped the outsides of his, and the very center of her rubbed over his erection, her core pressed tightly to him.

And the heat.

God.

Melinda flowed over him like molten lava, scorching hot, unbelievably sweet, her fingers and lips as grasping, as seeking as his.

He wanted their clothes gone, wanted naked skin to naked skin and himself engulfed by her flames.

A tiny, still-rational part of his brain intruded. He tried to shut it up, he really did, but it got louder instead, more insistent, until he had to listen.

And agree.

This wasn't right.

The time, the place. He'd promised to wait.

Besides, he couldn't take her here, in the middle of the family room on a rented condo's couch, where anyone could walk in at any moment and catch them together. Especially not their first time.

She deserved something special, she deserved care and time and attention. She deserved the best of him, the best he could give her, and right here, right now, was not it.

Damn it.

"Mel," he said, groaning her name against her lips. And again when she continued raining kisses over his mouth, his jaw, his cheeks and eyelids. "Mel."

Regretfully, he removed his hands from beneath her pajama top and smoothed it back into place over her hot, luscious skin, then dragged his fingers through her silky hair.

"Mmmmmm," she said.

Melinda gave him one more smacking kiss on the lips, then settled against his chest. He laid his head back against the couch's arm, every muscle in his body giving out.

Restraint had its costs.

Along with a serious case of sexual frustration, he didn't think he'd be able to drag up the strength or energy to move any time soon.

Then again, there was something to be said for snuggling on the couch with the woman he loved draped over his length, her breasts pillowed against his chest, her sweetly scented hair ticking the base of his throat.

There were worse sacrifices.

Melinda went back to drawing shapes on his chest, and they dozed for a time, the faint music of the New Year's Day parade lulling them in the background.

"Where is everyone?" she asked after a while.

Jacob squinted at the clock on the DVD player above the TV. Almost four o'clock. It was later than he'd thought.

"I don't know," he said. "I thought they were going to watch the football games, but they're not next door, or we would've heard them by now. Maybe they went to the lodge or skipped it all to go skiing. There's a lot of fresh powder again after yesterday's storm."

Melinda tensed against him, and he cursed himself for bringing Dane into the room with them with the mention of the day before.

He opened his mouth to say something, but she deliberately relaxed her muscles, hugging her arms around him and tucking her hands beneath him, between his body and the couch.

"We should talk," she said into his chest, the words muffled. "Some more. About all this."

"I know."

There was a long, quiet pause, while they each seemed to debate what to say first. Then, as one, they shifted up until they sat facing each other, their knees touching and hands held. Eyes searching.

She smiled at him, though it was shy around the edges.

"Pretty weird, huh?" she said, and he huffed out a laugh.

"Yeah."

Raking his hands through his hair, Jacob clasped her hands again, and said, "Listen, Mel—"

At that moment, the front door burst open, and a crowd of noisy people seemed to fall through the opening. He and Melinda dropped hands and scooted apart as they prepared to face the horde.

They came in stamping and blowing, complaining about the cold and rhapsodizing over the deep powder, bickering about the outcomes of the day's college-bowl games. Christian had evidently lost a bet with Wendell involving first-pass rights with a cute girl they'd met in the lodge earlier. He wasn't happy.

Melinda exchanged an amused glance with Jacob. Those two were forever arguing over girls, though never seriously. At least not so far.

Relief that she and Jacob seemed to be, at least for now, back on a fairly even keel, with the added bonus of some mind-blowing kisses rattling her memory banks, Melinda greeted everyone with a smile.

"Hi, guys," Jacob's dad called to them where they sat on the couch, watching as everyone stripped off their gear and made a general mess in the entryway. Bill's tone said everyone should behave normally, as though yesterday never happened. "You two have fun today?"

"Hey," they said back in unison, catching each other's eyes and looking away again quickly. Pointedly not answering *that* question.

Melinda couldn't imagine how Jacob's dad, or anyone, would react to a relationship between them. That was one of the questions she wasn't ready to answer.

"I call dibs on the first shower," Bill said over his shoulder. No one seemed to be paying any attention.

Nancy, on her way to the other condo, poked her platinum-blond head through the door, ducking beneath Stan's arm to catch Karen and Lois's attention.

"Give us about an hour next door," she said. "I'll make up the trays over there, and we'll meet you back here. Send one of the kids over to grab the extra drinks after you're settled."

"Will do," Lois said.

"Can you send Danny down to the mini-market for more chips?" Karen added. "Someone—" she cast a meaningful glance at her husband, "—finished off the last bag."

"What?" Stan said, all innocence.

"Sure thing," Nancy said, waving as she headed next door.

Wendell and Christian disposed of their gear in the laundry room, then came over to the couch and dropped down on the coffee table facing Melinda and Jacob, studying Melinda's face with identically pained expressions.

Wendell said, "Ouch. You almost match my sweater."

He grasped the front of said sweater and pulled on it, drawing it to their attention.

It was, characteristically, a wild riot of colors and clashed horribly with his bright red hair. Oranges mixed with reds, mixed with purples, yellows, and greens.

"I do not," Melinda said, half laughing, half indignant. "Nothing could look as bad as that sweater."

"Yeah, so shut it, Wen," Christian said, shoving at his friend. Jacob merely rolled his eyes.

To Melinda, Christian asked, "Does it still hurt?"

So much for pretending nothing had happened.

"It's fine," she said. For their benefit, she made her best gangster face and said, "You should see the other guy."

Wendell snorted. "I did see him, rolling on the ground in agony. Remind me never to piss you off." He winked at her and grinned, and she felt better again, Dane's shadow receding to the back of her mind.

Christian shoved Wendell again. "Too right," he said. "No one messes with our girl."

Seemingly satisfied, Wendell patted her on the knee, Christian patted her on the head, and they both gave Jacob oddly meaningful looks, which he ignored. Then they made their way into the kitchen to guzzle water and snag carrot sticks from the tray Karen was busy arranging.

Jacob reached for Melinda's hand and squeezed it surreptitiously. "Too right," he said, echoing Christian, and smiled.

"Don't you forget it," she answered, determined to keep

things upbeat.

The look they gave each other spoke of many things they couldn't voice out loud with everyone around them. Even though they still needed to talk things over, Melinda's nerves had settled again.

They would work it out.

"You two up for a party?" her mother called from the kitchen. "We're having a do-over for New Year's Eve."

Jacob, all energy again, bounced up from the couch and pulled Melinda with him toward the kitchen.

"Absolutely," he said, reaching for his own handful of carrot sticks and smacking Wendell's freckled fingers out of the way.

"Good," Karen said.

Wendell thwacked Jacob on the back of the head, then followed Christian back to the couch and changed the TV station to a late-afternoon football game.

Her mom continued to chop and arrange the carrots and celery, though she studied Melinda and Jacob closely. Her eyes filled with pain momentarily as she surveyed Melinda's bruises, but she quickly sniffed back her emotions. She focused on Melinda's eyes, instead, and Jacob's. Seeming to approve what she saw in their depths, she gave them each a smile.

"All right, then." Pointing at Wendell and Christian with her chopping knife, Karen said, "Jakey, take those two hooligans next door and see if Nancy needs any help."

Christian, overhearing her, whined, "Aunt Karen, the game's on!" Karen ignored him.

Melinda chuckled at the frown her younger cousin tossed first at her mother, then his own when he heard Aunt Pat's warningly intoned, "Christian," issue from the table where his mother sat slicing avocados.

"Mel, I need you to wash up the radishes and cherry tomatoes, please," her mom continued, "and hunt up the ranch dressing, then make some of those cheese squares your dad likes. Let's get this party rolling."

"Did I hear cheese squares?" Stan asked, dodging Jacob to snag his own handful of carrots and celery. He winked at

Melinda.

Though she would have preferred more time alone with Jacob, Melinda played along, grateful for the effort everyone was putting into recreating New Year's and the sense of normalcy.

"Okay, Daddy," she said, giving Stan a kiss on the cheek. "I'll get right on them. I just need to brush my teeth first."

She didn't look at Jacob, but he caught her drift.

"Yeah, me, too," he said.

Karen checked the watch on her wrist for the time. "You went all day without brushing your teeth? Dr. Parker isn't going to be happy with either of you on your next visits if you do that again. And you, big guy," she added, digging tickling fingers into Jacob's ribs and making him dance away, squealing like a girl, "won't be happy if you have to have another cavity filled. Remember what happened last time."

Jacob shuddered, and Melinda smirked at him. Her best pal didn't mind needles when they were meant for someone else, but try to stick him with one…

"Ha," Christian said from his spot on the couch. "Yeah. How'd that go again?"

Clearing his throat, Christian gave a high-pitched, warbling scream before falling back against the couch cushions, chortling hysterically at his own humor, while Wendell issued a longer, ululating version.

Melinda bit the insides of her cheeks—hard—to keep from laughing with them, though she knew her eyes gave her away when Jacob pinched her nose.

"Watch it, pipsqueaks," Jacob said, his brows lowered and topaz eyes glinting with promises of retribution, though his lips quirked. "I can get my hands on a needle or two for you clowns easily enough."

"Yeah, yeah," the boys said, waving dismissive hands in his direction before returning their attention to the game, unconcerned.

"Anyway," Jacob said to the room in general, "I was seven."

"Ha! You were eleven if you were a day," Melinda said. She gave him a saucy wink.

Jacob pokered up, his arms crossed. "Lots of kids don't like needles."

"Uh-huh," Karen said, reading Jacob's face perfectly, a smirk of her own riding her lips. "Lots of big kids, too, I hear. Go brush."

"We're going," Melinda said, plucking Jacob's sleeve, still struggling not to giggle as they headed for the bathroom. She squealed and jumped when he whacked her across the butt.

Closing the door behind them, Melinda leaned back against it and stared at Jacob, the grin fading from her lips.

Thinking of the familial invasion and the interruption of their discussion, she said, "That was…"

"I know," he said, reading her expression. "There's nothing we can do about it now."

"You're right," she said with a sigh. "But—"

"Yeah. But."

They brushed their teeth, and Melinda smoothed the tangles out of her hair while Jacob ran a wet comb through his. Finished, they faced each other again, and the seconds ticked slowly by.

At the same moment, they moved forward, moved into each other, wrapped their arms around each other, and clung.

Melinda tilted her head back, raising on tiptoe to meet his seeking mouth. She thrust her fingers into the hair at his nape, and he wrapped the length of hers in his fist and held on, pressing his hands into the small of her back.

They sank into the kiss with mutual groans, rubbing their bodies against each other in mutual frustration.

Knowing they had only moments, they poured everything they could into the kiss, and when they broke apart, they were both breathing heavily.

Melinda's lips stung, full and puffy from his mouth, her skin lightly abraded by his unshaven cheeks, but no one would notice it under the bruises.

They stared at each other for one long, weighted heartbeat, then reluctantly exited the bathroom and went to help prepare for the party.

"There's our champ," Danny said when he walked in the door of the condo, making a beeline for Melinda. He pulled her straight off her feet and kissed her lightly on each cheek before setting her down again. "How ya' feeling, Rocky?"

"Better," she said, giving his arm a squeeze. "Thanks."

"You're not on any meds or anything, are you?" he asked.

"No," Melinda answered with a frown. "Why?"

She did have a pile of pills in her suitcase, thanks to the totally unnecessary prescriptions the doctor had given her last night, which her mom had filled while they were out during the day. Just in case, she'd said.

Melinda had the impression the doctor had freaked out that Dane's attack on her had happened at the resort and wanted to make absolutely sure she was well-medicated, as if that would make up for it.

Whatever the reason, she hadn't taken anything.

"Good," Gabe answered instead, coming in behind Danny. He snagged one of her favorite fruity wine-coolers from the ice bucket on the kitchen counter, shook it up, and twisted off the top before handing the bottle to her and gently ruffling her hair. "Drink up. It's New Year's, after all."

"Thanks," she said, clinking bottles with the beer Gabe held in his other hand.

He winked at her, his deep green eyes gleaming. "I live to serve."

Melinda snorted, but smiled back. Danny and Gabe toasted her with their bottles, then moved on into the family room, joining Wendell, Christian, and Bill to watch the game. Her dad stood at her mother's elbow, sneaking food every chance he got, getting his hand smacked repeatedly for his trouble.

Jacob and his mother had gone next door to help haul trays and drinks for Nancy. Since Melinda had already finished the chores her mom had given her, she'd taken a few free minutes to change out of her pajamas and freshen up. Now she sat at the kitchen table, one bare foot braced on a second chair, painting her toenails a bright, sunset pink, and watching the antics of her family and friends.

No amount of makeup would completely cover the bruising or the scrapes on her face, which looked much worse than it actually was, thanks to her Irish heritage and pale skin. And her jeans and dark-purple sweater were a far cry from the red dress she'd worn the night before. But she felt better, and more festive, for having made the effort.

"Hey, it's the Terminator," Rick said, sliding into the chair opposite and scrutinizing her face.

"Movie one or two?" she wanted to know.

"Neither," Eddie disagreed, taking the seat next to her cousin. "Rambo. You've definitely got the Rambo vibe going on."

"All right, boys," Lois said, walking through the condo's open door with Jacob on her heels, both laden with trays. "Leave the girl alone and come help me with these."

Rick and Eddie jumped up to take the food from Lois's hands, leaving Jacob to balance his overfull trays on his own, while Melinda frowned thoughtfully after them, trying to decide which movie tough guy she'd rather be known as. None of them seemed quite right.

"What about Dirty Harry?" she asked the room at large, to a chorus of loud nos.

"Why not?" she asked, offended.

"You don't have the *cojones* for Harry, sweet pea," Gabe said from the couch, then shoved a handful of corn chips in his mouth.

"But the Terminator, Rocky, Rambo..." She trailed off meaningfully.

Gabe shrugged. "Not Harry."

"Not Terminator," Eddie repeated his earlier opinion. "It's the same thing. Him and Harry are calm, cool, deliberate. Rocky and Rambo—they're temper and flash, emotion. Unpredictable. Like a woman, only badass."

"Hey!" all the women in the condo chorused, Aunt Pat loudest of all.

"Dude, did you just call Rambo a *woman?*" Danny asked, astounded.

"Son, did you just call a woman not badass?" Aunt Pat asked Danny, who wisely clamped his mouth shut.

"I think Eddie's got it right," Jacob put in, with a grin full of secrets only for Melinda. "Hot-blooded badasses are the ticket, more like you."

"Hmm," she said, slightly mollified, though she'd been pretty damn proud of her calm, cool, and deliberate action in kneeing Dane in *his* tiny little *cojones.*

"Rick," Karen said in a scolding tone of voice as she came back into the kitchen, "save some of those for Stan."

Standing at the kitchen counter with his mouth full of cheese squares, Rick leaned out of reach of her mother's swatting hands and tapped the side of his nose, tilting his head as he studied Melinda thoughtfully.

"I dunno, Mel," he said. "We already established you're a little crazy, so I'm thinking more Martin Riggs."

Melinda narrowed her eyes at her cousin, but after thinking it over, nodded decisively.

"I'll let the crazy part pass," she said magnanimously, "but I can live with that one. Riggs it is."

The *Lethal Weapon* movies made up one of her favorite series, and Mel Gibson's character in them was a quadruple threat—tough, tender, funny, and sexy—even if nowadays he was way old. If she couldn't pull off Dirty Harry, she'd settle happily for a female version of Martin Riggs.

Eddie's dad and Uncle Allan squeezed through the door next, another cooler grasped between them, which they trucked down the short hallway to the storage area.

"What's in the cooler, Dad?" Eddie asked. "We already brought over all the drinks."

"Never you mind, son," Peter said, coming back into the kitchen and clasping his son on the shoulder. "It's for later."

Swinging behind her chair on his way back to the other condo for more trays, Jacob leaned close to Melinda's ear and whispered, "If you're Riggs, does that make me the blond he gets together with in the second movie, or the brunette he gets in the third?"

Melinda snorted out a laugh, but he was gone before she could come up with an answer.

26

The party went on until the wee hours of the next morning.

Zach called in the early evening, a welcome surprise since they'd just talked with him at Christmas. They shifted to FaceTime so everyone could get in on the call.

Predictably, her mom teared up a bit, and Melinda did, too.

She missed her big brother.

It was so great to see him, and he looked relaxed and happy, though he'd had seven fits when he first caught sight of her face and heard the story of New Year's Eve. She was glad when they got past that point, though she noted Zach kept glancing at her in concern whenever she was on screen.

After a dinner made up mostly of finger foods—in astounding quantities, though the guys pillaged the trays like a plague of locusts descending—the surprise in the extra cooler turned out to be a chocolate ice cream cake, Melinda's favorite. Nancy and Peter had driven all the way to the town at the bottom of the mountain to make the purchase earlier that day.

The cake, like everything else, disappeared in record time.

They watched the evening football games, played a few

games themselves, listened to music. Conversations sprang up everywhere. Laughter rang. Groups shifted, blended, broke apart, reformed in new combinations.

Melinda scanned the condo, contentment settling in her heart. She'd enjoyed the big New Year's Eve party the night before. Well, at least until the end. She loved large gatherings, big, dressy events, lots of noise and people. But this—her family and friends all in one place, comfy and casual, sharing the night together, just them—this was her favorite sort of party.

After the final bowl game, they put the first *Lethal Weapon* movie on, in honor of Melinda. She bowed for their applause, and the last shred of Dane's specter vanished from her mind. Yes, he'd knocked her around, but that was as far as it had gone, and the lingering fear over what might have happened disappeared as well.

Later, Rick badgered his brothers into presenting a short one-act play like the ones they used to do when they were kids, although this one was a lot more risqué.

Melinda held her belly in giggle-pain, howling with laughter when Danny threw down a dance-off challenge in the middle of it and came out the clear winner over Gabe, Eddie, and Wendell.

During a brief lull in the evening, Rick grabbed Melinda by the hand and dragged her off to the hall bathroom, closing the door behind them and pulling her to sit on the side of the tub.

"So, Riggs," he said, and made her laugh. "How're you feeling?"

Because his eyes went serious when he asked, she answered him the same way. "I'm good. Really."

"Good," he said, then wrapped her up in a hug.

His blond curls tickled her nose, but her eyes went a little teary. For all his wild antics, Rick could be every bit as sweet as Christian, as older-brother-ish and protective as Danny. The three of them, along with Jacob and her brother, were her champions.

She was surrounded by them, really, including Eddie, Gabe, and Wendell in their number, and her Honeywell cousins, too. Each one of them was so different, but at their cores, they were all genuinely good people.

Her heroes.

She was a lucky girl.

Momentarily overcome, Melinda sniffled, and Rick cleared his throat and patted her back.

"Scared me," he said, squeezing her a little tighter. "All of us."

"Me, too," she whispered.

Rick held onto her another minute, then gave her a heartier pat and sat back to scan her face again, suddenly brisk.

"But you're good, so we're good, right?"

"Right," she said, pulling her composure back together.

"Great. Then can I ask you a favor?" His blue eyes twinkled merrily, which should have given her warning.

"Of course."

"Can I borrow your makeup and try to copy some of this?" he asked, waving at the *this* that was her bruised face.

The belly laugh took her by surprise every bit as much as his request.

"Sure," she said, rolling her eyes but still laughing, standing to grab her makeup bag.

"Thanks," Rick said, moving beside her and pawing through her eyeliners and shadows. "Hey, this purple's perfect."

He turned to the mirror and brushed a healthy swipe of the powder across his right cheek, studying the effect.

"I've got a post-fight scene in a thing I'm doing next month," he explained, "and pulling off this look would be awesome. The girl who's doing the makeup's not so good with the blood-and-guts stuff."

"Have at it," Melinda said, waving her hand.

"Here," he said, grabbing her around the waist and hoisting her onto the counter. "Tilt your head to the left so I can get a good look—no, not that far, just, yeah right there. Now don't move."

Well used to Rick's fascination with her makeup, Melinda tilted and turned at his direction while he played. He had to crouch down to see himself clearly in the mirror due to his height, which only made it funnier. There was something about watching her tall, muscular, ultra-handsome, very masculine cousin fool around with her products like any one of her girlfriends that always put her in a good mood.

"So," he said a while later, as he fluffed blusher on his temple over several layers of her favorite eye-shadow to deepen the bruising effect, "what's going on with you and Jake?"

Melinda startled, her eyes flying wide as they met her cousin's in the mirror.

Oh, that was sneaky.

He'd lulled her into relaxation with the small talk and makeup-artist routine, then pounced when she'd least expected it, and it was too late to cover her obvious reaction.

That didn't mean she wouldn't give it a try.

Settling an innocent expression on her face, she said, "What do you mean?"

Rick snorted with disgust. "Melinda, whatever you do, don't try for a career on the stage."

She folded her arms over her chest and glared, affronted, her nose in the air. She was so not discussing this with him, or anyone, until she and Jacob worked out what was what. Rick went back to fluffing her blush brush over his face, studying her mulish expression and clamped lips in the mirror.

"The silent treatment, huh?" Blush, brush, fluff. "Okay, then, let me tell you what I know."

Snapping the blush compact shut, he tossed it back in her bag and turned to face her directly, leaning his hip against the counter.

"I know Jake hasn't been able to keep his eyes off you for months," he said, then paused when her eyes went round. "What, don't tell me you haven't noticed."

"Months?" she mouthed, almost silently.

She'd thought this whole thing was a recent development on his end. Months? How could she have missed it?

Her mind supplied the answer.

Mitch.

She'd been wrapped up in Mitch and hardly noticed anything outside their own little circle.

If she had seen, if she had known... Would it have changed anything? Impossible to know, though it gave her a funny thrumming under her heart.

Why had Jacob never said anything?

"Yes, months," Rick said, talking over her thought process. "I know *you* haven't been able to keep your eyes off *him* your whole life, and—"

"What?" Melinda interrupted, unwilling to expose her feelings in front of Rick before hashing them out with Jacob. "Don't be stupid, I never thought about him that way. We're friends."

The memory of every secret-marriage fantasy she'd ever had about Jacob danced through her head, one frame after another speeding by and putting the lie to her words, but they'd been just that—short, sweet, innocent little crushes, quickly buried under the weight of their friendship and the sure knowledge that their futures would never mesh.

And okay, she'd never said anything to Jacob, either, but that was because she'd known those fantasies had no hope of becoming real. Their friendship had always been the most important thing in her life.

It still was, if it came right down to it.

Wishing for anything more was just…

Was just…

Well, it was exactly what they were doing right now, wasn't it? Hoping. Wanting. He'd declared his love to her, and despite how things had gone earlier, she loved him desperately, so it was different now. Real. Or it could be.

If she was brave.

Oh, God.

"Don't *you* be stupid," Rick said. Unaware of her inner turmoil, he took a washcloth and scrubbed off all the layers of makeup. "You forget how well I know you. Of course you thought about him that way. You guys have danced around it for years."

Years, Melinda thought, suddenly very glad she was already sitting down.

"When you brought Mitch home," Rick continued, "we all thought that was the end of it, so thank God that's over."

Surprised yet again, Melinda gaped at him. "You guys liked

Mitch."

"Eh," he said with a shrug. "We liked him for your sake. I always thought he was sort of a slimy git, but that's not the way to start things off with someone you might end up related to eventually."

"But..."

"I never took you and Jake seriously until I got hit in the face with it—which is sort of how you look right now, by the way—but now it clicks."

Melinda sat staring at her hands, clasped loosely in her lap, wondering if someone had spiked the single wine cooler she'd had earlier. She felt half-drunk, as though the counter and floor kept shifting beneath her, and her head swam dizzily, but it was information and emotion overload causing it, not the alcohol.

"Hey, kid," Rick said, placing a hand on her shoulder and waiting until she met his gaze. His expression now was repentant. "Have you two not talked about this yet?"

Melinda could only shake her head. Then nod. Then shake. They had. Sort of. Okay, yes, but... Not really. Not fully.

Oh, God.

Why did hearing about it from Rick make is somehow more real, more scary?

"Ah," he said, and pressed his forehead to hers. "Sorry. I just wanted to tease you, I didn't realize... Christian said—"

Melinda's head popped up, eyes narrowed. "Christian? What does Christian have to do with this?"

"He said—that is, he talked, uh..." Straightening, Rick cleared his throat. His blue eyes went shifty. "Maybe I should just..."

Watching her warily, he stretched a hand behind him for the doorknob, obviously hoping to escape the conversation. She wasn't letting him off that easily.

"Richard Dean Carlisle," she said, jumping down and pointing to her vacated spot on the counter. "Sit."

Ducking his head, Rick did as bade, hopping up on the tiled surface and swinging his feet like a naughty four-year-old. "You sound like my mother."

"Now," Melinda said, disregarding that comment and

leaning into his space, "what did Christian say?"

Rick ran a finger under his collar. "Only that he talked to Jacob and we were right and—"

"Who's 'we' and right about what?"

"Danny, and, um—"

"Danny, too?" Melinda rubbed a hand across her forehead and the sudden ache blooming smack in the middle of her eyes. "You guys are worse than a bunch of gossiping girls, you know that?"

It took some more grilling, but finally it all became clear. She wanted to smack them upside their handsome blond heads for interfering, though she supposed her cousins had their hearts in the right place. And if they were right, Jacob had had feelings for her for a lot longer than she'd suspected. Maybe he hadn't planned to marry her when they were four, the way she had, but still…

"I cannot believe you guys talked to Jacob about all this and not me," she said.

Rick shrugged, unconcerned. "Guy code."

"Guy code? How about family code, dork?"

"Girls are heartbreakers, Mel," he said, pointing a finger and scratching the tip of her nose. She batted his hand away, though guilt stabbed through her mind. She didn't want to break Jacob's heart. "Men have got to stick together. Besides, Jake's practically family, too."

"Huh," she said, "I'll remember that the next time any of you are dating someone."

"Now, Mel—"

"And by the way," she added, firing up again, "if no one liked Mitch, a little heads-up would have been nice!"

Now he had the grace to look abashed.

Hunching his shoulders, he said, "We thought you were going to marry the guy. Would you have listened if we'd said anything?"

Considering him, Melinda searched herself for truth. And sighed, relenting.

"No, probably not. I thought… Well, it doesn't matter what I thought."

Seeming to believe he was safe now, Rick slid off the counter and hugged her.

"Mitch didn't deserve you, sweetie," he said. "Jake does. No one belongs together more than you two. Even if the whole thing is weird beyond words and cracks me up."

Jacob deserved a lot more than her waffling. She couldn't let Rick see the conflict in her eyes. She and Jacob loved each other, belonged together. She believed that without question. But man, the logistics were a bitch.

She set it aside to think about later.

"Thanks," Melinda said, then pushed her cousin away with a playful huff. "And shut up."

"I mean it," he said.

"But..." Melinda paused, shifting awkwardly, the worry getting the better of her.

Did she really want to ask the question burning a hole through the center of her heart? More importantly, did she really want an honest answer?

"What?" Rick asked, checking his face in the mirror for any last traces of makeup and flicking his curls back into place.

"Is it... Do you think it's bad, or, I don't know, says something, you know—" *Spit it out, Melinda.* "—says something bad about me that it seems like I've gotten over Mitch so fast? Maybe this is all rebounding, because you know Jacob just broke up with somebody, too, and—"

"Mel," Rick interrupted her babbling with a dramatic eye roll. "My God, you think too much."

Tossing his second washcloth into the hamper, he straightened to his full height, brushed his hands off, and became very businesslike.

"All it tells me is that you're smarter than the average girl, which I already knew, and Jacob's maybe smarter than the average guy, which is a huge surprise—"

"Shut up."

"—but seriously, where's it written that you have to pull your hair and gnash your teeth over a breakup for any particular length of time? That kind of thing plays better on the stage."

"I don't know," Melinda said, frowning at her nails. "It

seems so unfeeling. So cold, to love somebody one day and be over them the next. Don't most people go through a mourning period? Even if the whole thing was a lie…" She trailed off lamely, confused and uncertain.

Gentle now, Rick hugged her again, and Melinda rested her cheek against his steady heartbeat.

"I think you did mourn him, intensely, for two full days," he said, "which is way more than the bastard deserved. I think you're a good, strong, loving person, whose natural tendency is to be positive and bounce back, not wallow around in misery. Especially misery caused by a guy who turned out to be a liar and a coward. And I think you deserve to be happy again, as soon as humanly possible, and for the rest of your life."

"You're sure?" she asked, chewing her bottom lip. This particular point seemed monumentally important.

"I'm sure."

"What about our families and everything? If he and I—"

"What? You guys aren't Romeo and Juliet, caught in the middle of feuding families. Stay away from daggers and poison and you'll be fine."

"No, it's worse! They're all best friends. *We're* best friends, and if we mess it up we'll destroy their friendships, too, not just ours. All of us, our whole group would be different. Think about it. Jake's your friend, too."

"Of course he is, so what?"

"Do you remember my friends, Carl and Donna? When they broke up, it was a disaster for everyone. And Jake's aunt and uncle are getting divorced and—"

"Wow, you've got a whole apocalypse going on in there," Rick interrupted, drilling a finger into the middle of her forehead. He gave her a wicked grin. "I'd be more worried about both of your sucky relationship track records."

"Thanks a lot. I'm serious."

"Me, too." He sighed. "Listen, Mel, first of all, give the rest of us a little credit. We'll handle our own relationships, however the chips fall. You can't avoid taking a risk because it might upset some people later."

"It's not only that," she protested. "I don't want to lose

him, either."

"Mel, he loves you. He told me so himself, and Christian, too. If you love him, that's all that matters. And give yourselves some credit, too. You've been friends your whole lives. Do you really think you'd throw that away because the romance didn't work out?"

"But—"

If you love him...

She did. So, so much. But sometimes love wasn't enough.

Opening the door at his back, Rick grasped her chin, leaning into her face until they were nose to nose.

"Follow your heart, not your head, cousin o'mine, 'cuz we already know how twisted your brain is." Before she could smack at him, he dropped a kiss on her nose, then backed away. "Now, listen, because you're right about one thing. Jacob's a good guy, and he's my friend. So don't screw it up."

Then he ran before she could hit him with her hairbrush.

27

Melinda followed Rick out of the bathroom slowly, her brows pinched together. What a bizarre conversation. Not that *bizarre* was unusual where conversations with Rick were concerned, but a knot of unsettled sensation had lodged itself somewhere between her lungs and her belly.

Half reassured, half not.

She sighed.

Follow her heart.

It sounded so easy, and maybe it would be if she could trust in a future that would make them both happy. She loved Jacob. She believed he loved her. What to do about it was something else again.

Rick was one to talk about the track record thing—he'd never had a successful relationship, either—even if he was right about her and Jacob. Neither of them had stayed with anyone more than a few months. Mitch was the closest she'd come to a real relationship, and their three months together had been built on a foundation of lies.

Then again, she and Jacob had already been best friends

their entire lives. That had to count for something, didn't it?

What made a successful relationship at their ages, anyway? Fun, friendship, respect, they had those. Loyalty, trust. Shared values. Similar interests, too. They loved each other's friends and families. She ticked each item off on mental fingers.

And they were *clearly* hot for each other, she added with a guilty snicker.

She was only twenty-one. Jacob, too. It wasn't like any of them, even including her older cousins or her brother or any of their friends, were looking to get married now.

They were only having fun.

But...

Melinda stopped in the middle of the hallway.

Married.

If she and Jacob got together, it could never be only about having fun, not with their history. Their families. A boulder seemed to crash land in the middle of her chest, the weight of it immense.

For a moment, she couldn't breathe.

She'd had shades of that thought before, yet now that a real potential future stared her in the face, it suddenly seemed much scarier.

It wasn't only about where they'd live or their careers, that was just the stage dressing and ignored the larger issue completely. They were fooling themselves. There was no way in hell they could get together, really together, and stay friends if they broke up. It would be too huge. They'd never survive it. A romantic relationship between them could have only two possible outcomes: marriage or disaster.

Could they survive those expectations, that pressure?

Were they ready?

Was she?

Rubbing a hand over her chest, Melinda sucked in a breath and forced her feet forward. There was only one way to find out, but the risks seemed insurmountable.

Reaching the kitchen, she flopped into one of the chairs at the dining table, smiling weakly at Aunt Pat, Lois, and Nancy, who had a deck of cards out, playing poker at the far end of the table.

"Okay, sweetie?" Lois asked.

Melinda avoided Aunt Pat's piercing, speculative stare and Nancy's anxious one, but nodded to Lois, not trusting herself to speak quite yet. What could she say?

Oh, sure. I'm just desperately in love with your son and thinking about all the grandbabies we're going to give you and Bill someday…

She swallowed the panicky laugh. Yeah, right.

The ladies studied her another moment, then went back to their game. Melinda aimed for casual, surreptitiously calming her breathing as she propped her chin in her hand and surveyed the crowd of people spread over the condo.

Her mother perched on the arm of the recliner where her dad sat, deep in conversation with Uncle Allan, Peter, and Bill. Karen had one arm draped around Stan's neck, and her fingers lightly toyed with the ends of his hair. He had a drink in one hand, his other arm wrapped casually over her mother's thighs, his big hand absently stroking the outside of her calf.

Love for her parents swamped her, made her teary. They were so wonderful together.

Neither of them were really paying attention to each other—they were involved in the group discussion—yet their body language spoke of not only their love for each other, but deep affection, genuine friendship, and an ease together that came from years and years of all three. There was such trust and security between them. Melinda wished she hadn't left her camera upstairs.

She and Jacob could have that. Had the potential for that. If they were brave. If they could sort out their goals and get past all those external hurdles.

His parents were the same, though perhaps not as touchy-feely as hers, at least in public. But she and Jacob both came from that sort of solid, happily-married background. Within the older generation of family and friends, they had plenty of good examples to follow for building a lasting relationship. And between them, they already had the history and affection, the ease and friendship, the trust.

Passion, too.

Yeah.

Sexual attraction was clearly not an issue, she thought again, and had to suppress another wild snicker as an image from earlier in the day burst into her mind, and a deeply sensual zing shot straight to her core.

It lit her up like a comet, every nerve end tingling. She gasped. She couldn't help it.

Melinda cast her eyes around quickly to make sure no one could read her emotions on her face, and gasped yet again when she found Jacob's eyes blazing into her own from across the room, burning her up with the golden flames dancing in their depths.

God.

Everything inside her tightened, trembled, twisted into a knot of need so taut it was nearly painful. She couldn't tear her eyes away. The space between them seemed to crackle, as though live wires writhed over the innocent carpet and bland linoleum, scorching everything in their wake.

Oh. Oh-oh-oh.

She made some sound deep in her throat, a sort of hum, then coughed to cover it when she caught Aunt Pat glancing her way out of the corner of her eye.

Jacob grinned.

Slowly.

Wickedly.

The memory of the kisses they'd shared flared brighter, sent the tingles spiraling. His expression said he knew exactly what she was thinking.

Wanting.

Needing.

He blinked, again slowly, his eyes half-lidded now as he stared at her, holding her prisoner with his gaze, and his lips parted. Just a bit. Just enough to have her thinking about his tongue. About the way he'd ravaged her mouth.

His eyes promised he'd do it again.

Melinda's hands began to sweat. Her breathing changed, still too fast, but deeper now, and she became acutely aware of the rise and fall of her chest, of her breasts lifting beneath her sweater, her rigid nipples brushing the insides of her bra cups.

Aching.

Hungering.

Jacob's gaze landed there, an almost physical caress. Swept lower. Her thigh muscles clenched. His grin widened. Went wolfish.

His eyes said he wanted—needed—too.

Jacob licked his lips, and oh, God, she was one hard heartbeat away from throwing all caution to the winds, leaping on him, and devouring him whole.

They had to stop this before she orgasmed right here, in front of everyone, in front of her *family*, in the middle of the damn condo.

She needed air.

Water.

An ice-cold shower.

He held her there on the strength of his gaze alone, motionless, yet quivering with need. He kept her poised on the dangerous edge until the quivers became a quake, until the quake threatened to shake her apart, to toss her right over that edge and out into space.

At the last possible second, he relented. The fire in his eyes banked to a smolder, and the intensity dimmed. His mouth quirked, a friendly grin. His dimples flashed. He winked at her before turning his gaze away.

Melinda collapsed back in her seat, equal parts raging, unfulfilled desperation, and shivering, helpless relief.

She'd had no idea he stocked that kind of fire power in his arsenal.

There would come a time she'd make him pay for it, too, she vowed, in every delicious way she could think of. She might even research a few more online.

For now, thank God, her temperature, her breathing, and her hard, pounding pulse were returning to normal, and no one seemed any the wiser.

But still, she craved…

Scanning the room again, she swallowed a slightly hysterical giggle. Seriously, how tuned out were these people? They'd just missed one hell of a show.

No, desire was not a problem for them. Unexpected, yes. And wonderful and amazing and so, just... Wow. Breathtaking. Soul shaking. But a problem? No.

Cautiously, Melinda rose to her feet, grateful to find her legs would hold her. Jacob's eyes met hers again, and she gave her head one quick shake, telling him not to follow her. She needed a minute.

She escaped upstairs and flopped on her bed, her arms and legs splayed wide, gulping air into her lungs the way she hadn't been able to downstairs without drawing unwanted attention. Eyes closed, she waited for her overblown system to finish leveling out.

Melinda ran her fingers through her hair and down her body, remembering Jacob's hands smoothing the curls down her back, sweeping across her bare skin. She'd thought his kisses were potent, and they were. Oh, they were. No question.

But *whew*.

She'd never experienced anything like what just happened. From simple eye contact.

Her pulse rate picked up again simply thinking about it, and her body cried out with unsatisfied needs. If he could do that with a glance, what would it be like when they finally...

Oh, boy.

She needed a distraction.

Remembering her camera, Melinda finally relaxed fully. Perfect. She could hide behind the lens for a while, keep a barrier between herself and Jacob. She couldn't afford for him to send her into orbit in front of everyone again. Not until they talked and either made things official... or backed off before it was too late.

Jacob watched from beneath lowered lids as Melinda descended the loft stairs twenty minutes later. She had her new camera around her neck and composure pasted over her face, but she didn't fool him. Even from this distance, he could see the pulse jumping at the base of her throat.

Good.

His was, too.

Holy crap, he'd thought his body was going to explode when their eyes tangled. The thrill of it, of taking her to that edge and knowing he kept her there, knowing she'd responded to him so fully, even while they were surrounded by people in the crowded room...

Not even touching.

It was incredible.

He'd deliberately set out to seduce her, yet at the end of it, she wasn't the only one so turned on she could hardly walk a straight line to the staircase.

Hot.

She was incredibly, astoundingly hot.

And that wasn't all, but... Was it any wonder he hadn't been able to keep her out of his head these past many months?

He'd never experienced that sort of compelling force before, that level of desperation. His craving for her was out of control.

Even now, with his body finally beaten back into submission, he could feel the threads of restraint straining against the need the closer she moved.

Melinda smiled at him as she lifted the camera to her face and snapped his picture. Jacob wondered what the photograph would show when she had it printed. Would she be able to read the lust in his eyes?

"Kidney bean," he said, so nobody around them would notice anything off. Hoping nobody would notice the sizzling intensity sparking off both of them in flashes and flares.

"Eggplant."

He hoped no one else said anything to him, because their voices were nothing but bees buzzing in his brain. His ears seemed tuned only to her voice, low and husky and just a little amused, and God, so sexy.

Just looking at her now short-circuited his system.

Moving around behind him, she trailed a finger inside the collar of his shirt along the base of his neck, and chills raced down his spine, then flashed outward to either side like an electrical storm. He shuddered visibly, and his whole body sprang with damp.

Aha, he thought over the vibrations coursing along his skin. *She still wants to play.*

Jacob reached backward, grasping for a knee or a leg, but she danced out of range, laughing at him. Though he let her go, she sent him a long, slow smile in return for the look he gave her. His heart kicked hard in his chest, but he grinned.

After that, she kept her distance, seeming to concentrate on taking candids of everyone, but he could still smell her, still feel the heat of her, no matter where she stood or sat in the room. He caught her watching him through the camera lens more than once.

Aside from missing her touch, missing her sitting beside him the way she usually did, he really wished they could find a chance to talk about everything. Maybe later, when everyone else was in bed.

Guilt stabbed at him, one sharp jolt. He should have told her about the internships. About Irvine. About all of it, before laying the whole I-love-you thing on her. Their differing goals and plans were the whole problem as far as Melinda was concerned, and he'd backed her into a corner without giving her all the information.

She wasn't going to be happy with him.

Then again, something surprising had shifted inside him this past week, unrelated to his feelings for Melinda. Something that might end up making both of them very happy, if he could wrap his head around the changes. But he had to be sure he was doing it for the right reasons. Lasting reasons.

He didn't want to make a huge mistake and wind up locked into a life he'd neither wished for nor considered.

"Did you finally figure it out, son?" his dad asked, sitting beside him.

Jacob stared at him quizzically. Bill only stared back, a meaningful look on his face.

"Figure what out, Dad?"

Leaning in close, Bill spoke for his ears alone. "That she's the one."

Jacob sat back, thoughtful now. He'd suspected, hadn't he, that his dad knew something was up. He never could pull anything over on that man.

Slowly, Jacob nodded.

His dad grinned, nodded back. Slapped him on the knee as he rose.

"Glad to hear it," Bill said. "Go get your woman, son. It's about time."

With that, his dad wound his way into the kitchen, whispered into his mom's ear. Her smile broke out like sunlight, and she looked his way, her eyes dancing. His parents toasted each other with the drinks in their hands.

Yeah, so much for keeping any of it under wraps. At least they were happy about it, which gave him a pleasantly glowing warmth under his heart. He'd never doubted they would be, but it was good to have some confirmation.

Now if only Melinda would be happy, too…

Tracking her with his eyes, he groaned silently. He knew what he wanted. But what was she really thinking?

Waiting had never been so hard.

Melinda moved around the room snapping her photos, including the one she'd wanted earlier of her parents, who'd luckily been in the same position when she returned from the loft. Her dad squeezed her hand as she moved around the group, taking shots at different angles.

She took part in various conversations as she went, including a heated debate with Eddie over whether or not Melinda needed all of her high-heeled shoes.

By the time the argument ended, she couldn't even remember how it had started—something Gabe had said about his sister Holly's shoe collection, possibly—but she'd made sure Eddie was well-schooled on the utter irrelevance of any man's opinion over the number of shoes owned by any woman.

"Unless your name is Christian Louboutin or Jimmy Choo," she said, poking him in the chest, "I don't want to hear about my shoes from you."

Eddie, his gray eyes dancing, merely grabbed her finger and gave it a friendly waggle. "Whatever you say, princess."

"Just you remember that," she said with an elegant sniff.

Shifting to scan the rest of the younger crowd, she found Christian and Wendell seated on the floor by the big window. They'd broken out the chessboard and had it propped on a footstool between them, though she couldn't see it clearly enough from her angle to tell who was winning. They were both frowning intently, Christian's straight blond hair falling over his eyes in bright contrast to Wendell's wild, wavy red mop and crazy sweater.

Melinda lined them up in her frame and inched closer, snapping several shots without them noticing. Checking the last one in the viewer, she despaired over Wendell's woolen abomination. Seriously, where on earth did he find those patterns?

She moved on.

Danny and Gabe stood in the kitchen, leaning their hips against opposite counters and talking in low voices between bites of whatever was left of the chips and dip, beer bottles in hand. She settled on the arm of the couch next to her Uncle Allan, who gave her an absent pat on the knee while he continued talking with Peter, Bill, and her dad.

Melinda took several quick shots of her cousin and Gabe, liking the way the lights shone on their hair, Danny's so light and Gabe's so dark.

Eddie, Rick, and Jacob wandered into the kitchen to join

the other two, digging in the fridge for more drinks. That was a whole lot of handsome male in one room. She snapped away, and they mostly ignored her as they talked.

Mentally planning out scrapbooks to give as gifts for each of their mother's birthdays over the coming year, she was about to lower the lens when Jacob shifted and looked squarely into the camera, his topaz eyes intense. Her breath caught, but she pressed the shutter almost without thought.

When he looked away again, she checked the shot.

It was a one-in-a-million photo.

Jacob stared back at her from the viewer, his bronze hair gleaming and lightly tousled, his carved cheekbones highlighted by the overhead lamps, his mouth unsmiling but lifted ever-so-slightly in a sensual curve, with only the barest hint of his dimples. His expression was serious, direct. Sensual.

Powerful.

By pure chance, she'd framed him perfectly against the tall, cream-colored kitchen cupboards, as though he'd posed before a professional photographer's backdrop. She noted some minor distractions on the counter beside him, but she could edit those out.

The photo was all about the man, and Jacob looked amazing.

Pursing her lips, Melinda returned to the family room area and sat next to her father, studying the photo. Stan entered some of his photographs in the LA County Fair's art exhibit every year, and she'd already planned to enter the one she'd taken of her parents and Jacob's on New Year's Eve.

If she could get Jacob to agree, she wanted to enter this one in the portrait division. She might be an amateur, but as deceptively simple as Jacob's photo was, she thought it might win.

28

They broke out the champagne at midnight and toasted each other's health and happiness, as if it was New Year's Eve for real.

Jacob and Melinda clinked glasses along with everyone else. He restrained himself from dragging her into a serious lip lock in front of the rest of the group.

Just barely.

He had plans for later, though.

Wendell and Christian, both underage, complained good-naturedly over getting stuck with sparkling cider, as usual.

By the time the party ended more than two hours later, after the occupants of the second condo headed next door, and his and Melinda's parents went to bed, Jacob felt like he'd run a marathon. His body had been in a constant state of sexual frustration, and even though he and Melinda had slept late that morning, they both were going on relatively little sleep given the late hour they'd gone to bed.

Coupled with the emotional frustration, it was no wonder he was exhausted.

Muscles aching, fuzzy-headed, he wanted nothing more

than to haul his ass upstairs, fall into Melinda's bed, wrap his arms around her, kiss her senseless, then sleep for twenty-four hours.

Christian and Wendell had already crashed in the sofa-bed, and Melinda had gone to brush her teeth. Jacob sat at the kitchen table waiting his turn. Despite the fatigue, he hadn't quite trusted himself to leave her alone if he'd gone in to brush his teeth at the same time.

And still, the weight of her not giving the words back to him hung between them.

He would wait, and she would think. There wasn't much he could do to alleviate the pressure, aside from treating things as normally as possible.

When she came down the hallway, all minty-fresh and ready for bed, her smile bloomed by slow degrees, and the deep, glimmering blue pools of her eyes never left his. She didn't stop, only stroked the underside of his jaw with a slender finger as she walked toward the stairs, that one subtle touch waking up every nerve and neuron in his body.

She said, "Pineapple chunk," in a deliberately teasing, deeply sultry whisper she cast over her shoulder, her chin lowered and her eyes heavy-lidded, staring at him seductively through her lashes.

He felt every one of those wide-awake neurons fry and die.

Melinda put one foot on the bottom step, one hand on the railing, and her pajama top lifted an inch, enough to show an enticing ribbon of pale, velvety skin.

Jacob opened his mouth like a fish out of water. Where did all the oxygen go?

He meant to say, "Curly-fry," in response, but his mind had simply wiped clean with that one little glimpse of skin, with her scent twining around him, and the only word that came out of his mouth was a whispered, "Beautiful."

Melinda stumbled a bit on the stairs in surprise. Her head jerked up to meet his eyes, and hers went wide and dark and so very blue. Her lips formed a small 'o' as pink rushed into her cheeks.

The two of them held there, frozen, staring, and then she

laughed, and it lit her entire face.

Her smile dazzled.

Blowing him a saucy kiss, she continued up the stairs. Jacob didn't even bother trying not to watch the sway of her ass as she climbed. He licked his lips.

That girl—he pounded a fist on his chest over his speeding heart. She'd poleaxed him, as his grandfather liked to say.

At least he knew one thing for certain. The heat between them was not even a tiny bit one-sided. Their future might be uncertain, but their bodies had no doubts.

She wanted him every bit as much as he wanted her.

Still recovering from the effect of her smile, Jacob wobbled a little when he stood to make his way down the hall. He took his time changing into his pjs, brushing and flossing, then brushing the knots out of his hair.

The scruffiness on his cheeks reminded him he hadn't shaved since early yesterday, so he took out his razor, dealt with it. Swiping a hand over his smooth cheek, he nodded. At least now he wouldn't scrape Melinda's soft skin when he kissed her.

And because the mere thought of kissing her sent an arrow of pure lust zinging to his gut, he took an extra moment to settle himself back down.

When he got back to the kitchen, he snapped the last light off, plunging the lower level of the condo into the mostly-dark of one small nightlight, the upper level into solid ebony. He glanced toward the tall windows. It was pitch black outside, impossible to tell if it was snowing.

Christian, he noted, had already thrown his covers off and had his top leg wrapped over Wendell's.

Jacob shook his head and continued toward the stairs. Rick fought, Christian cuddled—forcefully—and Danny, he knew from experience, talked in his sleep. Loudly. He also walked once in a while, which had scared Jacob to death when they were kids, to wake finding Danny standing over him, sound asleep and chattering away, in the middle of the night.

What was it with Aunt Pat's kids? He felt sorry for their future wives. But… He shrugged. At least he didn't have to sleep with any of the three anymore.

Not his circus, not his monkeys.

Making his way to the head of the stairs, Jacob fumbled toward his bed in the dark loft. He tossed his clothes in the general area where he believed his laundry bag to be, then sat on the edge of his bed facing Melinda's.

Wanting her so much it hurt.

Patience had never been his strong suit, but he'd promised to give her time.

Even though he wished she didn't need any.

Regardless, tonight he looked forward to snuggling up with her, sharing a few hot kisses, maybe a caress or two, even knowing it would remain mostly innocent. She wasn't ready for more, and as turned on as she made his body, his brain wasn't functioning at full capacity. He could sense it trying to shut down, like an appliance on the verge of a power outage.

Yawning hugely, Jacob leaned forward and stroked his palm down Melinda's arm from shoulder to wrist, then laced their fingers.

"Mel," he whispered.

No response.

"Mel?"

Leaning a bit closer, Jacob placed his ear just above her nose and mouth.

Sure enough, the deep, even measure of her breathing announced what he should have predicted. She was sound asleep.

Jacob mentally smacked himself. Of course she was. The girl was even more exhausted than he was and needed a good night's sleep. And he'd taken his time getting ready for bed. The combination of a couple glasses of champagne, sheer fatigue, the quiet, and the nice, dark loft had worked their magic and lulled her under.

Disappointed that he wouldn't get to sleep with her tonight, he nevertheless was glad she'd get some rest.

Still, he was unable to resist the siren call of her lips, and pressed his, feather light, to her mouth for a good night kiss.

She said, *"Mmmm,"* and shifted toward him in her sleep.

"Goodnight, Mel," he whispered. And because he could, he

added, "I love you."

Climbing into his own bed, Jacob pulled the covers up under his chin, automatically turning on his side and tucking his knees up to keep his feet from hanging off the edge all night long. He matched his breathing to Melinda's effortlessly, the steady rhythm soothing in the peaceful quiet of the dark condo.

Just before he dropped off to sleep, he thought he heard her murmur, "'Night, Jakey."

They woke early to leaden skies and winds already kicking the icy cold into every tiny crevice and crack on the building. The whole condo seemed to shiver.

Oblivious to the cold, relieved that Jacob seemed determined to keep everything easy and normal between them, Melinda stared into his eyes across the small space separating them, their hands linked. Not speaking, not yet, but enjoying the slow waking together.

From downstairs, Melinda heard her dad complain, "I don't know why I bothered checking the weather reports before we left. They haven't been right above ten percent of the time."

Melinda and Jacob chuckled quietly. Karen answered in a soothing voice, her words unintelligible. No one else seemed to be awake yet, though her parents had clearly been after coffee, as the rich, dark scent filled the loft.

"It's hard to believe today's our last day," Jacob said, breaking the silence but keeping his voice low.

"I know."

"What do you want to do today?"

Contemplative, Melinda didn't answer right away.

It was her last day to challenge herself on the expert slopes, to push herself past her comfort level on the lifts. If Jacob would go with her, she could handle it. Even though he might not be totally happy with her this morning, despite how normal he seemed at the moment, he'd take her if she asked him. He was always encouraging her to ski with the guys.

She bit her lip. Did he know she was afraid? She hoped not. She didn't want him to think she was a coward.

More importantly, she didn't want to *be* a coward.

Did he think her cowardly for not telling him she loved him right back?

There were only two things in her life that truly scared her. Heights. And Jacob, and what it was going to take for the two of them to really make a go of this budding relationship between them.

She'd gone to sleep last night thinking about those fears. And missed opportunities, which had made her think of Seth, who would never get another chance to conquer a phobia, tackle a challenge, or jump for the gold ring.

And she'd thought about bravery.

Her dad always said cowards let their fears hold them back. The brave might still fear, but they met their fears head on.

Melinda intended to meet hers, and she could start on at least one this very day. The lesser of the two, perhaps—facing down a mountain didn't hold a candle to her fear of losing Jacob and their friendship—though it still ranked high on the list.

Mind made up, she lifted her gaze to Jacob's. He watched her, waiting patiently for her to speak.

"Will you take me on the black-diamond trails with you today?"

Jacob's eyebrows hit his hairline.

"Seriously?" he asked, the beginnings of a grin stretching his mouth wide. When she nodded, he said, "Yeah, of course. Are you sure?"

She nodded again before she could change her mind. "Only the black-diamonds, not the doubles."

One step at a time, she reminded herself. She could tackle the doubles wherever they went next year.

"You got it," he said enthusiastically, and bounced out of bed, slapping her on her rump. "It's about time. Come on, let's get ready."

When she stood, he pulled her in for a kiss that lifted the top of her skull straight off, then bounded down the stairs, whistling.

She had to wait, fanning the heat from her cheeks and the dazedness that had to show in her eyes, before she could follow without risking a parent or cousin knowing exactly how Jacob had started off her morning.

He made her ache in places she hadn't known she could ache.

Unfortunately, Melinda's bruises had come into their full array of colors and looked worse than ever. She hoped her layers and goggles would disguise the worst of them. She tested the goggles in the bathroom to make sure they didn't press too uncomfortably on any still-sore areas, relieved when they seemed fine. She could always tell people she'd smacked into a tree.

Though their whole group had been up late the night before, last-vacation-day fever had infected them all. Everyone was ready to head to the shuttles uncharacteristically early.

"Sweet Jesus, it's freezing," Bill said, stamping his feet while they waited for their transportation.

Even their excellent gear wasn't enough to keep the wind-chill out completely, especially when standing still, and the sky seemed to get lower, darker, and heavier by the minute.

"Definitely another storm coming in," Peter said, scanning the clouds. Nancy had burrowed into his chest, seeking what little warmth she could find. "Looks like a bad one."

"According to the weather people, it's supposed to blow in and out fairly quickly," her dad put in, his arms wrapped around her mother, "but I've lost all faith in those people, so who the hell knows."

Melinda shivered and hoped the weather people were right. She wouldn't last out there very long if the weather worsened too much, and she wanted time to acclimate to the higher lifts and tougher slopes.

"Let's hope the winds don't get too much worse," Danny put in, doing partial jumping-jacks in place, along with Gabe, to keep his blood moving. "They'll close the lifts."

The shuttle finally arrived, to general relief. Melinda and Jacob sat together, as they usually did, and held hands covertly while the others made plans for how to get the most out of their final hours of vacation. There would be no night skiing that evening, since they'd need to get the cars loaded for the morning's drive.

When Jacob announced he was sticking with Melinda for the day, the guys grumbled and rolled their eyes, but otherwise didn't remark on the change, though Rick and Christian both winked at her. Melinda had to fight a blush. Jacob's dad grinned, and all four women gave them speculative glances, but thankfully kept quiet and continued on their way.

They'd agreed to meet at the lodge for lunch at one, as usual. The rest of the guys, plus Aunt Pat, headed for the expert, double-black-diamond runs. Jacob led Melinda toward a black-diamond lift line. She did her best to ignore her mother's surprise as they skied past her and Karen noted where they were headed.

Once in line, the nerves set in again. Melinda pushed them firmly to the back of her mind. She'd be with Jacob, and he rode these lifts all the time. It would be fine.

They didn't talk much while they waited their turn for the lift chair. It was too cold, the wind too biting, to be comfortable standing around chatting. The lifts would be worse, sitting still and moving through the frigid air. She shuddered and moved closer to Jacob.

Finally, they skied into position for their chair. Was it her imagination, or did this lift seem to move faster than the intermediate ones?

She had no time to worry about it, because almost as soon as she got set, the chair arrived, hit the backs of her legs, nudging her into the seat, and they were off.

"Oh," she said involuntarily as the chair swung more than she liked in the swirling wind and seemed to shoot straight up from the ground to the top of the first tower, which was much higher than the lifts she was used to.

"Okay?" Jacob asked, though his voice was muffled through his scarf and the multiple layers he'd piled on.

"Yeah," she said, determined for it to be true.

"Freakin' cold," he added.

Melinda merely nodded and stared straight ahead, though that didn't help much, since each tower they moved toward seemed higher than the last, raising them farther and farther from the ground and up along the steep side of the mountain. Cold as she was, fear-sweat sprang beneath her arms and slicked her palms inside her gloves. Unpleasant tingling increased in her extremities.

Jacob told jokes and made her laugh, at least a little, helping to distract her from the heights. If he could keep that up all the way to the top, she might make it off without a problem.

Then the lift jerked to a stop.

The chair continued to swing in the wind, and the two of them sat, stuck at a standstill far above the ground.

"Oh, man," Jacob said, tilting his head back. "Not a good sign first thing on our last day."

Melinda's free hand vised on the bar next to her. She concentrated on sending her heart back into its chest cavity from where it had lodged itself in her throat.

Swallowing convulsively, she breathed slowly, deliberately, in through her nose, out through her mouth.

It's no big deal, she told herself. *This happens all the time. It'll start up again any minute, and you'll be fine. Just don't look down.*

As soon as the words formed in her head, of course she looked down.

Melinda's whole body seemed to freeze solid. She couldn't even gasp through her locked-tight lips.

They were so *high.*

In defense against the view, she closed her eyes, but that made the attack of dizziness even worse. Popping them open again, she stared resolutely straight ahead at the backs of the skiers on the chair in front of them, who seemed to be chatting serenely and taking in the view as though nothing was wrong.

Okay. Okay, okay, okay. You're securely seated on a sturdy chair, with Jacob right beside you. Hanging from a sturdy cable. Just breathe.

But cables break…

No, no, no. You'll be okay. You'll be okay. Please, God, let it be okay…

The cold seemed to increase exponentially every ten seconds they sat there, waiting for the chair to move forward again. What was taking so freaking long?

Jacob was still speaking, though his words wouldn't process through the buzzing in her head. The tingling in her feet and hands increased, until she worried she'd have trouble maintaining her grasp on the bar and her poles, or standing if they ever got to the end of the lift.

Slow breaths, slow...

Shame bit at her. If Jacob noticed, she'd have to tell him now. She could only hope he wouldn't think less of her for her stupid, irrational fear.

How much longer was it going to take for them to fix the problem?

A tiny, shameful part of her hoped they'd have to close the lift, and that would give her the excuse she needed to put the rest of this testing day off until her next time out skiing.

Of course, they'd have to get down somehow, and there were other black-diamond lifts...

The waiting was making her crazy. If they didn't hurry up, she was going to totally lose it.

29

"Mel?" Jacob asked. He leaned toward her, but she didn't answer.

Determined to keep things light and low-pressured between them today, he'd deliberately talked a lot of nonsense. She hadn't responded to any of his jokes since the lift stopped.

"Mel?" He patted Melinda's thigh.

She jolted in surprise, her eyes flying to his, wide and scared even through the protective covering of her goggles. He frowned back at her. Something was definitely up.

"Hey," he said, patting her again. "Are you okay?"

All that came from her lips was a sort of high, thin keening, even as she nodded. Then shook her head. Then nodded again.

"What's wrong?"

Shifting so that he had one arm around her shoulders, Jacob peered into her face, concerned.

"Sweetie?"

At that moment, the chair jerked forward. She startled again, violently, but her obvious relief to be moving again was so great that whatever paralysis had had hold of her lifted. She tried to speak.

"I-I-I—" she stuttered, stopped, seemed to gather herself.

Melinda leaned into him a little, so he pulled her closer.

"I'm afraid of heights," she mumbled, just loudly enough for him to hear her over the wind. Clearly ashamed.

Confused, Jacob said, "Yeah," and waited.

She looked up at him. He stared back at her quizzically.

Dragging in a wavery breath, Melinda said, "When I was younger, I fell off the diving board, and—"

"Yeah, I know," he interrupted. Where was she going with this?

"What do you know?" she asked, surprise in her voice now.

"Mel, I was there that day, don't you remember? I saw the whole thing. I followed you home."

"You—what?" She gaped at him, obviously confused. "You were there? I—"

"I saw that stupid kid bounce the board, saw you fall." And, he distinctly remembered, he had nearly swallowed his heart in fear. She'd landed so fucking close to that concrete. "I saw the lifeguard pull you out. And I followed you home, to make sure you got back okay, 'cuz you were pretty shaken up."

He had been, too. He'd even had nightmares about it a couple of times.

Melinda frowned at him. "I have no memory of that at all."

"So you're afraid of heights. So what? Lots of people are. It's not like you let it stop you from doing anything."

"I do, though."

"Like what? Who cares if you don't go bungee jumping or dive out of airplanes."

"I let it stop me from taking the black-diamond runs. Until today."

"Is that why..." Jacob trailed off.

That was why she stuck to the lower slopes. He'd always supposed it was some silly lack of faith in her skiing abilities—hence the classes every year—but he should have known better. She was one of the most confident people he knew, and a strong skier. Always had been.

Now it made sense.

Melinda stared at her gloved hand fisted around her ski poles, making him frown again.

"So why now?" he asked.

She blew out a breath, the only indication the rise and fall of her chest, as the exhalation flew away soundlessly in the wind.

"I don't want to be a coward," she said, low. "I don't want you to think I'm a coward."

Girls. They got the weirdest ideas.

"I don't think that, not at all. You come out here, every year, you ski, you ride the lifts. It doesn't matter what hill you're on. What matters is you're here."

"That's not all, though," she said, still not looking at him. "This thing with us—it scares me, Jacob. A lot. But I don't want to let fear hold me back, hold us back, from what might… I just—"

Now he hugged her, just one arm around her shoulders, but he pulled her in as tightly as he could. He wouldn't deny it hurt not to have her jump in with both feet, but he'd had months to come around to the idea of them together, even if the final push had come in a sort of blinding flash. They had plenty of time to work it out.

"There's no rush," he said, "and no pressure. We'll figure it out together."

The end of the lift approached, finally, and they disembarked, skiing down the path away from the lift exit and around toward the slope.

"Are you going to be okay with this?" Jacob asked, indicating the run.

It looked like a normal black-diamond slope to him, nothing too fancy, nothing too steep, but Melinda's face had blanched as they'd skied forward.

"You don't have to prove anything, you know," he said when she didn't answer right away. "No one thinks you're a coward, least of all me."

Melinda took a deep breath and nodded.

"The lifts are the worst," she said. "Skiing, at least I'm on my own two feet. But I don't go that fast."

Jacob looked back at the slope. She wouldn't have a lot of

choice on this run. There wasn't room to do much of her usual slow back-and-forthing. Expert-level skiers had to go for it or roll to the bottom. He hadn't even taken her to the true top of the slope yet, this was only the midway station. There was another lift that went on up to the run's peak.

He opened his mouth to say so, then thought better of it. Best if he didn't influence her expectations one way or the other.

"Let's go," she said.

Melinda sucked in another breath and, ignoring her inner coward, prepared to break her neck. The expert run stretched out below her skis seemed impossibly steep, and narrow, and full of obstacles.

On one side of the trail, a sheer rock face, heavily draped in snow and ice, extended straight up the mountain, only a few weedy trees clinging here and there to soften its edges. On the other side, the trees grew in dense lines to the edge of the slope and trailed away toward the valley.

Moguls and high piles of snow dotted what she could see of the descent, which appeared to angle nearly straight down, but the trail curved around to the left out of sight, making it impossible to know what else she'd face.

She had no one but herself and her monumental pride and ego to blame if she died.

Melinda tried to laugh at her melodrama, but her little internal joke fell flat—since she feared she might do exactly as she'd thought and not survive the mountain.

It was too late now, and Jacob was waiting patiently for her to make a move. If this was her last hurrah, at least she'd spend her final moments with Jacob.

With that cheerful thought riding foremost in her brain, she nodded to Jacob, and tipped her skis over the edge.

He took the lead, and she followed him as best she could. He moved like lightning down the impossibly steep grade, even though she suspected he'd deliberately slowed his usual pace to try to accommodate hers. His form was amazing.

She'd never seen him move quite like that, almost like an Olympic skier. The crisp sound of his skis cutting through the snow and ice flew to her ears over the howl of the wind.

Gradually, as they flashed around curves, hurtled over moguls, avoided trees and other skiers, the exhilaration seeped through. Her lips curved into a small smile, then grew into a grin, then her gleeful whoop echoed down the slope.

It was incredible, amazing. Almost like flying. In some places *actually* flying off the ends of the jumps and down, down, down.

Because they'd started out so high up the mountain, the slope seemed to go on nearly forever, and Melinda gloried in every foot of it. How many years had she deprived herself of this nearly sexual pleasure?

Too many, but never again.

This might be their last day in Utah, but she determined to head out to Big Bear or Wrightwood as soon as possible—as often as possible—once they were home, and master their black-diamond runs all through ski season.

Melinda swooshed to a stop in a wave of snow beside Jacob, still laughing, warmed through despite the wind-chill, on top of the world.

"Let's go again!"

Jacob, a smile tugging at the lips he'd exposed by pulling down his scarf, leaned forward and kissed her smack on the mouth.

"You got it," he said, and led the way to another black-diamond lift.

Melinda chattered all the way up, her hand locked tight on the bar, but otherwise ignoring the height of the chair. The exhilaration running through her veins was something she'd never experienced to such a feverish extent.

Pride, victory.

Joy, made all the richer because she'd shared the experience with Jacob.

It was a heady drug, and she mentally urged the lift to faster speeds so she could partake of it again and again. The day would be over before they knew it. She wanted to get plenty of runs in.

This time, she took the hill faster, stayed closer on Jacob's flying heels. The run was slightly wider than the first one she'd tried, so she had more room to maneuver. The moment they reached the bottom, she grabbed Jacob's hand and tugged him back toward the first lift. Then again, and again.

The next time they reached the top of the lift, they disembarked just as the gray sky darkened even more, went leaden, and opened wide. Snow dumped down on them in heavy buckets. The meager morning light seemed to die completely, the winds picked up, and soon it seemed they were skiing through a snowy tornado just to exit the lift area.

"If this keeps up," Jacob shouted over the suddenly howling wind, "they'll have to close the mountain."

She followed Jacob away from the lift. Instead of turning to head down the slope again as she'd expected, he led her to yet another lift. She had to tilt her head back to follow its lines up the sheer face of the mountain, where the first tower disappeared at a dizzying height inside the storm.

She said, "Oh, shit."

"What?" Jacob yelled, leaning in closer to hear her.

Melinda shook her head, closed her eyes, and counted to twenty, hoping the dizziness would pass before she had to get on the lift. She'd already conquered two slopes. Multiple times. This one was step two of the challenge, the true top of a black-diamond run.

You can do it, Mel. You can. Just breathe.

There were four groups ahead of them waiting for a chair.

Then three.

Then two.

The last couple went, and it was their turn to ski into position for the next chair.

This lift was definitely faster. It took off with an audible whoosh, even over the sound of the storm, and Melinda rocked back in the seat as it traveled up, and up, and up some more, snow blanketing them in sheets, then blowing off, then blanketing them again.

"I wish they had enclosed gondolas here for days like this," Jacob said, his voice still raised, though they sat close together. "They're a hell of a lot warmer."

Nodding her agreement, Melinda shifted closer to Jacob, not for warmth, which was pointless in the wind, but for the extra sense of security.

She'd almost stopped worrying about the lifts. They trucked along smoothly enough, despite the winds, exactly like the beginner and intermediate ones, and the snow was so thick, she could no longer see the ground in any case. It helped reduce the fear.

Until a new realization intruded that made the lift-heights issue seem quite trivial by comparison.

She would shortly arrive at the top of the mountain, safe and sound, delivered by the speeding chair. Then she would have to let go of the handle, let go of Jacob, and ski down it.

In the blinding storm.

It was one thing to take an expert run with relatively clear visibility, even as steep and twisty as their first slopes had been. And she'd loved them. But this one would be steeper yet, twistier and longer yet, and visibility on the mountain was rapidly reducing to zero.

She hadn't intended to increase the challenge level on her phobia quite so suddenly or so dramatically.

"Still okay?" Jacob yelled.

Anxiety already had razor-sharp claws sunk into the back of her neck. Her throat worked up and down while she tried to unlock her rigid mouth to answer him. It stayed locked shut.

However much she wanted to deny it, her heart was pounding, racing, and her limbs tingled in that unpleasant, about-to-black-out-from-fear way she only associated with heights.

But she would not let him see her cower again after the triumph of the first two slopes.

She nodded, dragged her courage up by the hair. Jacob would never let anything happen to her, and she'd already proved she could handle an expert run. This was simply a different slope, that was all. Higher, yes, but the same skill level.

They reached the end, hopped off the lift, and she followed Jacob blindly, her eyes focused only on the back of his black ski jacket. The snow came down in sheets, and the wind pierced. If nothing else, skiing down the mountain would warm them through.

Jacob pulled to a halt right before starting the descent. "Just follow my lead," he shouted, and she nodded gamely to show she understood.

He shoved off, and she prepared to do the same. From behind her came the sound of someone shouting, and she turned her head at the last minute to look back at the lift operator. The woman waved her arms, as though urging them back to the lift, but it was too late. Melinda had already tipped forward. Her weight shifted, sending her plowing down the slope after Jacob, who was already nothing but a black blur through the snow, though he wasn't too far ahead yet.

The last thing she heard as she dropped over the edge was, "Mountain closed!"

Crap.

If they'd closed the mountain, that meant only one thing. Visibility had gotten so bad that it was now dangerous to ski, which she could have told them herself. The unexpected storm had become a blizzard.

Trying to stay calm, to focus on Jacob and the terrain, Melinda fought her footing, fought the rising panic. New winds seemed to have sprung up from nowhere, far stronger than any they'd experienced all week, and with no particular direction or pattern. They buffeted her first on one side, then the other, until it was a struggle to remain upright.

The narrow trail boxed her in to such an extent that she could barely turn to control her speed, and the snow flew past faster and faster. Yet no matter how fast she skied, Jacob seemed to get farther and farther ahead, until he was only an indistinct speck at the edge of her vision.

"Okay," she said aloud, her words whipped away by the winds, "okay, okay, okay. Focus, Mel."

She talked herself forward, though she didn't know the trail, didn't know the terrain. Moguls took her by surprise. So did jumps. She fell once, but managed to stay in her skis by some miracle, and at least the fall slowed her down a bit. With the mountain closed, she didn't have to worry about anyone crashing into her from behind, either.

It was a small relief.

Her skis caught air down a particularly steep section, and once again she managed to keep her feet upon landing. Just barely. Her depth perception was all screwed up thanks to the snow and the darkened day.

Then the slope narrowed even further, until it became a single-person trail, mountain on one side, trees and a dangerous drop-off on the other. She was going too fast, but there was no way to slow down, no place to stop, no cover. She tucked into her skis to ride it out, body as protected as she could make it, and shot down the path at a breakneck pace, her heart rate matching her headlong flight.

This was insane. Far more than she'd bargained for. The euphoria of the first slopes had long since faded.

Now she simply wanted to survive the mountain.

Melinda flew out of the end of the narrow path. The slope widened out again, and there, finally, was Jacob, waiting for her off to the side. In the driving snow, she might have missed him altogether but for his shout and the waving of his ski poles at the periphery of her vision.

"Thank God," she said to herself, and plowed to his side of the trail and a bit below him, pulling up short on a tiny strip between two soaring trees. She couldn't see their tops in the storm.

"Hell of a ride, right?" Jacob said cheerfully, stepping sideways down the mountain to get to her side.

"Right," she managed. "They closed the mountain."

"Really? How do you know?"

She told him about the lift operator, and he shrugged.

"I'm not surprised in this weather," he said. "This might be the worst conditions we've ever skied in."

"I think so," she said dryly.

"Come here," he said, and pulled his scarf and several layers down.

More than willing, Melinda freed her own mouth and leaned in for his kiss. It warmed her right down to her toes and up to the top of her head.

"That might hold me 'til later," he said an inch from her lips. "Better have one more to be sure."

She laughed at him, but wrapped her arms around his neck and sank in, disregarding the snow piling up on them both.

"All right," Jacob said, muffling his face again. "I think we're close to the level of the first lift, so we're almost halfway down. You ready?"

Only halfway? Her muscles already quivered with fatigue.

Resigned, Melinda nodded and shoved off after him. At least the lower part of the slope would be somewhat familiar, even if she couldn't see it.

They shot past the exit for the lower lift a few minutes later. The turnabout tower hulked in the storm, already deserted, eerie looking in the dim light and meager visibility. Security lights glowed above but illuminated nothing through the snow.

The whole trip, from top to bottom, seemed to take hours.

Finally, finally, they made it to the end of the run.

The ski patrol was out in force, checking people in as they came off the various slopes, making sure everyone who'd been out when the storm broke was accounted for. Melinda wanted nothing more than to collapse in a heap at their feet.

Instead, she followed Jacob around to the lodge and headed into the women's locker room to drag off her outer layers and put on her after-snow boots, which were lovely and toasty on her half-frozen feet.

Staring at herself in the mirror as she tended to her hair, she couldn't help grinning at her reflection. She'd done it. She'd taken that mountain, had done even more than she'd anticipated, and checked one huge fear mostly off her list today. Maybe her heights phobia wasn't magically cured, but she'd beaten another level.

Pride swam through her system, along with a surprising jolt of purely sexual energy that made her want to find Jacob and throw him down on the ground to have her way with him right that minute.

Down, girl, she told herself, though her grin in the mirror stayed sharp and wicked.

Conquering the mountain left only her relationship with Jacob remaining on the list of major fears to tackle.

Surely one a day was sufficient.

Once they got home, away from the party atmosphere of vacation and the nonstop togetherness with so many people, they'd have time to be together, alone, and figure everything out.

She hoped.

Finished fussing, Melinda met Jacob in the main room. She sat beside him on the edge of the fireplace, waving to the rest of their group, who were crammed together over several tables and inter-mixed with strangers.

All of the tables and chairs were already full of skiers waiting to see if the storm would pass by, but she didn't mind. The closer they sat to the fire, the better, at least until her frozen muscles thawed.

Jacob had already ordered hot tea for them both and handed her a large, red ceramic mug with the lodge's logo on the side. She breathed in the steam, then drank deep, relishing the heat as the liquid spread its warm glow through her belly.

"Thanks," she said, trying not to visibly shiver when he sneakily danced his hand over her knee.

"Welcome," he said, and grinned roguishly.

Who needed tea or fire when Jacob was around? One touch, and her whole body went volcanic.

Jacob's eyes twinkled as he studied her over the rim of his own mug. He knew exactly what he was doing to her with his playful fingers.

"So…" he said, giving her knee one more squeeze, then removing his hand so she could breathe normally. "What did you think?"

Melinda took a very deliberate breath to settle the butterflies he'd set winging around her belly with a simple stroke.

"I think I kicked that phobia's ass," she said, and clinked mugs with him when Jacob cheered her. "And I think I'll wait to tackle those expert runs again on a clear day."

He laughed. "Sounds reasonable."

"Jacob?" A small, elderly woman interrupted them, putting a hand on his shoulder.

"Neta!" Jacob said in surprise, and jumped up to kiss the woman on her wrinkled cheek. Tucking her hand into the crook of his arm, he turned to Melinda. "Neta, this is Melinda Honeywell. Melinda, Neta Smalls. She's the woman I, uh—"

"Bowled over with his charm," Neta broke in smoothly, casting an amused glance at Jacob, who flushed. "It's lovely to meet you, Miss Honeywell." She smiled at Melinda, then turned her bright eyes on Jacob. "Is she the one, young man?"

"Yes, ma'am, she is," he said.

"The one what?" Melinda asked.

Neta merely smiled again at Jacob. "Excellent choice," she said. "I do hope you'll keep in touch and let me know how things are going. You have my email?"

"I do."

"Good, good. I'd hoped to see you once more before leaving." She lifted a cheek imperiously for him to kiss again. "Clyde and I are heading out tomorrow morning, and I wanted to say goodbye, and not to worry. You're going to go far, I know it."

"Thank you, Neta. It was great, um, meeting you," Jacob said a bit awkwardly, no doubt thinking of the way he'd met her, crash landing on the slope.

"It was a real pleasure," she answered with a saucy grin. "It's not every day a handsome young man knocks me on my ass."

Jacob coughed explosively to cover his shocked snicker. Neta merely patted his arm.

"Now, enjoy the rest of your time," she said, "and take good care of this young lady."

She winked and was gone, before Jacob could say, "I will."

"Wow," Melinda said. "She doesn't mess around, does she?"

"I told you she was a spitfire," Jacob said with a chuckle. "Lucky for me."

Melinda looked at him, seeing the shame and worry lurking in the backs of his eyes, despite his smile.

"Do you want to talk about it?" she asked.

He stared at her for a long minute before nodding his head. "I do, actually, but not now. When we get home, okay? I have a few things to work out, and I'd like your input."

"Okay," she said. That wasn't the response she'd been expecting, but he seemed all right, so she let it go for now.

"Thanks."

"So now what?" she asked. "Will they open the lifts again, do you think?"

"They're still saying this storm's going to blow through. I don't know. It looks pretty fierce out there."

"Felt pretty fierce out there."

"Too right," he agreed. "You know what else feels pretty fierce?"

Her eyes caught by the flames dancing in his, Melinda shook her head.

Jacob leaned closer so he could whisper in her ear, making her shiver. "This need I have to kiss you until you melt. Right here, right now."

Her breath caught on a tiny moan. "Jake…"

He laughed again and stroked a hand down her freshly-braided hair. "The first chance I get," he said, and his eyes made it a promise.

"The first chance *I* get," she corrected him.

She smiled when the flames in his eyes flared brighter.

30

As it turned out, the storm did not blow through, and after having an early lunch at the lodge and waiting through conflicting weather reports, their group agreed to call it good, head back to the condo, and start packing for their departure the next day.

Just as well, Melinda decided. Her muscles still quivered with the stress and exertion of that last run.

Luckily, they'd chowed most of their food items, as usual, so there wouldn't be much to organize in the kitchen once they got through the last day's snacks, dinner, and breakfast the next morning.

She and Jacob escaped the chaos of the rest of the condo to pack up their belongings in the loft.

They engaged in idle chatter, perhaps threaded with a little nervous laughter. Perhaps flirting a bit more than usual, and maybe a bit more meaningfully. It was all essentially normal, though the underlying, deeply sexual tension kept her pulse rate deliciously high.

They snuck in a few quick kisses, too, when they were sure

no one would come up and discover them. There was so much going on that they didn't risk it often.

Once they were finished packing, they headed back downstairs to help everyone else finish up. With all of them pitching in, it didn't take long to load what could be pre-loaded into the cars and to set the two condos to rights, with everything ready for a quick escape in the morning.

Just before dinner, Melinda took a final armload downstairs. She stretched her hand forward to pull the door into the garage all the way open, as someone had left it ajar, but stopped when she heard her name.

"Rick said Mel seemed worried about it," a masculine voice said from the other side of the door. Danny, she thought.

"Worried? Why?" Eddie's voice, sounding surprised.

"What happens if they break up and blah blah," Danny answered. "With the families and everything."

"Girls," said Gabe with a snort, and she could hear the eye roll in his voice.

"Well," Eddie said in his reflective way, "it makes sense. It's a big change, and not only for them. What did Rick say?"

"The same thing I'm going to tell her the next time I get her by herself," Danny answered. "We'll deal. We're all family, Jake included, and if they don't work out, they don't work out. Family doesn't change."

"I don't think it's gonna be an issue," Gabe said. "I didn't see it initially, but…"

"Yeah," Eddie said. "They'll be good together, as long as…"

"As long as what?" Gabe asked when Eddie broke off.

"Hm?" Eddie asked. "Oh, nothing. Nothing."

From her spot behind the door, Melinda frowned, but the guys were still speaking.

"Besides, if Jake hurts her the way that dickhead Mitch did—" Danny began.

"—they'll never find his body," Gabe finished.

Eddie snorted. "He won't."

"Well, girls, now that Mel's love life is settled…" Gabe trailed off and there came the sound of a trunk slamming. "I'm ready for a beer. You?"

Amused, touched, comforted, Melinda made a production of opening the door before they could get there and catch her eavesdropping.

Handing over the last bag, she beamed a smile at each of them, and when they came upstairs, she had their beers already open and waiting.

Following recent, sad tradition, once the chores were done, everyone gathered around the kitchen table in a loose circle prior to their final evening meal of the trip. Karen, Lois, and Nancy poured drinks and passed them around. Once they each had a glass, Bill cleared his throat and drew everyone's attention his way, as it was his turn to give the toast.

"Tonight is January second," he began. "In a perfect world, we'd be celebrating a twenty-first birthday right now. A bright young man would be having his first taste of alcohol—or his first legal one, at least."

Bill paused to allow the low chuckles and a few sniffles to subside. "He should be here. Making our lives, and so many others, better because of his company. Instead, here we are, missing him, as we have every day since his passing. Wishing more than anything that he were still here with us, instead of looking out for us from above. A moment of silence, please."

Bowing her head along with everyone else's, Melinda sought blindly for Jacob's hand, comforted when his fingers clasped hers, strong and steady and warm, though they both sniffed deeply to hold back tears.

When the moment had passed, Bill said, "Thank you," and everyone raised their heads, all eyes a touch brighter than they'd been. "Raise your glasses."

Around the circle, every glass lifted, and they moved closer to each other instinctively, free arms around each other so that everyone was joined, a unit.

"To Seth," Bill said, raising his glass yet higher. "May he ever dance with the angels and keep the Lord laughing with all his best jokes."

"To Seth," they echoed, and clinked glasses all around before drinking to their friend's memory.

Parents hugged children, and children hugged friends and cousins. Someone turned the music on, and gradually everyone began talking again.

As she always did, Melinda found a reason to lock herself in the bathroom for a quick, hard cry, and her own prayer for Seth. Then she fixed her makeup, smoothed her hair, and rejoined the group, with an extra hug for Jacob.

Uncle Allan brought out his deck of cards and performed a few new magic tricks he'd learned over Christmas—one of his favorite activities—and had them all exclaiming over his sleight of hand.

The guys went with their fallback conversation, arguing over sports, and the noise level rose back to normal, if a bit subdued.

Though the week had been a lot of fun overall, and she was in no particular hurry to get back to real life, Melinda's heart lifted at the thought of going home. With their friends and family all around, the strain of concealing her feelings for Jacob wore continually on her nerves.

She wanted normalcy and privacy to clear her mind and heart, and she wanted real time alone with Jacob. The best she could hope for at the moment was a quick snuggle and a lengthy kiss before bed.

Their final night of vacation could not come to a close soon enough.

Dinner consisted of leftovers and snacks, but nobody complained. Jacob scrounged enough cold cuts to make a decent hero sandwich, shared a last bag of chips with Melinda, and let her talk him into splitting a brownie, too, since Eddie snagged the next-to-last one before Melinda could hold him off with her fiercely-wielded fork.

Afterward, they sprawled over the condo floor and furniture to watch a movie—Twister this time, in honor of the day's blizzard.

When the credits rolled, bodies shifted and stretched in preparation for heading to bed.

Jacob waggled his eyebrows at Melinda behind her dad's back and made her blush. He grinned at her reddening cheeks, hoping their desires were well aligned, because he knew exactly what he wanted to do as soon as they got up to the loft.

"Hey, I forgot," Wendell said to the room at large, "do we have dates for camping yet? My mom called earlier. My cousin's getting married in Connecticut at the end of June, and I have to go."

"We're looking at a couple options," Melinda's Uncle Allan said, mid-stretch so that his voice went up three octaves at the end. "Everyone's calendars get trickier every year, but sometime in July, most likely."

"July?" Eddie said. "Won't Jake be gone al—"

Jacob slanted Eddie a fierce look, cutting him off mid-word.

"Uh, that is…" Eddie tried to change tack, apology all over his face.

Too late.

Lois looked between the two of them, her eyebrows raised into her hairline. Jacob hunched his shoulders, dreaming of a hasty retreat as his mom pinned him in place with her patented Shrink Stare. But it was the look in Melinda's eyes, the sudden stillness of her body, that made his feet feel rooted to the spot.

"Gone?" Lois said. "Gone where? Why? What's going on?"

Shit, shit, shit.

So much for telling Melinda in private. So much for telling her *first*, so she didn't hear about it this way, in front of the entire freaking group. For a usually quiet guy, Eddie had sure picked a winning moment to flap some loose lips.

Goddamn it.

Sighing, Jacob ran a hand through his hair. There was nothing to do now but toss his cards down and hope it didn't cost him the jackpot.

Low voiced, Eddie said, "Hey, sorry, man. I didn't mean to—"

Jacob jumped up from the couch and clapped Eddie on the shoulder.

"It's all right," Jacob said. "I should've said something before now."

Moving in front of the TV, he clasped his hands in front of himself, bouncing a bit on the balls of his feet while he tried to think of the right words to say. The weight of every eye in the room seemed to press down on his shoulders.

"Okay," he began. "I have sort of an announcement to make."

Melinda raised her eyebrows at him, but he couldn't quite meet her gaze. He stared at a spot beyond her left temple instead.

The rest of their party glanced around at each other and at him again before settling back into their places, faces lifted to his expectantly.

What was going on? Was this the secret he'd been keeping? Melinda's stomach plunged to her toes. She frowned at him and opened her mouth to say something, she had no idea what, but Jacob finally caught her eye and gave a small hand gesture, waving her quiet.

Crossing her arms over her chest, she dropped back into her seat. She crossed her legs, too, for good measure, then realized she was bouncing them the way Jacob did when he was stressed and forced herself to stop.

"Jacob?" Lois said, staring at her son when he remained silent, frowning at his hands.

Finally, he lifted his head and looked straight at his mother, as though no one else was in the room, though he addressed them all.

"I've been sitting on some news," he began. "I wanted to wait until after the trip, but this is just as well. It's probably the last time we'll all be in one spot for a while, and I wanted to tell everyone together, anyway. So…"

Melinda tensed as though waiting for an axe to slice her heart in two. What was this secret and why had he been hiding it for so long?

"I've been talking with some people at UC Irvine over the past six months or so," he said, "and they encouraged me to apply for a couple of new opportunities—some internships and stuff."

Frowning, Melinda stared at him, more confused than ever. School stuff? Why did he seem so nervous?

Jacob cleared his throat. "I got accepted to all of them—"

"Oh, Jake, that's fantastic, congratulations!" Lois said.

All signs of maternal concern had vanished. She clapped her hands, beaming around at them all in delight. Jacob held up a hand.

"The first thing is—well, if it's okay with you guys," he said, looking at his parents, "I know it's more money, but if we can swing it, I'll be transferring to Irvine in the fall."

Melinda gasped, but Bill and Lois's exclamations of pleasure and pride in their son buried the sound. He wasn't going back to Fullerton for their senior year?

Irvine wasn't that far, really, but…

He wouldn't be on campus.

Or in the local coffee shops.

She wouldn't see him every day, or be able to pop into his place whenever she wanted.

And he was doing this *now,* just when they were… were…

God.

Her throat felt tight, like she couldn't quite swallow past the lump inside. Biting the inside of her cheek to keep from crying, she stared hard at Jacob's face, ignoring the looks Christian and Rick tossed her way. She had a feeling Jacob's opening words were only the tip of the iceberg.

"It's sort of late to transfer, isn't it?" Danny asked.

Gabe said, "Won't you lose credits?"

Waggling his head from side to side, Jacob said, "Not exactly. I mean, yes, but that's where the rest comes in. They're really mixing things up over there, very forward thinking, trying new ways of educating their premed and medical students, turning out doctors with a lot of extra experience and training."

"Dude, that's so cool," Wendell put in.

Melinda glanced once at Eddie, but he only frowned at the tip of his foot where it dug a pattern into the carpet, clearly regretting opening his mouth.

"What's the rest?" Uncle Allan wanted to know.

"The internships. One this summer, one next, plus a short one over break next Christmas. They're taking really small groups of premed students overseas, in teams, to shadow their top doctors. We'll get field experience in hospitals all over the globe and in clinics in remote areas that are medically underserved."

"That sounds like an amazing opportunity, son," Bill said.

Her dad said, "It sure does," and Peter nodded, both of them clapping Jacob heartily on the back. Her mom kissed him on both cheeks.

"Well done, Jacob," Aunt Pat and Nancy said in unison.

"It really is," Lois said, dabbing at the corners of her eyes. "We're so proud of you, honey."

"I don't understand, though," Karen said, her head tilted as she stepped back to study Jacob. "You're not a doctor yet. You're not even in medical school. How can you treat patients?"

"We won't be operating or issuing orders or anything," Jacob said, "this is more like being a fly on the wall on the front lines, getting to help out while doing a lot of observing, writing reports, non-medical assisting, but with more access. We'll be going to school, too, the whole time. There'll be a lot of homework, labs, all that sort of thing."

"So, emptying bedpans and cool stuff like that. What's the benefit, other than the glamorous experience?" Gabe asked.

"Everyone who successfully completes all three internships will get some extra points for consideration if they apply to Irvine's medical school, for one. I'll still have to pass my MCATs and everything, but this'll be a big bonus on my application.

Being at Irvine for senior year, I'll be able to meet people who can help me get where I want to be when the time comes. Since Irvine's my top pick for med school, anyway, this could be the key."

"Any drawbacks?" Rick asked.

He was frowning, his eyes moving between her and Jacob. Melinda avoided catching his gaze. Christian stood with his arms crossed over his chest, a scowl on his cherubic face.

"Yeah, why'd you wait so long to tell us?" Wendell put in. "Rick told us about his play the minute he heard."

Now Jacob looked at her. Melinda stared stonily back, waiting for him to say what she'd already figured out.

"It means I'm not going to be around very much. Like, at all. There'll be some breaks, but it'll be over a year total. At least."

His gaze implored her for understanding, but it was all she could do not to run out of the room. How could he have kept this to himself, how could he not have told her? All his talk about love and wanting to be together. How could they be together if he wasn't even around?

She'd broken her own rules, ignored her common sense, and fallen in love with him like a fool.

And now... He was leaving her.

Melinda wanted to kick herself. Wasn't this exactly why she'd never let herself pursue her daydreams about Jacob? She *knew* he wanted the traveler's lifestyle, never in one place for long, no home base, always on the go. She'd believed it wouldn't be an issue until he actually became a team doctor at some distant time in the future, but no, he'd found a way to make it happen years earlier.

Irvine was nothing new. She'd known he'd wind up there to get his medical degree. It was a year earlier than expected, that was all. Yet it brought their differences front and center in a way she could not ignore, no matter how much her heart wanted to be with him.

This was only the beginning.

How could they possibly be together when their foundations, their basic needs and desires, were so totally incompatible?

Talk continued around her, but Melinda no longer heard anything anyone said. Numbness descended, and she welcomed it, thankful she didn't have to fight her tears in front of everyone. Tears would come later. Now... she didn't feel anything at all.

Just empty.

The same way her future looked, stretching out for decades in front of her. How cruel, to discover her best friend was truly her soul mate, to feel the sheer mind-bending power of that pure joy, that love, only to lose it almost immediately. All in less than a week.

Now what could she look forward to? Years and years spent pining for someone she loved but would never have.

Sure, she could toss away her own dreams and follow him wherever he went. Or stay where she wanted to be, contenting herself with his presence whenever he blew through town. Either way, she'd be lonely and miserable. Eventually they'd come to hate each other.

Well, she wasn't having it.

She'd put a stop to it right this second. Thank God they hadn't gone any further with their little relationship experiment. A few kisses, that was nothing. They could come back from that, pretend it was vacation-induced temporary insanity and return to friends-as-usual.

If her heart weighed like it had turned to a thousand-pound cement block, well, she'd deal with that later.

Her cousins kept trying to grab her attention, but Melinda ignored them. She didn't want to talk about it. As soon as she could escape without anyone making note of it, she said goodnight to the room in general and made her way to the loft. Christian tried to waylay her with a hand to her arm, but she shook her head and kept moving.

Jacob—still engrossed in conversation with his parents—would be a while, which gave her time to figure out what she'd say when he came up.

Melinda sat on the edge of her bed facing the window, one hand wrapped around her waist and the other rubbing the sore spot over her heart.

Outside, the mountains soared upward, vague shapes gone slightly blue in the greater dark and steadily falling snow.

She stared and stared.

No solutions came. Her mind stayed stubbornly blank except for the endless questions circling in ever-increasing frustration.

Was she being stupid, clinging to her desire to live in Pasodoro? She tried to imagine her little dream house, the way she so often did. It always brought her pleasure, a sense of security, and confidence in her goals. Her future.

Now it stood empty and desolate without Jacob inside it to make it a home.

How quickly she'd placed him there in her mind. How quickly her daydream children had become his children. *Their* children. How quickly she'd given over every part of herself to him. Every wish, every goal, every dream.

Without even realizing the loss.

She'd jumped in with both feet after all, and it was only now, with the waters closing over her head, that she realized she didn't know how to swim.

"Hey," Jacob said softly from behind her, making her jolt. She hadn't heard him on the stairs. "Are you okay?"

Melinda shrugged, finally noticing the downstairs had gone dark and quiet. Everyone had gone to bed. She'd sat blindly staring out the window longer than she'd realized.

"Are you mad?" he asked.

She shrugged again, then shook her head. Though the numbness was starting to wear off, anger was not among the emotions beginning to clog her lungs.

Sitting beside her, Jacob stared out the window, too, and blew out a slow breath. He reached for her hand, again slowly, almost hesitantly, as though he feared she'd jerk her fingers away. His shoulders seemed to relax a bit when she folded her hand in his.

Neither spoke, both of them continuing to stare out the window. The silence in the condo deepened until Melinda swore she could hear her heart and Jacob's beating in time together.

Jacob cleared his throat. "I'm sorry, Mel."

Still not looking at him, she said, "Why didn't you tell me before?"

She gave herself points for the steadiness of her voice, despite the hurt winging through the widening cracks in her composure. No tears dampened the corners of her eyes, another point. She was beyond tears.

When he didn't answer, she added, "You've been keeping this to yourself for months. Months, Jake. I thought we told each other everything. Even more so—" *Now,* she meant to add, even more so *now,* but she couldn't get the word out.

"I know."

He squeezed her hand, then let go, propping his elbows on his knees and dropping his head into his hands. Melinda willed herself statue-still.

"I started to a few times," he said, rubbing his fingers through his hair. "More than a few. At first, I didn't want to tell anyone until it was a sure thing. Then I wanted it to be the right time. I almost spilled it the night before we left to come here. At dinner. Then Rick got his phone call, and I didn't want to detract from his news. It seemed easier to wait until after the trip."

Easier for you.

More hurt pushed through the frozen shell surrounding her emotions.

"You told Eddie."

And not me, how could you not have told me?

"He's my roommate, Mel. I had to tell him. He needs time to find somebody before I move out."

"Okay, but—"

Steady, she cautioned herself when her voice went thick. *Keep it impersonal. Keep calm. Just the facts.*

"This week—what happened with us—I knew I needed to tell you, Mel…"

"But?"

Cold. She was so cold. Inside and out, all over, her whole body. She wanted Jacob's warmth around her, yet as close as they sat on the bed, they might as well have been perched on distant, ice-bound mountain peaks.

"Look, it's not like I'm going to Afghanistan for three years or anything," he said. "I'll still be around. Maybe not as much as either of us would like, but it doesn't have to be this big of a deal."

"Not a big deal? No, of course not," she said, firing up. "Not for you. You'll be off gallivanting across the world, doing what you've wanted to do from the beginning. While I'm what? Waiting around for you to grace me with your presence as time allows?"

"Doing what you want to be doing," he said pointedly, "where you want to be doing it."

"Alone," she countered. "If we're going to be together, I actually want us to be, you know, together. Otherwise what's the point?"

"I want that, too, more than anything—"

"That's not what it sounds like," she said.

"Then come with me."

"Then stay."

"Mel!" he said, blowing out a breath that was half laugh, half pure exasperation. "God, you're impossible."

"So are you. You should have told me all this, Jake, before we started anything. This is a big deal for you, I get that. I would have helped you celebrate, even though I'd miss you so much. And right now I'd only have to worry about missing my best friend instead of my heart ripping out of my chest."

"Melinda," he said, and now his voice was low, full of regret. He took her hand again, squeezed hard. "You're killing me."

"Same goes," she whispered.

Silence wrapped around them again, each caught in the web of their own thoughts.

"Everything happened out of order, you know?" Jacob said. He gestured widely with his hands, as though encompassing the entire mess of their relationship. "And fast. I didn't want to blow it before we even had a chance to try."

"Why try when you knew this was coming?" she asked, aware her voice was starting to hitch. "Why take us down that road? This is exactly the sort of thing I meant, Jacob, our goals are too different. We don't—"

"Don't say it," Jacob said, twisting around to kneel on the floor in front of her, his hands gripping her thighs. In the near dark, his eyes glimmered. "Don't."

"But—"

"I knew you'd be upset," he said, his voice getting faster the more she pulled back. "I know it's not ideal, and the timing sucks, but this doesn't really change anything."

Melinda drew a careful breath, painful bands tightening around her heart. She nodded. "You're right. It only moves up the inevitable."

"Melinda," he said, his voice now as raw as she felt inside, "don't do this. We can make it work, I know it. If you'll give us a chance. I have some ideas—"

There was only one question she needed an answer to. "How?"

How? It was such a small word for such a big question.

Melinda held her breath, hoping against hope that Jacob would have the answer. Some way for them to be together despite everything. He hesitated as if he would speak, then only shook his head, and her heart cracked wide open.

He slid his palms along the sides of her thighs, wrapping his arms around her and pulling her closer.

Tighter.

A big, strong man, offering her all his strength, all his comfort, and she wanted it all, but a sob trembled on her lips, knowing he was not to be hers. He overwhelmed her, undid her. Destroyed her.

Jacob dropped his head into her lap and held on as though he'd never let her go.

He said, "We'll find a way," but she already knew there was no way, no solution that would give them both what they wanted and needed from their futures.

It took everything she had not to reach out to him, not to run her hands through his hair, over his shoulders and down his back, not to hold onto him as tightly as he was holding her. Pain razored every nerve ending.

She told herself it was better to start the separation now, better not to pretend, even as every cell in her body seemed to cry out in need.

"Jacob," she said, her voice low, her throat throbbing with unshed tears. She allowed herself one small touch, a hand to his shoulder. "We should get some sleep."

In answer, he squeezed her more tightly yet, but finally, finally he sat back on his heels. With one arm still around her, he grasped her chin with his free hand, forcing her to meet his gaze.

"Look at me," he demanded when she closed her eyes to escape the intensity of his all-seeing stare.

She obeyed reluctantly, knowing he could hear her shallow, unsteady breaths, the pounding of her heart. Could he tell how close she was to giving in, to throwing her arms around him, tossing away her dreams, and promising to follow him wherever he might lead?

Anything to escape the pain of losing him.

Staring deeply into her eyes, he held her there for one long moment. Then he reached up, leaned forward, and kissed her senseless.

It was like being tossed into the middle of a whirlpool. The room seemed to revolve around her head, and she spun with it, no awareness of up or down or right or wrong.

There was only Jacob and his blistering kiss.

When he broke the contact, she gulped air like a drowning person. The kiss might have lasted an hour or a day. A month or a year. She had no concept of time. She heard no sound but her own thundering heart, tasted nothing but the sweet saltiness of his lips. Felt nothing but his hard, strong body pressed to hers. He filled her vision. His scent filled her lungs.

He'd stripped her of every one of her senses and filled the empty spaces with himself. It was too much, and she started up in a panic, overpowered, but his hold on her kept her in place.

"Understand one thing," he said, his voice a whisper now, though it echoed like a gong in her mind. "I love you. And this isn't over." Standing, Jacob kissed the top of her head, and said,

"For now, get some rest," as though everything were completely normal.

He made his way to the other side of the room where he rustled around, presumably getting into his pajamas, before dropping heavily onto his bed.

Melinda sat where he'd left her, her mouth opening and closing like a fish. No words came to her lips. No words came to her mind, either. She'd never been kissed all the way brainless before. Jacob had brushed the ragged edges of it yesterday, but...

Wow.

Melinda stifled the somewhat hysterical giggle that wanted to rise into her throat. He definitely knew how to kiss, but she wasn't sure she cared for the total loss of intellect and basic motor skills.

Weak limbed, she forced herself to move, shifting to climb beneath the covers. Out of the corner of her eye, she spied Jacob, his arms crossed behind his head, staring straight up at the ceiling. His knees were drawn up, tenting the blankets, to keep his feet from dangling off the end of the bed.

Mimicking his position, she stared at the ceiling as well.

Disconnected images and nonsensical phrases floated along the paths of the brain cells Jacob's kiss had unraveled. She stared until her eyes watered. No answers appeared upon the wooden beams above her head.

When her body cried out for Jacob to come sleep with her again, she told it to shut up.

The silence in the loft deepened, thick with tension, but neither of them moved, and neither of them slept for a very long time.

Just as she was finally about to drop off, she heard him murmur, "Goodnight, shortcake."

She didn't answer, but in her mind, she whispered, "G'night, pickle relish."

Jacob rolled his head back and forth along his seat's headrest, wishing they were already home. The trip was taking for-freaking-ever, even without any delays like the ones they'd had on the drive to Utah the previous week.

The blizzard of the day before had blown itself out sometime before midnight, and the plows had worked all night, so the roads were in decent condition, though edged on both sides by some of the largest piles of snow Jacob had ever seen.

No, by any rational time-keeping system, their return trip took the standard six hours it should have. It was only in his mind that time seemed to slow to a crawl.

Melinda sat in the SUV's passenger seat, and he'd taken his usual spot behind her, neither of them wanting to make a change in their seating into an issue. They'd gotten through breakfast by being scrupulously polite, though both of their mothers had inquired if they were coming down with colds thanks to their pale faces and tired eyes.

Jacob sighed. If only it were as simple as a cold.

He figured it was painfully obvious to anyone with more than two brain cells to rub together that he and Melinda were at odds. No one said a word.

Eddie—who'd already pulled Jacob aside several times that morning to apologize again for his big mouth—and Rick had parked themselves in the backseat this time, proclaiming a temporary boycott on grown-ups and their choice of driving music. Christian and Wendell, who didn't much like the 'ancient' 1980s music preferred in the younger generation's vehicle, but who'd brought their handheld games in any case, settled in the smaller car with Aunt Pat, Uncle Allan, and Eddie's parents.

It hardly mattered, since the music stayed off and the car cruised forward in heavy silence. Danny had woken with a migraine and was camped out in the middle seat next to Jacob, his head back and his eyes closed while Gabe maneuvered the SUV through the light traffic.

The car stayed quiet until they stopped in Las Vegas for a quick lunch—In-N-Out again, much to Christian and Wendell's delight—and they got out to stretch their legs.

By then, Danny's medication had done its work, and he was feeling better, though he still looked pretty beaten down.

Back on the road after lunch, Gabe turned the music on low so as not to disturb Danny, and talked to Melinda about school, their summer plans, and the races he had coming up.

Jacob listened with half an ear, wondering what it would be like between himself and Melinda by next summer—camping together, going to Rick's play or Gabe's races, fishing at Eddie's, or any of the events he might be able to make with his new schedule—if they hadn't sorted out their relationship.

Rubbing a hand over his heart, he stared out the window. Somehow, they had to fix the mess they'd made, and despite what Melinda had said, the only fix he was interested in was the one that ended with them together.

He should have told her his ideas last night. Instead, he'd let nerves get in the way, had convinced himself she wasn't ready to hear him yet, that it would be better to wait until he was sure. Until he had everything solidly in line.

Wasn't that the sort of thinking that had gotten him into this mess in the first place? Holding back. Keeping secrets. Well, he'd learned his lesson, finally. He'd make it right.

Though the clock seemed to move backward, the scenery sped by. It was mildly depressing to be back down out of the mountains, away from all the gorgeous snow and scenery. Back to the brown, winter-dead desert.

Even Vegas, for all its flashy nighttime glamour, seemed dull and tacky in the bright early-afternoon sunlight.

But it was familiar, and close to home, and he was plenty ready to be back in his own house, his own room, his own long-enough bed.

It would be even better to have Melinda there with him. And he would, he vowed.

Somehow.

There were scary, exciting, pulse-pounding possibilities in the wind. It would be up to him to make them happen in a way that would make them both happy.

So much had changed in the past ten days. Surely she'd lived an entire year instead of less than half a month. Even looking at Jacob in the car's mirror had Melinda's heartbeat racing, her breath coming shallow and fast, nerves and needs tangling over her skin and grinding against the despair that threatened to drag her down into a deep, dark pit.

She had a lot to think about in the coming weeks.

The trip home flew by, a welcome difference compared to the drive to Utah. And she thought about Jacob the entire way, even as she talked with Gabe or listened to the quiet music on the radio.

It was already dark when they wound through Victorville at just after five in the afternoon, the height of traffic hour. They passed by Hesperia's Main Street exit in favor of the less congested Ranchero Road, following it all the way out to Hesperia Lake before making the turn into Pasodoro.

Skirting the quiet town square, with its old-fashioned globe lamps still ringed with Christmas lights and hung with festive wreaths, they crossed the bridge over the dry Mojave riverbed and finally pulled up to the gate in front of their house.

From the lead vehicle, her dad hopped out to deal with the lock. Beyond the gate, the house glowed in the automated house lights, the warm peach stucco, burnt umber roof tiles, and pretty, landscaped yard a welcome sight to Melinda's tired eyes.

Gardening in the desert could be challenging with the extreme temperatures, rocky soil, frequent droughts, high winds, and the ever-present fire danger, but her mom managed to create lasting beauty out of her carefully selected plants.

With her mother's artistic vision and her dad's business flair, their company thrived along with the foliage, and the land around their home showed off their hard work.

Every time she came through the front gates, Melinda's heart filled with pride and contentment. It was good to be home.

"All right, troops," Stan said once they were all parked and stretching outside the cars. "Time to divide and conquer."

Her dad gave out his standard post-vacation organizational orders, including an invitation for anyone who wanted to stay to a last group dinner before heading home, then paused for an extended stretch of his own before tossing a set of keys to Rick.

"Grab the dogs from the sitter, if you would," Stan said. Turning back to everyone else, he clapped his hands and said, "Okay. Let's do this."

It didn't take long to divvy up the gear, even with the return of the joyful dogs running and jumping about, but the group was so worn out, no one decided to stay for dinner.

Soon, the others were back in their own vehicles, waving as they drove down the long driveway and out the gate. She didn't even get to say goodbye to Jacob, though she wasn't sure what she would have said anyway.

As his parents' car passed by the spot where she stood with her mom and dad, watching everyone leave, he called, "See ya later, cheese puff," out the window, and sent a tiny curl of warmth back into her heart.

Following her parents and the rowdy dogs into the house after the gate closed behind the Tanners and their taillights faded from view, Melinda wished she could go straight upstairs and sleep for a week. Maybe then, when she woke, she'd find everything back to normal.

Instead, she helped her dad put their snow gear away in the garage, then helped her mother prepare a quick dinner, and thought about Jacob.

She ate, cleaned up, unpacked her suitcase, and thought about Jacob.

She started the laundry, caught up her social media pages, downloaded her photos from the trip, and thought about Jacob.

He stared intensely at her from the shot she'd taken in the condo's kitchen during their New Year's Day party. It looked even better on the bigger screen of her laptop than it had in the camera's viewer. As she'd known it would. She was definitely entering it in the fair's competition.

God, he was sexy.

And sweet.

And wonderful.

And she loved him so much she wanted to scream at the injustice of it all.

Why couldn't she have fallen this hard for someone who wanted the same things she did?

If Mitch had been true to her, she might never have discovered the devastating intensity of her feelings for Jacob. She might never have learned the truth about the depth of true love, or the way it could shred the heart.

She knew now.

And the worst of it was, because she did love Jacob, she wanted him to go out and conquer the medical world. She wanted him to have his dream career, and everything that went with it, even though that meant them not being together. She wanted what was best for him, no matter what it did to her.

Love sucked.

She put the last of her things away, glad that her parents had given her some space after the first few concerned glances they'd tossed her way, then wandered into her bathroom.

She looked like hell.

Aside from getting no sleep the night before, the bruises from her tangle with Dane were starting to take on a green-and-yellow hue at the edge of the darker colors.

"Ack," she said to her reflection.

Deciding to take a bubble bath, she ran the water hot, then slipped in, soothing her sore muscles in the steamy heat.

And she thought about Jacob.

Feeling naughty and daring, she ran soapy hands over her body and dreamed they were his.

She knew now, exactly, the way his eyes would smolder when he looked at her, kindle when he touched her, flare when he kissed her. She wanted to see them burn.

Her hands stilled, and a lump formed in her throat.

What was she going to do?

Only silence answered.

Later, after forcing herself through a halfhearted yoga sequence, Melinda tucked herself into bed in her darkened room, her head cradled on her hands, and thought, and thought, and thought about Jacob.

If only there were a way…

It seemed strange to go to sleep in a room without him now. She missed him being there, even in a separate bed.

Melinda rolled over, seeking elusive comfort.

Her cell chimed, the sound loud in her quiet room. A text message. She grabbed the phone hesitantly—she'd deleted another spate of messages from Mitch over the past several days, each from different numbers, all of which she'd blocked. She wasn't in the mood to see another one, but the text was from Jacob. One simple message that set her heart aglow.

:I love you, buttercup. G'night. <3:

Grinning ear to ear despite herself, she texted back.

:'Night, licorice whip. <3 <3 <3:

It wasn't *I love you*, exactly. She often signed texts to him with those little emoticon hearts. She shouldn't hope, shouldn't let the spark of pleasure build a bonfire in her belly. Yet no matter how often she repeated to herself that there was no hope for them, she couldn't stop the blaze.

She loved him, and he loved her. And if anyone could figure out a way forward, it was Jacob. He'd asked her to trust him. To give her heart to him freely. Even as her mind whispered *but-but-but…* her heart sent all her love winging across the night sky, straight to Jacob.

They had to find a way.

Smiling, hoping, Melinda sank into sleep, surrounded in her dreams by Jacob's strong arms. Her smile lasted all night.

Jacob studied the little hearts in Melinda's text and wondered what she was thinking. If she was already in bed. If she missed him the way he missed her.

Being in that loft together all week had almost felt like living together. Without the fun stuff, obviously, but still.

His room seemed dark, quiet, and lonely without her smile, her laugh, her scent.

His whole life would feel that way if he had to go on without her now.

Before, he'd acknowledged that he'd miss her wherever he went. That it would suck not to see her for months at a time.

Now that they'd torn down their friendship barrier, surviving without her felt impossible, like trying to leave his lungs behind. If she was vital to his happiness, how could he be happy without her?

He'd spent that hellishly long drive home tossing everything around in his brain, working all the angles, seeking a way through their impasse.

Once at home, he'd sat down with his parents and spilled the whole sticky mess into their laps. Together, they'd tossed it around some more.

His mom, with her shrink's cool logic, and his dad with his gut instincts, had thrown their confidence behind him one-hundred percent, as they always had, and they'd come up with some damn good ideas, too. They'd helped him face some truths about himself, things he'd never consciously considered before.

According to his mom, he'd never been ready to consider them before.

Well, he was ready now. More than his relationship with Melinda had changed on that ski trip.

He had a lot to think about.

Jacob pulled up a recent memory in his mind, the victorious

smile on Melinda's gorgeous face right after she completed her first black-diamond run the day before. Her eyes had blazed with triumph, and her smile had burned hot enough to melt the polar ice caps.

He had so much to tell her.

Now that they were home, vacation over, decisions made, it was time to get serious.

32

Though they hadn't even been apart a full day, she missed Jacob.

A lot.

Melinda woke missing him, and it only got worse as the morning wore on.

Her parents had headed out to the nursery early to catch up on the piles of paperwork and stacks of phone messages that would have built up while they were gone, even during the slow winter season. There would be orders to place, appointments to make for landscaping consultations in preparation for spring planting, the endless bookkeeping, a thousand other things.

Afterward, as part of their longstanding post-ski-trip tradition, instead of coming home, they would go to the Pasodoro Inn for an evening of fine dining and pampered relaxation, complete with a night in their favorite suite. It was their annual Christmas gift to each other and helped them smooth the transition from the week of skiing back to regular life.

Melinda didn't mind having the house to herself overnight

to unwind in her own way every year, so it worked well for all of them. Sometimes she'd have all of her girlfriends over for a raucous slumber party, but she wasn't in the mood for that this year.

Instead, she intended to spend most of her day putting the house back to rights so her parents wouldn't have to deal with it—including taking down as many of the Christmas decorations as she could manage on her own.

Tomorrow she'd meet her mom and dad at the nursery, and for a few days after that, to help them clear the rest of the business backlog.

Before she knew it, Christmas break would be over, and it would be time to head back to school. It seemed incredible to think she'd left Cal State Fullerton in mid-December with one boyfriend, yet had almost returned with a different one.

And not just any boyfriend.

Jacob.

Thinking of school made her think of next fall, when Jacob would be at UC Irvine, and she'd still be at Cal State. Without him.

It was irrational to get so upset over him changing colleges. He would have been there the following year anyway, for med school, and during non-traffic times, the two schools weren't even a half-hour apart. It wasn't like he was leaving the state. But she'd still had at least eighteen months to work up to the idea of his moving farther away.

Her get-used-to-it timeframe had been cut in half.

When her entire life consisted of fewer memories without him than with, it amounted to a big, unhappy change in her daily routine. And that was before taking a romantic relationship into consideration.

Hoping to blank her mind with chores, Melinda threw on her oldest, rattiest sweats, turned the music up to scream, and got to work.

She finished unpacking and organizing everything from the trip, emptied the last of the ice from the coolers, ran more laundry. She did the breakfast dishes, then spent a half-hour playing with Baxter and Buddy, sending them into doggie bliss, and wore them out enough to keep their noses out of the Christmas boxes when she started taking down the ornaments and lights from the tree in the living room.

She was seated at the dining room table, winding up the last of the garland and about to head upstairs, when she heard the front door open.

Buddy and Baxter, who'd been sleeping at her feet, took off down the hallway in a blur of black fur and scrabbling paws, barking joyfully and drowning out the voice of whoever had entered the house calling her name.

"In here," she yelled back, pushing away from the table to see who was there.

Her heart beat a little harder than necessary, wondering if it was Jacob, and she stared at herself in the mirror over the buffet in despair. She looked like a chimney sweep.

Poking her head around the corner, she caught sight of her visitor. Surprised, she said, "Hey, Eddie."

Melinda ignored the totally vain flare of relief that it was not Jacob who had caught her looking like she'd been crawling around inside the fireplace. Not that he hadn't seen her covered in dirt and sweat before—they camped together every summer, after all—but still.

"Hey," Eddie replied, looking up with a smile as he continued to rub the dogs' ears. Their tails thumped wildly against the carpet, their tongues lolling out the sides of their mouths in sheer delight.

"Are you looking for Rick? I haven't seen him today."

"I came to see you. Got a minute?"

Now doubly surprised, and twice as curious, Melinda said, "Sure," wondering what was up.

Though she and Eddie were good friends, and hung out regularly as part of the rest of their group, it was rare for him to seek her out privately.

"Kitchen?" he asked, tilting his head in that direction.

"Sure," Melinda repeated, following him into the other room. "Would you like some tea or something? I can make hot chocolate."

Eddie, out of all the guys, had the biggest sweet tooth, but though his smile widened when she mentioned the cocoa, he said, "Tea's fine."

As at home in her kitchen as his own, Eddie took a seat in the attached breakfast nook while she put on the kettle. The oval trestle table—big enough to seat eight, or ten in a pinch—was surrounded by chairs and low, built-in benches. It sat in a cozy alcove with a bay window facing the front of the house.

Melinda dealt with the tea things, arranging cups, spoons, both sugar and honey—she knew her friend!—milk, and a shaker of cinnamon on a tray, then depositing it on the table.

Comfortable with silence, Eddie kicked back in his seat, his hands stuffed in the pockets of his favorite, ancient brown leather jacket, and watched the birds flitting from branch to branch outside the window.

"There's a pFeddUp meeting tomorrow night, my mom wanted me to remind you," he said.

pFeddUp—Partnership For Eliminating Distracted Driving—was the nonprofit Seth's parents had started after his death.

"I'll be there."

When the kettle whistled, she placed it on a trivet on the table and added a package of Scottish butter cookies, hiding her grin when Eddie's eyes lit up and his mouth kicked upward at the corners.

She took a seat beside him and watched out the window, too, while they stirred their tea and nibbled cookies in the quiet kitchen. She'd always found Eddie to be a restful sort of person.

He was great with kids—patient, kind, funny, the kind of guy even the troublemakers seemed comfortable seeking out to confess their secrets to. She'd only seen him truly riled a handful of times, and it had always been in defense of someone else, but those few times were sort of legendary.

It was a foolish person who picked on someone smaller or weaker in Eddie's vicinity.

Some people found it odd that he and Rick were such good friends, given their polar-opposite natures, but that was part of what made their friendship work so well. Plus, they had the same affinity for kids, which made them both extremely popular summer camp counselors.

Now Eddie was working toward opening his own camp in the foothills outside Pasodoro where his grandfather had left him some property. It would take him years to make it the way he wanted, but she had no doubt he'd succeed with it, and kids would come from miles around.

Someday, her own children would go to Eddie's to ride horses, fish, hike, swim, and all the other fun stuff kids did at camp.

She'd grown up doing all of those things on his parents' property, simply because they were all friends, but Nancy and Peter's focus had always been the horses. They'd never offered the types of activities Eddie planned to provide to the general public, with the recent exception of the annual rodeo for Seth Mazer's memorial scholarship fund.

Melinda had thought the rodeo might eventually migrate to Eddie's property, as well, but his land was too far out of town to make it practical.

"So," he said finally, blowing across the top of his tea. "You and Jake."

Trust Eddie to get right to the heart of the matter. No beating around the bush.

"Yeah?" she said cautiously.

She rested her head along the high back of her seat, turning her face to look at him. Eddie twisted toward her, sitting forward a little, one elbow on the table, his other arm draped along the top of her chair, his gray eyes intent.

"I want to apologize for springing his news on everyone. He wanted to tell you first, Mel. You should know that."

"Not your fault," Melinda said, sipping her tea.

"So what's the problem?"

"What do you mean?" she hedged, then caved when he only gave her his patient stare. "Okay, okay. In a nutshell?"

When he nodded, she said, "I'm in love with him. He's in love with me. And it's never going to work out."

She said the words matter-of-factly, as though their truth weren't tearing her apart inside. Eddie's eyes said he saw right through her.

Eddie considered her for a full minute before straightening to take another sip of his tea. He set the mug back on the table, folded his hands in front of himself, and lasered her with his gaze.

"You're both idiots, you know that?" he said. While Melinda spluttered, he held up a hand and kept talking. "First, everyone knows you love each other. But since it took you two dummies long enough to figure that part out, I'm going to help you with the rest."

"I hardly think—"

"Uh-huh," he interrupted, wagging a finger in front of her face, "that's exactly the problem. Thinking. You think too much here—" he drilled the same finger into the middle of her forehead, "—and not nearly enough here." His finger jabbed a spot above her heart.

Crossing her arms in defense, Melinda frowned at him. "How is that helpful?"

"Don't get your tiara in a twist, I'm getting there."

Gentler now, Eddie's eyes softened, and he tugged affectionately on a lock of her hair that had come down from the messy bun she'd thrown it in halfway through her chores.

"When did you decide you were going to spend your entire life here in Pasodoro?" he asked. "When did Jake decide he had to get out?"

Melinda frowned at him. "He's always wanted to leave. And I've always wanted to stay here," she said. "Why would I want to go anywhere else? Everyone I love is here."

"Not everyone," Eddie corrected. "Rick will be off to Hollywood or New York, and who knows with the rest. Do you really think all your cousins are going to stay here? Or all of our friends? If home is where the heart is, and your heart's with Jacob…"

Staring into her tea, Melinda mulled that over. Of course, he was right. She'd turned a blind eye to the truth, but there was no way everyone she loved would stay in Pasodoro. Jacob and Rick weren't the only ones who'd set their sights on faraway places.

"You think I should go with him."

"No. I think you guys should ponder when and why you

made the decisions you've made and whether they're still valid. You might surprise yourselves."

"I wish you'd just say what you mean. It's not like you to be cryptic."

"Some things you have to discover for yourself, princess."

Melinda scoffed. "If I was really a princess, I'd have my knights force you to talk."

"When did you get so bloodthirsty?" he asked, the humor back in his eyes. "Come on, budge up," he added as he nudged her out of her seat.

Once they were both standing, Eddie pulled her in for a hug, pressing her head to his shoulder for an extra moment. Melinda soaked in the comfort that was such a part of him, even when he was being mysterious and annoying.

"Did you talk to Jake about this?" she asked when they pulled apart.

"Nope," he answered, grabbing both of their mugs and rinsing them out in the kitchen sink. "That's for you to do. So go do it."

Tipping her an imaginary hat, Eddie sauntered out of the kitchen.

"Charge your phone!" she called after him, and heard him laugh.

"Yeah, yeah," he said, and a few seconds later, the front door closed quietly behind him.

Melinda stared unseeing at the empty archway from the kitchen into the hallway, not exactly sure what had just happened or what she was supposed to do about it.

"Thanks a lot, Eddie," she muttered, then went upstairs to take apart her little fake tree in her room.

Carefully packing away her homemade ornaments, she smiled at the ones that had photos of herself and Jacob together or Jacob by himself. One of her favorites was a shot of Jacob, Rick, and Eddie, the summer they were ten. The photo had captured them in mid-jump off the rock ledge at Deep Creek, about to splash down into the clear, green-blue water, identical mile-wide grins on their faces. They wore swim-trunks and nothing else, their bare, boyishly thin and hairless chests gleaming in the hot desert sun.

Melinda envisioned the last time she'd seen Jacob without his shirt on, only a few days ago at the condo in Utah. He'd been walking down the hall in nothing but low-slung jeans after taking a shower, rubbing a towel briskly over his dark, wet hair.

He was still Jacob, the boy she'd grown up with, the boy she knew almost as well as she knew herself, but some things had changed in quite… scintillating ways since their shared childhood.

Gone was the hairless, skinny chest and soft, childish belly. Jacob the man had a firmly muscled chest, abs sculpted like fine marble, and just the right amount of crisp, dark hair trailing down the center of his flat stomach before disappearing enticingly inside the waistband of his jeans.

Remembering, Melinda's belly spasmed with lust.

Yet the biggest change of all wasn't something that could be seen with the naked eye. It lived in both their hearts, and had the potential to tear them to pieces.

Thinking over her conversation with Eddie, she frowned.

Talk to Jacob, talk to Jacob.

Of course she'd talk to Jacob.

She just didn't know what good it would do.

Because she was filthy from her tussle with the dogs and sweaty from all the chores, Melinda took a quick shower, threw on her favorite jeans, and pulled a dark burgundy cable-knit sweater over her head. She added the gold Celtic-knot earrings Jacob had given her for Christmas two years ago, and the Goofy watch from this year, and paced her room.

And thought.

And fretted.

And stalled.

And thought some more.

Regardless of the danger to her friendship with Jacob—to their families and friends and their entire circle—and unwise as it might be to act on the emotions swirling inside her, she had to admit the deep-down truth to herself.

Jacob was it for her.

And since that was the case, she wasn't going to be happy

anywhere on earth unless they were together.

As much as the idea of leaving Pasodoro made her sad and scared, the idea of living there without him was unbearable. Jacob was the one with the big career aspirations, goals that would require him to travel far and wide. She couldn't ask him to give all that up. But if she removed the specific location of her dreams from the rest, she could still have almost everything she wanted if she went with him.

She'd still be a nurse-midwife, she'd still be helping her fellow women through one of the most transformative periods of their lives, helping them cope and adjust and giving care to her community. She'd still make a happy home for herself and Jacob and their future children.

Okay, so those children wouldn't grow up with their grandparents and cousins right down the street, in a town where almost everyone would know and care for them. They wouldn't walk to Ollie's Ice Cream Parlor or go to events in Pasodoro's town square. And maybe they'd have to find a different camp to go to instead of Eddie's, and she'd have to meet new friends to share her life with. Maybe there would be some birthdays and holidays that the extended family would miss out on, but…

Belly pitching, teary-eyed, Melinda collapsed on her bed, all her strength streaming out of her muscles.

She was in love with Jacob. Her best friend in the world. It wasn't rebounding. It wasn't simple lust. It wasn't a childhood or teenage crush she would out grow. And, miracle of miracles, he loved her back.

It should all be simple! It should all be happy!

So why was it so monumentally painful and complicated?

Scrubbing the tears from her eyes, Melinda sat up, and her gaze landed on her Cal State sweatshirt. Huffing out a breath, she considered the blue-and-orange logo on the front. Moving to Fullerton for college her freshman year had been hard, even with Jacob there, too. Harder than she'd anticipated.

Nearly three years later, she still missed being home, even though she enjoyed school and all the friends she'd made. She loved Orange County. She loved all the things there were to do there, all the opportunities. Still, the idea of leaving her life in

Pasodoro behind for good felt like ripping off a limb.

But the idea of not being with Jacob felt like ripping out all her vital organs.

She could live without a limb. The organs? Not so much.

Standing again, she moved into her bathroom to splash her face with water, then gripped the edge of the counter with her hands, leaning close to the mirror to look deeply into her own eyes.

What she saw there told her the decision had already been made.

If she had to choose between everything in Pasodoro and Jacob, she'd choose Jacob. Every time.

The truth didn't lessen the pain she felt over the decision, but the certainty centered her, confirmed it was the right choice, no matter how difficult.

Love trumped all.

Now that she'd made her decision, excitement filled her up, energy tinged with hope and nerves and urgency. It rushed inside her like water flooding the Mojave River, too big to contain in her body.

Too big for the house.

She needed the air, she needed to get outside.

She had to tell Jacob!

Too wound up to sit still, Melinda paced her room. She wanted to call, then worried over what to say. She tried out a few lines, discarded them, tested a few more.

Nothing sounded right. She had to get it exactly right, she had to…

She had to stop.

But…

Melinda paced some more, muttering under her breath, until she finally swiped a hand across her field of vision.

"Stop," she said aloud.

This was insane. She'd never in her life worried about calling Jacob, or had to gather up her courage to talk to him. She wasn't about to start now.

Grabbing her cell, she hit her speed dial and ignored the quick, nervy little pitch in her belly.

"Hey, chocolate curl," Jacob said.

"Lemon drop," she responded, so happy when he answered in his usual, boisterous tone that she did a little dance in place. "I like that one, by the way."

She hoped he could hear the smile in her words and not the nerves.

"Thanks," he said, humor in his voice now. "I figured you would. It has the word 'chocolate' in it."

"Exactly."

A short, uncomfortable silence, so unusual for them, fell across the phone line.

"So how's the home-again organizing going?" he asked, as though everything was normal.

She tried to answer the same way, though the nerves were now crawling up her throat. "Pretty much done. You?"

"Yep, done. Good to have a few more days at home before school."

"Yeah. Um, anyway," she said, twisting a lock of hair around her index finger, "I was calling to see if you were busy or—"

"I'm not busy," he interrupted.

"Okay," she said. "Um." Why was this so hard all of a sudden? "Good. Then I was wondering if you, uh, want to go for a walk?"

If she didn't get out of the house in the next three minutes, the top of her head might blow off.

"Sure. Give me ten minutes, I'll be right there."

Ten! Oh, God.

They hung up, and the nerves kicked up her spine. Ten minutes sounded like forever.

She pulled on her boots and bundled up against the winter-desert chill—nothing compared to what they'd experienced in Utah, though still bitey, especially with the winds blowing.

But that only took two minutes.

Oh, God, oh, God, oh, God.

She was going on a walk with her best friend, damn it. And she was going to tell him she loved him. And would go with him.

Anywhere.

Which would make him happy, since he loved her, too. There was not a single thing to be nervous about.

Except their entire relationship hung in the balance of the outcome of this particular walk.

She breathed in, breathed out.

It would be okay.

It would.

It had to be.

She hoped he would kiss her again.

Now there were excited tingles running up and down her spine instead of the damn nerves.

Much better. But still unnerving.

Melinda's hands sprang with damp, the way they did when she wandered too close to the edge of a steep drop.

Hurrying back into the bathroom, she brushed her hair again, then freshened her lip gloss. Finished, she slapped on a warm hat, wrapped a scarf around her neck, and headed out the front door to meet him, expecting to still have a few minutes to wait.

Only he'd surprised her. Jacob was there already, faster than usual, maybe out of eagerness to see her.

But he wasn't alone.

33

Shock made Melinda draw up short, and her stomach seemed to bottom out.

Jacob stood, tall and oh-so-handsome, his car door still open behind him, squared off like a gunslinger at high noon with Mitchell Gaveston.

Shock stole Melinda's voice. What was Mitch doing here?

"Mel," Jacob said, moving to intercept her

She held up a hand, her eyes on Mitch, and Jacob stopped in his tracks.

"Melly," Mitch said, speaking in that cajoling way he had, stepping toward her with a wide smile.

She used to find that tone playful. Now, combined with the use of the hated nickname only he ever called her—and she'd never been able to make him stop—it scraped like a serrated blade down the length of her spine.

"Don't call me that," she snapped, holding up her other hand to stop him from moving any closer.

"Melinda," he corrected, and smiled his hangdog smile. The one that had seemed so self-effacing and endearing when they first met, and now struck her as calculated. "Sorry. It's so good to—"

"What are you doing here, Mitch?"

Out of the corner of her eye, Melinda noted the still-as-stone watchfulness in Jacob's stance. Others might mistake it for poised control, but she knew underneath that pseudo-calm exterior, his muscles coiled tight, ready to spring.

It bolstered her confidence, even as she determined to get Mitch out of here before he tested Jacob beyond his limits. She didn't want the two of them coming to blows.

Not that she'd mind tossing her own right-hook Mitch's way—he so deserved it, the bastard—but it would be better for everyone if they could end this like grown-ups.

As fast as possible.

Mitch shrugged, went for charming and innocent, his lips turning up at their corners. His sandy hair waved in the breeze as though he'd engineered it precisely that way.

"You didn't return my calls," he said. "I knew you were coming home yesterday, so—"

"So you took it upon yourself to force your presence—" Jacob interrupted.

"Jake," Melinda said sharply, slicing her eyes his way, cutting him off. "I'll handle this."

Jacob crossed his arms over his chest and pokered up. Jerked his chin once to indicate his assent, though he clenched his jaw so tightly, it would be a wonder if he didn't crack any teeth.

Shifting her gaze back to Mitch's dark-brown eyes, Melinda said, "So you drove up here to, what, hear me tell you in person to get lost?"

"Now, Melly—Melinda," Mitch quickly corrected himself, stepping forward again.

Jacob gave a low growl.

"Stay where you are," Jacob said, his voice level enough, but tension in every line of his body. "And don't touch her."

Mitch, who'd been steadfastly ignoring Jacob up to this point, finally shifted his gaze from Melinda's to scan his eyes disdainfully down Jacob's much taller, leaner body.

"This doesn't concern you, boy," he said. "Why don't you run along and—"

Jacob leaped, but Melinda did, too, landing in the middle of the two men, her outstretched hands slapped against both straining male chests, keeping them apart by sheer will.

"Stop it! Stop now," she yelled. "Jacob, back. Mitch, get back."

She knew they could get around her easily, but having her jump between them seemed to have brought them—at least temporarily—to their senses.

Both men snapped straight, their arms falling to their sides, and each stepped carefully back.

Jacob slid his left hand down her arm and twined their fingers together, pulling her to his side.

Mitch frowned now, noting the move.

"What's really going on here?" he asked, his voice laced with suspicion.

"What's going on," Melinda said evenly, disengaging her fingers from Jacob's and moving a step away, giving him a subtle motion of her hand to keep him still and silent while she addressed her words to Mitch, "is I want you to leave. We have nothing to say to each other."

"Melinda—"

"No." Now she sliced her hand through the air. "You made your choice when you went back to Christina. If that was a mistake on your part, then I'm sorry it didn't work out, but you can't bounce back to me, or between us like a ping-pong ball. You made your choice. We're done."

Considering her, Mitch tilted his head, and his expression went ugly.

"It looks to me like you didn't waste any time bouncing along, yourself," he said nastily, a sneer on his face now. He waved a hand, indicating Jacob. "I always knew there was something going on with you two. You want to play the injured party? What a slut."

"That's it," Jacob said, and charged, his fist already drawn back, but again, Melinda jumped between the two.

"Jacob, no!"

She faced him full on this time, her back to Mitch. Both hands splayed on Jacob's chest, she pushed him backward one hard chest-slap at a time, and his expression was so surprised, he let her maneuver him all the way back to his car before he managed to protest.

"You heard what he called you," Jacob spluttered, finally grabbing both her hands in one of his, holding them captive against his taut belly.

"Yes," she said, very evenly, very deliberately. "I did. And I repeat. I. Will. Handle. It." Melinda emphasized the last by jerking her hands free and poking Jacob in the sternum. "Stay. Here."

His hand shot out, recaptured and tightened on hers.

"Melinda, let me stand for you," he said, and the look in his eyes burned something pure and hot and wonderful right through her heart.

Gently now, pulling one hand loose, she placed it against his cheek. Looking deeply into his eyes, she said softly, "Stand *with* me, Jake."

She held there, waited until his gaze softened. Finally, he nodded. Still sharp, still angry, but silently consenting to act as her second against their common opponent.

Satisfied, spinning on her heel, Melinda marched back to Mitch, never questioning that Jacob would listen to her. Of course he didn't stay where she'd left him. She heard his equally angry steps stomping right behind hers, but he'd leave Mitch for her to deal with now, even if he didn't like it.

"He's not very well trained, is he?" Mitch asked, smirking over her shoulder at Jacob. "Down, boy."

Mitch laughed, deliberately insulting. His eyes went wide and shocked when Melinda stepped right up into his face and slapped him for all she was worth.

He opened his mouth to speak, but Melinda overrode him, pushing him now, until he slammed into his car and had to lean backward over the hood to keep any space between him and her fury, her poking finger drilling into his chest.

"Look at me, Mitchell," she said when Mitch's eyes still wavered between her and Jacob. "At *me*."

Slowly, insolently, Mitch met her gaze, the smirk still on his mouth despite the angry red mark of her palm print on his ruddy cheek.

"You have the nerve to come up here, whining and weaseling in my face, calling and texting me over my entire vacation, claiming to want me back. After what you did, you have the nerve to accuse *me* of being the slut when you cheated on me for months with that bitch, Christina?"

Surprise lit Mitch's eyes, and he started to say, "How did you know—" before he caught himself and clamped his lips shut.

Melinda closed her eyes and straightened away from him. *Well. That settles that question.*

"Look, Melinda," Mitch said, seeming to see an opening now that she'd stopped for a second. "I'm sorry I hurt you. I never—"

"You're a pig," she interrupted, looking at him again, seeing him clearly for possibly the first time.

She searched her heart for hurt, for regret, and found only indifference.

What a relief.

"You didn't hurt me," she said, "or only for a minute. You opened my eyes. Everything we had together was a lie. I know that now, and it's wiped away any feelings I thought I had for you, good or bad. Now I have truth, and it's better than anything I could have imagined."

Mitch reached toward her, but Melinda merely raised her eyebrows. He lowered his arm. She stepped back, straightened her sweater. Reached behind her for Jacob's hand. And stood a little taller when his fingers wrapped instantly around hers, strong and sure and supportive.

"I don't care what you do, or where you go, or who you go there with," she said. "As long as it's far from here. Goodbye, Mitch."

Turning, she walked away, Jacob at her side, without a backward glance.

Once through the front gate, Melinda and Jacob jogged across the street and onto a narrow dirt path leading away from the road. The track snaked over open land toward the low bluffs above the Mojave riverbed.

They walked side by side, their destination a matter of long habit and mutual preference, taken by silent consent.

She heard Mitch's car spin out when he sped through the gate and took off down the street that would lead him out of town, but she neither looked nor cared.

If she'd needed any reassurance, Mitch's surprise visit had definitively proved she could move forward with a clear mind and a clear heart, with no shadows lurking in any darkened corners. Shadows couldn't survive the pure light of joy that had flooded every nook and cranny of her soul along with her love for Jacob.

Mitch's role in her life was truly over, the chapter closed.

Now it was time for not only a new chapter, but a whole new book, page one of her life with Jacob. She planned to savor every word.

Though those words wanted to pour from her lips in a rush, she held them back. Just a bit longer. She wanted the moment to be perfect.

Juniper and Joshua trees dotted the view, along with a few scattered houses in the distance, fragrant smoke curling from their chimneys. No one else seemed to be outside. The sun shone brightly in a pale blue sky, though the wind whipped cold air through their many layers and pinked their cheeks. Black birds wheeled overhead.

They walked in comfortable silence, their shoes crunching loudly on the small pebbles littering the ground, holding hands as they traveled along the well-worn trail. It pushed its way through mounds of brush and cacti and drought-dry dirt.

There was no need to hurry or to fill up the peaceful hush with small talk. It was like being the only two people on earth.

Finally, they reached the edge of the bluff above the Mojave River and followed the curve of the trail north toward the memorial garden.

A front entrance to the garden, easily accessible from the road, led to a small parking lot. There, a tall, decorative arch marked the beginning of the rocked-in walking trails through the park, but Melinda and Jacob liked to approach the spot the way they always had, long before it became an official location.

The arch had *Seth Mazer Memorial Garden* engraved across the top and the date of the garden's establishment on a second line beneath the name. The garden itself was scattered with drought-resistant plantings, a few small shade trees with benches beneath, and a small gazebo in the very center, with a bronze statue of Seth in its own little circle in front.

Stepping over the low, decorative fencing that marked the outer boundary of the garden, they made their way to the statue first, where Melinda ran her hand over the bronze boy's hair, as she always did, brushing away the latest layer of endless dust deposited by the desert winds.

Seth's parents had commissioned the statue after his death and had donated it to the garden. It depicted him running, looking back over his shoulder at the kite flying just above his shoulder, his face lit with a happy grin. Melinda had supplied the photo the statue was based on, taken by her father on a long-ago summer's day in Pasodoro's downtown square when they were eight. She and Jacob had been in the shot, as well, flying kites of their own right behind Seth's.

The land for the garden had been donated to the city by Seth's great-grandparents, Asher and Evelyn Davis, the founders of Pasodoro and owners of the Pasodoro Inn and Resort, where her parents were staying that night.

Her parents had designed the garden and supplied all the plantings, and almost everyone in town had come out to help with the cleanup and landscaping at one point or another. Eddie's parents had commissioned the arched entry. Jacob's dad had designed and helped build the gazebo, along with everyone in their high-school graduating class.

The city had approved setting aside a small portion of their property taxes to help with maintenance and upkeep, but mostly the garden continued to be tended by volunteers, a labor of love.

Melinda and Jacob stood by the statue for a few moments, then Jacob gave her hand a tug, and they walked toward their favorite spot, a double-sided bench overlooking the riverbed on one side and facing the gazebo on the other, placed on the exact spot where she, Jacob, and Seth had often sat to contemplate life.

The Mojave, mostly an underground river, only rarely flowed above ground, when heavy rains and high snow run-off from the mountains caused severe flooding.

When it raged, it became a dangerous, fast-moving river responsible for road closures, loss of property, and the tragic drownings of animals and humans alike if they ventured too near its banks.

They sat close together, their legs stretched over the sandy ground, leaning against each other as they stared across the dry riverbed toward downtown Pasodoro, the clock tower just visible about the trees.

"You okay?" Jacob finally asked, his fingers still woven through hers, their joined hands resting on his upper thigh.

Melinda nodded, rubbing her cheek against the shoulder of his black jacket. "Yeah. I'm good, actually. I think I needed to see him one more time to really believe it was ended, and like I knew the things I needed to know. If that makes sense."

"That's good," he said.

"Yeah."

Shifting, Jacob scooted around a bit until they faced each other, though he kept hold of her hand. His tawny eyes pierced hers, seeming to glow with the warmth of the sun beaming down as he studied her face.

"So do you?" he asked when she stayed silent. "Do you know the things you need to know?"

Not taking her eyes from his, Melinda said, "I do. I do know."

Jacob's hand tightened convulsively around hers. The expression on his face, so hopeful, so hesitant, so full of feelings for her, burned itself into her heart. She would never forget this moment as long as she lived.

The moment when everything changed.

Melinda placed both hands on his face, one on each cheek, gently, softly, and stared into his gorgeous eyes so he would see the truth in hers.

So he would know.

Leaning forward slightly, she took a deep breath and said the words that would launch a brand new life for them both.

"I've loved you my whole life. I'm so incredibly in love with you, and I'll go wherever you go, because there's nothing I want more than for us to be together."

Nothing moved, no one breathed. Only the flaring of light in his eyes indicated he'd even heard her as she shifted closer still, as she wrapped her arms around him, as she pressed her lips to his in a kiss to seal the words, her lips moving over his in promise.

Then she kissed him again, once, twice, thrice, and whispered, "I love you, Jake."

She opened her eyes, and his were so close, so beautiful.

Her Jacob.

He swallowed audibly.

"You do?" he finally said in a whisper as low as hers, his gaze searching, full of surprise and hopefulness. "You will?"

When she nodded, a smile blossoming across her lips, Jacob's big body seemed to gather in, then explode all at once, a detonation of joy. He threw his head back, tossed his arms up in a victory V, and shouted, "YES!" at the top of his lungs, and all she could do was hang onto him for dear life while the storm of energy shot through his body.

She was still laughing when his mouth crushed down on hers in a kiss more passionate than anything they'd yet shared.

Caught up, suffused with a happiness so pure it seemed to pour from her in waves of shimmering gold, Melinda threw herself into the kiss. Every thought, every emotion, every need and desire twined together into one delicious flood of sensation, and all centered on Jacob, on his kiss, his touch.

He laid her back on the smooth bench, cradling her head in

his hands for a soft spot to rest, and kissed her for a long time.

Kissed her thoroughly.

She no longer knew where her mouth ended and his began, or whose breath belonged to whom. He was hers, and she was his, and that was the only thing that mattered.

When they finally came up for air, both panting, Jacob helped her sit upright, and they leaned against each other again. A bit drunkenly now, Melinda thought, with so much passion swirling like the headiest of intoxicants through her body, and his, too, if his breathing was any indication.

"So," she said, when she could finally speak.

"So," he echoed. "I guess we need to make this official, huh?"

"I guess we do." She smiled at him, letting him see the love pouring from her, all for him, and he smiled back and squeezed her hand.

"All right, then," he said, and clearing his throat, Jacob straightened up and put on a very serious face. "Melinda Anne Honeywell, will you be my girlfriend for real? And will you love me, and let me love you, and will you be with me? Will you be mine?"

As serious now as he, she answered, "I will. And you, Jacob Robert Tanner. Will you love me, and let me love you, and will you be mine?"

"I will," he said, and sealed it with another kiss. "I love you, Melinda."

"I love you, Jacob. Forever."

"I have something for you," he said, a little awkwardly now. "It's not—I don't want to—oh, hell. Here."

Digging in his pocket, he thrust a small box at her and had her heart pounding suddenly in the back of her throat.

Raising her eyes to his, she asked, "What is it?"

"Open it, you goof."

Nerves danced again in his eyes, setting hers flying, too. What had he done?

Opening the box carefully, a little fearfully, Melinda stared at the delicate amethyst and diamond ring nestled in black velvet.

"Oh, Jacob," she said, "it's so beautiful. But I—what…"

"It's a promise ring," he said. He took her hand again. "I love you, Mel. More than I realized before, actually. This, what we have, it's the real thing. I know it. And I want to marry you someday."

"Jake," she said, and it came out as a gasp and a laugh, love and nerves and joy all tangling inside and stealing her breath.

"I need you to know that, right at the beginning. I want to marry you. I want us to be together, really together, forever. A house, kids, the whole thing. If that's what you want, too."

He broke off, his expression questioning and nervous again, until he registered her teary smile and breathed out a sigh of relief.

"Okay. Good. That's good." He laughed a bit, and she laughed, too.

"Yes," she said, "yes, yes, yes, Jacob, to all of it. Always."

"I really hoped you'd say that."

He kissed her, and this time was again different, more sure, more steady, and still more joyful, so much so, she thought she might burst from the power of their combined emotions.

When he broke the kiss, he pulled her into his chest and held her head against his heart.

"How—" she started, "I mean when? When did you do this?"

"This morning," he said. "I was getting ready to call you when you called me."

"It's so beautiful," she said again, staring at the sparkling ring in her hand.

"Will you wear it?" he asked. "Until we're ready for the real thing? I know we still have things to talk about, but I want to make this commitment to you now. I want to make this promise between us."

In answer, she asked, "Will you put it on?" and tugging off her glove, she held out her hand as Jacob slid the ring into place.

It fit perfectly.

"Okay," he said.

"Okay."

They grinned then, big, dopey, foolish grins, and hugged, holding on tightly to each other, as tightly as possible.

Boyfriend and girlfriend. Promised. Amazing.

Yet there was one more question to ask and answer, one more hurdle for them to overcome before their relationship would truly cross the bridge from friendship-land into the land of lovers.

It would be a huge step. And a little scary. But they'd come this far...

"Jake?" she said, keeping her voice small and a bit hesitant.

"Hmm?" he murmured into her hair.

"The lovemaking thing," she said, and felt him go still as marble in her arms.

"Yeah?"

Oh, there was so much caution in that single syllable! She had to stifle a nervous giggle. He pulled back so he could see her face.

"I asked you to wait..." She trailed off, watching him closely.

Jacob dropped his forehead to hers, blowing out a breath that was half strangled laugh, half groan. He grabbed both of her hands and clutched them between their bodies while he seemed to struggle with what to say.

Finally, he lifted his head again, met her eyes.

"Then we wait," he said, making it as simple as that. "I love you. Not for your body, though I love that, too, and I want you more than I want to keep breathing. I can't pretend it'll be easy, but I promise not to push. I love you, Mel, and I want it to be right for both of us. Okay?"

Jacob.

Her man.

Such a good, good man.

She'd known that was exactly what he would say. It was exactly the right thing, the best thing he could have said, and he meant it, she had no doubt. It was all there in his eyes, in the way he looked at her, even in the way he kissed her. In the way he devoured her whole, yet never took her past the line he thought she wasn't ready to cross.

And it was all she needed to hear to set her last fear free, to know that now was the time to cross that line, tear down that final barrier, and show him the true depth of her emotions—not only her love, but the trust, the certainty, the boundless desire.

The need.

It was time.

"Take me home," she said.

34

Jacob struggled to control his breathing and the rampant needs rioting through his body.

God, he wanted her.

It would be torture to wait, knowing Melinda was his, knowing she loved him, knowing she wore his promise ring. Knowing someday she would be his bride.

She brought out passions in him he'd barely scratched the surface on before, things he'd not even known he was capable of, needful of, and he wanted every one of them—and more—with her.

Now.

But if she needed time, he'd find a block of wood to chew down on and wait.

Somehow.

In the meantime, at least he could kiss her and drive himself stark raving mad that way.

He leaned forward, intending to do exactly that, but she evaded his mouth and hugged him instead. Then she rose, brushed herself off, and held out her hand.

"Come home with me, Jake," she said, and he realized it was the second time she'd said it. And there was a look in her eyes...

What did she mean? Did she... No, she'd said to wait. Hadn't she?

Rising, confused, he took her hand and followed her out of the park, back up the sandy trail toward home.

The wind whipped tendrils of her dark hair from beneath the cap and scarf she had on, and her cheeks were rosy with cold. Melinda looked sideways at him and smiled, and he smiled back, but didn't know what to say. She had a new look in her eyes, one he couldn't decipher.

"What do you think our parents will say?" she asked after a while.

"Oh, um," he said, sidetracked for a moment from his lustful musings. "Well, mine are pretty happy about it."

"They are?" A happy glow filled her eyes, wide and deeply blue as she stared up at him.

"They guessed during the New Year's Day party, or maybe even before, I don't know. And then... Well, I think they've sort of wanted this, but didn't want to push."

She nodded slowly, seeming to ponder the ground beneath their feet as they moved along at an easy pace.

"I think my parents may sort of know, too, or have been wanting it. At least, my mom said a few things recently that make me think they might."

"Well, then," he said. "Everyone's happy."

Because he could, he leaned over and kissed her, just quickly, as they walked.

"Everyone's happy," she said, and her smile lit him up more than the sun.

When they got back to the house, she pulled him with her up the stairs and down the hallway to her room. She closed the door behind them and leaned against it, staring at him.

"Kiss me, Jacob," she whispered.

Eager to obey, Jacob moved in to her, grasped her hands and held them in one of his up above her head. The other he wrapped around her waist, holding her trapped there for a long beat.

Their eyes stared deeply into each other's, as though they could see each other's souls. He watched as her breasts rose and fell with each rapid breath, watched the way her eyes went limpid and dark, the way her lips parted, waiting for his mouth.

When he couldn't stand it another second, he released her hands, ran both of his down her sides, and hauled her up against him, picked her right up off the floor. She wrapped her legs around his waist, her boots digging into his glutes, and he pressed her back into the door and fused his mouth to hers in a searing kiss.

It burned every thought out of his head, every human need out of his body, save her. Air, light, food, drink, he needed none of them, only Melinda, only her mouth attacking his like a fever, nip for nip, bite for bite, tongues dueling for supremacy as they invaded each other's mouths.

It came on so fast, he could hardly keep up. It was all flash and fire and driving need powering through him, slashing his control to ribbons.

Dizzy, desperate, Jacob tore his mouth from hers and melded it to the pounding pulse in the base of her throat, nibbling, licking, sucking the spot while she writhed in his arms and moaned his name, her breaths panting in his ear.

Her taste flooded him, hot, spicy, intoxicating. His sanity hung by a thread.

"Take me, Jake," she gasped. "Be with me now. Please."

Her words barely penetrated the sexual buzz filling his brain, but he shook his head, sure he'd misheard her. Misunderstood.

"What?" he asked. "But—"

"Jacob," she groaned when he let her slide down his body, but he needed space, he needed to think, to focus, and he couldn't do that with her slithering over him, frying all his nerve-endings to ash.

"Wait," he said, gulping air, "just wait. What?"

"Please be with me, Jacob," she said, her words coming between breaths every bit as short as his, her blue eyes trained on his face like high-powered beams, seeming to glow from within.

"But you said—"

"I said to take me home. Please be with me, Jake, here in my room. I can't wait any more."

His head still reeling, trying to wrap some sense around her words, he shook his head again, but it wouldn't clear.

"What about your parents? If they come home—"

"They're at the Inn for the night," she said, already pushing his jacket back from his shoulders.

Something was trying to leap inside him, leap right out of him, but he had to make certain...

"You're sure?" he asked, holding her face, holding her gaze, seeing only love and desire shining in her eyes. "You're sure, Mel?"

"I love you," she said simply.

The leash snapped. They leaped at each other again, and now it was frantic, hands and mouths battling, no finesse, only greed as they snatched at each other's clothes and shoes and stumbled across the room.

He tore the cap from her head, yanked off the scarf. They fell where he tossed them, but he didn't look or care. She finally pulled off his jacket, and it hit the floor a second before hers landed on top of it.

Jacob said, "Wait, here—"

And she said, "No, let me—"

They tore at each other.

Hopping in place, he dragged off his boots, then hers as she shifted foot to foot, one hand on his back to hold herself steady. Gloves and socks and jeans disappeared, his sweater and hers, and he barely remembered to grab the condom in time before his jeans vanished in the maelstrom of fabric flying around her room.

Then suddenly they were standing in front of each other in nothing but their underwear, his boxers and her matching purple bra and panties, their chests heaving with their exertions.

The ring he'd placed on her finger shimmered with fire in the light.

For the first time, he noticed she wore the little earrings he'd given her last Christmas, the Goofy watch on her wrist.

His eyes skimmed over her as she scanned him, head to toe and back again. When their eyes met now, a little shyness had crept back into her gaze, and she giggled in a very un-Melinda-like way.

He said, "My God, you're beautiful," and watched the red seep from the tops of her breasts up into her cheeks and the tops of her ears.

"So are you," she whispered.

Melinda stood before him, a vision in lacy purple, all slender lines, pearly skin, high, firm breasts, and smooth, narrow belly. She wasn't tall, at least compared to him, yet her legs seemed to go on forever, and all he wanted was to touch and taste every inch of her, starting at her delicate feet and working his way up.

Slowly.

Over decades.

Until he knew every precious centimeter of her better than she did. Until she became part of him, and he of her.

He reached, she jumped, and they fell across her bed in a tangle of limbs. They cracked skulls and laughed, but they didn't stop.

"Move this way," she said, trying to nudge him to the left, but he said, "No, here," and rolled with her until she lay trapped beneath him, her hair tangled around them both and her fingernails scoring his back.

Ferocious need driving him like a whip, Jacob sank against her, sank his teeth along the pounding cord in her neck, and scraped. She arched against him, his name falling from her lips in a chant, her hands shoving at his boxers.

Mindless, he didn't even bother trying to figure out her bra clasp, simply dragged the cups down and swallowed her whole as she cried out and dug her fingers into his hair, pressing him closer, and closer yet, urging him on. Her rigid nipples tasted like honeysuckle, and he feasted like a starving man, first one, then the other, while she cried *yes-yes-yes* in his ear.

Jacob had a moment to think he'd try for that finesse next time before the storm unleashed completely.

He ripped her panties off.

Desperate, he dragged his mouth down her writhing belly,

buried his tongue inside her and rode out her wild bucking, his hands clamped to her buttocks, her strong, satin legs vised around his shoulders.

She screamed, "Jacob!" as she came, the waves of her orgasm crashing over them both. She tasted like heaven, and he wanted more.

Melinda thrashed against him as he drove her up again, the breath sobbing from her lips when she shattered a second time, her body dewed with sweat, both of them drenched in passion.

"Take me," she said, begging the words. "Jacob, take me now, please."

He could hardly wait.

With a final kiss for her pulsing center, he reared up, smoothing his hands from the outside of her calves to her thighs, a firm, possessive caress. He dealt with his boxers, the condom. Then he stroked his hands along the insides of her legs, where her skin went unimaginably soft, and pressed her thighs wide, brushing the damp curls he'd wetted with his tongue and her pleasure.

He held there a moment, drinking in the sight of her beauty spread before him in the golden afternoon light while she vibrated beneath his hands, and her thighs gripped his urgently, driving him forward.

"Hurry-hurry-hurry," she gasped, but still he stared.

Melinda Anne Honeywell, you are unbelievably beautiful. And you're mine.

Her body was a gift, one he'd never tire of unwrapping. One he would cherish all the days of his life. All silken limbs and strong, sleek muscles, velvety, sensitive skin quivering for his touch, his mouth. The scent and taste of her intoxicated him.

The sight of her breasts, rosy-tipped with succulent nipples, the scorching heat of her sex drove him wild.

And her mouth.

Oh, God, her mouth.

He promised himself years of exploration, decades to discover all the hidden mysteries, the nuances of her lips.

His best friend. His woman. His love. Forever.

"Jacob," she pleaded.

"Melinda," he answered. "I love you."

Slowly, slowly, he slid his length inside her. She rose to meet him, closed around him like the tightest of fists, and what little restraint he had left disintegrated.

It was wild, chaotic, magnificent, and when she came again, he followed her instantly. His shout tangled with hers, and they collapsed together, a sweaty, sticky, helpless jumble of shaking limbs and racing hearts.

When they could breathe again, when they could peel their eyes open, they stared at each other in awed shock.

Slowly their smiles spread, and the smiles became laughs, and their laughter shook the bed.

Then they wrapped their arms around each other tightly and loved each other all over again.

Much later, Jacob reached up and brushed back the wisps of hair their lovemaking had teased into her face, then wrapped her back in his arms, their naked bodies pressed intimately together, and Melinda's heart swelled at the look in his eyes.

God, she loved him.

"What made you change your mind?" he asked.

"Oh," she said, her eyes on the beautiful ring on her finger, on the promise of it. Her heart sang, overfull with love and joy. "A couple things, I guess."

She told him about Eddie's visit and his cryptic message. Jacob watched her carefully, his gaze intent.

"After he left," she went on, "I realized that no matter how bad I want to stay in Paso, I won't be happy anywhere without you. Not even here. I had it switched around in my head before. That the perfect life was here, and if you'd only cooperate, everything would be great." She smiled a bit ruefully. "But it's like you said. It's not the place, it's the people in it. You're the most important one."

"Mel," he said, pressing his forehead to hers. "You stagger me."

"He made me see something else, too. That most of what I was clinging to so hard had to do with Seth."

"Seth."

Nodding, Melinda linked her fingers with Jacob's and laid her head on his shoulder, thinking about their spot looking out over the river and imagining Seth there with them, as he had been so many times over the years.

The hurt would never really go away, the missing of him, but she could let this one thing go now. She believed Seth would approve.

"I always wanted to stay in Paso," she said, "but after he... after he died, it became sort of an obsession. Everyone was so sad, all of us, and his family nearly came apart. Life seemed so fragile all of a sudden, in a way it never had before. The way it could change just that fast. I figured, since none of us know how much time we'll really get, I'd better spend as much of it as possible with all the people I love the best."

She smoothed her fingers over Jacob's bare chest, then pressed a kiss to his shoulder.

"I'd raise my kids here," she continued, "so they'd know the same sort of childhood we had, that security, knowing everyone, being close to family, all of it. Like staying here would be protection somehow, and if something bad happened, it would be the best place for them to be, so…"

She trailed off, running out of words to describe the way those ideas had nested in her heart and mind and become their own truths.

The way she'd let yet one more fear rule her decisions, just like her fear of heights, or giving love a chance with Jacob.

"I guess that all sounds sort of stupid," she said when Jacob stayed silent.

"No," he said, and there was a strange note in his voice. "It sounds sort of familiar, actually. Eddie's a smart guy."

"What do you mean?"

"When we got home yesterday, I dumped our whole relationship deal on my parents, and we talked it out for a long time. My mom gave me basically the same advice Eddie gave you." He played idly with her hair as he spoke, but Jacob's eyes stayed on hers. "When Seth died, you locked everything down. I wanted to run. Freshman year…"

Melinda stroked a hand down his arm for comfort, twined her fingers with his. "I know, Jake."

"Yeah. Well… afterward, I realized that wasn't the way to go, but I still had this need to escape. To just get out. Coming home, even for visits, hurt."

How could they have been so close, yet never talked about this? She'd always taken comfort in going home, in the reminders of Seth all over Pasodoro. For her, those reminders kept him alive in some small way. She'd had no idea Jacob found them so painful.

"Do you still?" she asked. "Is it still that way for you?"

"Sometimes. I handle it better now. We're always going to miss him, but that doesn't stop just because we're not at home. It's the people, right? The thing is, we carry them all with us no matter where we go. So why not go where we're actually happiest?"

Confused, Melinda tilted her head back to see him more clearly. "What do you mean?"

"You said you'd go anywhere with me," he said. "Did you mean it?"

Now she frowned. "Yes. I hope we can still come back to visit often enough, but—"

"What if you didn't have to leave?"

"I don't understand what you're saying."

Suddenly edgy, Melinda sat up, and Jacob followed. Feeling vulnerable, she dragged the sheet over her nakedness. Jacob reached for her hands.

"Mel, when I was in the ER with Neta and her husband in Utah, we had a lot of time to talk, and then talking with my parents sort of drove it all home." He took a breath, watching her closely. "The team doctor thing, that lifestyle, that was all about escaping. I love sports, and hanging out with pro athletes sounds cool, but the people I really want to help, the ones who *need* my help, aren't those athletes."

"They're not?"

"They're old people. Like your grandparents and mine, and all the ones I've hung out with through the years at the retirement home. People like Neta and Clyde, who the doctors don't listen to half the time, just because they're old. They need me. I can do some good for them, really help them."

Excited now, Jacob continued speaking, but Melinda could hardly take in all that he was saying. In her mind's eye, she watched a film strip of memories, all the times Jacob had gone out to the retirement home or the extended care facility, all the hours he'd spent doing chores for the old folks, playing board games with them, or simply talking.

He'd worked a lot with kids, too, like Rick and Eddie did, but it was always the older people he gravitated toward.

It made perfect sense to her, but what did it mean for them?

"So," he said, drawing her attention back into focus, "it's still medicine, but now I know I'll be working where I really need to be."

"Where is that, exactly?" Melinda asked, and held her breath.

"Here, Mel. I want to be home. With you. I want to have that house you're always talking about, I want our kids to grow up in it and have our families and friends all around. I want a life with you, right here in Pasodoro."

"You—you do?"

"The next few years will still be tricky. I still want to go to UCI, and the internships are an important part of that. There'll be residency stuff and all the rest. You still have a lot to get through, too. I thought, for starters, maybe we could get an apartment together next fall, somewhere that's a good halfway point between Fullerton and Irvine so the traffic isn't so bad for either of us. And then, eventually, when we're ready to set up shop for good, we come back here."

Melinda stared at him, completely flabbergasted.

"Mel?"

"Do you mean it?" she whispered, her voice all but

deserting her. "Really?"

Cupping her face in his hands, he leaned in and kissed her mouth, her nose, her forehead. "Yes. I mean it."

"You're sure?"

"I'm sure."

"Oh, Jacob!"

With a cry of happiness that came from the deepest depths of her heart, Melinda tackled him flat out, raining kisses all over his laughing face.

Soon enough, the laughter turned to a different emotion. Naked skin heated, went molten. Lips sought and answered. Hands teased and torched.

They were awkward and fumbling, smooth and graceful, fast as lightning and slow moving as a lazy summer stream.

They laughed and played and whispered and loved, all through the evening and long into the night.

When the sun kissed the morning sky, Melinda's delightfully exhausted mind stuttered and stammered and finally shut down completely. She was sensation only, emotion only, no thoughts, no rationalizations, not even any hopes or fears.

They were beyond the physical, beyond touch and sex. He was Jacob, and she was Melinda. Together, they were elemental, natural, essential.

She rested her weary head on his strong shoulder, and Jacob's arm came around her automatically. He pressed his lips to her forehead and murmured her name, and she snuggled against him, thoroughly content.

She would have followed him anywhere for love. In love, in joy, she would follow him home.

~ THE END ~

THANK YOU!

Thank you for reading *Snow Angel!* If you enjoyed it, please consider helping other readers find this book:

1. Lend this book to a friend!
2. Leave a review on Amazon, Goodreads or your favorite review site! It makes a difference, and is greatly appreciated.
3. Request that your local library purchase a print copy so that other readers can discover Chantilly's romances.

Be the first to know about new releases and fun reader perks by subscribing to Chantilly's announce-only newsletter at www.chantillywhite.com/contact.html#newsletter

Acknowledgements

It takes a writer's village for me to get a new book out into the world, and I love thanking everyone who so generously gives of their time and superior smarts in helping me. They're there for me, no matter how busy they are in their own lives, and I'm so incredibly grateful. These people are AMAZING. Neither *Snow Angel* nor any of my other work would have seen the light of day without their direct influence.

In no particular order:

Jami Davenport, for convincing me to write a series. We've batted around a lot of ideas over the past year +, and I swore over and over that my brain just didn't "think" in series, but when *Snow Angel* barged in the door, insisted I stop what I was working on to write it, and oh, by the way, informed me it was the beginning of a looong series, I knew lurking just behind the book's beginnings stood Jami, grinning and saying, "I told you so."

Laurie Temple. Where to begin? She is THE WOMAN when it comes to editing. She's able to step back from a story and really grasp the big picture, then drill down to the fine details. She finds the character inconsistencies, the plot holes, the arcs that aren't working, and she does it all kindly and with a smile on her face. Not to mention she's very speedy, which is great for me, since I'm always running behind schedule.

Lydia M. Sheridan, for being the sole reason *Snow Angel* got done when it did. You, quite simply, ROCK.

Lori Lyn, Joan Satterlee, Lydia (again!), and Missy Blanchard, for being a shoulder to cry on when I need one, an ass kicker when I need that, and a friend all the time.

Joan Satterlee, again, for sharing her takeaways from a

recent plot class and saying the magic thing that tripped the bell in my head and solidified the ultimate source of Melinda and Jacob's conflict, making *Snow Angel* SO much stronger.

Anthea Lawson, for being the master of everything—business, craft, tech, whatever it is, she knows it! And miraculously, she shares it generously and repeatedly. For being an amazing friend and critique partner, even when she's so insanely busy she barely has time to blink, much less take a breath.

Lavada Dee, for the gift of her time and a final, super-speedy beta/edit after I made all the changes recommended by Laurie and Anthea, and for finding the most amazing details to tweak, all of which made the manuscript stronger, better, and cleaner.

My college-girl, for being my first reader, and for loving the story and the characters, for being my cheerleader as I was writing, even when that meant spending so much time working while she was home for the summer from school. For snuggles and movie nights. For kicking around story ideas and giving me an honest critique. I love you, sweetie pea.

My oldest, for being the grownup. For keeping the family going, for bringing me endless bottles of Pepsi, for helping to give me a fresh perspective, and for geeking out with me on a regular basis. For giving me a final beta and strengthening the end of the book. For buying my books with her own money and reading them, even the sexy ones I said she couldn't read, and for trying to leave me sweet reviews, even though Amazon won't let her. I love you, kitten nose.

My baby boy, for talking writing craft and story with me, for sharing his own thoughts on that craft, for getting the whole creative process. For his amazing art, for helping me figure out the fine details on book cover creation, for always being supportive even though his mom writes "that sexy stuff." For making me laugh, holding my hand, amazing hugs, and warm snuggles. I love you, Smiley Guy.

Last but definitely not least, my guy, my hubby, who loves and supports me every day, even when I spend every second of it inside a story instead of taking care of things around the house, who cooks and cleans and organizes even after a long day/week/lifetime at his "real" job, who still calls me beautiful and almost makes me believe it. I love you, Wolfie.

One final note: absolutely any errors still in the book are new ones I must have introduced after the above edits and feedback, which were flawless, and the blame for them rests solely on my shoulders. My team rocks!

>I love you all, always,
>*Chantilly*
>October ~ 2014

Author's Note

During the spring of 2014, I was busily writing a paranormal romance novella called *Remember Me*, which has been listed on my website as "Coming Soon!" for over a year.

At least.

I LOVE that story. I really do. And I intend to finish and publish it before the end of the year (still 2014—it may not be a great idea to put this in print in case something happens again, but…)

As I was writing, as often happens with me, this new idea landed **BA-BLAM!** in my brain and simply refused to go wait quietly in its story-idea corner.

So I caved.

Yes, I gave in, thinking *Snow Angel* would be a 6,000-word short story, not too long or too much trouble to pound out, then I could get right back to *Remember Me* and continue on as though the little interruption had never happened.

Uh-huh.

One-hundred-twenty-eight-thousand words later…

Snow Angel turned out to be the longest book I have ever written. It's also the beginning of a whole new series, *High Desert Hearts*, and I'm so excited to keep writing in this world! I fell in love with these characters. I hope you did, too.

Eddie's story is next, and I can't wait to dive into it. I adore Eddie. Adore. But… Poor guy, he's in for some trouble. Of the female persuasion.

But first, I swear I'm going to finish *Remember Me* no matter what.

I also have a collection of stories from my college days to get out, but they are NOT romance! Not, not, not. They're more literary, dark and gritty, social issues, all that sort of thing. Do not pick them up if you're looking for more romance. You will be disappointed, and probably angry, and you'll want to leave me all sorts of nasty reviews for putting you through those angst-filled, non-romance stories. Please don't do that! Wait for *Remember Me* and Eddie's story instead. We'll all be happier.

Eddie's story, *Desert Damsel*, will be out in Spring ~ 2015.

Be sure to join my newsletter for publication news and reader perks! Here's the address:

http://chantillywhite.com/contact.html - newsletter

I also love hearing from readers, so if you're feeling chatty, about books or life or whatever, drop me a line at Chantilly@chantillywhite.com, and as always, thanks for reading!

About Chantilly

Like her readers, romance author Chantilly White lives in the real world, but she also knows the value of escapism. As a shy, too-sensitive girl in a new school, Chantilly discovered the priceless ability to escape her surroundings through reading the latest romance novel or by taking pen in hand to write her own stories.

Reading and writing have been a joy ever since.

Now Chantilly loves providing the same joy to her readers. *Pure Hearts ~ Sinful Pleasures* is more than just her tagline. It's her promise. Whether they're looking for a sweetly fluffy romantic tale or a spicy-hot romp, a sweeping historical romance or a contemporary love story, Chantilly White's readers know when they delve into one of her stories, they will be transported to a world where love reigns supreme and everyone gets their happily-ever-after.

Guaranteed.

Always a storyteller, Chantilly holds a degree in Creative Writing and English Literature from the University of California at Riverside. Now living in the Pacific Northwest with her husband, three children, and three crazy cats, she is a member of Romance Writers of America (RWA) and several local and online chapters. She serves as President for the Olympia RWA chapter in Olympia, Washington.

Check out Chantilly's website at http://ChantillyWhite.com for even more new works as they become available.

Sign up for Chantilly's announce-only author newsletter at http://chantillywhite.com/contact.html#newsletter and be first to learn about new releases, contests, and special extras. Friend her on Facebook, Twitter, Pinterest, and Goodreads, too!